Marilyn Ellner is the author of *Ali and Abe*... her first novel of suspense and romance. She is a wife, mother of three and has been a stylist for 33 years along with the owner of two boutiques. Her favorite hobby, when she isn't creating projects out of concrete and wood, is creating stories and putting them to paper. *The Phantom Funeral* is extra special for Marilyn because many people believe the Phantom is a true ghost that haunts the small 33 year old historical town where Marilyn grew up.

To my Dad – You inspired me to be a reader as I was growing up. When I lost you, I felt your presence and push to write this story about what you loved…the history of our small little town.

To my husband, Bear – You don't always get the crazy things I do and all the irons I have in the fire but in the end…you support me and take it all in stride. I Love You and Thank You!

To Danny Ellner, Dan Dinges, and Lilly Vanderford – May we imagine your stories to continue on!

Marilyn Ellner

THE PHANTOM FUNERAL

AUSTIN MACAULEY PUBLISHERS™

LONDON * CAMBRIDGE * NEW YORK * SHARJAH

Ordering Information
Quantity sales: Special discounts are available on quantity purchases by corporations, associations, and others. For details, contact the publisher at the address below.

Publisher's Cataloging-in-Publication data
Ellner, Marilyn
The Phantom Funeral

ISBN 9781685625108 (Paperback)
ISBN 9781685625115 (ePub e-book)

Library of Congress Control Number: 2023901099

www.austinmacauley.com/us

First Published 2023
Austin Macauley Publishers LLC
40 Wall Street, 33rd Floor, Suite 3302
New York, NY 10005
USA

mail-usa@austinmacauley.com
+1 (646) 5125767

To Lisa Durbin-Leonard for giving me the idea…love you dear friend!

To Mary Gregson, Ruth Pope, Tina Siefmerman, Tania Barbeau, Angel Mollet, and Kathy Brewer…without you all I wouldn't have moved forward. Thank you for being there for me!

Prologue

Early Morning Hour of 4 July 1754

The night would have been in complete darkness if not for the full moon's bright light spilling over the rippling currents of the river in the hour past midnight. The reflection from the water added an eerie glow along the path that bordered the river's bank. To a stranger, the path would be hard to follow, but strangers venturing out this far into such an isolated area was unheard of.

Yet the one figure leaning against a large oak tree, several feet into the brush, was no stranger to the area. Pulling away from the large trunk, the man adjusted his waistcoat after releasing the long row of buttons exposing the roughness of a linen shirt. Lord, how he hated the heat of summer in this place he liked to compare to hell. Even in the midnight hour, the weather was excruciating. He almost preferred the bitter winters that came with the territory.

It didn't help that belonging to the French Military delegated his attire to consist of a hooded knee-length capote coat. Then there was a blue, cocked, tuque wool hat that had a wide ribbon sticking out the top that graced his head. As he leaned back against a tree, he took the scratchy wool garment off his head and swiped his hand back and forth through the ribbon. "Good Lord," he whispered, "who in the hell thought up these atrocious styles?"

Placing the hat back on his head, he looked down and brushed away a fallen leaf from the thick linen of his shirt. He felt restricted in the heated attire. Even his underdrawers consisted of thick material and frills. Yet, he was grateful that his boots were knee high because living in the wilderness, one needed to keep one's feet and lower legs protected, mostly due to the flooding which was common when prancing along the Mississippi River.

Out of boredom, he dusted at a small speck of lint on his waistcoat. Looking down, Edwin Berger was glad to see he didn't soil his clothing or boots when he got out of his canoe. It was such a tedious job climbing out of a wooden box while the river's current wanted nothing more than to suck a body in. Thank goodness, he had a cove to pull into where the current wasn't quite as swift.

It had to be done because it was all part of his plan and he planned to see it through, to the end, no matter how long it took. In order to see it through though, he had to take chances and make sacrifices. He was thorough in his planning and was smart enough to know every plan needed to have an escape. So he traveled to the bank, by way of the river, to hide his borrowed canoe in the thick brush along the small cove in case he needed to make a quick escape. It was well planned on his part because if anything would fail, he would head across the river to Saint Genevieve and take off on one of Gaston Smith's horses. He was sure the blacksmith would be pretty sotted, as he was most nights and would be clueless to anyone stealing one of his animals.

If his plan failed, he figured he'd take his time and follow the river south and maybe head to New Orleans. Yet that was only a last resort if something went wrong with his perfect plan. He chuckled to himself because he was sure his plan would do as it must.

"Where in the hell is he?" He whispered to himself as he pulled away from the tree. He was starting to get edgy. He lifted the cocked hat and wiped the sweat from his forehead with his coat sleeve. Running his hands through the back of his head only reminded him he needed to take a knife and chop at some of the dark, curly length because it only contributed to making him perspire more.

He smiled as he once again thought about his plan. The plan that was going to unfold soon…very soon. Looking at his pocket watch, he estimated that within the next hour, he would have his vengeance.

He wondered if maybe he had a sickness. Shouldn't it bother him that his plan for the night was to kill his friend? He didn't really feel he had any sickness of the head though. No, he didn't believe that because it was a much-deserved death coming. His pal, the mightier than thou Dane Geofrey, deserved to die on this very night.

He chuckled and wondered if his friend had any idea he was going to die. The fool truly thought Edwin was his friend. That friendship was only one-sided, of course. Edwin wasn't sure how the other gentleman couldn't see the hatred in his eyes. Then again, Dane wasn't one to have enemies so why suspect anything?

It really was sad that he had to resort to murder, but Edwin knew he couldn't keep the ever perfect Dane in his life. Since arriving here, Dane's persona tended to make everyone invisible, and he was tired of being invisible. Dane was that person whose stance and height reeked of authority. Yet not to Edwin, he had no desire to bow down to the younger man.

He wasn't sure why everyone put Dane Geofrey on such a tall pedestal. He may have been born at the fort, but apparently, the family moved back to France after the first fort was built. Probably because Dane's father, one of the main contractors in the construction of the original fort, knew what a disaster the fort turned out to be. The wooden buildings damn near washed away into the swift river. It was bizarre to wonder why a man of wealth would petition to come to this hellhole to work. Yet, apparently Dane's father was young and had a passion for building things.

Right after the first fort was finished, old man Geofrey married the daughter of a fellow soldier. Within a year, Dane was born and the family moved back to France right after the birth. Not long after the builder departed with his family, the first fort slowly started washing away from the intense flooding along the banks of the mighty river.

Eventually, construction was started on the second fort. This structure was placed a short distance away from the river. Unfortunately, the new wooden buildings couldn't compete with the harsh weather. One would think it was time to move on down river after so many bad attempts, yet greedy France wanted a huge territory ownership in this New World and wasn't giving up. Finally, in early 1750, the construction of a limestone fort was drawn up. When talk of this newest fort was to be constructed, Dane's father, now a Baron, arrived with many slaves to help with the building. He came without his wife and children.

A few years into the construction and halfway finished, Dane Geofrey and his brother, Antoine, arrived at the fort and nothing has been the same since. Just the look of Dane Geofrey screamed authority. Apparently, his real name was Daniel, but he preferred to be called Dane. Edwin was sure that was because it sounded even more dignified.

His charm and strength couldn't be matched. The younger man had it all. Edwin had to endure the sighing and whispers of the young ladies at the fort going on about how handsome Geofrey was with his emerald green eyes, sandy brown hair, flawless tanned skin with perfect white teeth behind a smile that melted their lonely hearts. It was rather sick the way the ladies fell over the man.

It wasn't just the women who thought Dane was perfect. He was well liked by the other soldiers and was recently made Lieutenant Commander. This angered Edwin because he felt the position should have been his…not Geofrey's. It was ironic though, not being chosen as Commander wasn't the reason behind Edwin's hatred towards the other man. Oh, it helped contribute to it, but his hatred came from Dane taking the one thing he wanted most…Liliane Bienvenue. The beautiful Liliane Bienvenue…or wait she was now Liliane Geofrey. Dane's beautiful wife of a week. The same woman who should have been his wife….his Lilly! The son of a bitch even got the girl.

Edwin's hands went into a tight grip as he pulled away from the tree and turned to look at the river. His teeth were clenched, as they did every time he thought of Lilly. The anger he felt was almost overwhelming. She was his Liliane, not Geofrey's!

He'd been chasing Liliane for months, biding his time. She hadn't really given him any clue if she was interested or not but he knew he could wear her down. Her father even gave him permission to court her…if she was willing. Yet, she apparently wanted him to chase her because she was playing hard to get.

He had a plan though. He had been determined to have her and would do whatever it took to make her his. If he had to compromise her and take what she wasn't willing to give, he would. Her embarrassment would never let her cry to her father or the fort community, but the thought of a babe growing in her womb would make her see things his way and agree to marry him.

Once they were married, she would learn her place. She would be the submissive, dutiful loving wife that was expected. She would be taught to pleasure him anyway he wanted. Of course, there was the part about her father being his Commander-in-Charge that made him tread lightly. Yet, he'd make sure she never told Daddy anything by threatening her with a petition for orders to relocate to Cahokia, a fort several hours north. She knew the rules of society. As his wife, she would have to leave her family and go with him.

Edwin was all about planning and in order to set his plan in motion he needed people to see the two of them together and think they were a pair. What better time to set his plan up than the upcoming annual Twelfth Night Ball that happens every January fifth, the eve of the Epiphany. The start of the Mardi Gras celebration. He would ask Liliane for the first dance and that would label the two of them as a pair.

The Ball was the perfect time to put his plan in place because there would be plenty of drinks for the attendees. Wassail Punch always made everyone's step lighter and their tongues looser. He would make sure Liliane had her fair share throughout the night.

Of course, he needed to balance the amounts of punch she consumed because she needed to seem alert when the King's Cake was presented. The King's Cake was the highlight of the evening. Every year, Baker, the fort's meal preparer, baked a large cake with four beans inside. After the cake was presented to the crowd, gentlemen lined up to receive a piece of the cake and hoped it contained a bean. The first one to find a bean was to be labeled 'King' for the next year. The King would then choose his 'Queen'.

After the King and Queen were found, three more beans were needed to be found and these gentlemen would also choose a lady to adorn their arm. This group made up the court. Of course, these positions weren't real but they provided entertainment throughout the community and gave bragging rights for the entire year.

Edwin's plan made sure he was the first one to find the bean. He bribed Baker with silver to give him one of the beans beforehand and as he'd eat his cake, he'd act as if he'd found the first bean. There would then only be three beans baked into the cake, ensuring there weren't too many found.

Of course, his plan was once he was made King, he would choose his Queen…and that would be Liliane. After their traditional first dance as 'King and Queen' was over, his plan was to pump her full of the Wassail and then ask her father if he could walk her home because she wasn't feeling the best. Then after getting permission, he planned to walk her not to her home but to the edge of the river…not far from where he stood now. It was then he'd made sure she was his.

Everything was in place and to his luck the weather was unseasonably warm the evening of the fifth. Edwin was excited as he put on his best attire. He even scrubbed up his boots.

The night of the Ball found his step was light and he was excited as he exited his quarter's. His plan was to get there right as the Ball started. Yet, to his dismay he became detained by the clergy needing help with a broken wheel on his wheelbarrow. He wanted to tell the old fool to find someone else but he had an image to uphold and needed to always look the proper gentleman…so he held his tongue. Plus, to say 'no' to a clergyman was not to be done.

Almost an hour later than he planned, he was shocked when he arrived at the Ball and watched it all blow up in his face. The first time he laid eyes on the golden boy was to watch him walk Liliane out to the dance floor for the first dance. This was his Lilly…no one else's.

With Dane's good looks and education, Liliane never gave Edwin another passing glance. She and her long, dark hair and beautiful brown eyes were no longer his to look upon. He knew deep down he was never going to get the chance to span her small waist or fill his hands with her full breasts or taste her soft lips.

No one knew of Edwin's anger that evening. No one gave him much of a passing thought. The buzz was too heavy with the news of Geofrey's sons being back in town and the oldest was looking polished and perfect with the Commander's daughter. To Edwin's dismay, she was just as lovestruck. Then to make matters worse, halfway through the evening the rumor circulating was Geofrey was here to replace Liliane's father, the Lieutenant Commander, from his position. Apparently, Jules Bienvenue felt he was getting too old for the position and had petitioned the monarchy to send a replacement. The replacement being Daniel Dane Geofrey.

Edwin was seething. That replacement belonged to him. He knew when the Commander gave him permission to court his daughter a few weeks ago, he was also sizing him up to take charge of the fort. Plus, he was more experienced and older than Dane.

The night was too much to bear. His hope for any restitution ended when he lost the bean in his pocket and couldn't find it. He couldn't find it anywhere. He was trying to keep his anger in control but almost completely lost it when Geofrey was the first to find a bean in his cake and he made Liliane his Queen.

The next few months haunted him. After the initial shock of losing Liliane had worn off, Edwin tried, he really did try and get over her. Yet, he found he couldn't. He had had plans and Dane had ruined them. He tried moving on and focusing on a different future. He even went as far as making time to flirt with other single women at the fort, but it wasn't like Fort de Chartres had many single women living there, so his options were bleak. Even the town of Prairie du Rocher, located a few miles away, didn't house any ladies that fared close to his Lilly. The pickings were few and far between in this godforsaken land.

Edwin wasn't anyone's fool though. In war it was smart to 'keep one's friends close and one's enemies closer,' and that was exactly what he did. He became pals with the mighty Dane. That way good ole' Dane wouldn't know what hit him when a lead ball struck him in the chest.

So here it was, the early morning of July fourth, the year of 1754, and Edwin found himself pacing along the riverbank of the Mississippi. He was waiting to take out the enemy. He was surprised to see his palms were sweaty. He took a deep breath and made his way back to the tree.

Lord, he hated the isolation of being out here instead of back in France. Yet he knew with being born a peasant, the military was the only way he would amount to anything. So here he was for the last four years, planted out in the middle of nowhere living amongst a half-built fort.

He wasn't even sure why they continued to rebuild the fort, the river was just going to wash it away again. The walls were being constructed very high from the limestone of the bluffs. At the corners of the walls there were turrets capped at each meeting point. The shorter wall had forty-eight loopholes to shoot from. He was told the air was smelling of war and they needed to be prepared. God, how he would love a good war! Sadly, as of yet, all he saw was an over populated half-built fort and a neighboring town that was so poor it was struggling to stay afloat…literally. What kept it alive was the fertile land that produced a fine crop of corn and wheat. The grain was shipped down river to New Orleans where the supply was in demand and the product could be bartered for much needed supplies to be hauled back up river.

According to the soldiers that have lived here for years, the place was mostly deserted until a few years ago a Frenchman named Renaut came here with his slaves and volunteers to search for precious stones. The area seemed like the perfect spot because the entire region was bordered by massive bluffs where the river once flowed.

Apparently they didn't find the stones and moved on, leaving many workmen and slaves from his entourage behind. Now the area was populated with breeds of all types. There were Frenchmen, Native Americans, Canadians from Quebec, and now the Africans. On top of all of that and to his disgust there seemed to be a few Englishmen staying in the area. This was annoying to Edwin because the area was a province of France. How dare outsiders come in and try to take over…especially the Englishmen? Of course, it didn't count that the Native Americans were here first and the Frenchman came and pushed their way into the area.

As far as the precious gems, what fools, he thought. They just didn't know where to look. Yet apparently good ole' Dane did. Edwin was sure Dane knew because a few months back he came across a bag of gold nuggets in Dane's possession. It wasn't by chance. He was snooping through the younger man's belongings. He was sure the nuggets weren't rocks he brought back from France because a few weeks later, when he looked in the wool bag again, there were more gold nuggets added.

Edwin didn't dare take any of the nuggets because he knew he needed to figure things out…make a plan. He also had questions, like where did the gold come from? He was afraid if he stole them Dane would become suspicious and put his guard up leaving Edwin no way to ever find out where the stones came from?

Sadly, he was no longer able to check if any more gold was added to the bag because Dane and Liliane married in a secret ceremony a week ago and now they live in one of the private quarters, as most soldiers did when they wed. Yet, he was sure Liliane knew where the mine was, he'd bet a month of pay Dane filled her in on everything.

The anger he felt when he found out the couple married was the final straw for him. He was sure they married because Dane compromised her just as Edwin had planned to do…only he was sure the little whore wanted to bed the golden boy. It didn't matter that Dane took what Edwin felt was his. His beautiful Liliane was now uncleaned because she had been touched by another. He planned to make her pay for that for the rest of her life…when she was his.

Once he calmed down, he decided he needed a plan. Of course, there was only one thing to do…kill Dane and get everything back. Plus, add a pile of gold for all the trouble. It was the perfect plan and now here he was waiting for Dane to come back home from what he was sure was a gold picking evening.

Ironically, he hadn't planned for tonight to be the night, but he was prepared for when the night would come, which ended up being tonight. It was late afternoon when he heard Dane explain to Liliane as they walked to the stables that he'd be home after the midnight hour. Edwin was sure the younger man was going to where the gold was located.

He had to control his anger as he watched Liliane nod at something her husband said as he leaned close to her and whispered in her ear before she kissed him goodbye. It was easier to believe the whisper was of importance more so than a promise of the night of lovemaking to come. Every time he thought of them together it burned a hole through his gut.

Knowing his face probably showed his reaction, he turned away from the scene at the stables before someone noticed his look of hate. His first instinct was to follow the newly appointed Commander, but that wasn't possible because he was in charge of the evening training with the men who were personally assigned to him. If he would have made an excuse to leave it would make the men look at him with suspicion when they found the younger man's body. Instead, he thought of a plan to kill Dane that night. He took every detail in as he watched him retreat from the fort heading east along the river.

Hours later, he wondered what was keeping the younger man. Darkness was deep except for the light of the moon. It was now well after midnight and Edwin was surprised Dane would wait this late to return. He yawned as a tired boredom settled around him.

After several moments he heard what sounded like a rider coming down the path towards the clearing where he hoped to take his aim. He decided against a musket because of the noise. They were close enough to the fort and he was sure the echo off the bluff may alert the soldiers on night duty. He went with the bow and arrow he traded with a native. This way it would also look as if one of the natives ambushed Dane. No one would suspect a soldier in the killing because they didn't use bow and arrows. He took a quiet, deep breath as he grabbed an arrow and fit it into the bow string.

Seconds after setting the bow, he heard the horseman coming closer. Straightening up, he pulled away from the tree and looked through the clearing. He was surprised to feel himself shaking as he lifted the bow. Taking aim, he waited until his enemy trotted through the opening in front of him.

Seconds later as he pulled back the bow string, he heard a female shout. Looking to the left, in the direction of the sound, he spotted Liliane with two other riders. She shouted her husband's name again which caused Dane to pause in the clearing. Not one to miss his chance, Edwin lifted the bow and sent the arrow flying, whistling through the air straight through the younger man's chest.

The silence seemed endless, yet only seconds later he heard Liliane's screams as she came running into the clearing, rushing to her husband lying on the ground. Did he kill him? He was pretty sure he was dead-on. He wanted to wait and see but wasn't sure who was with Liliane and he didn't want to stick around and find out.

Turning back towards the direction of the fort he spotted a soldier through the edge of the brush. "Son of a bitch," he whispered as he ran along the river bank. In no time he heard the shouts to stop. Of course, there was no stopping him as he made his way to the canoe and jumped in as he pushed off sending the boat into a full rocking motion.

He kept his back to the soldier so as not to be recognized. The canoe was still rocking and he had a hard time getting it under control with the swift current. After a few moments the boat flipped and he plunged into the water. He kept one hand on the canoe so he wouldn't lose it. With all his strength he grabbed each side and stuck his head above the water inside the flipped canoe and used every bit of his strength to hang on.

What was only a few minutes, yet seemed like hours, the canoe got caught up on a fallen tree laying in the water from the bank. The impact was so hard Edwin had to let go of the canoe and grabbed at the branches as the canoe flopped up above the branches. He wrapped his arms tight around a bigger branch as his legs were being pulled under with the current. It took him several minutes to try and pull himself up but the current was too swift. In the next instant Edwin Berger gave his body to the mighty Mississippi River. His final thought was…*I didn't plan for this.*

Chapter One

25 October 2022

The driver turned down the radio as the jeep approached the sleepy little town that sat near the Mississippi's bank. She briefly wondered what had made her natural instincts want to turn it down. It wasn't as if she had her window lowered, so why the need for silence? Was it the calmness of the small little town? Maybe it was, because there wasn't much movement going on this early Tuesday morning and she wanted to blend in with the peace and tranquility.

Lillian Bienvenue, or Lilly as her friends and family liked to call her, smiled as she looked out the window at her father's hometown. She loved the feeling this place put in her heart. The way the bluffs bordered the town as if to protect and preserve it. Slowing the jeep down to a snail's pace she looked at the clock on the dashboard and decided she had time to drive around before meeting her family for lunch.

Prairie du Rocher goes back three hundred years and is considered a village, but referred to as a town by the locals. The town holds a remarkable amount of history. Unfortunately much is undocumented because it was settled in 1722 and during that time period the country was very raw and primitive making it difficult to document all the events taking place.

Of the few written documents, it was known that the town was settled because of the historical French fort, four miles away. The first wooden fort was built in 1718, completed in 1720. The fort didn't stand erect long due to flooding. This happened a second time to a second fort before it was decided to erect the structure with limestone from the bluffs. The project was completed in the 1750s. While most of the structure has fallen to ruins, there remains several different areas of the foundation of the limestone fort intact and even recently there has been a replica of the fort reconstructed to house a great tourist attraction for visitors to the area.

Many documents from that era are still intact. Including items from the first Catholic Church, Saint Anne. These documents are now housed at Saint Joseph's, the present-day Catholic Church located in the small town. From these documents, it has been determined that Prairie du Rocher was three hundred years old. It was no surprise that the town held many celebrations and events throughout the year to celebrate the tricentennial. As winter was approaching, the celebrations were coming to an end. Lilly wished she could have attended the festivities but her job was too new to get the time off.

As the jeep turned the corner, Lilly came across what she always felt was the town's foundation. It wasn't like a normal town where the focal point was a City Hall or Courthouse. No, not in Prairie du Rocher, Illinois; here the foundation was Lisa's Market Street Grille.

Lisa's was one of the reasons people made the drive to the historical little town. The restaurant had charm and the chicken was famous. It was also appealing to many because the newly renovated restaurant was also in a building that was over a century old. The beer garden only added to the appeal.

Lilly smiled as she pulled the car over to look at all the renovations the place had gone through in the last few years. The last time she was here, two years earlier, Lisa was expanding the restaurant and bar. Now the place was huge with a fenced-in beer garden on the side and a large extension to the back for additional seating for the restaurant. She was excited to check out the restaurant when she met up with her parents and siblings for lunch.

The village looked good after a year of celebrating three hundred years. There were events that took place every weekend throughout spring and summer. Her parents came for a few of the events and would group facetime with her and her siblings when they were in the heart of it all. Usually her grandfather was in the background participating in the events. Lilly wished she could have been here to see his reenactments. Once he portrayed an Indian Chief and another time a constable. On her many calls to him she knew he enjoyed the roles very much.

Looking to her left she spotted the summer kitchen and small cemetery that was the only remaining building that once held the beautiful Brickley Mansion before it mysteriously burned down in 1970. The other end of the lot still housed the old historical Creole House. This small quaint house is considered one of the oldest houses still standing in the state. The entire front of the block was sectioned off by a wrought iron fence.

Looking at the yard, Lilly sighed and thought about the once beautiful Brickley House. She wished she would have had the opportunity to see the house before it burned down. History was her passion and in Prairie du Rocher there was plenty of it. She fell in love with all the stories of her daddy's home town.

The tale of the Brickley Mansion was unique in itself. A house was erected because of a winning lottery ticket sold in Chicago. The ironic part about the house is that it should have been called 'The Leigh Mansion.' It was actually built by Abraham Leigh, the local Mill owner, and Brickley was his partner. The story itself was crazy because it actually all started in Chicago in the late 1860s. A man by the last name of Cosby, a wealthy distiller, wanted to mark his place in history. He felt that the town needed more culture and he invested greatly into the building of a massive Opera House. The design and structure was above anything of its kind in the day. The building cost over six hundred thousand and housed over three hundred pieces of artwork.

The problem was, two years after it opened, Cosby became broke with the maintenance and upkeep of the building. About to go under, Cosby announced he was going to host a nationwide lottery with the first place prize being the Opera House itself and the other prizes were three hundred pieces of artwork that graced the lovely Opera House walls.

Tickets were five dollars each, which was a large amount for a ticket in 1866. There were 210,000 tickets sold. The first three hundred tickets pulled were for the artwork and the final ticket drawn for the Opera House was won by none other than Mr. Leigh of Prairie du Rocher. Mr. Leigh became the owner of a massive Opera House in Chicago.

Ironically, Mr. Leigh didn't wish to have any part of the Opera House and actually settled on a cash prize of two hundred thousand dollars. Cosby was happy to pay him using part of the proceeds from the lottery and was happy to once again have the Opera House in his ownership. He took the remaining money from the tickets sold and glamorized the Opera House once again.

Incidentally, a few years later in 1871 Cosby turned on the Opera House's gas lights for the first time and a few hours later the entire building was engulfed in flames from The Great Chicago Fire. It was a coincidence that the Great Chicago Fire started right after the Opera House turned on the gas lights, but how ironic that Cosby put so much into the house just to watch it burn to the ground?

Back in Prairie du Rocher, Abraham Leigh had a beautiful mansion built right under the bluffs with the winning money. Not long after it was constructed, tragedy struck and Mrs. Leigh passed away. Leigh decided to move away from Prairie du Rocher and sold the home to his partner Brickley. Leigh died not long after the sale while on a trip to Ohio. Brickley Senior, left the house to his son F.M. Brickley and wife. It was this family that resided and entertained inside the elaborate house.

The Brickley family was known for housing some extravaganzas in its day. Mr. Brickley apparently had no problem showing off his wealth. The locals like to talk about the parties. Yet eventually F.M. died and asked that the house be donated to a charitable organization. While that wasn't to be the case, the house stood for many years…vacant. Until it mysteriously burned down on 5 April 1970. To a town the size of Prairie du Rocher, the Brickley Mansion was a showpiece…their pride and joy. So it had to be a disappointment when the house no longer existed.

Pulling her jeep away from the shoulder, Lilly sighed at the sadness she always felt when she thought about the fire destroying history that early morning. To this day, fifty plus years later, no one has ever come forward with the answer to what caused the fire.

One thing was sure, her grandfather wasn't enamored with the house. Several years ago she asked him about the house and he snorted and implied it wasn't that impressive. Which was odd for her grandfather to reply because he loved history and took pride in the older houses throughout town.

On the other end of the two-acre yard still stands what is considered a very old house. One of the oldest in the state of Illinois. She was happy to see the historical Creole House looking fit. It amazed her that the old wooden structure was still standing two hundred plus years later. If she remembered correctly, a doctor built the house. Later the house was purchased by Mr. Leigh, before he won the lottery. It was a few years later that he won the lottery and built the mansion and if the stories are true…Brickley moved into the Creole House after Mr. Leigh moved into the Mansion.

Of course, as with most things marked in history, there are always conflicting stories of people, dates and times. One thing was sure, when she was a child, she always had fun playing out behind the Creole house and in the wooded area by the bluff. She just had to make sure she didn't get caught trespassing.

She'd have to ask her father his take on the date of the Creole house's birth to be sure, but she thought it was around the 1800s. If anyone would know, it was her father, the American History Professor...now turned Archeologist. Of course, growing up with both her parents being history teachers, history was pretty much embedded in her head. She had been taught early on the importance of appreciating the old buildings and structures along with the amazing stories of times past. While she didn't share a passion for teaching history as her parents did, she had a passion for writing about it. She actually loved writing about everything, so becoming a journalist just made sense.

Turning the corner past the small-town library, she spotted another small mansion. The Conrad House. The three-story mansion didn't fit in the middle of such a small town, but the smallness of the little town surrounding the building probably contributed to the massive size. That or the fact that it was built dead center in the middle of Main street.

The Conrad house had some great stories attached to it. There were many conflicting stories about the house. One being that Mr. Conrad never lived in the house, that he passed away while it was being built.

Her favorite rumor was that in the early 1900s Mr. Conrad owned the grocery store that sat across from Brickley Yard. His competition, Schicker's Mercantile, was on Henry and Main street. Everyone coming along on Main or Henry via horse, carriage, or on foot would stop by the Mercantile first. So Mr. Conrad approached the town board and offered to build a beautiful house that will bring tourists to the small town. The catch was, he could build it on any of his properties and it just so happened he owned part of Main street. The town agreed, never thinking Mr. Conrad would place it right smack dab in the middle of Main St. It is believed that when people came from out of town they had to reroute around the house and it was just easier to go to Conrad's store than out of the way to Schicker's Mercantile.

Lilly smiled when she read the sign declaring the house to be a Bed & Breakfast. She always wanted to go inside and explore the three stories of history. Every summer she spent in Prairie du Rocher she became wistful when she came upon the house. Maybe if she ever made her way back to Prairie du Rocher, after this visit, she might just book her stay at the B & B.

Several minutes passed as she drove through the small town weaving in and out of the streets. She loved the cute gazebo in the middle of town. It was here where her parents got married. When her mother talked of their wedding, she would explain how the park was newly donated to the town. Eventually the Beautification Committee raised the money to put a gazebo in the middle of the park. Her grandfather pulled some strings to see the wedding happen and a few months later there were white chairs set up on the lawn with yellow flower petals gracing the ground. Lilly would sigh when her mother's spoke of her favorite part of the wedding…the white horse and carriage that pulled up to the park entrance, delivering her to her new husband.

Her father, Greg, grew up in Prairie du Rocher. Greg had a strong love of the past and decided to become an educator of history. When he graduated from Illinois State University it was with a doctorate in History and a double major in Archeology. He felt the two would go hand in hand.

His first and only job as a professor was at the University of Kansas City where he met Lauren Miles. Within a few minutes of meeting the couple fell in love. In no time they married and had Lilly and her two siblings. The wedding took place here because her mother's family was from Indiana and Prairie du Rocher was halfway between Kansas City and Indianapolis. Plus Prairie du Rocher was an adorable quaint place to have a wedding according to her mother.

The Jeep headed in the direction of the elementary school. What she really wanted to see was the school's playground that was across the street from the small school. Because of it being a hazard for kids to walk across a public road, there were cones positioned to block the street from any traffic during school hours. Lilly took the detour and pulled into the parking lot adjacent to the playground. She smiled as she looked at the newly remodeled playground. After putting the car in park, she sighed as she thought about all the hours she spent here as a child.

She had to admit the remodel of the playground was nice, but not as cool as it had been when she was a kid. The now castle with turrets was once a human hamster wheel-like thing that you ran inside forever if you had the stamina. Yet she and her best friend Rissa, a local girl, had been content just sitting inside the wheel.

The high tower to the left used to have a fireman's pole that you could slide down. She was happy to see the rope bridge was still intact. She smiled as she thought about the many great times they had hanging out at this playground.

Looking over at the school she was glad it wasn't recess for any of the children yet. She was sure it wouldn't be long before the kids would be on the playground, especially because it was such a beautiful fall day. She loved how the leaves were turning into so many vibrant colors.

Glancing around to make sure she was alone, Lilly stepped out of her car and took a deep breath to fill her lungs with a large dose of fresh country air. Kansas City wasn't necessarily smoggy but there was definitely something about the country air. She stretched out the four and a half hours of aching muscles from the drive. *Wow,* she thought, *I need to get back into yoga...I'm definitely out of shape.*

Of course, to anyone passing by, the last thing they would think when seeing a beautiful, brunette girl walking over to sit on a park bench was that she was out of shape. The jacket and jeans didn't hide the sleek, slender body. They would notice her long legs, and the soft curves in all the right places.

Truly if someone at that moment was to approach her, they would encounter a real beauty. Not just the flawless skin sprinkled with freckles and dark brown eyes or even the full mouth with dimples on each side. After taking in the initial outer appearance, they would be drawn to the charming, smiling eyes of a woman with a true heart and an old soul.

Lilly was glad she wore jeans as she sat on the cool metal park bench. She looked around for a few minutes, taking in all her childhood memories. Small towns were great for city kids to visit but if you didn't find fun things to do, you'd get bored real quick. Yet she was lucky because she and her family spent most of their summers in Prairie du Rocher and she always found new adventures in the little town.

Looking up, she smiled at a memory that hasn't surfaced in many years. Lilly found a bestie, her name was Rissa...short for Clarissa Mollot. Rissa lived next door to Lilly's grandparents' house and was almost a year younger than Lilly. Yet that didn't matter to the two girls and in no time they became fast friends. Rissa had this awesome red hair while Lilly's was a boring brown. Every time they saw each other, after spending most of the year apart, the first thing they would say is..."I want your hair." While the other would reply "No I want your hair."

She smiled at another blast from the past. What was it...twelve, maybe thirteen years ago when she developed her first crush? A couple years after becoming summer friends, Lilly was fourteen and just graduated from eighth grade. The first thing she did after greeting her grandparents was go and find Rissa. Knocking on Rissa's door she was sad to learn that Rissa was still in school. Prairie du Rocher had quite a few more snow days than Kansas City and they were in session for another week.

Well Lilly wasn't going to let that stop her. Every day, for the next week, she could be found on the playground across the street from the school waiting for the final bell of the day to sound. On Rissa's final day of seventh grade, Lilly was so bored and anxious to hang with her friend that she arrived at the playground about thirty minutes before school was out. The last hour of the school day never allowed the kids outside for recess so she wasn't worried about running into a bunch of school kids or teachers.

As a rule, the girls would meet at the hamster wheel. It was their clubhouse of sorts. That day she had a bag with a couple sodas and some snacks for the picnic they were planning to celebrate Rissa's last day of school. Grandpa even snuck in a few candy bars. That pretty much sealed the deal that he was the best grandfather ever.

Lilly was out of breath when she approached the playground. Without even looking she plopped down on the edge of the wheel to catch her breath. It took her a few seconds to get her breathing under control before she opened her backpack to grab the teen magazine to pass the time.

As she turned to settle herself inside the wheel, she gave a shrieking scream when she spotted a boy sitting inside the other side entrance of the wheel with his back on one side and feet on the other.

"Hello." The boy said before she could recover from being startled.

Lilly was mad. Who was this boy invading her and Rissa's territory? Why does someone always have to come along and ruin the good things? It didn't matter that he was kind of cute...he wasn't supposed to be in their space.

The silence was awkward after she jumped out of the wheel to put a little distance between her and the intruder. When she didn't reply, the boy swung his way through the wheel and sat on the edge of the wheel next to where she stood and stared up at her. She stared back. Once the anger started to diminish Lilly looked into the greenest eyes...planted on the cutest face of any boy she had ever laid eyes on. He was perfect with his sandy brown hair, and tanned face with perfect lips. She wasn't sure why but she liked his mouth.

The strange feelings he stirred inside her made her even angrier than before. She put her hands on her hips and asked, "Who are you and why are you here?"

The boy smiled and stood up to stand in front of her. "The names Tripp and you are?" He asked with a lop-sided grin.

Lilly didn't know what was wrong with her. She wasn't usually shy and as a rule she was polite to everyone. So why this sudden anger? It wasn't like she didn't have crushes on boys…well mostly it was her favorite singer, Harry Niles. Yet this boy was making her feel weird things and warm all over. Even her palms were damp.

She wanted to tell him to leave and was on the verge of it when she looked intently into his eyes. They took her breath away. Next thing she knew she heard herself say, "My name is Lilly."

Chapter Two

Tripp looked past her towards the school. "So why aren't you in school?" He asked in a deep voice that didn't quite fit his boyish look.

Lilly followed where he was looking before turning back to look into his beautiful green eyes. "I'm actually not from here and my school got out a week ago." Her nerves kept her babbling on. "Why aren't you in school and how old are you?"

He gave her a cocky grin. "Same as you, my school was out last week. I'll be fourteen soon and heading to high school."

"I'm also a Freshman." She stated matter-of-factly, letting him know she was on his level. "Where do you go to school?"

"Champaign, Illinois." He smiled. "You?"

"Kansas City."

"Wow, that's kind of far. Are you here for the Rendezvous?"

"No," She paused. "I mean we go, but my family stays here with my grandparents over the summers." She looked away awkwardly before asking, "Why are you here?"

"My dad is doing the re-enactment at the fort this week. I tagged along." He looked around, "It's kind of boring here."

Lilly wanted to be cool and chill like him. "I know. But at least my parents let me do whatever and my friend Rissa, she goes to school here and her last day is today, she and I hang." She wanted to slap her forehead for running on and on. She was sure she didn't sound very chill at all.

He took a few steps back and sat on the edge of the hamster wheel again. "So what do you mean by hang?"

She couldn't tell him they had picnics at the playground or played behind the Creole House. She didn't want to look and sound like a dork around this really cool guy, "We chill. You know, we're girls. We paint our nails and listen to music." Man, she was bombing this. "What do you do while you're here?"

He picked up some of the pea rocks that covered the playground floor and tossed them absentmindedly. "I don't know. I haven't been here in years. Too busy with summer sports." He looked at her. "Now that I graduated eighth grade, there aren't any school sports for me this summer. So my dad asked if I wanted to come along this year and I said sure. I was bored at the fort and asked dad if I could walk into town and he was fine with it."

"You walked here from the fort? Is that where you are staying?" She was curious.

"Yep, it's only a few miles so it didn't take long." He shrugged before tossing more rocks. "We camp out."

"Really? Do you stay in one of the teepees out there?"

"Yep." He was glad she was interested and sounded excited that he stayed at the fort but didn't want to let on. If she knew he came into town yesterday and saw her and her friend hanging out around town and that was why he came back here, she would think he was a stalker. Maybe he was, he thought. She was the most beautiful girl he had ever laid eyes on. He wanted to meet her, but had no idea how to approach her. He was bummed when she never looked his way when he followed her and her friend into the town grocery store the day before. Yet, his luck changed as he heard her tell the clerk they were buying a bunch of snacks because the two of them were going to have a picnic at the playground the following day as soon as her friend got out of school.

Of course, he knew he was going to have to be at the playground nonchalantly the following day. He even came early to beat her there. He hadn't expected her to arrive early. Yet that worked out even better because now they were talking.

Her eyes were excited as she asked about the teepee. "Can I come and take a look inside sometime?" She rushed on before he could answer. "I always wanted to look inside one but my father said it wouldn't be polite to ask."

He gave her a cute dimpled grin. "Sure. My family won't mind."

Lilly smiled down at him as he stared up at her. Neither was aware of the awkwardness any longer. The ringing of the school bell broke the silence between the two. In no time, Rissa joined them and Lilly made the introductions. It was all history from there. The duo became a trio for the next week. The girls would walk the four miles to the fort to hang out in the teepee. Yet most of the time it was Tripp who came into town and hung at her

29

grandparents' house. She was sure it was because he liked how her father and grandfather picked his brain about being with the re-enactors.

Lilly smiled over the long-ago memory of meeting Tripp. She often wondered whatever happened to the handsome boy who made her feel the first stirring of womanhood? She was sure the crush was only one-sided. Tripp was a flirt but never declared his undying love for her. Yet he did kiss her once…her first kiss.

She remembered emailing back and forth a few times but that eventually went away when her computer crashed and she no longer had his email. Then school became too busy to even think about it. She didn't receive her first phone until that August when she started freshman year.

High school took over and all the hoopla that came with it. It was ironic that she never remembered or he never told her his last name or gave her his phone number. She didn't think to give him her number because she lived in Kansas City.

Thinking about that sweet kiss she remembered how oddly it came about. It was the last time she saw him. Lilly never told Rissa about it because she was embarrassed. Or maybe she just wanted the memory to be all hers.

Tripp was in town and he came by the house and asked if she wanted to take a walk. She thought he had already left to go home, so she was excited to see him at the door. He said his father was letting him say goodbye and would meet him in town in an hour.

They walked across the levee to the creekside behind the old grain elevator. Tripp never said a word as he took her hand and they followed the creek for a few minutes. She remembered being nervous and giddy because he had her hand. They came to a secluded spot and sat on the bank. Tripp was quiet so she thought she should be quiet as well.

After what seemed like forever Tripp broke the silence. "I've had dreams about this spot." He looked down the stream. "This spot and a few others." He nodded towards the end of town where the railroad tracks laid. "Across the tracks and even at the fort."

"What do you mean?" She was curious.

He looked at her. "Like I've dreamt I was in this spot and someone came here and killed me." He looked away. "That's why I wanted to walk this way before I left. I wanted to see why I keep dreaming this dream. It's weird because I knew exactly where to go." He picked up a small twig and tossed it into the creek. "In my dream there wasn't a levee and I was riding a horse. The other dreams I've had I died as well. It was really creepy because I was always pierced in the chest by a blade." He looked at her and grinned. "I think I've spent too much time at the fort."

Lilly smiled and wrapped her arms around her bent knees before resting her head on them facing him. She thought he was the most handsome boy in the whole world. He was by far cuter than Harry Niles.

She wanted to tell him that his dreams were no big deal, they were just dreams. Yet she knew all about how dreams could confuse a person. Whenever she stayed at her grandparents' house she was always dreaming about crazy things like going back in time to the colonial days. She never really remembered the dreams in detail. She just figured she had these dreams because her father was always shoving history down their throats.

As she sat there and remained silent Tripp thought she was thinking he was losing it. "Lilly, please don't think I'm crazy. I've only been having these dreams since I've been here. I'm sure everything will go back to normal when I go home."

Lilly didn't want to be reminded that he was leaving. "I don't think you're crazy Tripp." She wanted to add, *I think you're amazing,* yet instead she asked, "What does it feel like being here right now?".

"With you…there's no bad dreams." Tripp was crazy about her and he really didn't want to leave before kissing her at least once. Leaning in he placed his hands on the sides of her face as she lifted her head and leaned into the kiss. She felt his soft lips on hers as she closed her eyes. Lilly felt as if she just died and went to heaven. The kiss was shattering to both of them. After several long moments Tripp was the first to move away. He put his arm around her as she laid her head on his shoulder and he laid his on top of hers.

The couple sat like that for quite some time before Tripp looked at his watch and realized they needed to be heading back. His dad was picking him up in town and they were heading home. As they approached the levee, Tripp paused and looked back at the creek. Lilly shivered because she knew he was thinking about his dream…his ghost.

He looked back at Lilly and kissed her one last time. "I'm going to miss you." He whispered as he grabbed her hand and turned away from his nightmares and walked with her into town.

Lilly cried herself to sleep that night.

31

The rest of the summer seemed dull after Tripp left. The next summer she only spent part of the summer in Prairie du Rocher because life got busy and the Bienvenue family had different commitments as their children got older. She and Rissa also lost touch after the summer with Tripp. Rissa's parents got divorced and she moved away with her mother. It didn't take Rissa's father long to move out afterwards. Rissa's only relative living in Prairie du Rocher was her mother's sister and Lilly didn't know her well enough to ask after her friend.

Then the following spring, Lilly turned sixteen, got a car and a summer job. Unfortunately she only made it back to Prairie du Rocher for weekend visits, here and there. Of course, the hustle and bustle of technology puts everyone in a whirlwind and next thing she knew she graduated with a journalism degree and a minor in Marketing and was working as a journalist in Kansas City. She often thought about her Prairie du Rocher friends but never tried to reach out.

The sound of a school bell ringing broke into her thoughts. Lilly jumped up and headed to the car quickly before she was mobbed by children running for the swings and slides. Getting back into her car, she backed out and took a back street to the church cemetery where her grandmother now rested.

Pulling in and parking, Lilly looked around at the beautiful gloomy place. She missed her grandmother Ashley. She was suddenly very aware that she was blessed to have the family she did. Having parents that were teachers gave her family the opportunity to spend summers with her grandparents in Prairie du Rocher.

When Lilly was small, her family did visit her mother's parents in Indianapolis. They were polite but not overly loving like the Bienvenue Grandparents. She remembered listening in on a conversation between her parents that her mother felt like her parents were put out every time they came to visit. They had a hard time adjusting to small children around. It seemed like over time the visits became less and less. Eventually only her parents went to Indiana and Lilly and her siblings stayed with the Bienvenue Grandparents.

The summer visits to Prairie du Rocher were special to Lilly. She sometimes missed her friends back in Kansas City but she loved being with her grandparents even more. Her siblings enjoyed it also because they were doted on by the grandparents. They loved the small town as well and found friends of their own while they were here visiting.

The summer after she got a job her family visits were less and less. Yet her grandparents made up for it by coming to Kansas City more. That made Lilly and her family happy. Her grandfather wasn't much for urban life, but he did like all the different history Kansas City had to offer. Yet after Lilly's sister, Angel, graduated from high school, Lilly's parents retired from the University and decided to join an archeology firm and travel around the country on archeologist digs.

Sadly within two years of her parents retiring and Lilly busy working on her career with the Kansas City Independent, the family's next visit back was for her grandmother's funeral. Lilly and her siblings were very close to their grandparents so it was heartbreaking when a deadly virus hit the world in the spring of 2020 causing the world to shut down for many months. The virus came through the country like a wildfire, spreading it's poison to many. It left a long line of death, especially the elderly, throughout the country…including Grandmother Ashley.

The worst part was the country was quarantined and there was no way the family could say goodbye. They did get to attend the funeral, but only immediate family was allowed. There was a ten person or less gathering mandated rule which included funerals. The family respected what was happening. They were just heartbroken that many people didn't get to say goodbye to Ashley Bienvenue.

Thankfully her grandfather, Frank, didn't get sick from the virus and the rest of the family was blessed to not have contracted the illness as well. Those were some very dark days for the world. Yet, the Good Lord walked many through it and a lot of valuable lessons were learned from that time.

Lilly's father had a hard time with his mother's passing. He regretted not spending the last few summers of her life here and has vowed he would not miss another one as long as his father was alive.

After she pulled into the cemetery and parked the car she grabbed the bouquet of fall flowers she bought at the nursery next to a gas station that morning. When she spotted the nursery, she knew it was a sign to bring Grandma some flowers. She chose a beautiful bundle and smiled as she smelled the flowers. Her grandmother loved fall and loved flowers even more.

Walking over to her grandma's grave she knelt down and placed the flowers in the vase attached to the stone. She ran her hand over her grandmother's name while she spoke to the lady she loved like a second mom.

Her conversation was one-sided but she didn't care. She pretended as if her grandmother were still alive and she went on to tell her how much she missed and loved her before saying a quiet prayer. Lilly wiped at her eyes and stood before turning towards her car to exit the cemetery.

Oddly, before she made it to the door, something alerted her to the older part of the deserted cemetery. Not sure why, but she felt a pull and turned in the direction and walked over to a group of very old headstones. If she had to guess, all the stones in this section were dated pre Civil War. Most were illegible with a number or letter here or there. Some of the stones had a last name only. After admiring the history of the older part of the cemetery, she turned to go back to her car. Yet, she noticed a beautiful granite monument with the name Geofrey engraved into it. The monument was placed inside a small section that had an iron fence bordering it.

One side of the fence had a slightly open gate and Lilly wasn't sure why, but she walked into the caged area. On the ground in front of the monument were three concrete rectangular plots. All three were dated almost a century apart. Lilly thought it was nice that someone took the time to preserve their family's gravesites.

Standing in front of the middle grave she squatted down to block the sun's reflection so she could read the headstone. *Lt Commander Daniel D. Geofrey, 28 June 1726–4 July 1754, Beloved Husband of Liliane. YOU WILL ALWAYS BE MY FOREVER.*

Lilly touched the stone as she read it and suddenly was knocked backwards as if struck by lightning. The impact knocked her against the gate wall and she fell into an almost unconscious state. It was like she was awake but she wasn't. Everything seemed foggy and blurred. She was confused by what was happening…and scared.

She couldn't open her eyes, yet she could see. People and images flash through her head. When her vision started to clear she looked around and thought she recognized where she was at. It was the fort…Fort de Chartres. There were people walking about, but it was as if she was looking at them but they couldn't see her. Was she dead? She didn't know, but she was starting to panic.

Suddenly, a young military man dressed in a historical military colonial costume, approached her with a smile. Was he a reenactor at the fort for the Rendezvous? He grabbed and hugged her before she could comprehend what was happening. Lilly was enchanted by how handsome he was. He was beautiful with sandy brown hair and light, bright green eyes. Hmm, she thought, if this is heaven…I'm good with it. Suddenly another face took his place. This one is a man smiling or more like sneering. He has dark curly hair and dark eyes.

She felt his evil as she noticed a hunting bow in his hand. She didn't know why but she knew she needed to get away from him. She struggled but he was hurting her with his tight grip. Everything became blurred like a confusing dream that jumps around. Suddenly, as if she was out of body once more, she sees herself crying over the green-eyed, handsome colonial man, as blood is covering his chest. She knew he was dying because she could feel it. Suddenly he spoke, "Liliane…my love. You will always be my forever." He coughs before whispering, "I will find you." She felt his presence slipping from her. She tried to pull him back but it was too late. She stared through the tears falling and felt so much pain…the pain of loss. She looked up at the evil man and just as he tried to reach for her she watched as he fell back and a large amount of water overtook him and pulled him away.

Lilly suddenly became alert to her present state and was confused as to why she was lying down on the cemetery ground. It took her a moment to clear her vision. She sat up but rested back against the iron wall. She reached up to rub the back of her head for fear she hit it against the fence. She was glad she didn't feel a bump.

She shook off the trance she was in. The October day came into complete focus but she was still rattled by what just happened. She reached up again to feel her head and still didn't feel any sore spots but was surprised to find her cheeks wet from tears. "What in the hell just happened?" She spoke out loud. There was no answer and she was glad there wasn't.

As she started to stand, she noticed a shadow fall over her. Looking down she noticed a patch of light settling on the monument that belonged to the Geofreys. She looks up to see the sun peaking in between the tall trees. She had an eerie feeling that she and this Geofrey guy had a connection at one time. Somehow she didn't feel it was a coincidence that he was married to a woman named Liliane.

Shaking her head, she wondered if she was losing her mind. She was spooked enough to know it was time to leave. Making her way to her car on wobbly legs she wondered if she wasn't just tired? She did get up early to make the trip this morning. Plus, it was one of the most hellish weeks of her life. So maybe she just needed to get some rest. She found she couldn't get to her car fast enough. She locked the doors before starting the engine and shifting it into drive. She couldn't get away from the cemetery fast enough. She didn't look back because she was afraid of what she might see. She felt her nerves slightly easing as she left the cemetery and approached the town once again.

Still a bit spooked, Lilly found herself pulling into her grandparent's driveway. She shifted the car into park and took a deep breath before looking up at the old, beautiful historical house her father, and his father, and so many more of her ancestors had lived in for almost two hundred years. She remembered always wanting this old house to be her permanent home as a child. She smiled as she looked at the beautiful mums blooming under the Magnolia that graced the front yard. Her grandfather explained to her on one of their many phone calls that he liked for there to be flowers around the tree all year long. He also stated that he liked yellow tulips there every spring since the day he put her grandmother to rest.

Lilly sighed as she laid her head back on the car seat headrest. She felt a tear roll down her cheek as she looked at the black wreath hanging on her grandfather's front door. She guessed she needed to plant more flowers next to her grandmother's flowers under the Magnolia.

Chapter Three

Several minutes passed before Lilly could compose herself. As she wiped the tears from her eyes, she looked out both windows to make sure no one saw her crying as she sat in her grandfather's driveway. She reached in the glovebox for a tissue before leaning forward to look in the visor mirror to see how red her eyes and face were.

Wiping away the signs of tears didn't do anything for her broken heart. Lilly sat back and sighed deeply. Looking through the windshield she stared at the house she always felt was a second home. The large two-story structure always brought her comfort when she stayed with her grandparents.

The house wasn't what one would call colonial, but it was definitely built in the mid-1800s and had a colonial feel to it. The wrap around porch was her favorite spot. How she loved listening to her grandpa's stories while swinging on the porch swing.

The backyard had a smaller shed-like structure that was still called the servant's quarters. Off the top of her head, she couldn't remember which great-grandparent of the past had actually built the house, but that 'great' apparently could afford a few servants. The house was big but not overly large, so to add a few servants would crowd the living space. He decided to build them their own quarters.

Over time servants were no longer the trend and the family hired people to come and work at the house, but not live there. The servant quarters were turned into an apartment for family members needing a place to stay when they came to town for a visit or as per her grandfather's case, a place to live when one no longer wanted to be under their parent's constant eyes. Apparently he lived there as a bachelor for a few years while his parents lived in the big house with his grandfather. Her grandparents had even lived in the little quarters a few years after they got married.

Grandpa had the stories. He would love to go on about what it was like living in the 'good old days' as he liked to call it. Her favorite tales were of her grandparents and their adventures growing up in Prairie du Rocher. Like the one where he put a bullfrog inside her grandma's desk in third grade. Or how he took her school lunch and replaced it with worms when she wasn't looking. Apparently Grandma didn't like him much and to his dismay he found he liked her too much.

So to stop the crush, he thought it would be smart to pull horrible pranks on her. It only backfired because she'd give him a hurt look and would say nothing as she walked away. Of course, that only made him think about her even more. Grandpa would say that in the end his pranks got him the prize because the most beautiful lady in Randolph County was now his wife.

Grandma rolled her eyes and shook her head. She would remind him that she chased him and had to bring him to heed because he hyperventilated at the thought of commitment when the time came. He'd hug her and declare that he had been a fool and that was something he'd always regret.

Lilly's fondest memories were of the two of them sitting on the swing with their legs rocking it back and forth. Her grandpa reminded her of that famous guy…Twain or the chicken guy…Sander's, with his white hair combed back and a thick mustache that slightly curled up on the edges with a patch of whiskers on his chin. Her petite grandmother aged beautifully with dark hair that Lilly was sure 'The Salon & Boutique' helped keep from turning a snowy color.

Lilly looked at her clock and realized she was late meeting her family for lunch. Her parents and siblings arrived in town last night. Her brother drove in from Urbana, Illinois and her sister from Oxford, Mississippi. Her parents came in from Pennsylvania where their current dig was located.

This morning they had to meet with the funeral director in Red Bud. Lilly couldn't come to town until last night because she had a big story deadline that needed to be submitted before the following day. Her boss would have been okay if she left yesterday but she knew she'd have to rush back to finish it. She felt it was better to finish it so she could take the rest of the week off.

Her momma was pretty sure they'd be done at the funeral home and would make it to Lisa's by lunch time. As Lilly pulled up and parked at the restaurant, she spotted her parents' car parked on the side of the building. She was excited to see her family. The last time they were all together was at Easter when they all met up in Kansas City. Her parents picked up her grandfather on their way from their dig in Gettysburg. Lilly hosted the Easter holiday in her parents' home because she was the only one to occupy it.

When her parents decided to become gypsies and move all over the country, they asked Lilly to stay in their house. They didn't know how things were going to work out so they wanted to sit on the piece of real estate until they could decide. She was the most reasonable choice because the other two lived in other states while she was still in Kansas City.

Lilly didn't mind because she loved the house and the extra room was nice compared to the small apartment she had been renting. It also helped that her parents refused any rent and all she had to pay for was the utilities…after she insisted. So it was a win-win.

Walking in through Lisa's bar, Lilly was impressed with the remodeling. The two-story building was over a hundred years old, but the architecture design was still well maintained inside and out. Lisa made the place very inviting.

After waving a greeting to the bartender, Lilly made her way into the dining room. She immediately spotted her family sitting at a table in the far corner. Lilly's father Greg and Lisa looked to be in deep conversation. Lilly bet they were catching up on family gossip considering they were third cousins. Lilly didn't wish to interrupt so she took that moment to look around and take in the newly remodeled expanded room.

The colors were a soft, inviting, antique yellow…accented with a deep rust. What she was most excited to see was the dining room walls that were covered in black & white framed pictures that appeared to be images of places and people of the small town. Looking closely, she recognized several places that were still standing. She couldn't identify any of the people because she was sure by their dated clothing they were before her existence.

"Lilly…over here." Lilly turned to see her mother waving her over to their table. Lilly made her way over to the group and right into Lisa's outstretched arms. Lilly hugged the owner and blushed as Lisa went on and on about what beautiful children Greg and Lauren made.

Lisa may be Greg's cousin but she became best friends with Lauren minutes after they met years ago. Lisa pulled back and gave Lilly a once over. "My little Lilly-Bear, you get prettier every time I see you."

"So do you Aunt Lisa." Lilly smiled because even though Lisa wasn't her real aunt, she insisted on being called Aunt Lisa. For all the years Lilly visited Prairie du Rocher, Lisa was the one constant. She was always there with her blonde ponytail and light blue smiling eyes. The best thing about Lisa was her love for the little town. The tourism traffic was steady because people from all over came to Lisa's.

Lisa patted Lilly's behind and told her to go and hug her parents. Lilly was happy to oblige her. Her mom was the first to jump up and give her a big hug and kiss on the cheek. "How's my sweet girl?"

"Doing well Momma!" She stated as she pulled back and looked at her mother. Since her parents moved away and she didn't see them very often she was more aware of her mother's beauty each time she did finally see her. Her mother's best feature, in Lilly's mind, was her green eyes that looked like soft jade stones. Her light brown hair was wavy and thick and stopped just below her shoulders.

Since they've become full-time archaeologists, her mother's skin had more color than in the years she was teaching. Her beautiful smile was surrounded by dimples and her nose was perfect. Her mother looked very young for her age with her slender shape and skin she took care of with pride. Lilly knew she worked hard on the sites and that kept her in shape. Lilly was so proud of her mother because she was beautiful inside and out.

After she ended the embrace, she looked over at her father with his arms stretched wide to give her a bear hug. Her father was her foundation. The bond the two of them shared was incredible. Looking at her dad, thinking the similarities between him and his father was almost eerie. Even as her father grayed…he still looked handsome with his soft blue eyes and easy smile. She had to hold back the emotions of losing her grandfather. Pushing them away, this was lunch with her family…there was plenty of time to cry later.

The next hug belonged to her brother Sawyer. Sawyer, her tall, slender, handsome, dark-headed brother who was two years younger and a recent graduate of the University of Illinois as an Engineer. He was 'the smart one!' Sadly he didn't hold any real interest in history, but he loved a good mystery. He's the kind of guy who wants to make the world a better place to live. She was sure, one day, he was going to make history.

Next came her forever true best friend in the whole world. Her little sister, Angel, was five years her junior but one of the closest people to her heart. She was adorable with her lightly-freckled face, dark eyes, and raven hair that made it easy for people to know they were sisters. All three children inherited much of their coloring from their Grandmother Ashley's family, yet also mixed well with their Bienvenue French Heritage.

Lilly hugged her sister tight and was overwhelmed at how much she had missed her since she started attending The University of Mississippi a few years ago. Ole' Miss got a real gem and Lilly had felt like a lost puppy the summer she moved home and Angel was getting ready to move into her dorm a month later. That was three years ago, yet felt like yesterday.

Lilly sat between her mother and sister which was a perfect spot because she had a great view of the black and white pictures that hung above her father and brother's heads. She turned to look up at Lisa, "Lisa, how is Jimmy Joe?" Lisa was married to the town funny guy. 'Jimmy Joe is full of piss and vinegar,' as her grandfather liked to say.

Lisa rolled her eyes and stated, "He's doing good and still full of piss and vinegar." Everyone laughed.

Lilly nodded at the black and white pictures. "I love the old pictures. Where did you find them all?"

Lisa smiled. "The locals. The older people were excited to have their photos on display."

"Well, I love it. I can't wait to look through them all." Lilly picked up her menu and didn't really look at it. "Hmmm…I think I'm in the mood for Lisa's fried chicken." She closed the menu and smiled at the rest of the family.

Her dad laughed. "No shocker there. We already put an order in for all of us to have chicken. It's a no-brainer that the Bienvenue family has been missing Lisa's chicken and needing their fill."

Before heading back into the kitchen, Lisa gave her condolences to the family. She went on to say how much Frank would be missed. It wasn't long after her departure, many locals having lunch made their way over to also give their condolences as well. That and of course, almost everyone had a story to tell. Lilly loved hearing the stories about her grandfather but sadly it made her miss him all the more.

Lunch lasted a lot longer than normal. Lilly had to laugh at the irony of a small town compared to a big city. In the city you'd once in a while run into one or two people you knew…on a good day. Yet in a small town everybody knew everybody and if you didn't, you were sure to know them by the end of your visit.

Greg repeatedly explained the funeral services to everyone who stopped by the table. In no time, she was sure everyone in town would learn that her grandfather was being laid out in two days' time. The funeral was scheduled for Friday morning at St. Joseph's Catholic Church and was followed by the burial at the cemetery where her grandmother was laid to rest. The same cemetery that freaked her out only hours before. She refused to even think about what happened out there. She was chalking it up to just being tired.

The family waved goodbye to many locals having lunch before making their way back to her grandfather's house. It was a given that they'd all stay at the huge house her grandparents had resided in for many years. She hoped it wouldn't freak her out staying there considering her grandfather just passed in the house a few days before.

She did have to admit that there were times in the past when she was a bit uncertain in the house, but it wasn't anything that scared her. It was mostly just odd dreams. She never really remembered the dreams, just remembered having them. When she asked her sister once if she had any crazy dreams while staying there, Angel stated she didn't but she was sometimes creeped out by all the noises the old house made.

Lilly pulled in the driveway next to her parents. Her father grabbed her suitcases and took them inside. Lilly climbed the steps to the porch and walked over and sat on the porch swing. Angel and her mother sat on both sides of her. Her mother was sharing sweet memories of Lilly's grandparents. She knew this was to help with the grieving they were all feeling and she was grateful for it.

She took a deep breath to hold back the tears. Her mother must have sensed her daughter's pain because she pulled her into a big hug. Angel joined in the hug and no one said a word for a few minutes while they quietly rocked back and forth hugging.

After several minutes she wiped her eyes and felt she was ready to go inside. She stepped across the threshold and was sad to realize her grandparents would no longer be there to greet her when she arrived for a visit. She looked around the foyer and to the left where her grandfather's study was located. To her right was the living room. She was relieved to see nothing had changed since her last visit. This helped her collect and keep her memories.

Her dad was leaning in the doorway between the two rooms that led to the kitchen and stairwell. He stated he put her bags in her and Angel's bedroom. Lilly suddenly wanted the norm of the room she always slept in. She followed her sister up the steps into the bedroom they always shared when they were here. There were actually enough bedrooms for each to have their own but the girls shared a room in Kansas City and every summer they were here they shared this same room as well.

"I can't believe Gramps is gone." Angel stated as she plopped down on the bed she always used. "It was so sad coming here yesterday." She looked back at her big sister. "I hated being here without you last night." She got up and walked over to Lilly who was standing in front of the window. She put her arm around her and laid her head on her shoulder.

Lilly rubbed her sister's arm. "I know. It seems like our lives are moving fast and everybody is getting older and leaving us." She sighed. "First Sawyer leaves for school. Then you. Mom and dad moved away in different directions. Now Grandma and Grandpa are both gone." Tears formed in her eyes. "I don't believe I deal with change well!" She stated before she laid her head on top of her sisters. No words were spoken for quite some time.

Chapter Four

As the supper hour approached, Lauren asked Greg to run to the town grocery store. Frank, being a bachelor, didn't have much food in the house. Greg smiled as he pulled up to one of his favorite childhood memories. The Old Conrad's Grocery building had been around since the late 1800s.

He wondered if the locals still called it Conrad's Grocery? When he was a kid, it didn't matter what new owner bought the business and renamed it, it was still always called Conrad's Grocery. It was the place where you'd go with a quarter and would walk out with a soda pop, some gum, and a bit of chocolate. Or at least that was the way it was when Greg was a kid. It was rather unique that it was still used as a grocery.

Greg always said Prairie du Rocher was a town for people who liked the simple life and predictable. Many people who lived here had roots that went as far back as when the French settled here in the early 1700s. They were taught early on to value the little things in life and to appreciate and preserve what they have.

In the last decade technology took over and the youth of today were so absorbed in newer, more exciting, mind-control habits. Their minds had to be stimulated every waking hour. Many children today can't handle being a part of the scenery, they fought to be in front shouting 'look at me.'

Of course, those people didn't usually want anything to do with the small towns and the simplicity that came with living in them. Greg knew in time the small towns would diminish, unless people started craving a simpler place and time.

Ironically when the nasty virus came along two and a half years ago, the same virus that took his mother's life, for all the bad it did…it also grounded people. It made families come together and get back to the basics as they were quarantined in their houses and surrounding yards. Many in the medical field fought like warriors on the front line while working with what little they had.

Greg's phone rang as he stepped out of his SUV. He sighed, as he always did when the phone rang. He hated the dang thing, but to live in this era, a cell phone was a must. Plus, his job required it. Not recognizing the number, he was hesitant to answer it. He hated telemarketers. Thinking it may have to do with his father, he decided to push the talk button.

The gentleman on the other end identified himself as his father's lawyer and was wanting to set up a time to go over the will. Greg explained that he and Lauren were only going to be in town until Saturday, but that they would be back mid-November. The dig they were on was close to being finished and they needed to be there for the ending.

The lawyer explained that he was leaving town Friday and asked that they meet sometime tomorrow. It was decided they would hold the meeting at Frank's house the following morning. Greg hung up and had to sit back down in his car to gather his composure. The reality of his father's death had just hit him hard.

His heart broke when he received the call Monday morning that his father had passed away. Frank loved his house so it was only fitting that he had a massive heart attack while watching television in the living room. Thank goodness he and his buddies always met at Lisa's for coffee in the mornings because when he didn't show, his friend Butch stopped by to see what was up. Greg knew it had to have been hard on Butch, after knocking and opening the door to shout Frank's name, to see his friend sleeping in his recliner, only he wasn't sleeping.

Greg was sure it was a heart attack because his dad had heart issues. The coroner's report wasn't back yet but he'd almost bet on it. Yet in reality it didn't much matter because his dad was gone and there was nothing he could do about it.

Lilly couldn't believe how tired she was a few hours later as she prepared for bed. Crawling between the sheets she looked over at her sister who was sitting legs-crossed on her own bed reading on her notebook. "So do you have a boyfriend?" She asked the younger girl.

Angel laughed as she looked up at her sister. "Where did that come from?"

"I don't know. I just feel like we've been so busy lately we haven't had any real time to talk. You stayed in Oxford all summer and I was busy at the Independent."

"No, I'm not seeing anyone." She sighed and looked towards the window. "There was a boy but he's graduating this year and going back to San Francisco. I felt it was better to end it before it got too far. I mean I hate long distance relationships." Looking at her sister she asked, "You?"

Lilly chuckled. "Nope." She rolled in the direction of her sister and propped her head on her hand and her elbow on the bed. "I don't think I'll ever find Mr. Right." She fell on her back and looked at the ceiling. "I mean I have the perfect man in my mind...but I can't find him."

Angel laughed. "That's a funny way to put it. Can't find him? Is he one specific person?" She sat the notebook aside and looked over at her sister.

"I don't know what is wrong with me. Like...I find it weird but I only seem to find myself attracted to men with emerald green eyes and light blondish brown hair." She looked over at her sister. "It's so weird. It's like I know he's out there but I can't seem to find him."

"Well he sounds hot...I think I want him too." Laughed Angel, before she felt the pillow fly into her face.

That night Lilly dreamed of her perfect man. As she drifted off into a deep sleep, she found herself inside what looked to be a barn-like structure. The inside walls were constructed of wood. There were lanterns hanging everywhere. The lights gave a soft, bright glow throughout the room. The room was a faded color of dark gray that was found on untreated wood. Her first thought was that everything was dull, yet beautiful in its glow.

Her vision had started out hazy but the room slowly focused in. She was excited by the decor of the room. There were huge pillars holding up the beams. Blue silk draped throughout the room. The chandelier in the middle took her breath away as she noticed they were lit with real candles that bounced dancing light around the room.

Lilly looked down and was shocked to see she was garbed in a gown...a ballgown of sorts. She wondered if she was a princess. She swished back and forth in the soft, silky, deep-blue material. The gown was detailed down to the perfect buttons.

The top of the gown was the same shade of blue as the skirt that draped out several feet from her hips and fell in gathers that met at the back of her waist. Looking from the front of her waist, she ran her hands across the beautiful flow of gold silk that emerged from the hooped undergarment pushing the material out and falling into a triangle that stopped at the floor. She couldn't resist putting her hands around her waist to confirm it was as small as it appeared. She lifted the skirt to see cute, but worn, booted shoes on her feet.

An embroidered gold pattern outlined the blue silk and matched the gold pattern that outlined the bodice of the dress. She was shocked to see her breasts were pushed high, almost under her chin, and very full. *Hell yes*, she thought. *I am loving this look.* She was just as shocked her breasts could look as big as they did. She lifted her hands to cup them and see if they were real. Luckily, she realized what she was doing and stopped herself. Her dress sleeves were very tight, giving her upper arms a snug fit before a wide drape of cloth emerged from her elbow and stopped at her wrist.

Reaching up she felt a soft piece of ribbon around her neck. She assumed it was a choker necklace of some sort, but not sure since there wasn't a mirror nearby. Reaching higher she could tell she was sporting an awesome updo. "Dang," she murmured to herself. "I wish I had a mirror."

Looking around for one, she was surprised to see people everywhere. People that weren't there minutes ago. Everyone was talking as they looked towards a stage where there was what appeared to be a band setting up.

Lilly found it odd that people all around her were speaking a language she didn't know yet she understood every word perfectly. She knew so much about this place. Yet how? Her memory was clearing up and she understood what was happening and where she was. She was Liliane Elizabeth Bienvenue and she was attending the Twelfth Night Ball held every January. The year was 1754 or wait was it October, 2022? More ironic was that she knew these people yet she wasn't sure how.

Standing in front of her, several feet away was her father, Greg only it wasn't him. It was her other father, Jules Delbert Bienvenue, her father in 1754. Yet he looked so much like her father…but different. Jules appeared to be the age of Greg, only he was dressed in a blue waistcoat filled out with ruffles from his undershirt and a gold trimmed kerchief. His breeches stopped at the knees and that was precisely where his stockings looked like they started. His shoes looked like dress shoes with a big silver buckle on the top, just like a pilgrim. Looking back up she spotted the pirate-looking hat on her father's head. Oddly, she even knew what the three-pointed hat was called…a Capotain. *Wow Pops, you look great,* she thought.

Lilly smiled and waved back at Sebastian and Josephine DuLois. Lilly had to admit she was a bit jealous of Josephine's dress. The couple recently came here from France and it appeared her trunks were filled with the newest and most popular fashion. Lilly planned to study the look later and would try to mimic it when she started her next gown.

Her very best friend, Hattie, waved at her as she was being presented to other attendees by her parents. When all of the formalities were finished, Hattie rushed over and hugged her. "Your gown is all the rage Liliane."

"Thank you but I believe it is you that is the rage." She looked at her friend's beautiful red hair all done up in an elegant coiffure. "I would give anything to have your locks!"

"No…it is I who lacks standing next to you." Her friend stated.

Lilly laughed. "We have to stop. Let's call a truce and admit it is Lady DuLois who shines tonight with her fabulous gown."

Hattie looked over at the lady and nodded her agreement.

Lilly smiled at her friend and suddenly thought about how much she looked like her friend Rissa. She frowned and thought that couldn't be because Rissa was her friend in a different century. Taking a deep breath Lilly decided to not think about it. She didn't want anything to tarnish her night at the Ball.

Looking around, Lilly was in awe at the beauty of the room. The more the people arrived the more the colors swirled every which way. This was the third Ball she was allowed to attend since becoming of age. She loved the dances and the merriment that came with the evening. Even the gentlemen drinking heavily in their cups made it fun. The flirting was exciting as the women batted their eyes and flirted with their fans.

In her excitement, Lilly spun around in her large hooped dress and thought this was going to be a glorious night. As she completed her spin, she came face to face with the most beautiful gentleman she had ever laid eyes on. She was sure he heard her gasp as she paused in her spin and put her hands, fan intact, against her heart. Never once pulling her eyes away from his.

The gentleman nodded to her. She was suddenly very confused. He was the man calling to her at the cemetery…wasn't he? She couldn't be sure. This man was so perfect with his sandy brown hair and the deepest green eyes that she was sure would make an emerald look dull. His smile was beautiful and he had dimples. Dear Lord, how she loved dimples. Wasn't he the one she was just describing to her sister about in their bedroom at Grandpa's house?

"Liliane," her father addressed her as he stood next to the gentleman. "I'd like you to meet Dane." Looking at Dane, he stated, "Dane, Liliane Bienvenue…my daughter."

Everything inside her melted as the man nodded and took her hand and kissed it. "Hello Liliane. With your permission can I address you as such?" At her nod he continued, "Please, call me Dane."

"Hello…um" was all she could say.

He chuckled at her pause and thought she was confused by his unusual name. "Dane is my second name because my given name is the same as my grandfather's name. It gets a bit challenging to know who was being addressed so it was easier to use my second name." Lilly wasn't sure what he was saying. She was too aware that his hand lingered on hers before letting it go.

Her father cleared his throat and broke her out of her trance. She slightly shook her head. "Hello Dane." She smiled and curtsied. "So what brings you to Fort de Chartres?"

"I have recently been assigned here. I only arrived this morning." Looking around briefly before his beautiful green eyes landed back on her, he smiled. "So far, from everything I have seen…there is so much unbelievable beauty here." Dane's stare was letting her know he was directing his statement towards her.

Lilly suddenly remembered Hattie next to her. "I'm sorry, I would like you to meet my friend Hattie LeFebvre."

Lilly noticed her friend looked just as lovestruck as herself when Dane bent over and kissed her hand. Lilly didn't know why but she was happy his hand didn't linger over her friend's hand. *Wow,* she thought, *am I feeling jealousy?*

Just then the band opened up with the first dance of the night, the Branle. Her father immediately left her to dance with her mother. Lilly didn't want to make eye contact with Dane because she didn't want him to feel pressured to dance with her. Yet she was elated when he bowed in front of her and asked for her permission to dance. She agreed as she watched Hattie being whisked away by another gentleman.

The Branle was a partnered dance, yet interacted with other couples in a circle. Many times she had to face Dane and look into his eyes. She was suddenly so shy she was sure her cheeks were red.

To hide her awkwardness Lilly would look around the room to avoid eye contact with the handsome Dane. She was glad she knew the dance well because she didn't wish to embarrass herself in front of him. Her mother and father loved to dance and in their free evenings they taught her and her brother Abraham the popular dances.

She was glad the fort's meeting hall was large enough to accommodate all the people in attendance and had enough room for the dancing. This was the only building that was large enough for the event. Without the table and chairs in the middle of the room the size was perfect for the flowing movement of the dances.

As the song ended Lilly found herself flustered again. Dane walked her over to where the punch was being served. She looked up to find the piercing green eyes staring deep into hers. "Please forgive me if I seem forward Miss Liliane, but how is it you haven't been spoken for…yet?"

Lilly could feel herself blush. Looking away so he wouldn't see her red cheeks, she noticed Edwin Berger lingering just inside the door. Lilly quickly looked the other way so as to not make eye contact. She always had such a bad feeling about Edwin. He creeped her out. She suddenly remembered dreaming of him as the devil at the cemetery. Lilly shook her head as she started getting confused. That hasn't happened yet…has it?

"Is everything alright? Did I embarrass you by my forwardness?" Dane asked and broke her out of her trance. "Please forgive me, fair Liliane." He looked genuinely upset.

Lilly smiled. "I'm sorry. I was a little lost there and no…I am not offended." She started to blush again. She wasn't really sure what he asked. Maybe she should be offended. She was relieved to see her father walk up. Hattie was right behind him.

The next several hours Lilly found herself dancing with many of the boys she grew up with. Dane didn't ask her to dance until the waltz was presented. She took his hand and stepped onto the dance floor.

Lilly tried not to think about how incredible it was to be in this stranger's arms. Her mind started drifting as she looked at his chest. She could tell he was well built. His tight chest muscles were pushing against his waistcoat. Lilly imagined herself unbuttoning all those buttons on it and slowly taking his kerchief off. Then next would be the white shirt. She fantasized about running her hands up and under it. Next she would undo the drawstring that held his…!

"Lilly? Hello?" Dane pulled her out of her thoughts as he swung her into the slow provocative dance. "Do you need to sit down? Your face looks flushed and the dance is only about half over?"

Lilly was so embarrassed. She smiled up at Dane and decided to focus. "I'm sorry. I was a bit sidetracked for a minute. What was it you asked me?"

Dane smiled and wondered if she was always this absentminded. It didn't matter if she was easily distracted, her beauty made up for any flaw she had. "I asked earlier why hasn't anyone spoken for you yet?"

Lilly's blushing started all over again. "Well it's not like I've met many men while living at an isolated fort. And you've met my father…he's a bit over protective."

"I never got around to asking him about his children when we met earlier today. Are you his only child?"

Lilly shook her head. "I have a brother. There were also two other girls but my sister died of scarlet fever a few years back and my mother lost another daughter who was stillborn."

"I'm sorry to hear that." He stated sincerely.

Lilly didn't want to talk about sad things. She wanted to talk about him. Just as she was about to ask him about himself the music ended. She let him lead her back to her father.

Dane spoke with Lilly's father for a moment before one of the men in the band stomped a stick on the ground and announced "The Virginia Reel."

Jules asked Dane to dance with his wife as he took his daughter's hand and walked with her to the dance floor. She was placed next to her mother in a line of eight ladies while across was each of their partners. Dane was next to Jules and across from her mother. Hattie and her father were a part of the eight sets.

The dance was a fun one where you and your partner stayed partnered but each couple would break away to swing arms with each person of the opposite sex in the group. Each couple weaved in and out until they met back up. Lilly wished they still had dances like this in her time.

Suddenly thinking about her time made everything start to swirl around. She looked up to see her father coming towards her just as she almost fainted. She knew she needed to focus on his eyes or she would lose sight of him.

As Jules approached his daughter, she stated she was alright. Dane asked for his permission to step outside with her to get some fresh air. Jules reluctantly agreed but asked that they go no farther than the front steps.

Dane guided her through the side entrance doors and motioned to one of the chairs placed on the porch. She stepped past him and grabbed ahold of the railing that surrounded the edge of the platform. She was shocked to see how surprisingly warm it was for January. As a rule, the winters here were bitter this time of the year. Yet this winter seemed calm and very unseasonably warm.

"Are you feeling better?" He asked several minutes later with much concern in his voice.

Lilly blushed as she hugged the porch post next to the steps while he stood on the step below her. He took his hat off and she wanted to reach out and run her hands through his hair. *Geez this man is driving her crazy.* "Yes, I'm sorry. I never faint. But if I wish to be honest, I believe I was close to it."

He wondered why sometimes she spoke oddly and if the French community here was acquiring an accent. "I know. One of the older ladies was pulling out her smelling salts before you would have had the chance to hit the ground." He joked.

She liked that they were eye to eye because he was on the step below her. She didn't flinch as he reached out and brushed a curl away from her eye. "You are the most enchanted creature I have ever seen."

"I doubt that. You've just come from France. I'm sure the ladies there make me look like a bag of flour."

Dane gave her a serious look. "Lilly, if I may be so bold and call you Lilly, no one I have ever met comes close to comparing to your beauty…inside and out. It's as if I can see into your soul. From the moment I first noticed you, you have taken my breath away."

Lilly thought he was smooth with the words. She didn't care, she was loving every minute of his sexy accent and beautiful face saying words every girl dreams of hearing! "Dane, I do believe you are trying to turn my head with all this flattery." She almost laughed out loud because she sounded like a damsel in a historical romance novel.

She smiled and tapped his arm with her fan. "I can assure you that I am not one of your ladies from France who believes in love at first sight." Lilly wasn't sure where these words were coming from. It was like someone was speaking for her.

Dane picked her hand up and kissed the back of it. "I promise you I haven't had time to flatter any others. Nor have I, until this moment, had the desire."

Many seconds passed as they looked into each other's eyes. Lilly wanted to taste his lips and decided to move in just as the door opened and her mother stepped outside and asked how she was feeling. Jumping back from him she reassured her she was better. Her mother announced the King's Cake was getting ready to be presented.

She strolled inside the building with her hand inside Dane's elbow. Had she looked to the left she would have seen the anger in Edwin's eyes. Had she looked to the right she would have spotted how happy her father was that she was with Dane.

The biggest tradition of the Twelfth Night Ball is 'The King's Cake.' Inside the cake are four beans…specially marked beans. The first man to find a bean is the 'King' until the next Twelfth Night Ball. He then chooses his 'Queen' for the year. The other three men to find beans make up the King's Court. Each man chooses a lady to be his partner. It was a fun tradition that didn't truly give any social standing.

Lilly, Hattie, and her mother watch as the men line up to eat a piece of the precut cake. Lilly frowned when she spotted Edwin first in line. Dear Lord she hoped he didn't find a bean. She wholeheartedly believed he would choose her.

Across the room Edwin was excited to be the first in line to get the cake. He made his way off to the side of the stage and reached in the left pocket of his breeches for the bean he hid there earlier. He started to worry when he didn't feel it in his pocket. He panicked and dug around in his other pockets. No bean there. He was sure he put it in the left pocket. He looked up and noticed a few women giving him an odd look.

Edwin knew he needed to calm down before he drew any more attention to himself. He patted his left pocket nonchalantly. Still no bean. *Son-of-a-bitch,* he thought as he looked up to see the new guy, old man Geofrey's son according to the other men, walk over to the Madam with the first bean. *I'm going to kill the bastard if he picks her.* He quietly promised himself.

To his dismay he watched as the man walked over to Lilly and bowed down and asked if she would be his Queen. He wanted to scream and beat something as Lilly smiled and nodded. She was supposed to be his Queen; not Geofrey's!

Lilly couldn't believe Dane got the first bean. After watching as he approached the Madam, she kept her fingers crossed behind her back hoping he'd ask her to be his Queen. She could hardly contain her excitement as he walked towards her and asked if she'd be his queen. Trying to play it cool, she nodded after he asked. All but one of the beans had been found. It was decided throughout the hall that Lilly's parents would fill up the last spot because her father was the commander at the fort. After the party was announced, the band started up with another waltz and Lilly couldn't have been more excited. She once again was in Dane's arms. The night couldn't get any better.

Then suddenly, as soon as the dance began, Lilly felt herself drifting away. *'Oh no, not yet,'* she thought as the colors in the room started to fade and everything was turning hazy. As she drifted away, she looked back and smiled as she watched herself dancing happily with Dane. She turned to look across the room. There was Edwin with a murderous look on his face as he watched the couple dance. Suddenly he turned to where Lilly was floating away. Lilly truly believed he could see her in her dream…if that made any sense. The smile he gave her was pure evil.

Chapter Five

Lilly woke up with a start. She willed herself back to sleep so she could continue the dance with the hot colonial guy. She tried but the reality of where she was told her it was only a dream. This bummed her out...*dang that was a nice dream.* She sat up in bed and was surprised to find herself shaking and soaked through from a cold sweat.

Looking over at her sister's bed she was relieved to see she was still sleeping. The bedside clock showed it was barely four in the morning. Not ready to go back to sleep, she grabbed her robe before making her way downstairs for a glass of water.

The first level of the old house put off an eerie feeling at such an early hour. Yet Lilly found comfort being in her grandparent's house. After taking a small drink, she emptied the cup into the sink and decided to go into her grandfather's study to find something to read. She needed to get her mind off the dream she just had. She didn't want to remember that the men in the dream were the same two men she envisioned at the cemetery the day before.

Her grandfather's study was one of her favorite rooms in the house. It was located to the left of the entrance into the house and always smelled of leather and a bit of that cologne the old timers liked. The best part of the room was it was loaded with history. The room was a bit magical to a history buff. She was sure there were first editions of some ancient best sellers lining the walls.

Looking around at all of his books she figured she should stay away from anything historical. She had a habit of starting on a place in history and not being able to put it down until she finished every word of it. History was an addiction for her.

She glanced around the room and noticed a book sitting on her grandfather's old desk. Suddenly she wanted to know what his final book was before he passed. She picked it up and was surprised to see it was a book on her family genealogy printed in a hardback. Rubbing her finger down it she wondered why she had never known there was a book on her family history?

The book looked new and she glanced around and spotted a box on the floor by the desk. Inside were several more books just like the one in her hand. There was a note inside from a self-publishing company thanking her grandfather for using their company to print his books.

Lilly pulled out the desk chair and was smiling at the thought of her grandfather going through the process of preserving their Bienvenue family history. Suddenly she had to give a slight pause and take a deep breath to fight back the emotions she felt when remembering she loved hanging out in the study with her grandfather. This was so much harder than she imagined losing both her grandparents in a two-and-a-half-year span. Everything was changing. She looked over to see the two photos framed on his desk. One was of her parents, herself, and her siblings. She smiled because the picture was pretty old. She was probably twelve at the time and the picture was taken on her grandparents' front porch.

The other photo was of her grandparents. The photo looked like it was taken only a few years before her grandmother's death. Lilly held the picture in her hand and ran her fingers over her beautiful grandparents' faces. "I miss you both so very much." She stated as she looked upward and wiped at her eyes. "Please know I love you both as much as anyone can love a person." Lilly stared at the picture and remembered her grandparents alive and well for several minutes before setting it back down and wiping away the tears.

She looked down at the hardback book. The first line was the book title, *Bienvenue Family.* Below that was the date *1698-2022* and the next line read *The New World.* She wasn't surprised by the 'New World' part of the title. Her grandfather always said his Bienvenue line started when they came here from France. She asked him to clarify and he said the name is too common in France. Yet there had only been his line to settle here so it was easier to keep track of the American line.

Lilly opened the thin book to the first page and smiled when she read the dedication. To my only child Greg Franklin Bienvenue, his wife Lauren Miles Bienvenue, and my three beautiful grandchildren, Lillian Elizabeth, Sawyer Francis, Angel Ashley Bienvenue. May you enjoy your history and one day find your story to pass to the next generation of Bienvenues.

Lilly smiled, how like her grandfather to create a book so the family wouldn't forget where they came from. It was because of him she and her father loved history. She hoped one day she'd have a story to pass on to her children.

The book started with the introduction of the name Bienvenue…its history and origin. It goes on to give a summary of any nobility with the Bienvenue name in France. Apparently she had a Baron or two in her past. Her grandfather added that the stories and information in the book have been passed down from generation to generation and he states that it is a known fact that tales can grow tall but that in the book he is trying to stick with what seems to be truth instead of fables. She smiled because she could see her grandfather using the word fables.

The actual book begins in the late 1600s and starts with a French Army Commander by the name of Jules Bienvenue. Jules was a strong figure in France and devoted to his King. He was young and dedicated to France. It goes on to say that Jules jumped at the opportunity to come to the new world in 1726 to command the post at Fort de Chartres.

Wait a minute, Lilly thought. *How weird was that? Didn't I dream my dad was named Jules way back then?* Lilly started getting weirded out. Did she just dream this? Or was it deja vu? She decided to shake it off for a bit. She didn't want to get spooked. Besides, maybe she dreamt it because her grandfather was always sharing stories of his ancestors and she could have subconsciously dreamed of these people because she knew of them through him.

Her grandfather didn't have any actual documented stories of Jules or the family, other than they arrived and lived at the fort. He went on to describe what life was like back then according to several early history books written about the fort. He described the fort as a wooden structure built in 1720. The reason the Fort was placed along the Mississippi was because France wanted there to be another large French settlement between Quebec and New Orleans that would be a stopping point in between when traveling the Mississippi. The fort was also built for trading up and down the river and also for protection against some of the Indian tribes.

The French in the area were peaceful with most of the local Indians as well, yet other tribes didn't like the local Indians or the Frenchmen. So there were constant battles and struggles causing the need for a structure to provide protection. He went on to write about a French explorer by the name of

Philippe Renaut. Renault was a Frenchman who was commissioned to come to the area to look for lead, precious gems, diamonds and gold. With disappointment, he never found any of the stones but he did find an abundance of lead…but mostly in the Missouri area across the river. In no time Renaut left the area leaving many miners and slaves behind.

The book continues to describe how the wooden fort was quick to fall into ruins and another one erected that also couldn't survive the harsh environment. In total there were actually four forts with the present-day one still standing. The first three fell to ruins because they were made of wood, The fourth was made of limestone from the bluffs giving the structure a better chance of surviving. Lilly chuckled as she thought of the 'Big bad wolf and the three pigs.'

Continuing on she read how a group of Frenchmen, contracted by King Louis XV, was given funds to acquire five hundred slaves to build the limestone fort and the cost was one million dollars. Lilly softly whistled, that was quite a bit of money for that time. Especially to erect a building so close to a swift river, prone to flooding. In conclusion, the fourth fort started construction in 1752 and was completed in 1756 and is still standing approximately four miles from the town of Prairie du Rocher.

Her grandfather was detailed and descriptive as he goes through the end of the 1700s with the French losing the Illinois side of the river to the English. He mentions how the fort becomes abandoned before he rolls into the 1800s. He describes the houses and style of dress in Prairie du Rocher. There is a nice writeup about the Creole House. The date it was built was still in question. Apparently many locals believed it to be around the 1800s yet some historians think it was mid-1700s.

He went on to describe the hardships people had to endure because of the cold winters and hot summers. It is written that after Illinois became a state in 1818 the people of Prairie du Rocher tried to establish a township but there was a struggle because of the low population.

The book goes on to explain how an aunt, several generations back, lost her fiancé by what the locals believe was the hands of The Fox tribe. He apparently was murdered near the town creek during a raid on the small town. Lilly's Grandfather wrote how his grandfather, many greats over, always believed it was an ambush by another gentleman who wanted to court the lady.

Lilly wasn't sure why but she suddenly remembered her and Tripp hanging out at the town creek the last time she saw him many years before. Odd, but he had a dream that someone killed him there. She felt shivers run up her spine and thought it was odd that a small boy dreamt about being murdered by the same place a murder took place years before.

Apparently that wasn't the only foul play in the Bienvenue family. Another aunt was being courted by a local boy. Supposably the girl turned the eye of a local bad boy and he didn't like her with anyone else. One evening her aunt's fiancé was walking her home after a movie, they were rerouted by knives and pistols pushed into their backs directing them across the track where her aunt watched her fiancé get murdered. Thank goodness the fiancé had a friend with them who killed the man before he could kill her aunt.

Geez, Lilly thought, *the women in the family aren't very lucky when it comes to men.*

Paging through and skimming over the book until she had time to really read it, Lilly liked how it mentioned all the highpoints of the town in the three hundred years of its existence. There was even mention of the Brickley Mansion with the Chicago Lottery. The Conrad house appeared several times in the book.

Lilly was excited to share the books with her family. She was sure they didn't know about it because they would have been just as excited and would have already mentioned it. She even smiled at how well it was written. If she had to guess, she would say she acquired her writing skills from her grandfather.

Flipping towards the end of the book she was surprised to see the sun was rising. Standing, she paged through to the ending to take a quick glance at what remained. She probably needed to be getting back to bed. Just as she was about to close the book, she spotted the Bienvenue Family Tree on the very last page.

Now this really piqued her interest. She always wanted to know her family tree but never had time to research it. She was happy her grandfather finished this before he left them.

It started with Jules, the same gentleman he mentioned earlier in the book. Jules had been a Lieutenant Commander in charge at the fort until 1754. He and his wife, Maria, had three daughters and one son. One daughter died at birth and another at a young age. *Weird,* Lilly thought, *I feel like I knew that.* Shaking her head, she moved on to read that the third daughter was named Liliane. "How cool," She stated out loud.

The couple's son was named Abraham. He helped preserve the Bienvenue family name by having three boys. Abraham's son Anton was the only one to have a son that carried the name to her direct line. His name was Gerald Anton. Lilly smiled at all the old names listed. Rarely did you hear Gerald anymore much less Anton. Gerald had several children but her direct line went through Gerald's oldest and namesake.

Lilly spent the next hour studying the tree and she noticed several interesting things. For example, the name Liliane was an aunt in the 1700s and again an aunt in the 1800s. Then in the 1900s there is mentioned an aunt named Lillian which is also how her name is spelled. She assumed it was because Lillian was more of the English/American version of Liliane. Also she found it a bit odd that throughout the book each Lilly never had children and only one had ever married. Also, the most odd thing about it was that each Lilly was born or died on April 23rd or November 1st. Stranger yet, when one Lilly died, another Lilly was listed as born...on the same day. There was a total of four Lilly's throughout three-hundred years but it was still very odd. Creepier yet the last Lilly to die was the same day she was born...23 April 1996. Did that mean she was going to die on November 1st? The thought gave her chills throughout her body.

She sat back in the chair and had to think about this situation. What were the odds that someone named their newborn after a great-great-aunt? Looking back at the first Lilly, she lived in France when she died and her great nephew named his newborn child after her, or she assumed after her, on the same day. Of course, there wasn't telegraph or phone service then so he probably didn't even know about the death until days, maybe even weeks later.

She wondered if her parents named her after her great-great-great aunt Lillian Bienvenue that died on the day she was born? Did they even know who she was? She didn't remember ever hearing about her father having an Aunt Lillian. Looking at her grandparents' picture she decided she needed sleep. Her emotions have been a bit crazy and out of sorts since she arrived yesterday. This was only adding to it. She wasn't dramatic by nature but this was pushing it.

Leaning back in the swivel chair she thought about how she really hoped this tree wasn't trying to tell her she was going to be an unmarried, childless, old maid one day. She picked up the book and then set it back down. This wasn't right…was it? She didn't know what to think.

She decided it was too early to be thinking about crazy family trees. She took a deep breath and rubbed at her very tired eyes. After clearing her vision, she yelped and pushed back in the chair when she spotted her mother in the doorway.

"Did I scare you Lilly-Bear?" Her mother asked with amusement in her eyes.

Lilly had her hands over her heart willing it to stop acting like it was going to pop out of her chest. "Yes ma'am, you did." She chuckled.

"I'm sorry." Her mother apologized as she walked into the room. "I was surprised to see someone sitting in here at six AM no less."

"I woke up around four and couldn't go back to sleep." She didn't tell her mother about her dream because she wasn't ready to try and figure that out yet. Instead, she picked up the Bienvenue Genealogy book instead. "Mom, did you know Grandpa was writing a genealogy book?"

Her mother nodded. "Yes, he wanted to surprise you all with it on Christmas." She looked over at the desk before walking over and picking up the book. "This is fabulous. Your grandfather finished it." She pressed the book to her chest. "This will mean so much to our family. I was afraid he hadn't finished it before he passed. I haven't been in his study since we arrived."

Smiling at her mother, she stated, "Wait until you and dad get a load of what I found in the book." Then it dawned on her that her parents may have already figured out the pattern. After all, her father was a history professor. Surely he would have checked into his own genealogy.

"What did you find, dear?"

She gave her mother a suspicious look. "Wait, did dad help grandpa with the book?"

Lauren shook her head. "No…well wait, your grandfather did ask him to look up a few things that he wanted verified about the history of the town. But for the most part your grandfather did it all on his own." She glanced down at the book she was holding. "To be honest, the only reason I think he even told your father about the book was because he didn't know the first thing about putting it in print. So he had to let him in on the secret." She smiled, "And of course, your father doesn't keep secrets from me…unless it's when he's sneaking junk food in the middle of the night." She rolled her eyes, "And then he wonders why his cholesterol is so high." She stated as she shook her head.

Lilly smiled as she grabbed the box of books and followed her mother into the kitchen. Her parents were always arguing about her father's diet. Her momma was health conscious…her father wasn't.

She was happy to see her father at the counter making coffee. Placing the box on the table, she walked over to him and she reached up to give him a kiss on the cheek before wishing him a good morning. He hugged her as he replied the same greeting.

Grabbing a cup from the cabinet, she turned to her parents and asked, "What made you decide to name me Lilly?"

Both parents gave her a confused look before looking at one another. Her mother shrugged and stated, "I don't really know." She looked at her husband. "Do you Greg?"

"I don't really remember. That was a while ago." He looked at Lilly. "What a weird question."

"I know and I'll explain why in a minute. But you both really don't know?"

Her mother shook her head. "I don't really think there was a reason behind it. When I was pregnant, I remember we couldn't agree on a name. Then in the hospital while I was holding you, one of us came up with Lillian." She looked at her husband. "Wait, I remember, Ashley and Frank came in and Frank said he just got a phone call saying his aunt Lillian passed earlier that morning. I think she was almost one hundred years old. I think it was you Greg who said you thought Lilly," she nodded to her daughter, "looked like the name Lillian and it would be a nice tribute to your great-aunt and I agreed," She smiled at her daughter. "From there it just stuck."

Before Lilly could say anything, her father walked over to the box Lilly just put on the table. "What's this?"

Lauren was the first to reply as she walked over to him. "Lilly found these in your father's study. They are the genealogy books that your dad was having printed."

Greg was excited. "That's incredible." He stated as he ran his hand over the binder. "I'm so happy he finished it." He smiled at Lilly. "This project gave him a purpose since Mom died." Looking at the invoice on the box, he continued. "I bet he needed to see this job completed before he went to be with her. According to this tracking, the books were delivered here the day before he passed."

Lilly felt sad when she heard the word passed. Trying not to dwell on it she decided to tell her parents about what she found in the family tree. Both parents were just as startled by Lilly's findings. Her dad was openly intrigued.

"Lilly," he stated as he flipped to the back of the book to look at the tree. "Grab a paper and pencil and let's play with this."

Lilly did as he said and sat next to him at the kitchen table while Lauren started on breakfast. The first thing on the list was Liliane from the 1700s. Lilly had him look closely at the births and deaths.

Liliane Elizabeth, 1 November 1732–23 April 1803

Liliane Maria, 23 April 1803–1 November 1897

Lillian Francis, 1 November 1897–23 April 1996

Lillian Elizabeth, 23 April 1996–

Greg was the first to comment on the pattern. "I feel like there is definitely something here. I am almost relieved to see different middle names. That would have made it even more eerie." He looked up at his daughter. "That is until I noticed you and the first Lilly share the same middle name."

"Eerie…try knowing you may die on a particular day." Lilly shivered.

Her mother leaned over her dad to take a look. "I just think it's weird that we gave her the name she was apparently supposed to have."

Greg leaned back and looked up at his wife. "I'm trying to think about what I remember about Aunt Lillian and that day. Dad said he just got a phone call from his Uncle Ezra explaining that Aunt Lillian passed away. I believe she died in her sleep."

He looked over at Lilly. "I don't really think I thought anything about you and her sharing the same name. I just remember liking the name and thinking it would be a nice tribute."

Angel and Sawyer joined the trio a few minutes later. Lilly and Greg filled them in on their findings. Within a few minutes everyone was on their laptops trying to find clues until Lauren made them turn everything off and put pencils down until after breakfast. Yet during the course of the meal, they discussed different theories of what it could have been. Some were far-fetched like when Sawyer suggested Lilly was possibly a vampire. That gave the family a chuckle.

Chapter Six

As soon as the meal was done everyone went about their morning getting ready for Frank's lawyer to visit. Sawyer came downstairs when he was finished getting ready and jumped back on his laptop. Several minutes later he called excitedly for Lilly and his father.

Both quickly trotted down the steps. Lilly was brushing her teeth and Frank was hopping on one socked-foot while the other sock was in his hand. Sawyer laughed at the picture they made. His mother and Angel were not far behind the pair.

"Sorry," he chuckled. "I didn't mean to make you rush." Sawyer stated.

Lilly, with a mouthful of toothpaste commented, "Weelre, din why'd you hout." She kept her hand over her foamy mouth as she made her way to the bathroom to rinse. A few moments later she walked back into the living room and sat down on the sofa arm to see what Sawyer found.

"Okay, so I was playing around with the 1700s Liliane's name and according to Grandpa's book she was married to Daniel Geofrey. They weren't married long, 28 June 1754 and he died on 4 July 1754. Nothing came up as a couple and Geofrey has at least fifteen generations of the exact namesakes so that is almost a dead end." He turned the computer towards her so she could get a better view.

"So then I typed in Fort de Chartres, and Lilly's husband's birth and death date…28 June and 4 July 1754…and this is what I found."

Lilly picked up the laptop and began reading. "Fort de Chartres and The Phantom Funeral." Lilly quickly read through the article about how a commander at the fort died because he and another soldier were in love with the same female. The commander of the fort had taken a bride and a soldier wanted her for himself. Not long after the couple was married the husband was ambushed and murdered. It was implied that the murderer was never caught.

It went on to say that due to the weather being hotter than usual the funeral was to take place that same night under the light of the full moon. The rising water also caused the Commander's funeral to take place in the town of Prairie du Rocher.

Sawyer searched around and came across an article going into detail about the funeral. Apparently there were documents at the fort that were written about the events. A scholar interpreted the French writing at the fort to English and they were later published in a book. There was a section about a murder of an officer and some very descriptive details of the funeral.

To summarize it Sawyer explained to the family, "No names were mentioned but the article continued on that this event leads to what some believe as the local ghost…the Phantom Funeral. Apparently the bride didn't attend her husband's funeral and for the next several centuries a funeral procession appears when there is a bright moon on July 4th. It is believed the Phantom is looking for his bride."

Her father interrupted his son. "I know that story. It used to be a fun one we would love to tell at campouts." He paused in deep thought before continuing. "Let me see if I remember…The funeral consisted of many soldiers following behind a wagon with a casket sitting inside. Leading the funeral were fourteen pairs of horsemen. The men on horseback were of rank and took their place accordingly. Rumor has it the bride was in danger because no one knew of the whereabouts of the murderer so she was sent immediately to France, missing the funeral."

Lilly smirked at how ridiculous the tale was before Sawyer continued. "Another article connected to the Phantom Funeral says it is believed that because the Commander's bride wasn't in attendance, a Phantom Funeral procession travels through time and is silently looking for the missing link…the bride of the deceased. The procession is believed to be leaving the cemetery with the casket still intact."

Lilly shook her head and smiled at her family. "People come up with the craziest things."

"Maybe, but Lilly," he looked up from his laptop at his sister, "our ancestor was Lillian Bienvenue, married to Daniel Geofrey at the fort during these dates. On page twenty-seven of Grandpa's book it talks about how Jules' daughter married the new Commander in charge. It goes on to say he dies on July Fourth and not long after Lilly goes to France with her family leaving her brother here to take over command of the fort. Daniel was probably killed early in the morning and buried in the evening." He looked at her once more. "If you ask me there is some kind of weird connection here."

Lilly looked back at the article and her tone became a bit sharp. "The story doesn't say anything about the year. What actually pulled up was July 4th and Phantom Funeral."

Sawyer gave her an odd look. "Okay, I'm only speculating here, so why are you getting all defensive?"

She looked at her brother and found she couldn't explain how she didn't want this to be true because she didn't want all these bad things to be connected to her. She sure as hell didn't want to be an old unmarried maid who was going to die on a November 1st…year unknown.

Shaking her head, she smiled at her crazy thoughts. "I don't know. I think it just freaks me out a little."

Sawyer smiled. "I love this stuff. I could play with this all day."

Lilly rolled her eyes and threw her hands up. "If anyone finds a pattern, it will be you!"

Her father interrupted the siblings. "I do know someone who maybe will give you a description of seeing the funeral once. Frankie Lang, an old friend of your mom and mine that was raised here, used to talk about how she once watched the ghostly funeral procession go through town."

Lauren appeared in the doorway. "You're right Greg. Frankie runs the You Bee You Boutique in town. If you kids are serious for answers you should stop in and see Frankie. She's a sweet lady. And if you do, tell her your dad and I say hello!"

Lilly didn't know if she wanted to know about the procession. Before she could reply to her parents Sawyer stated, "So the pattern of an actual full moon isn't necessarily the entirety of a full twenty-four-hour day. I looked at dates that people say they spotted the procession and compared to different full moon calendars and the actual full moons have been known to be the third or even the fifth of July. The full moon on the day the soldier died at the fort was the third rolling into the fourth. So I am assuming it's saying the procession comes into play when it's close to his death date and the moon is full or almost full. Remember a moon is only full for a minute then it decreases. It is believed the procession happens every year, yet there needs to be a bright moon to see the procession." He clicked on another link. "So the next Fourth of July, that has a full moon sometime on or around the 4th is…" He looked up from his computer. "2023…next year there will be a full moon on July 3rd at 11:40 pm. I wonder if that would be considered enough of a full moon for the funeral?"

Lilly shook her head and shrugged. What did it all mean? Geez she loved and hated puzzles…but this one kind of scared her because it seemed personal. Her family started talking about wanting to see the Phantom Funeral and it was decided they would all meet here next year for the Fourth of July to try and see if the tale was true. Lilly wasn't sure why but the entire thought freaked her out a bit.

Seconds later Lilly jumped out of her seat when the doorbell rang. She laughed when she noticed everyone else had been startled as well. Her dad chuckled. "Let's think about Phantom Funerals later, right now we have to have a meeting with Dad's lawyer."

Greg opened the door to her grandfather's attorney Peyton LaCrete. Lilly smiled and was surprised to see the lawyer was younger than she thought and actually very handsome. He had light brown hair and pretty soft hazel eyes. His smile was charming and he was built tall and thin. He looked to be around thirty.

Lilly rolled her eyes as she watched Angel bat her eyes at the man and give him a once over. *Dear Lord,* she thought, *when did her sister learn to be so bold?* She pretty much chalked it up to being a college student.

After the introductions were over and everyone was on a first name basis, her mother led the way to the kitchen table for the meeting. Drinks were offered and distributed before everyone got down to business. Lilly sat next to Angel, across from her parents while Peyton and Sawyer each took a chair at the ends.

It didn't take Peyton long before he got right to business. "Let me first start by saying thank you for meeting me on such quick notice." Nodding to Greg and Lauren he continued, "Greg, you mentioned you will be leaving town Saturday morning and I am leaving Friday after the funeral so I felt as if this is something we should complete beforehand."

He stood and handed a packet to each of them. "In case you aren't aware, you all are Frank's only heirs." Lilly was happy the lawyer used her grandfather's nickname, making this tough situation seem a bit more personal. "I want to add that I have only been a lawyer for four years and in those four years I have never met a man who was more proud of his family and his heritage than Frank." He smiled and Lilly felt a few tears fall before seeing her mother place a box of tissues in the middle of the table.

Peyton gave everyone a few moments to gather themselves before continuing. "Peyton had a trust and it is pretty much ironclad. He wanted everything to be divided evenly between you all. He felt his grandchildren were just as important and equal as his Son and daughter-in-law. Let's begin on page four,"

He gave everyone time to flip to the page. "There is a list of all his assets minus his house and a second life insurance policy. The list is everything that can be divided once any incurring debt is paid. I will add that there shouldn't be much. His funeral was prepaid and he also died at home so there isn't going to be any large medical bills pending." He asked everyone to flip to the next page.

"Frank had a large life insurance policy as you can see. That will also be divided equally between the five of you. Twenty percent to each Grandchild and forty percent to Greg and Lauren."

Lilly was shocked at the amount her grandfather left behind for them. She couldn't help but be a bit excited. This was going to pay all her student loans off and she maybe she could even think about trying her hand at freelance writing. *Wow,* was all she could think until she remembered something Peyton said. "Peyton, what will happen to the house?" She panicked when she thought about them never getting to be in her grandparents' house again. "We don't have to sell it…do we?" Her expression and voice showed her concern.

Peyton smiled at her before looking at her father. Lilly was confused at why all of her family was smiling at her. She suddenly became upset. "You all cannot be fine with us selling Grandma and Grandpa's house? Is that why you're smiling?" She became very angry and before they could reply she looked at Peyton. "Then I will take all my inheritance and buy this house. I refuse to let someone else live in OUR family house."

She started to rise when Angel put her hand on her shoulder to stop her. Lilly looked at her father and noticed his smile was gone but he still had a twinkle in his eyes. "Lilly, I think you know us better than that to think we would sell off this house. It's been in our family since the day it was built in the mid-1800s."

Lilly felt really low. She should have known better. What was wrong with her? Peyton continued after she mumbled her apologies. "Lilly I actually like that you've shown such passion for this place." Lilly looked at him and wondered why he was glad she showed interest in the house?

Peyton continued. "Lilly, your grandparents wanted you to have the house."

This time Lilly did jump up. "What?" She said with complete shock.

Peyton smiled. "Yes Lilly. Your grandfather left you a letter." She looked down as he placed the letter in her hand.

Lilly looked around at everyone. "This isn't fair. I can't take this." She motioned to the house with her hands.

Sawyer spoke up. "Yes, you can. And before you continue, we want you to know that we all knew about this and we are all completely fine with it."

Lilly looked around at all their nods and smiles. Then it rolled into her brain about the upkeep and location. "Wait, how can I take care of a place like this?" She gave her parents a panicked look.

Her Mother spoke up. "Your grandfather will explain things in the letter. As for your father and me, well we discussed it and what we are hoping for is that you move here and freelance." When Lilly started to protest her mother stopped her. "I'm just saying what we hope for. Anyhow, we would love to sell the Kansas City House."

"What? Wait, I like it there." Lilly looked like a deer ready to bolt.

Peyton had the decency to ask to be excused for a few moments. Lilly was sure he didn't feel it was his place to be in the middle of this family discussion. She was happy he excused himself.

Her father came over and pulled out the chair next to her. "Lilly, your mother and I have dreamed of traveling the world discovering the past. And owning a house is just a nuisance to us. We've always known what this house means to you. We all have." He nodded to her family and when she looked at each of them, she could see they agreed with him.

"So your grandparents wanted you to live here when they were gone. Plus, it will be a home base for all of us."

Lilly didn't know what to say. Taking a deep breath she had to admit she would like to live here. So many things ran through her head…like there weren't a ton of jobs to be had in the area. Yet she has always dreamed of freelancing or even writing a book.

"Dad, I'm not sure I can do it." She whispered loud enough for everyone to hear her. Her father hugged her and reassured her she could as her sister, not to be left out, reached over and joined in the hug.

Peyton came back in a few minutes later. Her father asked him to continue. "Lilly, with the house comes a chunk of money to help you with the upkeep. It's not a huge amount but enough to see to all the little things your grandfather didn't want to mess with." He grinned. "Starting with the roof. He said he wasn't in the mood to hear any banging in the morning…so he left that to you." He chuckled.

Lilly wasn't really listening. She kept staring at the letter and wished she could go hide in her grandfather's study and read it. The letter meant more to her than anything else. It was like he was going to talk to her one last time.

As soon as Peyton left, the family made idle chit-chat for a few minutes before Sawyer excused himself because he wanted to play around with Lilly's genealogy. Angel and her mother started preparing for lunch. This gave her and her father a few minutes alone to migrate to the parlor and talk.

After sitting across from each other her father began by saying, "Lilly, I don't want you to feel pressured into living here and I want you to know all you have to do is say the word and we won't sell the Kansas City house and you can go back there. Either way we will still keep this house."

She looked up at her sweet father. If there was one thing she was, it was blessed with a great family. It almost made her cry to think about how much they loved and believed in her. Even her grandparents, in death, were giving her the opportunity to follow her dreams to be a freelance journalist. And her siblings weren't the least bit fazed that she was inheriting the same as they were and much more. "I'm sorry if I was a brat earlier. I think this all smacked me pretty hard."

He grinned. "You grandfather wanted us to all know his thoughts but he didn't want to tell you in case he lived for a lot more years and you'd put everything on hold waiting for this old house to become yours. When I told Angel and Sawyer about it, they instantly agreed the house should go to you. Sawyer likes being an engineer in Champagne and there isn't much around this old historical town for him. And Angel has always said she wants to live in a big city. So we've always known this wasn't for her. But they were both happy to think of this place as the place where we can all meet up. Because, even though you kids didn't grow up here, I think you all still consider it home in one way or another,"

Lilly looked around at the crown molding and arched doorways. She did love this old house and she loved this old town. She couldn't believe she was being offered this chance. She jumped up and rushed over to her father and hugged him. "Thank You so much and of course, I'll live here!"

They talked for a few more minutes about how her parents planned to go back to Kansas City in a few weeks and get the house ready for market. She planned to meet them there for a few days and help. It was decided that since her grandparents' furniture was a bit dated, she would take the furnishings from Kansas City. Her parents were going to hire movers to bring the big stuff to the Bienvenue house.

Lilly stated to her father that she was probably going to call her boss tomorrow, after the funeral, and explain she was moving. Then she would start figuring out this freelance stuff. As for her few Kansas City friends, she hoped they would stay in touch. It just seemed like living in a big city, people came and went. So her friend list was pretty short.

Giving her father one last hug, she made her way to her grandfather's study. She knew she would have to start thinking of the room as her study but for now she was fine still thinking of it as her grandfather's study. Closing the door, she sat down in the same chair she sat in earlier that morning. She ran her hand over her name written in her grandfather's handwriting on the front of the sealed envelope before opening it.

My Sweet Lilly-Bear,

Well, if you are reading this it's a pretty good indication that I am FINALLY with Grandma Ashley. Don't be sad because I can promise you I am happy. Every day since she went to meet our maker I wake up and ask him if today is going to be the day I get to be with her? And every night I am sad that it wasn't. Your grandmother and I have a special Love. I have loved her all my life. Love is a funny thing. Sometimes you never know when it's sitting right in front of you and other times that same thing is something that you can't bear to let go.

With your grandmother I experienced both. We always had a back and forth crush from grade school on. I know I told you the tales but it wasn't always the cute boy and girl puppy love stories. Your grandmother and I hit a kind of a dark time. There was a time when I wanted to find out what was out there and treated her as if she didn't exist.

Actually you asked me once about the Brickley Mansion and I was abrupt and stated that the house was overdone. Well now I am going to let you in on a secret about the mansion. The mansion was beautiful but it holds a bad memory for me and your grandmother.

It all started back in 1970. All of us young men were a rowdy bunch after serving our four years in the Army. Not the disrespectable mean kind but more of the drinking and gambling kind. I had only been home for a few months and I'll be the first to admit I was kind of bored with the drinking and tired of losing my butt at the card table. To be honest I had been living that lifestyle since I enlisted. Me and my Army buddies were always throwing dice, betting cards and tossing back cold ones whenever we had any time off. So that probably explained the boredom after being home a couple months.

Earlier that year I started to pal around with a distant family member to the Brickleys. Badger was his name...Edward Badger. He wasn't one to sit at the tables so we found other things to do in town...mostly chasing skirts. Oh, don't get me wrong, it was just flirting and dancing...your grandpa has a big respect for women and I didn't hang with the loose ones if you know what I mean.

Anyhow your grandmother had more than just a passing fancy for me since I returned. Ironic isn't it...I was sweet on her all those years yet she didn't return the feelings until after I came back home. But by then I was too manly for that frivolous nonsense and just wasn't ready to reacquaint myself with the flirting games we played over the years. I wasn't ready for the altar at that point in my life...or so I thought. Ashley was a year behind me in age and she was more than ready to settle down as most girls her age did at that time. I knew to get involved with her was a forever deal and I wasn't ready to make that deal. I mean when you are a handsome buck like me...you want to play the field for a while.

Lilly chuckled and realized she was crying again. *Geez,* she thought as she found a box of tissues, *will it ever stop?* Wiping at her eyes she was still smiling at her grandfather's comment, 'handsome buck.' Gosh, how she was going to miss him!

Moving on, my ole buddy Badger took an interest in Ashley. And little girl I can't explain it but the green bug of jealousy slapped me hard when I noticed Badger hanging with MY Ashley. Of course, I was too manly to act like I cared. But it broke my heart to see Ashley looking at Badger as she used to look at me.

On top of that there was something about Badger that wasn't there before he started courting Ashley. There was an evil in his dark eyes. He reminded me of a wolf to a lamb. Maybe that look had always been there but I didn't notice it until he was with my Ashley.

Lilly-Bear, Badger always bragged about being cousins of the Brickley family...the ones that used to live in that big old house you asked about. He didn't live in the abandoned house but somehow he had a key to it...so I believed him when he said he was related. Heck there hadn't been any Brickleys in the area for years. It was crazy but the house was left standing for many years, unoccupied, but fully furnished. Badger, myself and a few of the boys would grab some beers and hang out in the old place.

Well, this is where it all gets crazy. One night Badger got angry with Ashley because she wouldn't give up the goods...if you know what I mean. Your grandmother was a true lady in every sense of the word. She was a lady waiting for marriage. Anyhow, Badger took Ashley to the mansion and was trying to impress her with what he didn't own. Well Ashley wasn't impressed; in fact, she was extremely uncomfortable and asked Badger to take her home. He was having no part of that and decided he was going to take what she wasn't offering. Yes, he was going to rape my Ashley.

Lilly, I swear this next part to you on every part of my being. I was just walking to the front of what you now know as Lisa's, only it was called the B & J Korral at the time. It was around two AM on 5 April 1970. I was mad at the world because I watched as Badger danced with Ashley while a band played in the tavern. The band quit around two. And I had to watch as Badger and Ashley took off from the bar. I remember I didn't drink much because I didn't want to do something stupid like confront the couple. I hung around the side of the building talking with my buddy Butch. After he went home, I walked to my car parked out front. There was no one left on the streets at such an early hour of the morning. Thank goodness the street lights were bright because if not, I am not sure I would have believed I saw what I saw.

Lilly…YOU approached me. YOU! My granddaughter Lilly. Of course, at the time I had no idea who you were. You were running towards me from the Brickley mansion's yard. You grabbed me and said, "Grandpa, you have to save Grandma? He's got her in the house and he's going to hurt her." I looked at you like 'who in the hell are you?' In case you are wondering, you were real…not ghost-like. And Lilly I am not making this up…I said to you "pardon me?" And you pointed in the direction of the Mansion and shouted "Badger…is hurting Grandma Ashley." When I still didn't move, you pushed me and said, "Go to Ashley!"

Well little girl that's all I needed to hear. I took off like a bat outta hell and jumped the iron gate and ran quickly into the Brickley Mansion. It took me a bit of time to get in through the locked door. After I entered, I looked around the lower level before I heard her above me screaming and tore up the stairs ready to do some damage. Lilly, he had her on the bed and her clothes were torn from her body and her face was bleeding. All I remember seeing was her beautiful face with blood on it. In hindsight, your grandmother put up a great fight and he didn't do what he set out to do.

I'm not going to paint myself as heroic, but let me tell you, you would have been impressed with your grandpa. I kicked that bastard's ass. He hightailed it out of there quicker than the old Mississippi after a heavy rain. I watched from the top of the stairs to make sure he was leaving. But then you won't believe what the bastard did? I watched, helpless, as the bastard took one of the oil lanterns he must have lit earlier to try and romance your grandmother with and tossed it, oil and all, below the stairwell. The lantern caused a fire immediately. The son of a bitch took off out the door and I ran back into the room and quickly covered your grandmother with a blanket and carried her to the top of the steps. But the house was so old the fire took to those old boards fast.

Little girl I was scared we would never get out. But the truest of all stories, you appeared out of nowhere and led us to a door at the end of the hall that opened up to the back balcony. There was a ladder waiting to take us down. You went first and I helped your grandmother down. Your grandmother never noticed you because her face was buried into my chest. Of course, I never mentioned it. I think I wasn't sure if what I saw was what I saw.

Your grandmother and I ran along the bluff and around the small cemetery behind the Creole House to get out of there without being noticed. We hid and watched as what seemed like the entire town gathered to watch the beautiful mansion go up in smoke. It was an unbelievable sight. The fire left behind nothing but four huge fireplace chimneys.

My Lilly, your grandmother cried in my arms as we made our way back to my apartment, the old servant's quarters, behind our family house. I clothed her and we talked. She asked me why it took so long for me to wake up? She said she couldn't have gone much longer trying to make me jealous with Badger. I was shocked. She said the only reason she went into the house with him was because he said there was going to be a party there when the tavern closed. He mentioned I was going to be there and that was the only reason she went along with his plan.

That night I declared my love to her. She also made me promise to not mention anything about being in the house. You see, your grandmother had a reputation to uphold and it wasn't proper for her to be alone with a man in an abandoned house...even though she was alone with me in my carriage house after. But no worries I made an honest woman out of her by the following weekend. We didn't need any fancy wedding. A small backyard wedding was good enough for us.

Old Badger never showed his face in town after that night. He had been bunking in the upstairs of Conrad's Store. A few days after the fire I asked Old Man Conrad if he knew where I could find Badger? I am not going to explain to you why I was looking for him. I want you to have only good thoughts about your Grandpa.

Anyhow Conrad told me the last time he saw Badger was the night before the fire. He said the next day he knocked on Badger's door to see what his thoughts were about the fire since it was a part of his family and when there was no answer, he opened the door and shouted his name. He looked around and noticed his clothes were gone. He thought it was odd that he left the day after the fire. He was also mad because Badger owed him two months of rent. I did try to find the bastard...almost to the point of obsession. I stopped when your grandmother put her foot down and I reluctantly complied.

We did find out later that there was no connection between the Brickleys and Badger. But I think I still had resentment towards the mansion because I can still picture my sweet Ashley laying on the huge bed with blood running down from her mouth and swollen eyes.

Anyhow I keep getting off track, which is fine because this is my final letter to you until we meet again.

Lilly didn't like reading that part.

Anyhow my sweet Lilly, it was you who warned me that day. I think I blocked out the memory because I wasn't a big believer in time travel or whatever it was.

Yet, I only realized it was you at your grandmother's funeral. I cannot forget the moment, it was when the service at the cemetery ended and it was time to say our final farewells. You were standing next to me holding my hand. I was supposed to lead the family to the casket before they lowered it into the ground. I couldn't move. As you walked forward you must have realized I didn't follow and you turned and said to me, "Grandpa...it's time. Go to Grandma." And I swear with all my being, in that moment, I flashed back to that night and could see you as clear as day and it was you Lilly who told me your grandmother was in trouble.

Lilly took a deep breath and put the letter to her chest. She remembered that moment at the cemetery when she had to coax her grandfather towards the casket. He did look at her as if he was seeing a ghost. She thought it was because he wasn't ready to say goodbye to her grandmother. How weird that he thinks he had a deja vu with her in it. Lilly didn't know what to think as she read on.

I know I probably sound like I'm losing my mind but I can assure you that I am as sharp as ever. That moment gave me hope on how to spend the rest of my time. I was determined to find out what happened that night. How did you get to be there when you weren't even born yet? Call it time travel, ghost, or a parallel universe but something happened.

Lilly that is why I am leaving you this house and everything in it. Because it is here that you can continue my research. I have found many interesting things in my family's past and most of it involves you.

I have a list of my findings in the library and I also have completed our family genealogy and am getting it made into a book as we speak. Look at the tree in the back...it's very interesting. Look at all the Lillys in the family.

Lilly, I also want to play a game with you. I left you a gold bracelet in my safe. The combination is at the bottom of this letter. I'm not sure if you have visited me that day in your time yet, or how it plays out. But if you ever find yourself talking to me on the streets of Prairie du Rocher the early morning of 5 April 1970 see if you know why this bracelet makes its way to be buried between the two front roots on the Magnolia tree in the main house front yard.

The story behind the bracelet is that it belonged to the first aunt Liliane of the family. Apparently she passed it to her namesake and I'm guessing so on and so forth. If there wasn't one it was passed down until there was one. This may be why there were so many Lilly's born in the family. The band is real gold and more than two ounces...so it has a bit of value...not to discredit the historical value.

The bracelet was given to my mother from great-aunt Lillian. She passed the day you were born. Apparently when my mother gave birth to my sister a few years before me, she gave her the middle name Lillian because she found out that my great-aunt would pass down the gold bracelet to any namesake. I guess a middle name was good enough for her because she passed the bracelet to my sister who ended up dying a few months later due to a bad case of mumps.

So the bracelet laid dormant because no one wanted to ask my mother what she did with the bracelet and remind her of her child's death. A few years later I was born and Aunt Lillian wrote to my mother and asked that she give the bracelet to me when I took a wife. As that time neared, I think my mother had a different idea. I found out about the bracelet because Aunt Lilly also wrote to me in my early adulthood and explained that she wanted the bracelet to stay in the family.

I asked my mother about the bracelet the day of my wedding and she told me she had no idea what happened to it...but how does one lose an expensive item? I wasn't always sure she was speaking the truth.

Ironically a few years after my mother died, Butch's mother passed. He and I got to reminiscing over a few drinks after the funeral. I asked him why his mother quit coming over for visits? He told me all he knew was that my mother accused his mother of stealing a gold bracelet from our house. Apparently she had it hidden in a hollowed out 'The Taming of a Shrew' book in our library. It seemed she showed it to his mother and the next day it was gone.

Cheri and my mother never spoke after they spatted some nasty words at each other that day. So after Butch told me this I went into the library and opened the book and saw the hollowed out pages...of course, there was no bracelet.

Then the strangest thing happened, I did eventually find it. I came across the bracelet the week after I lost your grandmother. It was buried between the two roots that stick up under the big Magnolia in the front yard. The roots are the ones that face the house. I have no idea why, but I decided to plant one of your grandmother's funeral plants there. It may be because we always loved rocking on the porch and would admire the big beautiful flowers the Magnolia produced.

Sorry I am once again digressing. Anyhow I was digging and up came the bracelet. You can only imagine my shock. I don't know how but I knew it was my great aunt's bracelet. I decided to have the bracelet inscribed. Actually, I'm getting ahead of myself. I have a favor, if you did indeed come to me on 5 April 1970, please go to the Bienvenue house and try and find out how the bracelet got to be under the tree. I feel you have something to do with this also...but I feel it hasn't happened to you yet.

I've decided to take a page out of my mother's book...figuratively. I would like for you to leave me a note. Maybe explain to me if you find the mystery of what happened to the bracelet all those years ago. I think it has to do with you and all these mysterious things in your genealogy.

Anyhow place this note in the book 'The Clock That Spun Backwards' on page seventy. I will periodically look onto the page. And only if you do this, then afterwards you look back on the same page and see if I have answered.

Also there is your aunt's diary. It is in a tin box on the top of my bookshelf. Please be careful with the book. It is quite old and worn but still very legible as it was placed in a metal case for many years. This book holds the answers to many early questions. Somehow I feel it's connected to you. Sadly, as much as I loved our family history, I never really took the time to read the journal. I knew it was there but part was written in French and I thought it was probably filled with fashion and frivolous things. I have since finished the logs of my aunts and find they do give much details about what occurred in their lives.

All of my investigations and findings are posted in my own personal journal at my desk. Lilly, I believe you are stuck in a form of history repeating itself. The name Geofrey is your connection but I am not sure what transpired between the two of you. So if you actually do go into the past and can get to the diary...please write the story of what happened so we can figure it out and fix it. But remember you cannot do anything that may change the course of history. I'd hate for England to have won the war.

This may all be crazy but I have done some serious research and have found several unbelievable things. An example is that my aunt Lillian Bienvenue, the one who died when you were born, paid to have several plots purchased in the town cemetery. While that may not sound crazy, what is crazy is that they weren't for our family. They were for the Geofrey Family. She even paid to gate their plotted area. She also added new headstones for the three Daniel Geofrey men, buried almost one hundred years apart. The middle stone was for the oldest death of Daniel D. Geofrey who died on July 4th, 1754...beloved husband of Liliane. How odd is that?

What's crazy is my Great Aunt Lillian died a spinster but in my family genealogy book I talk about how she was engaged to a local boy and he was murdered as she watched the entire incident. I have found that her fiancé was none other than a Daniel Geofrey...a direct ancestor to the Daniel Geofrey of the 1700s. She never journals in the book after the death of her fiancé, so I only know of what has been passed down. I will also add that her namesake, Liliane of the 1800s also lost her fiancé and his name is also Daniel Geofrey. Those are the three men buried together at the cemetery that your aunt had redone. Because I don't want to confuse you, just read my book and the writings of your aunts' in their book. If you wish to see the plots, they are next to each other with a large monument above the stones that says Geofrey.

Lilly's heart started racing as she thought about the cemetery the day before. There had to be a connection. Oh, dear Lord...what has she gotten herself into? This has to all be connected. There was a reason she was drawn to the graves. She felt like something was broken and her ancestor wanted her to fix it.

One last thing my dear Lilly, I would advise you to keep this crazy stuff to yourself for you may be committed if you try and explain it to anyone. This is why I didn't speak of it to you on one of our many phone calls since your grandmother's passing. I was afraid you'd have your old grandpa placed in a home.

My sweet girl please tell Angel and Sawyer how much I love them also. And your father and mother who I've cherished with my entire being. And Lilly, please don't think your grandfather is crazy...well maybe a bit in my old age. If you are not comfortable, please do not venture on this quest. But if I know my little Lilly-Bear...you will be all over this.

Remember I love you my sweet girl and conquer whatever it is that prevents you from finding the love like I have with my Ashley.

With all my Heart...Grandpa

Lilly sat back and looked around a bit spooked. 'What the hell is going on? She sat back and closed her eyes. Maybe she was having an odd dream. Maybe she was in a coma and dreaming all these crazy things. Lilly looked up at the ceiling. "Grandpa, you were losing your mind, weren't you?" Yet that was the part that worried her. Her grandfather wasn't one to believe in ghosts and déjà vu. He was smart and very practical. "Damn," she whispered. He knew her well enough to know she wasn't going to leave this alone.

When did her boring life get so crazy? Hell, she had only been in town for a day and everything was nuts. It all started when she went to the cemetery. She decided she had way too much happening at once and decided to give her brain a break...but first she wanted to see what her grandfather left her. She made her way over to the safe and used the combo at the bottom of the letter to open it. Right there in front was a velour box the size of her fist. She knew this was the box her grandfather spoke of. Opening it up she looked at a solid gold bangle bracelet. It was very pretty, yet slightly worn with a faded, small grooved pattern in the middle and a fleur-de-lis on each end. Yet it was over two hundred years old and had been buried so that was probably why it seemed a bit rough.

Lilly took it out of the box and walked over to the desk lamp and turned it on to see what it was her grandfather had inscribed to her grandmother. She was shocked to see it wasn't to her grandmother but to her. It read...*My sweet Granddaughter Lilly...may you untwist your destiny. Love Grandpa Frank.*

Her grandfather had it inscribed to her, not her grandmother? Wait, were there any other Grandpa Franks? She looked at the tree to make sure. She was happy to see there wasn't another Frank.

Lilly decided to look in the book her grandfather wanted her to leave a letter in. 'She smiled over the title *The clock that spun backwards*, because it implied going back in time. She was sure her grandfather purposely put it next to *The Taming of the Shrew*. While the clock book had no messages for her, she was chilled to see the pages hollowed out of the *Taming of the Shrew* book. Yet the more she thought about it the more it made her chuckle to think about how smart people were back then. She would one day have to take the time and see if there were any more hollowed books in her grandfather's library.

Next, she decided to find the diary. She looked throughout the large bookshelves at all the books and wondered how she was ever going to find a diary. But to her surprise she spotted a metal case on the top shelf in the middle. She wasn't surprised to see a footstool right below it. Either her grandfather was preparing her to find it or he was checking to see if she wrote anything in it during his time here.

The entire concept was crazy. If he's gone, how can he see what she was supposed to leave for him if she somehow went into the past. But if she goes back to a time he's still living, then he hadn't passed yet and would see it before he did pass? *Oh my,* she thought. *Am I even considering what he's suggesting?*

Suddenly she remembered the dream she had just hours ago and she was chilled. She walked over to the window instead of retrieving the diary. She looked out without really seeing. She remembered dreaming about the Ball they have in town. Only it wasn't at the American Legion Hall they use now, but somewhere dated. She could picture her father and mother at the Ball. There was also a brother...maybe.

Lilly breathed in sharply as she remembered the handsome man she was dancing with. What was his name? Surely it wasn't Daniel? *No, she* thought. *What was it? It started with a 'D'; Dean? Dave? No, it was Dane. Yes, that was it. But Liliane's husband was a gentleman named Daniel...Daniel Geofrey.* She wondered if Dane was short for Daniel in the 1700s. *Wait...what was the middle name on the headstone?* She couldn't remember but knew she would probably have to go back out there sometime but wasn't in a big hurry to do so.

As she looked out the window she smiled and remembered the beautiful dresses and the dancing. Oh and then the cake? Had this Dane really gotten the first bean which made him a King? Yes, she did dream of this. He even chose her for his Queen.

Lilly sighed at the romance of it all. She was twirling around the study as she remembered the dancing when she was suddenly interrupted by her mother's knock on the door before she opened it. "Lilly, you have company."

Lilly turned to watch a beautiful redhead appear through the door and say, "I want your hair."

Chapter Seven

Lilly had to stare for a moment before it hit her that the beautiful creature standing in front of her was her childhood friend, Rissa. She shrieked and ran to hug this grown woman who had once been the very best of all her friends. She pulled back and stated, "No, I want your hair." They hugged again as her mother quietly closed the door as she exited the room.

Lilly pulled back and looked at the redhead. The years have turned the gangly, freckled face girl into a beautiful, petite, very thin yet curvy lady with incredibly long flowing auburn hair. "Rissa, you are absolutely beautiful." Motioning towards the sofa she stated, "Come sit, we have so much to talk about."

Rissa looked at the beautiful brunette in front of her and was sure she would be jealous if she was the jealous type. She was glad she battled those insecurities in college and learned to love herself for who she was and how she looked. Now she looked at her gorgeous, tall, tanned friend with flawless skin…with only a little jealousy. Seriously, anyone who looked at this girl would have to be a little jealous.

Rissa always knew her friend would turn out gorgeous. That was one of the reasons she blew off all her friends every summer…she always felt she had a special person in her life when she was with Lilly. Plus how cool was it to be friends with a worldly girl who was a year older and from a big city like Kansas City? They became the best of friends and spent almost every waking hour together, for two months, each year. In all that time they never got into so much as an argument. Rissa hoped they could be that close again.

Lilly couldn't contain her excitement. "Tell me everything. Last I knew you moved and we lost contact."

Rissa smiled. Lilly hasn't changed much. She was always direct and to the point. She always asked a million questions and was the most inquisitive out of anyone she had ever met. Rissa wasn't surprised when she read her friend was now a journalist. That was right up Lilly's alley. "Well, as you know, my parents got divorced. So we moved to Red Bud for a year, then Mom moved us again to Freeburg. Mom's still there and remarried. Dad made it as far as Smithton and never remarried. I think he landed there to be close to us but not too close to Mom. He passed away a year ago from cancer."

Lilly could see Rissa was still hurting deeply from this. "I'm so sorry. I always liked your dad. I just didn't know him well."

"Thanks. He had a hard time when Mom decided she was tired of feeling like a single parent. He just worked too much to play husband and father." She gave her friend a sad smile. "He felt he needed to work a lot to support us. It was a 'damned if I do and damned if I don't' situation." She paused before continuing. "Anyhow, my brothers are both married and enjoying their families. My mom and stepdad are snowbirds and getting ready to head to Florida for the winter." She grinned. "And me and my fiancé, Zeke, are fixing up and moving into our old house next door."

"Really." Lilly became very excited. "You guys still owned the place?"

"Yep. You know my dad...he would never sell anything he could make more off by renting it out." She smiled. "He knew how much I loved it here so he left it to me." She rolled her eyes. "But let me tell you...renters put wear and tear on a place."

"I bet."

Rissa shrugged. "It's a good thing Zeke is a carpenter."

Lilly threw her hands up in the air and laughed. "Okay, so who is Zeke?"

Rissa chuckled. "Zeke and I met while he was flipping a house and I was contracted to do the inside design work."

"Oh my gosh," Lilly interrupted. "Are you an interior designer?"

"Yes ma'am, and I'm not too shy to say I am a fabulous one!" She stated.

"I'm so excited...okay you can go on with your arrogance." She grinned.

Rissa chuckled. "So anyhow, we both were in each other's way...a lot." She grinned. "To be honest I thought he was a pain in the ass and always under foot." She sighed, "But then something changed and I found I liked having his charming butt underfoot. And we've been together ever since. That was almost two years ago."

Lilly hated to admit it but she was green with envy. She wanted to talk about a guy like that. But hell, she had never met anyone close to that. It was weird, she has had a few boyfriends in the past, but it never seemed to last long. It was like she was looking for someone to make her face light up the way Rissa's did when she talked about Zeke.

Rissa pulled her from her thoughts. "Enough about me…I came here to tell you how sorry I am about you losing your grandpa."

Lilly smiled. "Thank You. Have you gotten to see him since you've moved back?"

"No, other than a wave here and there because we haven't really moved back yet. We just started working on the house a few weeks ago and that's mostly in the evenings when we aren't flipping other houses. We actually started our own business a few months ago. So we've only been here a few hours here and there. But I was going to make my way over and ask about my bestie." She grinned at Lilly before giving her sad eyes. "Now I wish I would have…even though I'm pretty sure he didn't remember me when I would wave at him."

"That could be. You have changed a lot and that would explain why he didn't mention to me that you were back in town." She smiled and continued. "Oh my gosh, so you're like those famous people on TV who flip those beautiful homes?"

Rissa laughed. "Not quite. Zeke and I aren't really the TV type. But yes, we do give complete makeovers. And the closest we come to TV is when we make DIY videos for fixer-uppers and post them."

Lilly was excited. She needed to update the historical Bienvenue house and now she knew of someone who could help her. "Wait…are you going to be living next door?" She asked her friend?

"Yes," She nodded. "We are planning to move in gradually over the next few weeks. I just finished a house and Zeke's next project is all exterior so I am not needed. I can't start my next job until he's done with this one because he's doing the interior with me. So I'll be packing and unpacking."

Lilly couldn't contain her excitement. She grabbed her friend's arms and was bopping up and down. "Rissa we are going to be neighbors. I am the current owner of the Bienvenue House."

"No way." Her friend nearly shouted as they both hopped up and down together.

The stress of the next two days was almost unbearable for Lilly at times. The funeral was long and depressing, yet bittersweet. The amount of people who came to pay their respects was unbelievable. Most of the older men held up the viewing line…not only because they were saying goodbye to Frank but because they were busy sharing stories about Frank to the family.

Lilly loved the turnout at the funeral. She had been afraid since her family was small there wouldn't be many to say goodbye. Her grandmother's funeral only allowed the very immediate family due to the virus hitting the world, so she couldn't compare anything to that. This time the line was out the door most of the evening.

The turnout swelled her heart…and her feet. All she wanted to do was take her heels off and soak her feet in a hot bath. She was relieved when her mother noticed her discomfort and suggested she take a break and prop her feet up for a bit in the family room the funeral home provided.

The actual burial the following day was dreary and cold. When the procession pulled up at the gravesite Lilly felt the chills crawl up her back. She couldn't help but take a glimpse in the direction of the graves she visited on the day she arrived. She was relieved to see nothing looked amiss in that area of the cemetery. She was a bit spooked and didn't want anything jumping up at her.

The burial was hard, especially when the six guns fired three rounds each, showing honor for her grandfather's service in the military for four years. Lilly couldn't hold back the rush of tears that seemed to constantly flow from her eyes. She would miss her grandfather dearly.

The luncheon following the burial was held at the American Legion Hall. It had been several years since Lilly had visited the hall. She would go with her grandparents to the Legion for all types of town events. This was where wedding receptions were held or Saturday evening bands would play. There was even a yearly Boy Scout Barbeque held there every Memorial Day weekend. The annual Twelfth Night Ball every January filled the hall with plenty of reenactors. Sadly she never got to attend the Ball because she was back in school by then. Yet her favorite event at the Legion was in the summer the Ladies Auxiliary would have Sunday Chicken and Dumpling dinners at the hall.

It was several hours later that Lilly sat down because she was wiped out. It took that long for the last guest to leave the hall. She was relieved when they all returned to the house. She knew tonight was the last night with her family until Thanksgiving. It was only a month away but she was already missing them. It was decided they would come to Prairie du Rocher for the holidays.

She had already spoken with her newspaper editor and it was decided she could take a short leave of absence until she knew for sure what she wanted to do.

Early the next morning Lilly wrapped an arm around the porch post as her other hand waved goodbye to her family. All three cars were going in different directions as soon as they left the little town. Her parents had the longest drive but they at least had each other's company. Angel had five hours in the car but she would be blasting her music the entire way. Sawyer would probably keep it quiet in the car as he mentally tried solving the world's problems.

Lilly looked over at Rissa's house and was disappointed to see no signs of life. Her friend's house was beautiful and as large as the Bienvenue house. It was pretty evident they were both built around the same timeframe with the unique edging and trim around the buildings.

Looking around she was overwhelmed at the quiet beauty the town took on in the morning hours. The bluffs stood tall and dominating like a mother watching over her children. Lilly stretched and made her way back inside. Having no definite plans for the day, she decided to look through her grandfather's journal and diary. She poured a cup of coffee before going into the study. Gathering the books she decided to take everything out into the living room. She figured she would be more comfortable on the sofa, lounging, while reading his notes.

In no time, she was absorbed in her grandfather's notes. He started around the time the family came over from France in the early 1700s. He noted that there was a Liliane Elizabeth Bienvenue born 1 November 1732 at the fort. She married Daniel Geofrey on 28 June 1754 and he died a week later.

Lilly sat back and thought about Lilly from the 1700s. The poor woman, how she must have felt losing her husband so soon. She wondered if they were in love or was it a marriage of convenience due to the low population at the fort? Call her a romantic but she felt it was for love.

She went on to read that Liliane moved away from the fort immediately after the funeral. She went back to France. She died on 23 April 1803. Living until the age of 71 was rather unusual in the 1700s.

The next entry was Liliane Bienvenue born 23 April 1803. Lilly still found that interesting. The day one Lilly died in France another was born in Prairie du Rocher. This Lilly had no entry of ever being married but she was betrothed.

Her grandfather noted that she needed to pay attention to the Lillys' death dates. Lilly still hadn't processed the dates since her father found the pattern.

She was sure it was because she didn't want to think about knowing the day of the year she may die. She scrolled back over each Lilly to see that each one lived to be old but never married except for the first Lilly from the 1700s. Did this mean she was doomed to never get married? But then again at least she might live to be old! She shook her head and couldn't believe she was even contemplating all this crazy stuff. It was all a coincidence. She was starting to believe her grandfather was slipping in his old age.

Then she remembered the grave. What had happened to her the other day? There was also that dream of her and a hot guy named Dane at the Ball. Her grandfather had little notes jotted down about events throughout the centuries but they didn't have anything in there about a Dane. Of course, her subconscious mind could have her dreaming about a man named Dane…but why?

There were notes about the Phantom Funeral. That made everything even crazier because her brother had just brought it up. Then again he may be researching the same sites her grandfather did. There were articles of people who spotted the procession throughout time relating the occurrences to the Fourth of July when the moon was bright and full or close to full. He also noted that the moon wasn't always on the actual full moon but could be off a day or two. He wrote that he felt the importance was in the brightness of the moon.

There were also notes about Illinois becoming a state in 1818. Next to that fact her grandfather placed a star and wrote how in 1822 a gentleman by the last name Geofrey was ambushed next to the town's creek. Apparently it was documented that it was from an Indian raid, yet locals believed that it was a premeditated murder from a local man who was in a fit of jealousy. His writings stated that some of his findings are rumors passed down from generation to generation.

Lilly was so absorbed in her readings she jumped in her seat when she heard the knock at her door. Putting her notes aside she went to the door and invited her friend Rissa in. Rissa looked around the living room and was instantly absorbed in the décor. Lilly chuckled because she could see her friend's head spinning on the things she could do to the room. "So what would you do with this room?"

Rissa spun around and looked at Lilly with a smile. "I'm a creature of habit. I can't walk into a room without thinking of what I could do to make it even better." She lifted her arms and indicated to the room. "There isn't much I would change. I always loved this house and would want to keep the vintage look. But…" she smiled, "I would still pop in some modern to accent the history and maybe not make the room so dated." She laughed. "I didn't come here to try to sell you on a job." She sat back in the chair. "So what's up?"

Lilly was so happy her friend was back in her life. Rissa had been attentive during the funeral and even organized the luncheon for everyone after the burial. That took a lot of stress off her family and they could focus on the funeral details. "Well, the family left today. So now you get to take their place."

Her friend smiled. "You know it. That's kind of why I am here. I am wanting to see if you are up for a night on the town? Of course, that consists of one stop…Lisa's." She chuckled. "But she has a band playing tonight and I thought the three of us could have dinner and then stay for some music."

Lilly wasn't really up for socializing. So much change had occurred in just one week. She just wanted to sit back and think over all the crazy things happening. Yet, she had to admit that the idea of staying in the house by herself for the first time kind of spooked her. Which was crazy because she had never been spooked in her grandparent's house. But then again she never really thought about Phantom Funerals and reincarnating over and over.

"I don't really know if I'm up for it."

"Lilly, we have lots of years to catch up on and you being stuck in this old house isn't at all good for you."

"Really," She rolled her eyes and smiled. "Why is that?"

"Because you will start hearing creaks in the floorboards and imagine ghosts are chasing you. You'll eventually become friends with your make-believe ghost and then you won't want to leave your house. You'll just stay inside with your twelve cats and peek out the window every five minutes when a car drives by."

"Wow…" Lilly lifted her eyebrows…if you only knew, she thought. "All that if I don't go with you tonight?"

Rissa smiled. "Yep!"

Lilly laughed. "Okay."

"Okay, you'll come tonight?"

"Yes, I'll go with you to Lisa's."

"Promise?"

Lilly grinned. "I promise."

"Good now you have to promise me one more thing!"

"I do?" Lilly asked. "What is that?"

"Promise me you won't get a cat."

Lilly tossed the sofa pillow at her. Her friend caught it and hugged it to her. Lilly suddenly wanted to tell her everything. Even though they haven't been in touch in years, she knew she could trust Rissa. Plus the young Rissa always loved a good mystery, especially if there were ghosts involved.

"Ris, if I tell you something, do you promise not to think I'm crazy?"

"Girl, I've always known you were crazy...so too late."

"Give me back the pillow so I can throw it at you again."

"I'm kidding. I promise you will still be my childhood bestie no matter what it is."

"Maybe it'll be easier if I just show you." She reached for the book her grandfather had printed as her friend moved from her chair to sit next to Lilly on the sofa. She opened the book to the family tree in the back and laid it across their laps. Lilly told her about all the women names Lilly in the tree. Rissa thought it was crazy. Taking the book from Lilly she looked closer at the dates and names.

Lilly decided it would be better for her friend to read her grandfather's letter than to explain it. She stood up and handed Rissa the letter. "I'm going to get us a drink and while I do I want you to read the letter Grandpa left me."

Rissa took the letter and by the time Lilly returned she finished reading it. "Oh my gosh Lilly, this is crazy!" She exclaimed.

Lilly walked over to the window and looked out at the little town. "I know. It's actually been a roller coaster ride since I got here."

"What do you mean?"

She explained about the cemetery visit and told her about the dream she had. By the time she finished she could tell her friend believed her and was a little spooked. "Rissa, do you know what the coolest part of the dream was?"

"Umm, probably having a hot handsome man treat you like you were Cinderella?"

"Well besides that," She smiled. "My dream had a best friend, her name was Hattie, but I'm pretty sure she was one of your ancestors. She was you through and through."

"How cool." She ginned. "I always knew we were destined to be soul friends."

"So now what?" Lilly had a lost look. "I don't know where or what I'm supposed to do about all of this." She indicated to the books and notes lying on the sofa and end table.

"Well, you are a journalist. Think of it as not personal but a mystery you need to write about."

Lilly nodded. "I agree. But I don't know where to start."

Rissa jumped up. "I do. How long before you can be ready for an outing?"

"An outing? Where are we going?"

"You'll see. Get ready and I'll be back to get you in five. I need to let Zeke know where we are going. He just got back in town last night so he's probably just getting up."

Lilly looked down at her sweats. "I can't go like this?"

"That's up to you but we are going in public…so I'd freshen up a bit." As she approached the door, she turned to look at her friend. "And bring a jacket, we will be outside." She stated before exiting the doorway.

Lilly did as her friend suggested and was ready ten minutes later. She walked across the street and hopped in the passenger seat as Rissa slid into the driver seat. As soon as they left town Lilly knew they were headed towards the old fort. Fort de Chartres was pretty much the only thing in this direction. Rissa was chatting on and on about the family tree and the different possibilities as they pulled into the fort parking lot.

Lilly was surprised at all the cars in the lot and when she took note of all the tents and teepees across the fort's lawn it dawned on her the fort was hosting the fall Rendezvous. As a rule, the fall Rendezvous wasn't as busy as the summer one. So the place was busy but not with visitors but more with reenactors hanging out by their tents and teepees.

Throughout the year the historical fort had events and reenactments where people from all over the world came and set up camp dressed as Indians, Frenchman, or maybe even a fur trapper. There were a variety of soldiers and colonial men who came and reenacted the ceremonies that took place at the fort in the 1700s.

The girls followed the path that led to the fort. They passed many traders trying to sell their wares to anyone showing an interest. Lilly stopped to admire some beautiful rugs that were woven from wool. Rissa loved the jewelry that was handcrafted and unique.

As the girls approached the entrance of the fort, Lilly looked up at the cool historical fort refurbished in all its glory. The two sets of entry doors were beautiful and unique with bars over the windows. Above the doors was the tower used to spot any incoming friends or foes. Over time many people have dedicated their time to making the fort a great place to visit by preserving and rebuilding the old fort. The results from all their hard work was exceptional.

When she was very small, she remembered coming to the fort while they were slowly renovating the place to look like the original fort. Most of the outer walls were just flat limestone foundations a few feet high that marked where the original wall once stood.

Now, after the renovations, some of the foundations had high walls in its place. The high castle-like walls were called Bastion. At each corner of the Baston there was a turret-like structure that stuck out from the outside corner called a Bartizan. This would allow the soldier to see out from both angles of the wall. Lilly knew she would have loved it if the Bartizan were in place when she was a child…she surely would have played a princess in need of rescuing.

As the girls walked through the entry doors, Lilly looked around at the buildings recently erected. Before the renovations, most of the fort's living quarters consisted of large basement-like holes in the ground with the short walls framing it. One of the favorite things for kids to do was jump down into the holes and try to climb their way back out. There were many times she and Rissa had to pull each other out or help other visiting kids out of the holes. But now most of the holes were sealed up. Yet she was glad to see a few still remained open. But she didn't think she was up for the task of climbing down into them.

Lilly looked back and up to the structure above the doors. "Oh my gosh Rissa, we have to climb the 'lookout tower' like we did when we were kids." Lilly said with excitement.

Rissa looked up and smiled. "I need to hit the bathroom before I climb those stairs. You go ahead and I'll meet you up there in a bit."

Chapter Eight

The girls separated as Lilly made her way up the steep ladder steps leading to the tower. She noticed the steps and handrail were newly replaced and much better than the old stone ones that were once used when she was a child. Yet the steps were just as steep as the original set.

Lilly was surprised no one was occupying the tower as she made it to the top. It was probably because there weren't a lot of visitors at the fall event. As a child the tower made her think of Romeo and Juliette. The four corners were the only parts that held up the tall roof. The sides were about five feet high inside and it was always a job to try and climb up and sit on the ledge. The front wall had two sections cut out where the cannons would be placed in case there was an attack on the fort. There were large stumps in the inserts so no one would fall out of the holes. Yet many used the stumps as a seat so it probably defeats the purpose.

She had so many memories of playing at the fort when she was a child. The tower was where she would be rescued by Prince Charming. The church that sat inside one of the buildings on the other end of the fort was where she was going to marry him and the basement holes were where she and the Prince lived.

She sat down on the edge of the lower cannon holes and rested her head on her hands that she placed on the stumps. Her eyes were heavy as she looked across the front fort lawn. The teepees and tents were very cool looking but the prairie land surrounding the fort was where the real beauty laid. In the distance sat the bluffs. She wondered what life was like back when this fort was built? Her imagination could almost pull up an image of it all. She smiled as she watched the people moving around in their vintage clothing. She closed her eyes to get a better picture. She was very tired and dreamy. Watching the reenactors, she smiled as they were pushing wheelbarrows and sharpening their swords. She smiled as she spotted her father walking out of the Commander's office.

Suddenly she bolted upright when she realized they weren't actors, that they were actually people she knew. She could see her father taking his position in front of the marching soldiers. She smiled as her brother Abraham was training with the other soldiers.

Lilly exited the tower so she could have a better look. She walked over and stood at the entrance of her and her husband's living quarters…only she was confused because she wasn't married…or was she? Suddenly she remembered she and Dane were married a few days ago and she needed to hurry in and prepare his noon meal. She quickly entered the kitchen and quickly looped her apron around her. She wiped her hands down the front of her apron and adjusted her skirt. She still couldn't believe how happy she was this past week since their wedding. Looking over at the bed made her blush. Who would have known a man could make a woman feel the way Dane made her feel? Lilly giggled and shook her head as she stirred the pot of stew hanging in the fireplace.

Lilly jumped as the door opened and her handsome sandy brown-haired, green-eyed, husband filled the doorway. She smiled as he closed the door and turned to her. Lilly was overwhelmed by this beautiful man. His tanned hard body made her melt. The reality spinning in her head said she didn't know this man but in her dreamlike state she knew every inch of his hard body.

Dane saw the passion in her eyes the moment he entered the room. He still couldn't believe she was finally his wife. The moment he met her at the Twelfth Night Ball he knew she was his destiny.

He walked over and pulled her in for a long hot kiss before grabbing her hand and leading her to the straw filled mattress used as their bed. Lilly gave a shy chuckle, "Dane, it's the middle of the day. We can't be doing this." She whispered half-heartedly as he reached behind her to untie her apron.

He kissed her long and hard before replying, "I have to have you, my love."

"But don't you have duties to attend to?" There was a small part of her that thought she sounded silly. But that was the real Lilly and the dreaming Lilly wished away the real Lilly as her husband slowly removed her clothing before picking her up and lying her on the bed. "My only duty in need of attending is making love to my beautiful wife."

Lilly watched as he removed his clothes and laid next to her before pulling the blanket over them. She closed her eyes and let the touch of his hands take over her mind. He knew just where to touch her to make her lose all control of her senses.

She thought about the past week they have been married, he taught her the ways of making love. Never did she imagine such a feeling could exist. Within a few moments her body exploded with pleasure over and over. She was sure her heart could never love as it did in that moment.

Time stood still as the couple laid together holding each other. Dane found it cute that his beautiful Lilly was suddenly shy. He kissed her neck and thanked the Good Lord again for giving him this beautiful woman as a wife.

Lilly was the first to break the silence. "Why are you done so early in the day?" She was surprised at how well she spoke in French. She wasn't sure she even knew French.

"Well, I am now the Lieutenant Commander, so I can work when I wish. Plus, as you know, I am never not in command or not needed. Yet today everything is calm so I decided to leave my post earlier than normal."

Lilly sat up and pulled the blanket to her chin. "Dane please tell me no one will know what we just did. I mean will anyone suspect we just...you know...since you've been in our quarters in the middle of the afternoon?"

Dane chucked and pulled his wife down on top of him. He was sure almost everyone who knew he was in his quarters knew what he and his sweet wife were up to. Yet he decided she didn't need to know that. He didn't want her embarrassed or upset so he reassured her no one would think the obvious.

Wishing they could lounge around but knowing they couldn't, the couple went back to their duties that needed to be done before the day's end. Because the moon was full, Dane decided that very evening would be a good time to do a little nugget hunting. Sitting down at the kitchen table he asked Lilly to join him.

He took her hands in his and looked at the heirloom diamond on her ring finger. "One day you are going to have a new diamond to replace this vintage one." He stated.

Lilly frowned at him. "I'm going to tell you right now Daniel Dane Geofrey this is the diamond I wedded thee with and it's the diamond I plan to wear until my dying day."

Dane loved how sentimental she was. "Lilly, I have to tell you something. It's a secret that only myself and Running Wolf know about." He stood and asked her to follow him to the cellar as he grabbed a lantern and led the way.

Lilly didn't like the steep steps down into the cold dungeon-like stone basement and wondered what her husband wanted to show her. He used the lantern light to light another lantern hanging on a wall. She looked around at the only thing in the room…wood for the fireplace. It was stored here to keep out of the rain.

"Dane, why are we down here?"

He smiled at her. "Do you remember how the elders talk about a Phillipe Renaut coming here, back when the first fort was erected, looking for gold and silver?"

"Yes, my father said he was the reason there was such a diverse group of people here because he brought over two-hundred miners and five-hundred slaves. And that after a few years all he found was lead. So he just got up and left…leaving behind many of the people who came with him."

"I do have one very intelligent wife." Dane smiled. "That is exactly what happened. But what many do not know is that there is gold in these bluffs."

She gave him a confused look. "What are you talking about?" She watched as he went under the stairwell into an arched storage area and took out a knife and ran his hand down the lime cemented rock until he found the spot he was looking for. He then proceeded to chisel out a section before pulling a chunk of the stone from the wall. He placed his hand inside a hole when the stone covered and pulled out a small wool bag. He walked over to Lilly and opened it, displaying a bag full of gold nuggets.

Lilly covered her mouth and put her hand to her throat. "Dane…" she exclaimed, "where did you get these?"

He smiled at her. "I found them in a cavern in the heart of the bluffs." He paused. "Well actually Running Wolf showed me where they were."

"Why would he do that?"

"I know it sounds crazy but he and I have become good friends. It started when I would go to the river to do a spot of fishing. One day he was at the spot I usually fished at. I didn't say a word, I just fished beside him. Well that went on for a few days then he had the nerve to show me the proper way to fish the swift river." He smiled. "I was offended for a minute then I caught on to his method in no time."

"But he doesn't speak our tongue?"

"True…but I have been teaching him some of our words as he has taught me some of his words. But truly, we seem to communicate just fine without knowing the other's tongue."

He chuckled as she looked at him with one eyebrow raised. "Seriously. This entire situation is crazy. It's like we are brothers. Not like I am to my brother Antoine, but like we are somehow kindred. That's the only way I can explain it."

He walked over to the wall lantern. "Lilly, Running Wolf showed me a cavern filled with gold. Shock doesn't even describe what I felt when we went into the small cave at the base of the bluff. The cave goes down into the ground. It's crazy though…it's like the river at one time pushed up into and washed away at the stone of the bluff."

Lilly picked up a stone to closely inspect it as he continued. "The crazy thing is Running Wolf has no use for the stones. He showed me because he thought they may be of use to me."

Lilly wasn't really sure what she was holding. She knew what gold was but really had no knowledge of its value. Growing up in a raw and primitive land she didn't have much use for precious metals. Yet she wasn't completely ignorant and knew people would lose their minds trying to get to the gold. In France the more gold you owned the wealthier you were. The wedding ring Dane gave her was the only jewelry she owned and all she would ever need. The gold in her band was similar to the rock but her band was much more polished. "Are they worth a lot?"

Dane smiled. "Put it this way Lilly, if anyone knew we had these they'd kill for them."

She handed him back the stones. "Then get rid of them."

"Lilly, you do realize we would be set for life. You could have the best of everything."

She put her arms around her husband. "I have everything I could ever want right here with you."

He loved that she was content. He once again couldn't believe how lucky he was to have her. He wrapped the nuggets back up in the wool cloth and placed them back in the hole before sealing it back up. He turned to his wife. "I'm not sure what I am going to do about the cave. I feel if I tell anyone then the place will be out of control with miners. If I don't tell, then the area could

97

become once again isolated. Yet having a populated area would be great for France to declare as theirs. We need more territory here in the new world."

"I just don't like that greed could cause people to get hurt over some pretty rocks."

"I agree. So together maybe we can figure it out. But right now, I need to meet Running Wolf and go back to the mine."

"What? Why are you going back to the mine? I thought we agreed to stay away from it."

He hugged his wife before extinguishing the wall lantern and leading the way up the stairwell. "I am actually only going one last time because Running Wolf is leaving the area and meeting up with his tribe for the rest of the hot months." He grinned. "I think he has a love interest in the tribe but denies it even to himself. Then he spotted the two of us in love and it woke him up to what he was keeping himself from."

"You know this without knowing his tongue?"

"We actually communicate well now. I use some of his words within our words and it's like we have our own language." He chuckled.

"Why are you going back then?"

"I feel I need to make sure I know where the mine is in case we decide to go public with it. I've only been there twice and still not sure of the way. I will meet Running Wolf where the fork turns left by the town's creek and then see if I can find the way without his help."

She hugged him close. "I really wish you wouldn't go."

He kissed the top of her head. "I know love. But I promise to be back just after midnight has fallen. The bright moon will guide me. I would rather return in the night instead of being spotted or followed during the lighted hours."

Lilly fed her husband the stew and walked with him to the river bank where the latest keelboat was docked. The boat had arrived earlier in the day from Quebec and was bound for New Orleans. One of the biggest reasons France wanted a fort in this area was for this purpose, a stopping point between the two territories.

Lilly has seen the keelboat many times, yet the structure still fascinated her. The boat was large and wide and had a shelter-like structure on the back that allowed for workers or travelers to sleep at night. The front and middle of the boat had oars protruding from the outside so many men could row it with several shift changes hourly. The keelboat was the only boat to go upstream while all other boat-like structures were built up North and sent down river only. They were disassembled after they were banked and unloaded then sold for scrap wood once they reached their destination.

As the boatmen were unpacking their wares that were to be delivered to the fort. Dane mentioned he wanted to take her to the market the following day to buy her something pretty. She smiled and said she was content just being his wife and didn't need anything else. He disagreed as they walked towards the stables. He hugged her goodbye and whispered sweetly in her ear, "Wait for me sweet Lilly, for I want to come back and love you all over again."

Lilly looked into his beautiful eyes with a similar promise. He saddled his horse and turned towards the direction of the river. He stopped and turned back to her and smiled, "I love you."

Lilly blushed and repeated the words back to him. She stood there watching him ride off with so much love in her heart. She wondered how she got so blessed.

Turning around she looked at the unique picture that laid before her. Soldiers were everywhere, but what surprised her was the women. They were everywhere doing everything. Many were tending to small gardens throughout the fort. Others were scrubbing laundry with washboards and buckets. It was very warm indoors so better to be outside tending to the laundry on a hot July day.

As Lilly walked throughout the courtyard, she was excited to see her mother exiting the chapel. She rushed over and startled the lady as she nearly knocked her to the ground to give her a hug. "My goodness Lilly, what has gotten into you." Her mother asked as she composed herself.

"Sorry Mother. I just miss you."

Her mother pulled back to look at her daughter. "Now dear, you were just with me yesterday. I'm guessing the transition of marrying and moving out of our quarters last week was a bit much."

Lilly smiled at the lady who gave birth to her. Or did she? It was weird but she reminded her of her mother but yet she didn't look like her mother. Lilly was getting that eerie feeling again that she didn't belong here. "Sorry Mother…I just miss you."

Her mother hugged her and asked quietly in her ear. "Is all well with you and Dane?"

Lilly smiled and nodded. "Yes indeed. He's amazing!"

Her mother smiled and loved the womanly glow her daughter had on her face. It melted her heart to know her daughter had married a strong dependable man who loved her very much. It was a wonderful thing when two people married for love and not just for station.

"Sweetheart, I must get your father's supper on the table." She gave her daughter a thoughtful look. "Do you mind running along and letting your father know we will sup in thirty minutes?"

"Yes ma'am…where is he?"

"Check the Powder Magazine…he was supposed to do the barrel inspection."

"Okay." She hugged her mother and took off in the direction of the Powder Magazine.

On her walk she suddenly had an eerie feeling she was being watched. Looking to her left she spotted Edwin Berger staring at her from one of the Bartizans. She wasn't sure what it was about the man, but he made her uneasy. From the moment he arrived at the fort she could always feel him watching her. She was aware he wished to court her at one time because he asked her father's permission. She informed her father she had no interest in being courted by Edwin and her father asked her to not lead the man to believe anything different. She agreed and did no such thing. Then Dane came along and thankfully Edwin must have sensed her heart was elsewhere for he no longer pursued her.

Lilly arrived at the Powder Magazine and softly called her father's name as she neared the door. Normally any other public place at the fort she would have just entered without a care but the Powder Magazine scared her. The building was built completely of stone in the shape of an arch. It was filled with nothing but barrels of gunpowder. She was always afraid if a spark appeared from a lantern or tobacco pipe…the building would go up in flames. Her father laughed and reassured her no one with a pipe would be near the building and lanterns weren't needed because you could see in just fine with the day's natural light from the doorway.

Lilly was surprised and happy to see her brother, Abraham, just inside the doorway. "Hello Liliane, did you need something?"

"Mother just wanted me to inform Father that supper will be served soon."

Abraham turned back to pass the message to their father before turning back to her to ask where Dane was. She didn't know how best to reply so she just stated he was fishing with Running Wolf. It wouldn't be a surprise to anyone that Dane was with Running Wolf. The Indians in this area made friends with the locals at the fort and the neighboring town of Prairie du Rocher. Most everyone was used to Running Wolf coming to the fort to do the trading for his tribe when his tribe was in the area.

"I have been in the mood to do a spot of fishing myself. Please let your husband know that I'd be interested in going along next time." Lilly nodded and wondered why she still wasn't used to people calling Dane her husband? She guessed that would come with time.

Just then her father came out and she ran into his arms to give him a big hug. "Hello, Father!"

Her father hugged her back. "How's my little girl? Is that husband treating you well?"

"Yes father. Dane has been wonderful."

He chuckled. "I figured he would be. That's why I chose him for you."

Lilly laughed. Her father liked to inform anyone who would listen that he was the reason her and Dane were in love. If you listened closely, you'd think he did all the work up until the wedding.

Lilly smiled as she looked at these two handsome men she called family. Her father was tall and robust. Her brother was very handsome and had been quite the catch with the women of the area. Yet he was no longer on the market. He married the lovely Lorena the previous year.

Lilly waved her goodbye to the men and decided to take a walk before going back to her quarters to wait for her husband. It was odd but the fort was the only place she had ever really been, but she felt like she had been to so many other places. There was an odd deja vu lingering over her on this hot July day.

Lilly looked up and noticed a soldier standing guard at the gatehouse which stood above the fort's entry doors. She looked around at all the busy people finishing up the day's work. She weaved in and out of all the living quarters and passed the cannons posted at their designated spots. She wasn't sure why but she was trying to take in as much as she could before it was completely dark out.

She loved the look and smell of the raw primitive land that surrounded her. The different smoke smells coming from all over. There were soldiers coming in from their hunt while others were training with swords. The stablemaster was brushing down a beautiful horse.

Lilly felt all warm and fuzzy inside. The day was hot and humid but she didn't care. Her skirt was heavy yet there was a coolness to the faded wool material. Looking down it probably helped that the style was cut low to show a slight amount of a female's cleavage. She chuckled and always thought it was odd that a lady couldn't show their ankles because it was improper yet they could have most of their breasts protruding out of the top of their gown. She was sure it was a male who made that rule.

Chapter Nine

As dusk settled over the fort, Lilly made her way back to her home. She thought the bright moon was a perfect glow to her evening walk. She was glad it was bright so it helped Dane find his way back with no mishaps.

Once inside she was bored and impatient for her husband's return. She went to the kitchen and cleaned up their earlier meal. When she was finished it was well past dark and she dozed off sitting in her rocker sewing on the tapestry she wished to hang in their quarters.

She was suddenly jolted awake a little past midnight. Where was her husband? Lilly started pacing and decided minutes later to quickly get dressed and head to her father's house. She felt something wasn't right.

Her father wasn't happy to be disturbed from his slumber until he realized what his daughter needed. He quickly dressed as she ran to her brother's house to ask for his aid. Several minutes later the trio left the fort on horseback in the direction she saw her husband take several hours before.

Not far past the fort walls, along the river path, Lilly spotted a lone rider quite a distance away. Her father was in the lead as they picked up the pace to see if it was her husband traveling in the distance. As they approached the rider Lilly was relieved to see it was Dane.

She shouted his name and took the lead from her father. Just as she neared him the glow of the moon showed what looked to be an arrow, soaring through the air and buried itself in her husband's chest.

Lilly screamed and jumped from her horse as her husband fell from his. "No!" she screamed again and again before falling to his side. Lilly put her hand on the sides of his beautiful face. "Dane...it's me." She cried as he looked at her and his hand softly wrapped around the back of hers.

"My beautiful Liliane." He whispered.

She looked at him confused. "It's okay my love." Her tears were falling and mixing in with the blood on his chest.

"I should have listened to you. I should have left it all alone. I think someone knows and that's why I am about to expire."

"No, no, no. Please don't leave me?" She cried.

"Liliane," his voice was a whisper. "Reach in my front pocket and take the bag and hide it."

She subconsciously did as he asked and quickly put the bag in her dress pocket, really not caring why he asked this of her. She was just thinking of how he was dying right in front of her.

"I was going to tell your father about the gold." His voice was getting raspier. "This would help the people here so much."

It dawned on her that he was going to die because he was trying to help the people. "No, please don't leave me." She whispered.

"Please Liliane, always remember my love for you." His voice was barely a whisper. Dane slowly reached up and wiped at the tears falling down her cheek. "My sweet love, you've owned my heart from the moment we met." He coughed. "I will find you again in another time…this I vow. I love you my sweet Liliane."

Lilly watched as he took his last breath. She kissed his warm lips and cried for several minutes as she laid her cheek next to his.

Moments later her father picked her up and hugged her to him as her brother approached. Abraham looked at the body of his sister's husband and had to hold back the strong emotions he was feeling. He walked over to her and pulled her away from their father and hugged her.

Lilly was the first to pull away and looked at her brother. "Did you see who did this?"

Her father said, "Surely it was a native. There's an arrow protruding from his chest."

Abraham shook his head. "No, it was one of our own. Honestly, I'm fairly certain it was Berger."

Father and daughter looked at him with complete shock. Lilly suddenly became so angry she shook. "Where is the bastard?"

Abraham explained that Berger jumped into a canoe and took off down river. He was fairly sure the canoe flipped but that was just past the bend so he couldn't be sure. He wasn't sure if Berger was still alive or not but he felt the odds weren't in Berger's favor but one could never be sure.

Lilly turned to her deceased husband and kneeled next to him before taking his hand in hers. "I promise you Daniel Dane Geofrey, you are and will always be my forever." She gave him one last kiss and stepped back so her father and brother could remove the arrow before lifting his body onto the back of his horse.

As they arrived back at the fort her father went to wake his most important confidants to discuss what was to be done next. Abraham took his sister to their mother before meeting up with his father. Lilly ran into her mother's arms and cried throughout the entire night. Her mother tended to her daughter as only a mother knew how.

Lilly cried until she slept. When the sun made its way into the small community it brought many unanswered questions. The one sure answer was that Berger was involved. The man wasn't at the fort and nowhere to be found. This confirmed to Abraham that it was most likely Berger he saw shooting the arrow and killing Dane.

There was no evidence if Berger had died in the river or not. Jules didn't want to take any chances of Berger coming back to harm his daughter. He felt that was the reasoning behind Berger's actions and couldn't stop blaming himself for not seeing the obsession the man had towards her.

Lilly confirmed she was never comfortable with the man. She told herself she didn't believe Edwin knew about the gold because he had been at the fort after Dane left. If he thought the Commander was going to line his pockets with gold wouldn't he have found a way to follow him? Not kill him before he knew. Unless he knew where the gold was and killed Dane because he wanted it all to himself? Of course, she had to keep this all to herself.

Lilly was sure deep down Dane's death was personal. The way he would stare at her sent shivers down her back. Maybe it wasn't her, maybe it was Dane becoming the Commander. Yet one thing was she was sure of, she wasn't going to ever tell anyone about the gold. Gold brought greed and greed brought death.

The family discussed what was to be done from this point on. Lilly was surprised when she heard that her parents were planning to return to France before the end of the year. Her father suggested they move their trip up and she would leave with them…that very day. She readily agreed. She needed to leave this place. Everything here reminded her of Dane.

Jules, by law, should return to his position as Commander if he was still in attendance at the fort, until another could be appointed. He spoke with the other officers and it was decided that her brother Abraham was to be the new Lieutenant Commander at the fort. Abe was honored and readily agreed. While the family was going to miss him, they knew his heart was here in the new colony.

It was also decided, due to the heat and the rising water, Dane was to be buried in Prairie du Rocher's Catholic cemetery that evening. The cemetery at St. Anne, just up the road from the fort, was under water from flooding. So the only other option was the small town's cemetery.

It was Abraham who suggested the family leave that very day on the keelboat heading to New Orleans. The trip was two to three weeks long and then in New Orleans the family would get on a ship for France. Lilly wanted away from the fort as soon as possible so she readily agreed. She didn't think she could see her beloved in a casket and she didn't want to stay at the fort for what could be months waiting for the next boat out.

Abraham delayed the boat for a few hours as Hattie and Lorena helped her pack her small amount of belongings. Her parents quickly prepared for the move as Lilly gathered up Dane's personal belongings. She kept a few things for herself and grabbed a few more personal items to take back to Dane's mother when she arrived in France. She then sent the rest to his brother.

Dane's father was as lost as she was and hugged her tight when she said her goodbyes. He agreed it was better they leave immediately in case Berger was still alive. He promised he was going to do everything in his power to find justice for his son. He asked that she let his wife know what took place and that he would be home as soon as everything was settled.

Abraham and Lorena waved goodbye to the family after a long round of hugs. Hattie and Lilly hugged for several minutes with the promise to meet again. Within a few minutes the trio was on the keelboat and heading down the Mississippi.

Hours later as the moon stood high, Lilly dozed off as she settled in under the shelter part of the boat. She dreamed of Dane's funeral...the one that was being attended to at that moment. It was as if she was floating and looked down at the procession leaving the fort and going towards the little town. She noticed Running Wolf standing in between the trees near the graveyard. He was watching the procession of forty wagons and thirteen pairs of soldiers riding side by side in front of a flatbed wagon with her husband's remains in a box on the back of the last wagon. As the locals spotted the entourage they walked behind the procession. They heard the story of the fallen Commander. Many had met the young man and were heartbroken to hear of his death.

Running Wolf remained in the wooded area as the procession made its way to the burial site. Lilly could feel his pain and sadness. She felt he was disappointed she wasn't there to put her husband to rest.

Smoke of the lanterns, leading to the grave, filled the air. She felt his confusion at the white man's ways. His people would have been there to say goodbye and to rejoice that the deceased was going to join the gods.

After the soldiers lifted the box and placed it in the hole something caught Running Wolf's eyes. Lilly looked to where he did and could see deep into the rising fog and smoke...the image of her love. This didn't surprise Running Wolf but it hurt Lilly. She could feel how lost her beloved was and his wonder at where she was.

Dane's spirit looked to Running Wolf with anguish in his eyes. His mind spoke to Running Wolf letting him know he was choosing the ultimate sacrifice...to stay in the parallels of time until he found his love and they would be together for all eternity. Running Wolf stared at the vision before sending him what the gods were saying...*you must remove the enemy before the enemy removes you.*

With that Running Wolf watched as the spirit of the procession turned and headed back to the fort...without the casket. They may have buried it but the spirit of the deceased is lost...looking for his true love. Running Wolf turned to the sky and looked directly where she was looking down from and she felt he could see her.

Lilly woke up with a start. She jumped up from the ledge she was sitting on. Thank goodness there was a large stump in the middle that permitted a person from falling. She looked around all lost and confused. Where was she? The last thing she remembered was climbing into the keelboat and dreaming about Dane's funeral.

She quickly looked down at her jeans and jacket. Wait, she ran over to the tall wall that looked into the courtyard of the fort. There was a bench in the corner so she stepped on it to see over the old stone. It was the same...only different. This place was similar to the original, only very different; more like a replica.

Lilly sat back down on the bench and had to collect her thoughts. Did she have another dream? Yes, that was it. Why is she dreaming these things? Could what her grandfather thought really be true?

Then she remembered Dane. The pain she felt in the dream became her reality. She almost cried over the anguish she felt. Lilly stood back up and began to pace again. She needed to get it together. Taking a few deep breaths, she decided to pass it off as just a crazy dream. Her grandfather had spooked her and now she was dreaming of it.

Her next thought made her sit back down. The Daniel Geofrey's grave she saw at the cemetery was the same person she kept dreaming about named Dane; Daniel Dane Geofrey. She just went back in time and lived out the death of her ancestor's husband. Lilly decided it was time to leave the fort. Rissa might get upset but she needed to leave. Hell, where was her friend? Did she already leave the fort because maybe Rissa couldn't find her when she returned.

Lilly ran her hand through her hair nervously. She had to have been in that other time for a day at least. Dear Lord, what if her friend reported her missing? Lilly looked around in a panic. Turning towards the exit she jumped as she spotted a handsome man stepping on to the threshold of the tower. Shock registered on her face as she stepped back "Dane?"

"Lilly?" He smiled. "No one ever calls me Dane." He smiled and took a step forward as she stepped back. "I'm surprised you remember my middle name? Hell, I'm not sure if you ever knew my last name."

Lilly wasn't listening to him because she was sure she was seeing a ghost. She realized this couldn't be her Dane because they were in a different time. "Do I know you?" She asked, completely confused.

This man grinned at her with perfect white teeth and sexy light green eyes...just like Dane's. She shook her head as if to clear it. Why does she keep thinking of some guy she has never met named Dane? At this point she was sure she was losing her mind.

"I hope you didn't forget me. For one week we were best friends." At her confused look he continued. "It's me...Tripp!"

Everything cleared up in that moment and Lilly no longer was stuck in another century. Thank goodness she could focus on what he was saying and she was remembering a young boy from a summer of her youth. "Tripp?" She took a step closer. "Is it really you?"

"Yes ma'am. How are you, Lilly?" He grinned.

Lilly, mentally shook her head to clear her stupor before reaching out and hugging her childhood friend. Damn, she thought, he definitely grew up if his hard body gave any indication. Lilly pulled back and looked up at him. "Dang Tripp, you got tall." She grinned.

He looked her up and down. "And you Lilly-Bear are still one fine lookin' lady. You were the hottest chick I'd ever laid eyes on back then. It's good to see that some things never change."

Lilly slapped him in the arm. "Whatever, you never thought I was hot. I think that's something I would have known as much as we hung around that week."

He lifted his eyes, "Really, why do you think I was hanging with you and Rissa when I could have been sneaking cigarettes and beer with all the boys here at the fort and chasing after the half-dressed squaws?" His grin grew. "Heck, you were my first kiss."

Lilly chuckled and blushed, deciding the conversation was getting too personal so she changed the subject. "Speaking of Rissa, she's here with me."

He grinned. "I know. She's the one who sent me up here." He smiled, "She hasn't changed a bit." He turned serious. "She told me about your grandfather. I'm so sorry. Frank was a great man."

She replied a thank you just as Rissa stepped over the last step unto the tower. Behind her was a gorgeous brunette. "So I see you found her." Rissa stated before turning to Lilly. "I couldn't believe it when I ran into Tripp."

Before Lilly could reply, the lady with Rissa walked over and looped her arm through Tripp's. Lilly knew at that moment the female was letting Lilly know Tripp belonged to her.

"Tripp sweetie, introduce me to your other childhood friend." There was a hint of animosity in her tone.

Tripp introduced the girl as Selene. He didn't say what she was to him so Lilly wondered if they were married or just dating? Lilly willed herself not to look at the woman's ring finger as she returned the proper greeting.

After that everything got awkward. There was small talk about what everyone has been doing since they last saw each other. Tripp held a degree in Applied Science in Land Surveying, Mapping, and Surveying Technology and was presently freelancing for a group in Northern Illinois. He was also a founding member of an organization that was trying to save the lands and homes along the Mississippi River. PORT was an organization specialized in aiding the Levee districts along the river. He had arrived earlier in the week to meet with different committees about the flooding in the area. He heard about the fall Rendezvous and decided to stay in town for the weekend before returning to Champaign the following day.

Lilly explained how her brother lived in the same area and told Tripp he should look him up sometime. Tripp remembered Sawyer from years past and agreed to give him a shout. Things got a bit uncomfortable when Selene asked if they were ready to go as she waved at the air as if to wipe away the dirt from the place. Tripp hugged the girls after exchanging numbers. Lilly could tell Selene didn't like that they were now connected.

As the couple left Lilly and Rissa looked at each other with lifted eyebrows before they both busted out laughing.

"What in the world does he see in her?" Rissa asked as she looked down from the tower wall at the retreating couples back.

Lilly joined her. "I don't know, but I hope she doesn't get any dust on her before she leaves the place."

The girls looked at each other and smiled before Lilly's expression became serious. She walked over to the inside wall that faced the inner yard of the fort. She grabbed the bench from the corner and pulled it over to the tall side of the wall that faced the fort's courtyard.

"What's wrong Lilly?" Her friend asked with concern as she joined her in standing on the bench.

"How long were you gone when you went to the bathroom?" She asked as she looked down at the yard.

"Ten, maybe fifteen minutes. I was talking to Tripp for a little bit before his girlfriend, wife or whatever she is, stated she was going to use the ladies room as well and decided to join me." She looked over the wall. "Like she couldn't find the bathroom on her own."

When Lilly remained quiet, Rissa started to worry. "Are you okay? Are you freaking out about running into Tripp?"

Lilly didn't say anything as she scanned the inside of the historical fort. It was crazy to her that she could now envision how the fort looked centuries ago. So much had changed. The modern replica fort look was so much softer than how the fort looked back then. She could now see in her mind the layout of a mid-1700's fort. The holes were basements that held the cold food to keep from spoiling and wood for the fireplace that was used daily for cooking. Nothing was ever tossed away because there wasn't much and everything was used until it was completely unusable. It was a harsh and primitive life.

Looking in every direction she remembered where the gardens had been throughout the fort. They were inside and outside of the walls. She could envision the people looking tired and overworked as they pulled weeds and dug into the black river soil.

While looking around she remembered what had felt like real moments just a few minutes ago was gone. It was odd but she knew what life was like back then. The dream seemed so real but everything back then seemed to lack the colors of today. The foundations of most of the buildings with the replicas on top and the ones that were left alone still had the limestone base in place but were aged from climate and time. The colors of the past seemed drabbier. The grass didn't seem as green as grass today. Maybe the colors were void because she was dreaming. Yet even with the colors more solemn and the hardships that were so much more intense back then compared to modern time with technology, she had to admit the serenity back then almost made her wish she never woke from her dream.

Minutes passed as neither girl said a word. Rissa knew her friend was trying to figure out something in her head. Lilly was silently identifying everything in the fort as it had been in her dream. It was crazy to think that her dream was only a few minutes in this time but had been hours in the past. It was as if time here stood still. It was even crazier that those hours gave her so much historical insight of what the fort life had been like back then.

It didn't take Lilly long to find what her mind now knew she was looking for. Her and Dane's lodgings. The house was no longer there and she was surprised to see the stone foundation was the only thing that remained. She was happy it didn't have a replica house or platform on top of it.

Looking around she was glad it was still just the two of them in the tower. It gave her a chance to process everything she was feeling. "Rissa," She turned to her friend. "Please don't think I am crazy but while you went to the bathroom and I was up here before Tripp arrived…" Dear Lord, she hoped her friend didn't think she was losing her mind and wanted to back completely away from her. "I think I had another 'out of body' thing!"

Her friend lifted her eyebrow. "Another hot guy?"

Lilly turned and looked back out into the fort. "Same hot guy…only this time he died in my arms." Lilly reached up to feel a tear on her cheek.

Rissa looked around to make sure no one heard them. Still alone, she asked her friend to explain what happened. Lilly went into detail about everything she saw and felt. It was so clear it almost felt like it just happened.

When she finished her friend hugged her before they both turned to look down inside the courtyard once again. "Lilly, something is definitely happening here."

Lilly smiled at her friend. "So you don't think I'm crazy?"

"Lillian Bienvenue, I've known you since we were kids and even though we haven't spoken in quite a few years I know who you are on the inside…and crazy isn't in there. So if this is happening, then we need to figure it out." She grinned. "Besides I always wanted to play Nancy Drew."

Lilly chuckled. "I think I've had enough excitement for one day, let's go."

"You sure you don't want to go explore the fort and see if there's more?"

Lilly shook her head. "My heart hurts and I just want some alone time to try and process all of this."

"I get it. Let's go."

Chapter Ten

Hours later Lilly walked into Lisa's with Rissa and Zeke. She looked at her watch and was hoping she could skip out after a drink or two. She hadn't wanted to go out but she promised her friend she would and Rissa was making her stick to the plan. She really just wanted to be home and sort through all the crazy stuff she had experienced at the fort earlier in the day.

Of course, that didn't happen after she returned home from the fort. She barely had her shoes off when two older ladies, Tammy and Ruthie, wanted to say hello with a casserole and a cake. Lilly thought it was sweet and explained that most of the family had already left but they joked that there was just more for her to eat now.

The ladies stayed for over an hour and by the end of the visit she knew quite a bit about the people in town even though she would never get everyone's names straight. When she mentioned this, they reassured her they had no problem showing her around so she wouldn't confuse anyone down the road.

By the time they left Rissa was texting her saying they were leaving in an hour and she wasn't taking no for an answer. So she hustled to get showered and ready. And almost exactly an hour later she was walking through Lisa's door with Rissa and Zeke.

She was relieved her friends didn't make her feel like a third wheel. Zeke immediately excused himself as he walked over to talk to a concrete truck driver who had done a few pour jobs for him. The girls headed out to the back patio to hear the band. They walked over to the bar and sat on a couple vacant barstools. The place was busy but not overly so, probably because the band had just started.

After ordering a couple beers, the girls toasted to meeting up again after so many years. They were oblivious to the looks they were receiving. The men were admiring and the women...not so much. In no time Lisa heard that the girls were at the bar and came out to give them a hug. She alerted the bartender, Ryan, to give the girls whatever they wanted…on the house.

Zeke came out a few minutes later to join them. Lilly looked around and had to admit she was very impressed with Lisa's patio layout. The bar was long and accommodating. The area was big enough to hold a lot of people. The stage was nice and big and could accommodate a large band.

The five-piece band was very good. They consisted of five men and a very talented female singer, who had no problem singing the latest top hits. Lilly was impressed that they also had a few of their own songs that they played and were definitely worth a recording. She was sure if they played their cards right, they could be playing at the Opry in Nashville someday.

As a popular ballad started Zeke pulled Rissa away from the barstool to claim the dance. Lilly smiled as she watched her friends. They made the perfect couple. She hoped one day she could find something close to what they had.

Lilly swiveled around just as a familiar face came toward her and asked if she'd like to take a turn on the dance floor. She smiled and looked up at Tripp before looking behind him and then around the patio. "Umm, I don't think your girlfriend would like that."

He grabbed her hand and pulled her towards the dancing couples. "She'll be fine because she's not my girlfriend. Plus she just got into a very long line at the woman's bathroom. I don't think she will be back for a while." He pulled her into his arms and she followed his lead and swayed to the popular song. "Besides, I'm just dancing with an old friend."

Lilly glared at him with a smirk on her lips. "Who are you calling old…mister?" She lifted her eyebrows before continuing. "And has anyone ever informed HER she wasn't your girlfriend? I think her claws would dig deep to whoever dared!"

Tripp laughed and called her a brat before pulling her close and led them both into the beauty of the lyrics.

Lilly softly listened to the popular words about finding a forever love.

I always find myself looking…could our paths have already crossed?
I wonder where are you now…what if our opportunity is now lost?
Have we passed each other…on a sidewalk or driving down the street?
Have we been in the same club…swaying to the same beat?

I'm so afraid I've already met you...and didn't know forever was in front of me.

What if our one chance has come and gone...a forever love of ours may never be?

Are we in a different time...possibly a parallel universe?

Are you listening to this song right now...along with me singing the same verse?

We could have been friends once...when we were young and small.

Maybe playing at the same park...laughing when one or the other would fall.

I'm looking for my forever, will we someday meet?

I want it to be exactly you, the one that is to be.

I know I'll know it's right because it won't feel wrong.

Your arms will tightly hold me as we sway to this slow song.

Have we just not crossed paths yet, maybe our time is yet to come?

Will I know that it's you? My heart is scared and numb.

I need to learn patience and storm through the weather.

To lose you I hope is never...I know you will always be my forever.

Time is what I needed...I finally see you in front of me.

Our one chance is finally here...and now a forever love is ours to be.

All the excitement spins around at the newness inside.

The way you make me feel makes it hard to hide.

I love getting to know you and the taste of your smile.

You make my heart flutter and race for miles.

Please Lord let this be the one I've been waiting for.

Please let what we found move forward to rise and soar.

I've found my forever. It took so long to finally meet.

I'm glad it's exactly you, the one that is to be.

I know deep down this is it because it doesn't feel wrong.

Your arms are tightly holding me as we sway to this slow song.

I'm glad we crossed paths and our time has finally come.

I've learned to be patient and my heart is no longer numb.

As the song continued on Lilly was taken back by the lyrics. She knew the song yet never really listened to the words. It was like they were written for her and this Dane she kept dreaming of. Yet it almost could fit her and this handsome man holding her. It talks about knowing each other before and playing at a park which could describe her and Tripp's past and the school playground. It also spoke about a parallel universe which seems to describe her and her ghost Dane. Yet Dane hadn't been a ghost when he was making love to her deja vu hours earlier.

Tripp was disappointed when the song ended and he led Lilly back to her barstool. "I like that song." He whispered in her ear, sending sweet goosebumps up her spine, before she slid back onto her seat.

Tripp was surprised that he and Lilly didn't speak during the dance. Yet he found he was content just holding his beautiful childhood friend in his arms. Crazy but the song almost felt like it was speaking to them. In a way it gave him an eerie feeling.

He was starting to feel like a big jerk, because he was here with one woman and was totally hitting on another. Yet, in his defense he never really invited Selene along, she pretty much invited herself. And he wasn't even dating the girl…not that she hadn't tried.

Selene recently started working with the non-profit organization he started a few years back. The company, Preserve Our River Towns, or better known as PORT, was created by Tripp and a few of his college buddies as a graded classroom project. The project was virtual and when it was all said and done, he and his two friends wanted to actually see it through because in reality it was needed. They even brought in a fourth person, Tripp's brother Jasper, Attorney at Law. Jasper was on board because he and Tripp grew up going to the historical sites with their parents and they developed a love for Mississippi River towns.

Over the next four years the group of surveyors set up the organization to fight for the people in jeopardy of losing their homes in the river towns along the Mississippi. These towns were truly the heart and soul of the United States before there was a United States…considering many of them were over three hundred years old and have so much history and charm. The PORT team believed it was worth the fight to get government help to preserve the history and protect the towns from the rising waters that could wash away everything, including their history.

The problem was parts of the government no longer wanted to pay to keep up with the maintenance. So PORT not only fought the government they were also trying to raise millions of dollars to help with the maintenance. PORT was strictly nonprofit; so the staff was all on a volunteer basis.

That was where Tripp met Selene a few months ago. She submitted an application to PORT to volunteer and after her interview it was decided by the partners that she would be a great addition especially because she had bookkeeping skills. To be honest she wasn't the type to be a part of their group. She was a bit materialistic and not very into the whole save the village thing. This made Tripp wonder why she was even interested in the organization.

About a month ago, Selene started showing an interest in Tripp. As a rule, he didn't believe in mixing business with pleasure. Yet there was something off about Selene wanting to be a part of the organization that made him suspicious. Tripp decided hanging out with the lady couldn't hurt if it helped him get to the bottom of her interest in PORT.

Yet now he was in a situation. He couldn't really tell Lilly that he was using Selene to see why she became involved with PORT. Yet what he wanted more than anything was to spend the evening with his teenage crush. To be honest when he saw Lilly at the top of the tower at the fort, he felt like he was kicked in the stomach all over again…just as he had been years ago when he noticed her for the first time the summer he spent in Prairie du Rocher.

"Do you want to know something funny?" Lilly asked.

"Sure."

"I was just thinking about you the other day."

He gave her a hurtful look. "Only the other day? I'm not sure I ever put you too far out of my mind." He said jokingly but wondered if there wasn't some truth in what he said.

She slapped his arm. "Quit, I'm being serious."

"Okay…go on. When and why were you thinking about me the other day?"

"Well, I arrived here Tuesday, I had a little time to kill so I took a ride and I ended up at the playground." She smiled. "I suddenly remembered the time we ran into each other that first day…on the playground."

Tripp lifted his eyebrows. "Ran into?"

"Yes, you remember how we met don't you?" She gave him a pouty look that said she'd be sad if he didn't remember.

Tripp chuckled and looked at her. "Lilly, there was 'no running into' about it. I saw you in town the day before and overheard you saying to the clerk you were having a picnic after school at the playground the following day. I wanted to meet you, so I happened to conveniently be there before you so I could 'chance-meet' you."

Lilly's mouth dropped open with laughter in her eyes. "Nice, and I was naive enough to be clueless!" She was shaking her head and smiling.

Tripp grinned and turned to the bar to order himself, Lilly, and the approaching Rissa and her date a drink. Introductions were made and Tripp found he liked Rissa's fiancé. After a few minutes of idle talking everyone got quiet as Selene approached the group. Tripp introduced her to Zeke, who she gave a warm greeting to, yet she barely acknowledged the ladies.

Lilly was still processing what Tripp admitted to moments before. He had a crush on her? Wow! She guessed it made sense considering their last day together at the town creek.

Rissa rolled her eyes as she noticed how Selene pushed herself in between Tripp and Lilly. Lilly almost busted out in laughter at the woman's audacity. She finally let out the laugh when Selene pulled Tripp onto the dance floor.

Lilly turned to comment about Selene's rude behavior just as a tall, dark haired, handsome man approached the group. He was smiling and she gave a hesitant smile back as he stood next to Rissa's stool and ordered a drink from Ryan. She was surprised as he handed her a beer. "My New Year's resolution was to buy the prettiest girl in every bar I enter a drink. And trust me…you are the prettiest."

Lilly lifted her eyebrows and gave him a small grin as she took the beer. "Thank You…but that could get you in trouble if the girl has a husband or boyfriend." She stated.

"And do you?"

Lilly chuckled and realized she played right into his hand. "Well done." She stated.

"And…?" He asked again.

Lilly didn't know what to think about this guy. He was definitely charming and quite handsome with his dark curly hair, brown eyes and easy smile. He was tall and built nicely. Yet something about him made her a bit uneasy. "I'm not sure how to answer that? My momma always said the less someone knows about you the better."

"Well, I would be shocked if you said you were single but there's always hope." He gave her a piercing look that sent chills up her spine.

Suddenly she became uncomfortable and was glad Rissa interrupted the conversation. "Hi, I'm Rissa and this is my fiancé Zeke." She shook his hand and Zeke followed.

"Edmond Brader." He shook hands with Rissa and Zeke before turning to Lilly with a smile and out-stretched hand.

Lilly shook his hand after giving him her name. She wasn't comfortable with the guy and wasn't sure why. Then again, she wasn't comfortable when it came to dating in general and always seemed to be uncomfortable when meeting a guy for the first time. While Zeke and Edmond started talking, Rissa turned her back on the men and mouthed to Lilly that Edmond was "hot." Lilly shrugged letting her friend know she wasn't interested. The girls turned their attention back to the men when Edmond asked if they were locals.

Lilly was hesitant to tell him much about herself so she just stated she was here for an extended vacation. Rissa looked back at her with a question in her eyes as Zeke explained how he and Rissa were new to town but planned to make it permanent. Lilly's eyes told her friend *I'll tell you later.*

"Are you just passing through or are you hoping to make Prairie du Rocher your home?" Zeke asked the other man.

"I'm actually from upstate, near Chicago." He replied.

"So what brings a man from a big city to little ole' Rocher...if you don't mind my asking?" Rissa asked.

He chuckled. "I'm actually here working with a federal engineering group to look into the maintenance of the levee system along the Mississippi."

Lilly wasn't paying much attention to the two men's conversation. She was busy chuckling at how bizarre the situation was around her. If someone was just passing by and didn't know there was a Fall French and Indian Rendezvous going on they would be confused by the dated clothing. On the dance floor was a Fur Trapper dressed in buckskin and dancing with a Squaw. In the corner was a group of five young ladies in vintage colonial gowns with most of their cleavage popping out, doing a shot of liquor. There were Indians with real mohawks and the only covering was a couple small loincloths to cover the most private parts of their body. Lilly was admiring the view of one of the Indian's, who wore the loincloth well, dancing on the dance floor in a circle with his tomahawk in hand. He was built very well and could pull off the nudity. Yet, it wasn't always sexy…sometimes there would be a half-naked Indian in the group that you really wish would put on some clothes.

The rendezvous was special in Prairie du Rocher. People came from as far as Canada and brought in a large amount of tourist revenue. Tourism helped keep the town alive which was an incredible feat in itself because three hundred years later the town was still very small and sometimes forgotten about. It was crazy to think that society and the government tended to treat people differently because they aren't a part of something big…when in fact being a part of something small makes one's passion and love of life…huge!

As Tripp and Selene rejoined the group Lilly almost wished they would just go away. Tripp said she wasn't his girlfriend but they looked awfully chummy to her. Selene smirked at Lilly to let her know Tripp was hers. Lilly really had bad thoughts about the woman and that was so unlike her. She almost made her own excuse to leave the place. Yet, this woman wasn't worth her having ugly thoughts. So she decided to push her out of her head.

As Tripp approached, she noticed an instant dislike between Tripp and Edmond by their body language. Interesting, she wondered what that was all about?

Edmond nodded at Tripp before stating, "I heard you were in town. Did you come to see the impossible?"

"Brader, I know what is here and what needs to be done." Tripp looked at the other man with disdain. "Were you down here rubbing hands together trying to count how many lives you can possibly ruin this time?"

Edmond shook his head. "I am not the monster you think I am. I'm the one trying to save these people from a levee break in the middle of the night…drowning them as they sleep."

Lilly could see the anger in Tripp's eyes before he replied. "People down here have been sleeping in their beds for centuries. You guys are on a power kick and all you want is to take away their livelihood and homes. Because the number of people along the river isn't as big as your large cities you think it doesn't matter. But it matters to these people." He lowered his voice. "It's not like there is a water wall about to burst."

Lilly was confused and yet she kind of figured out that this had something to do with the town's levee system. She looked around to notice that people were starting to edge closer to hear what was going on. Even though she knew this wasn't the time or the place.

"Edmond?" Lilly drew the man's attention to her. "Would you like to dance?"

Edmond smirked at Tripp. "I don't have the time or the desire to discuss this with you. As you can see, the beautiful lady wishes to dance with me."

Lilly didn't stick around to look at Tripp's expression. She knew she took a chance on him being mad at her but the last thing she wanted was for the two men to go to blows at her friend's restaurant. Yet stepping into Edmond's arms she felt a cold chill run up her back as he smiled at her. Lilly wished she would have let the two men duke it out instead of putting herself in this situation.

"So lovely Lilly," He started as he swayed to the slow tempo. "I am most sorry you had to witness that nasty little scene back there."

Lilly suddenly thought he reminded her of what she pictured the devil to look like. "What was that all about?" She wanted to understand the argument. If she was going to live in this town, she needed to be aware of what was happening here.

His grin was slick and almost ruthless. "Well Geofrey and I have a disagreement when it comes to the river bottoms." Lilly felt him stepping closer so she stepped back a bit without losing a beat. "I truly believe the levees are not held together well and I am afraid they are going to break one day causing many people to lose their lives by the break."

Lilly was confused. "So Tripp doesn't think it will happen?"

"Correct. He wants to keep patching the levees and hope they will just keep standing erect as they are. Yet the government has worked extensively to see if it was possible to keep the levee system as it is. Unfortunately it no longer works."

"I don't understand, why doesn't it work?"

"There's so many water sources dumping into the Mississippi. This makes it fuller and more rapid. Plus you have global warming and everything north of here is melting and dumping into the river. This in turn is causing the levees to become weak and leaving water leaks in them which can cause a major break leading to not only flooding but could wipe out the little town here."

Lilly was taken aback by the information. What did this mean to Prairie du Rocher? What did it mean to the people who were born and raised here and still living here? What did it mean to the farmers who had their livelihood in the fields that were planted every year? "So what is it you want to do to make this better?"

"Lilly, the river is mean. You can't control it and tell it what to do. It's a part of nature and needs to be able to flow where it needs to flow."

"So you think the answer is to remove every homestead and town in its way no matter that you will be destroying everything these people know and love. It's their homes…their history! Destroying our history, not just the locals but United States history. This town is one of the first settlements in this country…the same as many of the towns along this river." She was getting heated. "There has to be a better way."

He had the audacity to smile at her like she was a small child. "I agree with what you are saying but that is why I am here…to find a way. Yet I cannot find a way that will not endanger people living along the river."

Lilly was relieved the song ended before she would let her temper get the best of her. She wanted to talk to Tripp and see what the other side of the coin was. He obviously felt there was a way around it or he wouldn't have been arguing with Edmond.

As she made her way back to the bar with Edmond in tow, she was bummed to see Tripp was nowhere near Rissa and Zeke. "Rissa where's Tripp?" She asked quietly so Edmond wouldn't hear.

Rissa looped her arm through Lilly's and stated to the men they were heading to the bathroom. Once they were out of earshot Rissa answered Lilly's question. "Oh my gosh Lilly, I think Tripp was seething that you asked Edmond to dance. He looked like he could have chewed nails." She walked through the bar and headed towards the other exit. "He and the she-devil left right after you went to dance. I shot him a text and explained that I was sure you asked Edmond to dance because you thought the two of them were going to come to blows."

"That's exactly what happened. Did he answer?"

"No, but he's probably still driving. They are staying in Red Bud so he probably hasn't arrived at their hotel yet."

"Rissa, don't get mad but I want to get out of here. I don't think I can be around that Edmond guy any longer." She shivered. "He gives me the creeps."

"I'm with you sista…I already sent Zeke a text saying we were heading home and to stall the creep for ten minutes before meeting us."

Lilly lifted her eyebrows. "Really? What did Zeke say?"

"Well let's just say I owe him extra favors."

The two girls were laughing as they quickly walked in the direction of their homes.

Chapter Eleven

Tripp was seething with anger. After seeing Selene to her room, he took off to take a brisk walk around the neighboring town of Red Bud. The town was fifteen minutes from Prairie du Rocher and was in no danger of the Mississippi floods. Red Bud was charming and the downtown looked like something one would see on a greeting card. Red Bud was quite a bit larger than Prairie du Rocher yet still small by most people's standards.

The walk was letting him cool off from the confrontation with Brader. If he truly believed Brader's intentions were good he would probably try to keep his cool when it came to discussing the levee problems along the Mississippi. Yet it was Brader that was responsible for a few towns having to relocate to higher grounds because they were no longer allowed to build or maintain a residence in the floodplain. He was good at approaching the homeowners while they were stressed and worried because their homes sat with six feet of water inside. That was when he manipulated these people into giving up everything.

Many towns were experiencing flooding for the first time ever because the river was now larger and stronger. This was mostly due to too many waterways dumping into the river. The government no longer wished to deal with the flooding, levee breaches, and maintenance that involved the small towns, yet were content with helping the larger cities along the river. Their answer to everything was to get rid of it instead of fixing it.

The levees needed repairs and a new system for control of the flooding. Instead of finding a solution, they wanted to erase the problem by forcing people to leave their homes and give up their livelihoods. It always came down to one thing…money.

That was why there was a need for PORT. It was created to help people fight against the big guys. Yet Tripp found the more he pushed, the harder people in power pushed back. He had a plan but he needed more people to become a part of his organization. Many voices speak volumes.

Tripp decided to head back to the hotel. He needed to leave early in the morning because he had a lot of work to do with PORT before he started his work week the following day. He was just bummed he didn't get to say goodbye to Lilly.

He had to admit it killed him to see Lilly dancing with Brader. Damn, Lilly with Brader. Was that even possible? He wondered if she knew him before today? She did mention at the fort she lived in Kansas City but now owned Bienvenue House. Yet they could have met down here before now. Brader was always in this area because he wanted to shut Prairie du Rocher down like he had done to a few other towns along the Mississippi.

After letting himself back into his room he grabbed a quick shower before heading to bed. He reached for his phone and smiled as he read Rissa's text. 'Our do-gooder Lilly was afraid you and the creep were going to come to blows so that's why she asked him to dance.'

Looking at the clock he realized it was too late to text the girls but he decided to do it anyway. His message to Rissa was a thanks for the heads up on Lilly dancing with Brader and that he hoped to be back in town again soon. She answered with a 'you better…we miss you already.'

His message to Lilly was a bit more personal. "So you want to take away my man card…huh? Just for that you owe me dinner the next time I'm in town. You have no idea how good it was to see you."

He smiled at her reply. "Didn't want anyone banging up Lisa's place. That guy is the devil. I'll have dinner with you only because I'm interested in what is happening with our levees now that I am a resident of PDR. Text me when you are coming back into town."

He grinned as he replied, "Now I have something to come back for! I promise it will be soon."

The girls decided to wait for Zeke on Rissa's front porch swing. Rissa turned to her friend and stated, "Spill it, Lilly."

Lilly looked at her friend oddly. "What?"

"What's up with you and Tripp?"

"I have no idea what you are talking about. Before today I haven't seen or talked to him since we were fourteen."

"Okay, then what's with the chemistry between you two? You could cut it with a knife. Selene could feel it as well as the rest of us."

Lilly shook her head. "I didn't get that feeling. I thought he was all over her."

"Please!" Rissa rolled her eyes. "He couldn't take his eyes off you and you were straining yourself not to look at him."

Lilly laughed. "I was not."

"Bullshit." Rissa laughed as she slowly rocked them back and forth on the swing. After a moment she jumped up and stated, "I'll be right back. I want to grab us a glass of wine."

Lilly continued swinging as she waited for her friend. She thought about Tripp and had to admit she found him amazing. He was everything she wanted in a man. Never had she met anyone who made her feel all tingly like he did. Well, no one else but the hot guy that was in her dreams earlier today while at the fort. Dane was just as sexy and in a weird way they both seemed one and the same…only he didn't exist!

It was funny, but sex wasn't something she thought of much. She did have a boyfriend for about a year in college and they had been intimate but it was nothing like what she felt in her dream. She wasn't even into the college guy, it was him who pursued her and she thought he was funny and sweet so she dated him. Yet she always knew he wasn't the one.

As far as crushing on someone hard, she'd have to say Tripp was her first and last serious crush. She just never really found that spark she felt with anyone as she had with him as a teenager. Geez, that was pathetic when she thought about it.

After seeing Tripp again, she realized where her obsession with sandy brown hair and green eyes came from. Tripp! It might also have to do with her ghost looking a lot like Tripp with the same coloring. Then there was that hot moment she had her hands all over her ghost earlier today…a ghost that looked and reminded her of Tripp.

She took a deep breath and was overwhelmed by the past few days. In less than a week she had lost her grandfather, quit her job, moved to Prairie du Rocher, found her old best friend, met up with her first crush, found out the parallel universe was playing havoc with her love life and had sex with a ghost. "Well, no wonder I'm tired." She mumbled just as Rissa was coming back onto the porch.

Rissa joined her on the swing after handing her a glass of wine. The two girls slowly rocked back and forth neither saying a word for several minutes. They just looked out at the quiet street glowing with soft light from the street lights.

Lilly was the first to break the silence. "You know he was my first kiss!"

"What?" Rissa looked at her with shock. "When?"

"When we were fourteen." She turned and smiled at her friend. "It was his last day here that summer." She sipped her wine. "He asked me to take a walk. We walked out to the town creek." She turned to look back at the deserted street. "He was restless and was explaining to me about how he was having dreams of being murdered."

"Geez...that's a lot for a fourteen-year-old!" Rissa stated.

"I know. So after sitting there and talking he told me he felt better with me by his side and kissed me." She smiled.

"Like a Kiss Kiss?"

Lilly smiled. "Yes and no. It was nice and let me tell you I just realized I have thought about that kiss over the years and I can say it was probably the most special kiss I've ever had." She continued before her friend could interrupt. "I don't mean like a passionate kiss but there was an intense pull that made me want to never let that moment end."

"Wow, why didn't you tell me?" Rissa felt a bit hurt.

Lilly grabbed her hand and squeezed it. "I was embarrassed. I was too cool to kiss a boy."

Rissa leaned back and continued smiling. "Wow, maybe you and Tripp belong together. Maybe you guys can rekindle whatever it is you have going."

"You forget he's with Selene." Lilly stated.

Before Rissa could comment Zeke climbed the steps to the porch. "Hello ladies. Thanks for leaving me with that odd duck."

Lilly leaned forward and was the first to reply. "I'm sorry Zeke...but truly he was creeping me out."

He laughed. "I get it. You should be creeped out...he asked me a million questions about you."

"Ugh, don't tell me that. I hope he isn't in town long."

"I have a feeling he will be making many visits to town to try and win the fair Lilly over." Zeke chuckled.

Rissa laughed. "He didn't call her that...did he?"

"No, but he does have an odd way of speaking."

Zeke claimed he was tired and said his goodnights. Rissa followed him in to refill their glasses. Lilly sat quietly on the swing thinking once again about all the surreal things happening.

127

Their street was a quiet one because it wasn't on any main roads. She was surprised to see a gray BMW driving past at such a late hour. She sucked in her breath when she realized it was Edmond. "How in the hell?" She whispered. He was looking over at her house while trying to be discreet. She was sure he didn't notice her on the porch across the road. She didn't move so he wasn't alerted to look in her direction. She just knew it was him and was really curious how he knew where she lived and why was he driving by her house?

Her first instinct was to jump up and run to her house and lock every door as he turned the corner past her street. Rissa came out then and she quickly explained to her what she saw. "That creeper is stalking you." She stated.

"I'm not going to lie…he gives me the heebie-jeebies."

"Lilly, why don't you stay here tonight?" When her friend shook her head Rissa continued, "Fine, go home and make sure you lock up. Tomorrow we can have Zeke's friend set you up with a great alarm system." She took a breath. "I don't feel comfortable out here."

Lilly shivered. "Me either."

The two girls hugged and Rissa called out to her and said to lock her bedroom door as well as she watched as her friend rushed to her house and locked up. Rissa decided Lilly needed more than just a security system and she was going to hook her up with double the security.

That night Lilly once again dreamed. She dreamed of herself as an elderly lady in France in April of 1803. She was having tea with her friend Hattie on one of her visits to France. Both women were older and apparently Hattie's granddaughter was married to Lilly's great-nephew. They were excited because the couple was expecting their first child. This bonded the two friends together forever.

Her friend came to France for one final visit as she was Ig too old to travel. Lilly never had the desire to go back to the America's so the friend's visits were the only time they got to see each other. Lilly could feel the sadness in her heart that this was the last time she would see her friend.

Lilly knew what she had to do as a great great aunt to the new baby. She handed Hattie her wedding ring. She nodded to the heirloom. "I had the inside of the ring inscribed…From My Beloved Daniel."

Hattie didn't need to ask what the words meant. She looked up at her dear friend with compassion in her eyes. "He was such a great man."

"He was." She replied as she slid off her small wrist a gold bracelet that she had made from the gold she took from Daniel's coat the day he died. She actually never intended to take any of the gold with her but it was left in the pocket of her skirt and she found it in with her clothing while unpacking in her new home in France. It took her a few years to break down and have the bracelet made. She commissioned the bracelet to be made with a beautiful lace pattern throughout the bangle and at each end a fleur-de-lis carved into the gold. This was to remind her of her time at the colony with her love.

She asked that Hattie pass these two items on to the baby the couple was expecting. She rose from her chaise lounge and walked over to her writing desk. She opened a drawer and flipped an inside switch that caused a bottom shelf to fall down close to where her knees were. She grabbed a tin box and pulled out a shawl-like material that was wrapped around what looked to be a book. She walked back over to her oldest friend and sat down. "I would like for you to give this to the baby also."

Hattie leaned over to see what it was Lilly was unwrapping. "This is a journal of my life. I don't know if anyone will want it or is even interested…but no point in leaving it here at my old age." She sighed and looked in the direction of the open window across the room. "I haven't written in it in years because my penmanship is a bit shaky these days. Most of the writings are the early days at the fort. Then of course, Dane." She sighed again and wiped at her eyes. "How I miss him still, as if he just left me today."

Hattie grabbed her friend's hand and squeezed it. "What you both had was something to be cherished forever. And losing him without answers has to be the hardest."

Lilly squeezed her hand back before pulling away. "Yes. He is, was, and will always be my forever." Looking at the book she softly wiped her hand across the top before handing it to Hattie. "Please see that it is passed to our youngest and maybe one day somebody will have answers."

As her friend left a little while later, Lilly suddenly felt the pain of losing her one and only love. Looking around she was glad she had come back to France. A widow she was and would always be but her work in their community had been rewarding. Marrying into the Geofrey family had given her some status that counted.

Financially, she was set because Dane was wealthy in his own right and had a few titles as well. Those titles went to his brother, then his brother's son. Dane's brother stayed in the Americas but did declare the titles for himself.

Several times she almost confessed to her brother, Abraham, on his few visits to France about the gold in the bluffs and the bag that was hidden at the fort. Yet she couldn't bring herself to do it. She felt the gold was evil and it was what killed her Dane. The bracelet was made to remind her of everything that happened. She didn't believe any good would come from anyone knowing about it. So she decided to take it with her to her grave.

She looked down at her bare ring finger and rubbed where she had just removed her wedding ring from. Funny but in the forty-nine years she owned that ring she hadn't taken it off until now. But something inside of her told her it didn't belong with her anymore, it needed to go back so she could reclaim it again. She laid her head back on the chair and decided she needed to rest her eyes…and with that she fell asleep dreaming about her beloved Dane.

Sunday morning brought sunshine to the beautiful little town. Lilly woke with the dream still very vivid in her head. She looked over at her bedside and picked up the gold bracelet she had removed the night before. Looking more closely at it, she confirmed this bracelet was from the 1700's Lilly? It looked like the one in her dream only now it was a bit worn. She wondered what happened to the ring Lilly gave her friend Hattie? She remembered it well because it had been on her finger when she envisioned herself with Dane in their house.

It was odd but it was almost like she was getting used to the dreams and deja vu because she wasn't as freaked out about the dream she'd just had, as she had been the other dreams. Of course, this dream didn't involve some hot handsome naked man.

Deciding she needed to start sorting out all the crazy things happening, she showered and got dressed for the day before heading into her grandfather's study. She decided to start at the beginning and that would be Lilly's diary. She looked around and spotted the metal box that she was sure contained the diary. She climbed up and grabbed the tin box.

Lilly wanted comfort and sunshine while doing the research so she took everything into the living room. Laying everything out she decided to send a good morning message in the family chat before starting. She wanted to make sure everyone was settling in as they got back into their routines.

She noticed there was a new text from Tripp this morning. She smiled as she reminded herself they were supposed to have dinner the next time he was in town. Opening it, she read, "Good morning. It was nice seeing you yesterday and last night." Her reply was short and sweet, stating how she enjoyed seeing him as well. They texted for a few moments before she got back to work.

Lilly knew it was time to get busy as she took pictures of her grandfather's notes before opening the metal box and touching the lace shawl-like material wrapped around the book. She suddenly had a cold chill crawl up her spine as she felt as if she had just touched this material a few hours ago in her dream. It was old and yellowed...but she was sure it was the same piece of cloth.

She pulled out a leather book. Like before, she remembered the book from her dream. She could remember clearly touching it before she gave it to her friend Hattie.

Opening it up she read the name Lilly Elizabeth Bienvenue. Below the name was the date, B. November~01~1732 AD. Even though the birth and death dates of the Lillys were embedded in her head, she still wrote it down on her notepad. She decided to mark down the dates to keep it less confusing.

Flipping to the first page, she was bummed to see it was all written in French. Yet to her surprise and excitement, she spotted a slip of paper between each of the pages where someone had rewritten everything in English. While she wished she could read the actual words from the owner, she was going to just have to be content that someone took the time to rewrite the words. She had to wonder if this was her grandfather's doing or a relative past.

The first entry gave her the answer. It read...

To anyone interested in the contents of this book, my name is Liliane Maria Bienvenue. The year is 1832. This book was left to me by my great-aunt Lilly Elizabeth Bienvenue Geofrey. The words in the first part of the book are hers and hers alone. In my adult years, while growing up in the Americas and in a present-day English dialog, I learned to speak, read and write the language of my ancestors so I could translate her writings to English because I felt since the book was in America it needed to be written in the language of the people. Plus, I was most curious about her life.

The book was passed to me by my Great-Aunt Lilly, the originator of the book. Along with this diary I received her wedding band (indirectly) and a beautiful gold bangle bracelet from her as well. As you will read, after my great-aunt finished her story and passed me the book I started my entries. But my entries did not come until I obtained the book in my early adulthood. It was at that time I only spoke with an English tongue. It took several years to understand the French language. And many more years passed before I was able to rewrite my great-aunt's words in this Diary.

I felt it was okay to continue the writings because I am also named Liliane and because I was born the day she died, 04~23~1803. My story, like Lilly Elizabeth's, is heartbreaking and dream shattering. If I could have read her language early on, I would have been in complete shock, in my youth, at the parallel happenings between her and myself. It was a bleak time yet I learned in life to move on and fight my way out of the dark places life can put you in.

Lilly decided she liked 1800's Liliane and she couldn't wait until she read her story. But first she needed to read Liliane Elizabeth's story. Getting comfortable she started on the first page.

18 September 1753

Journal de Liliane Elizabeth Bienvenue, Fort de Chartres, The New World.

The writing on these pages come from my personal experience of being born into a raw and untamed area along a rapid river in a territory that is called The New World.

My Father, Jules Delbert Bienvenue, Lieutenant Commander of the fort, was born in France and came here with our King's Army to help oversee the building of the King's Fort. The fort we actually reside in is the third fort in this land and it has yet to be finished. The first two were made of wood and could not withstand the intensity of the flooding that is common here. This newest fort is being erected with limestone taken from the rock of the bluffs that sit high above us looking over us like a protective mother.

Life at the fort can be very boring but we make do. Life is also hard work even if you are the daughter of the Commander. The men have many responsibilities tending to the fort and the desolated area. The women have much responsibility tending to the men. We work the gardens, spin wool for clothing, and there's always sewing and cooking with the preparation of the food to be done. That is just to name a few of the chores expected. I have heard from several women who followed their husbands to the fort from France that life is harsh here compared to home. Yet this is the only home I know as I was born here. I have never been to our mother country. So of course, I've never experienced this luxury they speak of so I cannot miss what I have never had.

Lilly went on to read several pages about life in the fort. To know the fort and to dream about the past gave her an idea of what Lilly was talking about. A few pages into the book caught her attention.

31 September 1753

Today brought in a beautiful Autumn day, but with it I had to tolerate the presence of Edwin Berger. I know it is not right to speak ill of anyone but I just cannot deal with this man-child. For some reason he has decided to take an interest in me. He even went as far as to ask my Father's permission to court me. I am ashamed to say that I was very upset with my father when he spoke of this. I didn't say anything but the look I gave him stated I have no desire to be courted by the man.

Father just said if I wasn't interested then I shouldn't give him any reason to believe I am...I assured him I had no desire. The man is an arrogant overbearing beast who cannot take no for an answer. He will learn the word through me because I have no desire to have anything to do with the boring braggart.

Lilly could suddenly picture the man. He was the devil-image she saw in her vision at the cemetery. He was also the man looking down at her from the fort's turret after Dane left to meet Running Wolf. She jotted down his name and wrote the word devil next to his name.

The next few entries did make her aunt's life seem a bit unexciting and Lilly was glad she lived in a time where there was so much more to see and do. While she thought living back then would be fun...for a minute, she wouldn't trade it for the comforts of today.

The next one that caught her interest was:

6 January 1754

Today is our annual Twelfth Night Ball and I cannot be any more excited. I love the pretty gowns we all wear. I'm sure my blue gown will be dated compared to Mademoiselle Josephine DeLois. I cannot help but be green with envy over the beautiful gowns the lady parades in. It is mostly due to her recent arrival that she has the latest fashion in her possession. I wish to mimic her style but I feel I am not very talented with a needle and thread. I am better with a saber or a musket.

While I sound sinful with jealousy over the lady's fashion I do so like the lady in question. She and her husband arrived a few months ago and I so enjoy her stories of my parents' homeland.

Lilly was incredulous when she read the next entry which was posted early the following morning.

7 January, 2:30 AM

I post the date only because I wish to remember everything about the most wonderful night of my life. Tonight I met the most magnificent man and I hope to be my future husband. Daniel Dane Geofrey.

Lilly went on to read about her ancestor's meeting with her future husband. The story was just as Lilly remembered it in her dream. It was so real to her she found herself smiling at the memory. She reached up to feel a tear run down her face. She was shocked to realize she was crying. She was sure deep in her heart these two would only be together for a short time. It was as if she could feel the pain this Lilly of the past was going to feel, yet already did. She sighed because it was all so confusing.

7 January 1754

I was ecstatic when my father approached me this afternoon and asked if he was allowed to grant Dane permission to court me. I wanted to scream "yes, yes, yes," but instead I nodded and stated that was fine. My father had a twinkle in his eyes and a smile behind his beard. I wasn't fooling anyone...my family could tell I was in Love!

For the next few months her aunt Lilly wrote about her courtship with Dane. Lilly felt deep down she knew these stories and had somehow lived them. Their romance was what every woman wanted to feel when it came to love. She went on to talk about his marriage proposal.

Apparently they had a special spot. It was about a mile up the Mississippi River in a little cove near the bend. He went down on one knee and declared his undying love for her. After she agreed, he gave her a beautiful diamond ring that had been his grandmother's.

The wedding was in secret because Lilly told her family she didn't want it to be a hassle. Yet she wrote that it was because she didn't want Edwin to do something to stop the wedding. She wrote that Edwin seemed to be around every corner when she wasn't with Dane. She also felt he was staring at her intently every time she was with her betrothed.

She didn't want to voice her concern to Dane because he thought Edwin was his friend. He also felt bad because he knew the man had an interest in her before Dane came along. She felt if she voiced her discomfort to him he may decide to end their relationship because of guilt. So she pleaded for a quiet ceremony and they were married at the end of June.

The next few entries were of the love she found being Dane's wife. A few entries later she wrote about Dane leaving that evening to hunt. She never said what he was hunting for, but Lilly knew. She had been there...in her dreams.

Her aunt Lilly went into detail about the loss of her husband. Lilly felt the pain her aunt felt because she had been there. It was crazy because she wasn't sure if it was just a dream or a hallucination. It was eerie to think how her grandfather figured out there was something off and had been correct.

She continued reading the journal while crying throughout the part where Daniel Dane Geofrey dies. Aunt Lilly had no proof that Edwin killed her beloved Dane but she knew in her heart, it was him. She went on to write that they were scared of what Berger was capable of and felt it best for her to get out of the area as soon as possible. It was a plus that the large keelboat was preparing to set sail that morning.

Lilly took a deep breath and got up to toss away her many tissues. What a sad story. It seemed the one thing through time was evil killing the innocent. She was hesitant to continue on but decided to move forward.

There hadn't been many entries in the book after that. Apparently her grief lasted for quite some time after returning to France. She met Dane's family not long after arriving and they embraced her with open arms. Eventually she overcame her grief and started becoming involved in different charities in their area.

Aunt Liliane never remarried and stated Dane was her one and only love. She had a nice, boring life and seemed quite content with it. Lilly felt sad for her ancestor. In her earlier writings she sounds so full of life but after losing Dane she seemed... sad. The last line her aunt Liliane wrote was...My only regret was that I never got to put flowers on my husband's grave. Those words made Lilly long to hug her aunt and promise to put flowers on the grave...whenever she had the guts to go back to the cemetery.

Chapter Twelve

Lilly sat back and looked at all the notes she wrote. So much was written yet so many questions were unanswered. She added her dream of Aunt Liliane giving her friend Hattie the ring, bracelet, and book. Yet she still had questions. Like why was she reliving her aunt's life? What does all of this have to do with her? What is missing?

Lilly decided to take a break for a little bit and grab something to eat. She needed to process what she knew. There was so much to think about.

An hour later she was back to work. She was reading Liliane from the 1800's entries. She liked to call her Lilly Maria. Lilly Maria gave a brief detail of her life before she obtained the journal when she was eighteen. She grew up in the town of Prairie du Rocher. Her great-grandfather was the first Liliane's brother, Abraham.

Lilly needed to understand what occurred in the area between the two aunt's lives. A few years after Dane's death the French Fort actually was turned over to Great Britain and many of the French soldiers went to other military posts. The fort was eventually abandoned between 1772 and 1776.

Lilly continued with the reading of her aunt's diary. Lilly Marie writes how their great-grandfather Abraham, Lilly Elizabeth's brother, lost his wife giving birth to their youngest son Anton. A few years later Abraham was stationed farther North. He didn't feel that he could take his three boys, between the ages eight and three into the harsh climate so he was relieved when Hattie offered to keep the children until he could come back for them. Hattie had married a trapper the year before and had a baby girl. She and her husband had just built a house made of bluff stone in the town of Prairie du Rocher.

A few years later Abraham came back and took the two older boys with him to New Orleans. It was agreed that Anton would stay with Hattie and her husband Luke because he never knew his real family and Hattie was the only mother he really knew.

Hattie and Luke never had any more children and they thought of Anton as their son. Anton learned the tanning of hides from Luke and eventually opened a small retail store in the center of the town of about sixty people. He married and had two children. Hattie's daughter also married and had four children. Anton's son married Hattie's granddaughter. They had two children, one being Liliane Elizabeth Bienvenue. The third Lilly.

Lilly was back and forth between the journal and looking up what the web had to say as far as the people, dates, and events that occurred then. She stopped to answer a few texts from her family and Rissa. Tripp didn't text her anymore but her boss did. She wanted to know when Lilly thought she'd be up to working on a few projects. Lilly explained she wasn't ready yet. She knew she probably shouldn't blow off her job because her boss was making an exception and sending her work. Yet right now she wanted to focus on her grandfather's quest.

After reading Lilly Maria's descriptions of the town and life in the early 1800's Lilly was excited to see the first entry of a Phantom Funeral.

4 July 1821

I want to document the most frightening thing that is rumored to happen in our small community. I have never witnessed the event but my friend Agatha did, only it was ten years ago on this day when she and her mother were leaving the Fourth of July festivities. I will write it as it was said to me.

Agatha's version: The hour had just chimed midnight and the date just turned to the day of our independence from England. The families in town were celebrating thirty-five years of being a free country. The festivities lasted for days due to the long hours of summer and the brightness of the full moon that shone. This was such a huge event…comparable to Christmas. Our community may be poor but we come together and celebrate well. There was food aplenty and dancing and singing that lasted for days.

I had turned nine a few months earlier and I was very tired and wished to leave the early morning festivities and seek my bed. My mother decided she would just leave my father at the festivities while we sought our beds. Papa was well into his cups and didn't wish to leave yet. Momma was sure he'd lose his way home.

As we were walking from the party outside of town in the direction of the old fort road. We came to the main road and noticed a bit of fog in the night air. The closer we walked the more we could see into the fog and we couldn't believe what was in front of us. There was what appeared to be a procession of many pairs of soldiers on horseback. Behind them were about thirty to forty wagons with a lone flat wagon that held a casket on the back. Behind the wagon were people walking silently as if in prayer. The procession was heading away from the town graveyard. The most eerie part of the tale was that no sound was coming from the horse's hoofs or wagon wheels. Plus why was the casket still on the wagon if they were leaving the graveyard?

I knew the image was ghostlike because the moon was full and one could see through the procession. I looked at my mother to see her reaction. She was as stunned as I. As the procession disappeared around the bend, I begged my mother to please take me home and she complied. The next day while we were in town my mother mentioned the incident to a few of the elderly. They confirmed that what we saw the previous night could have happened. They called it a Phantom Funeral. Apparently a well-loved Commander at the fort many years before, was ambushed and murdered in front of his new bride. The murderer wanted the bride for himself, but because the murderer was recognized he quickly escaped from the area and was never found. The bride's family left the fort immediately because they didn't trust the murderer wouldn't come back and do harm to the bride. The elders went on to explain that a Native friend of the Commander confided to the Commander's brother that a Phantom of the funeral will appear when the moon is bright on the commemoration of his death. This will keep occurring until the curse is broken and evil passes before good and he can once again be with his true love.

Lilly was curious if there was a full moon on that day. She searched for full moons in 1811. She pulled up a page and typed in July. The moon was completely full on the second. The next day is considered a 'waxing gibbous' and shines one hundred percent. Lilly Maria says the hour was after midnight and the day just turned into the fourth. That made sense because Sundays were more of a day of rest and celebrations during that time period…of course, these small-town people must really like to live it up if they went into the early morning hours.

Deciding to keep going, she typed in her search engine 'July 1754 full moon.' She wasn't surprised to see the moon was full on the fourth. So it appeared that the Phantom showed its face whenever the moon was overly bright around the Fourth of July.

She knew Dane died on the Fourth because his tombstone clarified that. Her visit to the past confirmed he died early morning on the fourth. Strange that it seemed like it didn't have to fall right on the Fourth as long as it was very bright on the fourth. Damn, she thought, this is all so confusing.

Lilly suddenly thought about the man her grandfather wrote about…the one who tried to hurt her grandmother and burned down the Brickley Mansion. What was his name? She looked through his letter and found the name…Edward Badger. She was curious if there was a connection. Yet her grandfather never died during his encounter and he apparently didn't think Badger did either so she wasn't sure there was a connection.

Lilly looked at the time on her phone and was surprised to see it was after nine pm and very dark outside. Her last break had been hours ago when she made herself a sandwich. Deciding she was done for the day, she locked up and showered before going to bed. Lying in the dark room she thought about everything she read and felt like she was no closer to understanding the mystery of why she was flashing back through time…a time she had never lived in?

The following morning was Monday and Halloween. The first thing she did was call the security company Zeke recommended and was excited when they promised to have her a new security system installed the following day. She then decided to bite the bullet and do what was nagging her in the back of her head…go to the fort and see if she could find where Dane hid the bag of gold in the stone. She didn't expect to find the gold because she was sure Liliane Elizabeth would have taken the bag with her to France. She just wanted to see if there was a hollowed out hole hidden within the stone wall.

With it being a Monday, she was sure the fort would be deserted. The fall Rendezvous was over and most of the reenactors went home the day before to go back to their everyday lives. Her plan was to go in the afternoon that way if there was any of the cleanup crew left at the fort they should be finished by then.

If there was a chiseled-out hole in the stone, under the stairwell, she figured it would be easy to find because Lilly and Dane's house was not reconstructed as most of the others. The only problem she had was once she jumped in the hole she was worried she couldn't get back out. So of course, she was going to have to recruit her partner in crime, Rissa, to help her out.

A quick text to her friend confirmed she would be happy to join her on a mission. Lilly smiled, she was glad her friend enjoyed the mystery of her family tree. Wait until she got a hold of the diary…she was going to go crazy.

A few hours later Lilly almost chickened out after pulling up to the fort. If there had been a car in the parking lot, she would have used that as an excuse to go back home. But unfortunately, there wasn't a soul around. Rissa could sense her friend's fear and made jokes to lighten the mood.

Lilly was sure the fear stemmed from her last visit flashing back to Dane being killed. There was also the stress of getting caught. Yet deep down what was bothering her was the fear of what she was going to find. If the hole was there then it really happened. If the hole doesn't exist then this may all be in her head. She just wasn't sure which way she hoped it would fall. Hell, she may not even be able to remember exactly where Dane showed her he bored the hole in the wall. It was chiseled out almost three hundred years ago…only she saw where he did it days ago.

The girls made their way inside the fort and walked over to the foundation where she envisioned Lilly and Dane lived. The plan was for Rissa to stay on the outside while she jumped into the wide open hole. If she couldn't climb back out her friend would help her with the sheet she brought along in her backpack.

After going through the entrance, under the tower and into the courtyard Lilly felt chills prickling her skin. Rissa followed her friend to the stone foundation. Both girls looked down into the hole. Rissa was the first to speak. "It doesn't seem as deep as when we were kids."

"I agree! But I am not as limber as I was back then." She stated as she climbed onto the wide stone platform that once supported the building's walls. She jumped down onto the small platform that would have been the top of the basement stairwell. Looking down she held onto the ledge and slid her body down the eight-foot stone foundation.

Dusting at her hands, she looked over to the curved archway that was about four feet deep and sat under the platform. This was where it was hidden but there were a lot of stones inside the hole. Now she had to figure out which one it was. She knew it was at Dane's eye level and on the right side of the wall so that narrowed it down.

Lilly asked Rissa to toss down the butter knife she had in her backpack. That was the only thing she could think of that would help pry open a stone wall. Lilly felt around the walls for any loose stones for several long minutes. She used her flashlight to see if any of the stone edges looked cracked and was disappointed to see most of them were. So she started pecking at the grooves. This went on for just under an hour. Every time she was ready to give up because her hands were tired from reaching so high, Rissa encouraged her to keep trying.

Lilly went back to where she started and used the butter knife over and over checking for any loose stones. "Rissa, why would I have thought this was going to be an easy task?" She shouted up to her friend in frustration. Time seemed to mold the rocks together tightly. What seemed like an easy job suddenly wasn't so easy.

A few minutes later Lilly found a break in the cement that held the rocks together. Putting the knife in a small slit she easily split the stone. Working her way around the rock about the size of a man's fist, Lilly finally pulled the rock free. "I think I found it, Rissa." She peaked out the doorway to look up at her friend who was sitting on the foundation's ledge.

Rissa hopped up and came closer to look down at her friend. "Is there an actual hole there Lilly?" She asked as she moved closer to get a better view from the top of the hole.

Lilly smiled as the rock came out and there was a dark hole inside. "Yes. So I am not losing my mind." She smiled as she held the rock up for Rissa to see. I'm going to take a picture of the hole before I put the rock back in case we ever need to see it again.``

Lilly took her cell out of her pocket and reached above her head to take a picture of the black hole and then the stone cover in her hand. She took a picture of the wall to mark the actual spot. She placed the rock back into the hole before looking at her pictures to make sure the flash didn't mess up. As she scrolled through the pics, she froze…right there on the picture of the hole, in the wall, showed a canvas bag of sorts inside the hole. The flash must have picked up the image. The bag looked like the same one from her dreams. Taking a deep breath, she pulled the stone back out with the knife and reached inside the hole with hesitation because who knew what else was in the hole and pulled out a canvas bag she was pretty sure she dreamed of.

With shaking hands Lilly pulled the bag out and slipped it inside the front pocket of her hoodie. She reached up and took one last picture of the hole to make sure there wasn't anything else in the dark space before replacing the rock in the hole. Just as she started to explain to Rissa what she found, Rissa stated in a loud whisper that someone was walking through the gates.

Lilly wasn't sure where she got the stamina from but she tossed the knife up at her friend and climbed up the wall like she was a teenager. She sat on the edge of the foundation and looked all innocent as a gentleman walked past them and gave a 'hello' before moving on.

Lilly wanted to get out of there ASAP. She doubted the fort had cameras but didn't want to take any chances. The girls made a quick escape and arrived at Lilly's house minutes later. Rissa assumed her friend didn't get to finish the hunt because of the arrival of the man walking through the fort.

Lilly asked her friend to come inside her house for a few minutes. Rissa joined in the living room as Lilly pulled the pouch out of her pocket. "I wasn't sure if there were cameras at the fort so I didn't want to mention this…but look what I found." She held open both hands that cradled the bag.

Rissa gave her an odd look. "Is that what I think it is?" Moving closer. "Lilly, do you think that's the gold Dane showed Lilly before he died?"

"I guess there's only one way to find out." She stated as they sat on the sofa and opened the bag and softly emptied the contents onto the coffee table. Both girls put their hands to their mouth as they stared down at a pile of gold nuggets.

Neither said a word for several moments before Lilly broke the silence. "How in the hell am I ever going to explain these?"

Rissa just gave her a dumbstruck look and shook her head. "Maybe they aren't real?"

Lilly shook her head. "I think they are." She started panicking. "What am I going to do with them? I can't tell anyone I dreamed about my ancestor's husband of three hundred years ago who told me where he hid a bag of gold."

"Why did we think this wouldn't be real? It never dawned on me that they would actually be in there." Rissa stated before moving on. "You can't tell anyone or people will be picking at every stone at the fort."

"I assumed my aunt Lilly grabbed them and took them with her to France." Lilly stood and started pacing. "Rissa, we can't tell anyone. Not yet anyway." She looked at her friend. "If you think Zeke is completely trustworthy then we can tell him…but that's it."

Rissa shook her head. "He is, but I think he would probably be glad to not know about this." She smiled. "He always tells me he doesn't need to know everything and that sometimes I tell him too much."

Lilly continued to pace. "Okay, so there is something way beyond me happening here. I apparently am being drawn into the past…but why?" She paused and looked out the window. "When my dad comes home for Thanksgiving, I'll show him the nuggets. He'll know what to do with them." She started pacing again. "The thing that worries me the most is that the gold came out of these bluffs. What happens if word gets out? People will bombard Prairie du Rocher and destroy our quaint little town."

"Then don't tell them."

She ran her hands through her hair. "I just don't know what to do. My parents aren't here and part of me is afraid of what my dad will say. He may want me to donate them to a museum. Yet I feel like they are a part of Dane and I don't know if I want to give them up."

Rissa looked at her oddly. "Lilly…you do know that Dane has been dead a long time and honestly…you've never really met the guy? You just dreamed of him."

"I know." She stated as she plopped back down on the sofa. "It's just that I've felt him. He was more male than any I've ever dated." She grinned at her friend. "I've even made love to him…in my dreams."

"What…you didn't tell me that!" She tossed the pillow at her. "And…?"

Lilly chuckled. "The best I've never had." She laughed as she hugged the pillow to her. "No lie, I remember it as clearly as with any guy in the present day." She buried her head in the pillow shouting, "I'm losing my freaking mind!"

The girls were silent for a minute before Lilly stated, "You know, he reminds me of Tripp."

Rissa smiled. "Hmmm…that's interesting." After a brief pause, she continued with excitement. "Lilly, I bet you Tripp can help. This is right up his alley."

Lilly thought about what her friend was implying. "I think right now I am going to lock these chunks of rocks in my grandfather's safe. Next I am going to finish documenting what I already know. Then I am going to go back to the real world and take a few freelance jobs my boss is trying to send my way." She put the nuggets back in the bag. "Maybe I'll call Tripp after the first of the year if I uncover more secrets of the Bienvenue family."

"Well I was thinking…Zeke is out of town for the night, why don't you and I go up town and grab a bite to eat and have a drink to celebrate Halloween." Rissa asked with a pouty lip and pleading eye.

"Damn, I forgot about grabbing candy." She sighed and rolled her eyes. "I'd feel bad watching kids in costumes go past my place and me not having any candy to give them, so I guess the only solution is to leave." She looked at her watch. "Let me shower and let's meet in like…say thirty minutes?"

"Sounds good!"

Lilly was shocked at how busy Lisa's was for a Monday night…and Halloween no less. Kids were Trick or Treating in the dining room and several people were having cocktails in the bar…Lilly and Rissa included. They were even singing along to Halloween songs with the jukebox.

As Lilly looked over at a group of ladies sitting at a table, she was excited to see they were playing the card game Euchre. She spun around to face Rissa. "Ris, do you remember when Grandpa taught us to play Euchre?"

Rissa looked over excitedly. "Oh my gosh, is that what they are playing?"

The girls grew up playing Euchre in the summers. It was Lilly's grandparents' favorite game. There were days they played it for hours.

Just then one of the girls at the table walked up to the bar and ordered a round of drinks next to where Lilly was sitting. The girl smiled at her so Lilly asked, "Are you guys playing Euchre?"

The girl nodded, "Yes, it's a favorite around here."

"Oh my gosh my grandpa taught Rissa and me to play years ago."

The girl gave Rissa a funny look and stated, "Clarissa Mollot…is that you?"

Rissa gave her a funny look as she studied her. A second later her eyes lit up in recognition. "Gina Heller is that you?"

"Oh my gosh." She laughed and went around Lilly to hug Rissa. "If I had paid any attention to you guys when you came in, I would have noticed that long gorgeous hair anywhere."

Rissa laughed. "Same, I would know you anywhere. You haven't changed." She looked at Lilly. "Gina and I went to grade school here. She was a grade ahead of me. I'm not sure if you guys ever met when you came here in the summers?"

Lilly and Gina exchanged pleasantries and decided they didn't remember each other. Gina asked the girls to come and watch the card game so she and Rissa could catch up. She introduced the other occupants at the table. Tania, Teresa, and Diane were all locals who were born and raised in the small town.

Apparently the girls like to meet up once a week to play cards and have a few cocktails. Their usual night was Thursdays…but because it was Halloween and they were childless they came tonight instead. In no time their new friends were dealing out the cards to the girls and they were laughing like they had known each other forever.

Lilly and Rissa had a great night with their new friends. They were excited when the girls asked if they'd like to meet up with them on Thursday? After agreeing the two girls decided to head back home. On the walk back to their houses they were giggling and refused to admit they were a little tipsy. But Lilly sobered up when she spotted a gray BMW parked down the side street from her house. She couldn't see inside the car but she knew who owned it. It had to be Edmond. There weren't many BMWs in Prairie du Rocher and the car was the same as the one the night before.

Not sure if he spotted them, she whispered Edmond's name in Rissa's ear and nodded in his direction before darting through a few backyards and coming up the backside of Rissa's house. Rissa unlocked the door and let her friend in. They didn't turn on any lights except for the soft glow from the home button on their phones to see where they were walking. They went into the front room and looked out the bay window to see if the car was still there. It was and the girls waited for over an hour for the car to leave. They were relieved when he finally pulled away. They were both very creeped out by the man.

Chapter Thirteen

Tuesday morning brought rain…lots of rain. The thunderstorm's noise was pounding into Lilly's head, waking her up just as the sun was trying to push it's beams through the wicked clouds. Her head was throbbing and she was sure it wasn't from the storm's screaming noise. She knew what she needed…food. Root beer, a couple ibuprofens, and warmed up leftovers did the trick. She fell back asleep around seven and woke up once again to a pounding noise…only this time it was Rissa doing the pounding on Lilly's front door.

She answered in her robe. "Lilly, are you okay?" she asked while walking past her friend. "I was worried about you. I've tried calling and texting in the last hour and you never answered. I started imagining things…like that creeper came back again last night and he…?"

"Okay, okay I get it." She chuckled as she walked into the kitchen with her friend on her heels.

Watching her friend make coffee in the dated coffee maker made Rissa laugh. "You really need to update your appliances."

"I know. Gramps was practical." She stated as she walked over to the counter where her phone was charging. "That's why I need you to start your next project and help me bring the place up to this century."

"Yay, I thought you'd never ask." Rissa smiled.

Lilly looked up from her phone. "I need to get going…the new security system is going to be here in about fifteen minutes."

"Okay, but then do you have plans for this afternoon?"

"Not really, just chasing ghosts." She grinned at her friend. "What's up?"

Rissa was walking to the door to let herself out as she called back to her friend. "You are going to go on an outing with Zeke and me. Text me when you're done with the security people and ready to go."

"Go where?" Lilly shouted back but her only reply was the slamming of the door.

"I cannot believe you would do this Rissa. I cannot believe you would stoop to something so low!" If Lilly would have known what her friend's outing was, she would never have agreed to go. Rissa knew she would be a sucker in an animal shelter full of puppies and dogs. She also knew she would never be able to leave without taking one home.

Rissa didn't want her friend mad at her but she knew Lilly would never agree to go to a shelter. She would make so many excuses to not commit. Yet Rissa remembered Lilly was a dog lover…the bigger the better she stated once when they were growing up. "You don't have to get one. I just want you to help me pick out one."

Lilly glared at her. "I'm calling BS. Are you saying we are here for you?"

Rissa smiled and nodded before walking down the aisle looking at the variety of dogs that were homeless. It broke her heart that some people didn't think dogs were as important as people. Or they'd commit to one and then realize they no longer wanted the responsibility and send them away. A person should have that happen to them once and then see how they would feel.

Lilly wanted to take home every one of the beautiful creatures. She cooed at each one of the dogs in the cages. A few minutes later a worker walked up and asked if she wanted information on adoption.

An hour later, Lilly was the new momma of a full-grown male Saint Bernard that she named Moose. He became hers the second the worker explained the dog had been at the shelter for months because it was rare for people to adopt extra-large dogs. Well, that was all it took.

It turns out that Moose was an inside dog and if she had to guess, he went through some dog training because he was well disciplined, housebroken, and very talented. The adoption center was letting adoptees take the dogs during the open house due to some emergency work needing to be done to the building. Lilly wasn't sure but she thought she heard the word asbestos. This made Lilly shiver. The worker reassured her the remaining dogs will be fostered out to families throughout the county.

Rissa and Zeke were the proud new parents of Maverick the Labradoodle. Maverick was big, feisty, and all over the place. He was approximately one year old and still very puppy-like.

Lilly was happy to have her sweet mellow Moose, but what in the hell was she going to do about the hair and slobber? And she was sure she was going to use up all her inheritance feeding him.

Fall in Prairie du Rocher was nice but winter could be brutal. The next few weeks Lilly and Moose were adjusting to each other. Lilly wondered how she ever lived without the sweet dog. He was mellow and very loving and she was definitely sure someone put him through some kind of training because he listened well. The one thing they didn't agree on was his walks. Moose, with his heavy coat, liked long walks in the cold temps…Lilly not so much. It was a good thing the southern Illinois winters could be freezing one week and unseasonably warm the next.

November was a busy month for Bienvenue House. Between the roof getting fixed and Rissa's remodeling of the house, life was hectic. Lilly's boss was putting a lot of work on her and she was glad to be getting a paycheck but she still had a lot of unresolved issues going on with her new life in the small town.

For starters she had to deal with insurance companies because there was past hail damage to the roof so the insurance company needed documented proof there had been hail in Prairie du Rocher in the last twelve months. Her new card playing friends all figured it to be about nine months ago in the spring. So she had to gather up all that information to present to the company.

Then there was the trip to Kansas City where she packed up everything she owned in three days. She lined up everything she was bringing back to Bienvenue house and marked it for the movers. Then after she arrived back in town she had to go through her grandparents' personal items and clothing to donate before clearing out any old useless furniture.

While she was gone, Rissa contracted Hartmann Painting to come in and paint the rooms. She couldn't get over how much Sandra and her crew did in three days. The rooms looked fabulous.

Then came Rissa's remodeling. Lilly was over the million questions her friend had about every little detail…yet she didn't want Rissa to take over because they had completely different tastes and styles. So that was exhausting work, choosing curtains, cabinets and faucets. She agreed the items needed to be replaced because she was sure the house hadn't been remodeled since the 50s. She was just afraid everything she had chosen may not complement each other but Rissa assured her what would and wouldn't.

Her reincarnating past, which is what she believed was happening to her, and Phantom Funeral life was put on hold until after she was caught up in her new life. She and Tripp dropped a few texts here and there but it was just a little cute, fun flirting. He didn't know when he was going to be in town next so she decided it was better to not get involved in a long-distance relationship.

She did have fun on what she and her new friends call Thirsty Thursday Euchre Night at Lisa's. She, Rissa, Teresa, Gina, Tania, and Diane had fun taking turns playing cards. The game only allowed for four players so sometimes on slow nights Lisa and bartender Bethany would join the group and make it a two-table game. Lilly learned a lot about the town from the girls. She met so many locals by hanging out with them.

Thanksgiving came and went with the family staying for a few nights. They were excited about the simple remodel Rissa did. The house looked the same, only updated and polished. Lilly couldn't believe how much she missed them and enjoyed every minute they were together.

They were all in love with Moose and he was just as crazy about all the attention he was receiving. She and Sawyer played around with the Phantom one afternoon. Yet Lilly couldn't bring herself to share with him everything she went through the first week of living in the town.

A few days into their visit Lilly, Angel, and their parents went to the little boutique in town called the You Bee You Boutique. The owner, Frankie Lang, was a friend of her parents. They all grew up and it was a nice visit the three childhood friends had while Lilly and her sister shopped for cute clothes and unique items a person didn't find in a typical department store.

While Lilly had her arms full of new clothes her father called her over to the counter where her parents and Frankie were talking. Her father included Lilly in on the conversation he was having with Frankie about the Phantom Funeral.

Lilly smiled at the tall, pretty lady with friendly eyes. She could tell in an instant why her parents would consider Frankie their friend. She had a way about her that made everyone she met feel special.

"So Miss Lilly, your daddy tells me you are doing a little investigation about our town ghost?"

Lilly was relieved her father came up with an excuse as to why she was inquiring. She nodded with a smile. "Yes ma'am. I've decided if I am going to live here, I probably should write about it."

Frankie nodded. "So let me see if I remember all the details. It's getting harder and harder as I get older to remember everything." She smiled at Lauren. "I'm trying to think about what year it was…I'm thinking it was in 1985 because I was around fourteen and my parents let me stock the shelves after hours at Bill's Grocery." She chuckled and looked at Lilly. "That's what the old Conrad store was called then even though half the town still called it Conrads."

Lauren chuckled. "I remember calling it that. Even though my parents were friends with Bill I just couldn't stop calling it that."

Frankie smiled at the memory before continuing. "Anyhow it was the night going into the fourth, I remember that because I had to stock a lot of fireworks that Bill was selling for the following Fourth of July festivities." She took a deep breath. "So as I was heading home…" she looked at Lauren then Greg. "Remember I lived out close to the cemetery?"

Greg nodded. "Yes, in the old Melrose house." He looked at Lilly, "That is considered to be one of the oldest houses still standing in the state."

Before Lilly could reply, Frankie continued on. "Anyhow, it had to be just before midnight because my mother expected me home from work by midnight. I remember running home because to be honest as kids we ran everywhere. Plus, I remember it being a bit creepy at night so I always wanted to get home fast. Anyhow, as I was coming around the turn to my house, the same turn that joins cemetery road I had to slow down because I was getting stitches in my side."

Frankie paused and shook her head. "I remember panting and just then I noticed a thick patch of fog near the cemetery. I stared at it for a moment before I noticed what appeared to be a couple horse heads emerging from the fog going into the direction of the fort. I was spooked and rushed over to farmer Don's barn and hid just inside the open lean-to."

She looked intently at Lilly. "Little lady, if I didn't see it with my own eyes, I wouldn't believe it. Those horses came into the clear with dated soldiers sitting on their backs. I watched as pair after pair trotted past me towards the fort road." She started nodding. "Then just as I thought it safe to rush home because there was a small break in the recession here came the horse drawn wagons. This went on for several minutes. I could see the people on the wagons. They were dressed in period clothes like you see at the Rendezvous.

That was actually what I thought was happening. I thought maybe the people at the fort were practicing for an event."

At her pause Angel appeared next to Lilly and had to ask, "Then what happened?"

Frankie looked at her, yet not really looking. "I remember feeling very chilled on such a hot night. And it was in that second I realized no sound was coming from the parade. The participants were ghost-like. You know?…like you could see through them. There were no sounds of horses trotting or wagons being pulled." She took a deep breath before continuing. "I remember being scared they were going to come and get me. But then I noticed a coffin being pulled by the last wagon. That confused me because why would a coffin be leaving the cemetery?"

She looked at Lauren. "I remember being sad for the deceased. And as the coffin moved on, I watched what appeared to be colonial people following behind the procession. They felt sad to me and I felt sad with them."

Angel couldn't contain the suspense. "Then what happened?"

Frankie ginned. "As soon as the last person walked by and the fog disappeared…I hightailed it the hell out of there."

As everyone continued to talk about what it could really have been, Lilly made a mental note to document everything Frankie had said. It was when they arrived at home, she excused herself and went into the study to look up the dates on her laptop. She wasn't surprised to see that 2 July 1985, there was a full moon…meaning it confirmed what Frankie said.

The day before her family was scheduled to leave, Lilly asked her father to join her in her grandfather's study. After following him in the room and closing the door she suddenly was really nervous about filling him in on everything. He sensed her anxiety and gave her a puzzled look.

She knew what she had to do to get the conversation started. "Pops I want you to read Grandpa's letter to me." She stated as she walked over to the desk and retrieved the letter.

"Are you sure? That was something from him to you and I'm not sure I am comfortable reading something so personal."

"Trust me…you'll understand why I want you to read it." She handed him the letter and went to stare out the window as he silently read it. It wasn't the letter part she was anxious about him knowing…it was everything that happened after.

She looked up at her father when he gave a quiet whistle. "Well, that is some letter." He stated, as he took off his glasses and put them back in his shirt pocket. "What do you think about all of this?"

She smiled as she leaned against the desk. "If you are wondering if I think Grandpa was losing it…? No, I don't."

Her father smiled. "Good, because I can assure you, he wouldn't have written you this letter if he didn't believe it to be true."

"Do you think it's possible?" She asked hesitantly.

"Lilly, I have been reading about history most of my life. I have been digging up people's past for the last few years and I can assure you I have seen and heard things that just don't make sense. So I personally don't think the dates and names in the family are a coincidence."

She smiled. "Good, because now I need to fill you in on everything else happening since I arrived here the day after we found out Grandpa passed."

She started at the beginning with her stop at the cemetery. She described in detail her falling and the vision she saw after. She went on about the Ball and her trip to the tower that led to the past when Dane died. She described her dream about living in France and the bracelet, ring and journal. Her father was fascinated.

"So what do you think is happening? What have you concluded from all of this?" He asked.

"I think myself and this Dane or Daniel Dane keep getting separated in time and are trying to find their way back to each other."

"Do you think you need to go back in time to find him and relive that period with him?" He asked as he leaned back on the sofa.

She smiled and shook her head at him. "Who would have ever thought we would be having such a crazy conversation?" They both chuckled. "I have been back twice and for some reason time won't let me stay there so I do not believe that is the case."

He gave her a thoughtful look. "You know this may not be real at all. Your grandfather may have been grasping at straws to keep him busy. Maybe he dreamed of you being here the night the Brickley Mansion burned."

She stood up and walked over to the safe and opened it. "I thought about that also." She pulled out the aged worn bag that housed the nuggets. Turning to her father, she opened the bag to show him her treasure. "That is until I went to the fort a couple weeks ago and found the gold Dane showed me hours before he died."

"Dear Lord." Her father whispered as he stood up and picked up a nugget. He put his glasses back on to take a better look. He looked down to examine it closer before looking back at her speechless and then back down again at the bag of gold. "Lilly," he was still whispering. "Do you understand what this means…on so many levels?" As he returned the piece of gold to the bag and sat back down with a flabbergasted look on his face.

"I think so." She whispered. "I was shocked when I returned to the fort a few days later and found the hole. Even more shocked that the bag was still there. Then I dreamed about Liliane Elizabeth, that's what I call the first Lilly, anyhow she never told anyone about the gold because she thought that was maybe what killed her husband and she wanted nothing to do with them."

"Have you told anyone of this?" He looked very worried.

"Only Rissa and I trust her completely."

"I agree, she can be trusted." He got up and looked out the window that faced the tall rocky bluffs. "This means there is gold up there and centuries later no one has found it." He turned to his oldest daughter. "People would kill for it."

"I know. I think that's what happened to Dane."

"What are your plans for that bag?" He nodded to the gold.

She liked that he wasn't demanding anything. He was letting her make the choice. "I don't think there's much I can do. They are raw and unpolished so I really couldn't explain where I got them."

"I agree and they are worth a small fortune so you can't let anyone know you have them…unless…" he looked deep in thought.

"What?" He had her interest piqued.

"If you ever want to get rid of them you can always say you found them in this house after your grandfather passed. I can always back it up that I knew he had them."

"But won't people think that there's a mine somewhere and Grandpa knew about it?"

"Not if I say the gold is the Bienvenue gold that came from France and has been passed down through the generations. And considering that we have to assume no one else has ever found the gold here before, they can't trace the origin to here."

Lilly was silent as she looked down at the bag. She looked at her father. "I don't know if I want to get rid of or sell the gold. I know it sounds crazy but I have a sentimental bond to it."

"I don't care either way. But if you keep them you need to keep them hidden and don't tell anyone about it." He smiled before continuing. "I won't be telling anyone…except your mother. She doesn't like me to keep anything from her."

Lilly laughed and hugged her father before putting the gold back into the safe. She turned back to her father. "It's rather odd but when I first got here all these things were happening and now the last few weeks I haven't been dreaming about any of it any longer."

He shook his head at her. "Hush little girl and don't borrow trouble. This could be the calm before the storm."

The following day the family left her once again. She was sad to see them go but they were expected back in a few weeks for Christmas. She couldn't wait because her father promised her between now and then he was going to try and research the Geofrey family history. His archaeology firm had a lot more information available to them than the internet.

Lilly's sadness was softened when Rissa showed up to wave them goodbye. They hugged her and promised to see her at Christmastime as well. Once all the cars took off in different directions…again, Rissa looked at her and ran up the Bienvenue House's steps. "Come on!" She stated.

"What are you doing in my house?" Lilly laughed as she followed her in.

She walked into the direction of the basement doors. "It's Christmas tree trimming time." She shouted as she disappeared down the basement steps.

December brought unseasonably warm temperatures and quite a few thunderstorms. Moose wasn't a fan of the weather and often jumped his large body up onto her bed when the thunder would start in the middle of the night. It was a good thing Rissa talked her into purchasing a king size bed when she decided it was time to take over the master bedroom.

The family came and went through the holidays. They arrived on Christmas eve and stayed until the second of January. The family, along with Rissa and Zeke, had a great New Year's Eve celebration with Lisa at the bar. Lilly was excited to introduce her family to all the locals she now called friends….especially the Rocher Girls.

Two days later she was waving goodbye once again. Even though classes were done for a few weeks, Angel had a job and had to go back. The same for Sawyer and her parents, their jobs were demanding and only allowed for so much time off.

Her father had found some information on the Geofrey family. It appears that the first Geofrey to the area was Baron Leonard Geofrey, father of Daniel Dane and Antoine. Daniel became a commander at the fort in 1754. Months later he passed on July fourth. He had been married to Liliane Bienvenue, her many greats over…aunt. Daniel didn't have any children, yet Antoine did. The name has been passed down and is still in existence. The last two members of the family that carry the name live in northern Illinois. Their names Jasper and Daniel Dane.

Lilly was shocked to hear that through the generations the last one standing was a Daniel. Once everything settled down, she was going to open that can of worms and find out about these Geofrey men.

She was adding that to her 'to do' list. But right now, she had to get ready for her first, modern day…Twelfth Night Ball. She couldn't have been more excited than she was when she slipped the huge full-length gown over her head. She felt like she was going to prom.

The dress was a Christmas gift from Rissa. She couldn't believe her friend got her such a beautiful gift. Rissa stated she wanted to go this year and she knew she could tempt her friend if she gave her the beautiful gown. Lilly laughed because Rissa knew her so well.

It was a good thing her friend was across the street because she had to come over and zip her up into the deep blue material that worked great with Lilly's coloring. The bodice was tight and uplifting making her breasts look very perky and full. The sleeves started snuggly at the shoulders until they reached her elbows before flaring out very wide to the wrist. The dress was similar to the one she wore in her dream, only this gown's colors were lighter and more vibrant.

Her waist looked small, but not as 156malll as when she dreamed of herself at the ball centuries ago. The skirt had a white lace material that started at the middle of her waist and sprayed down into a large triangle that stopped at the floor. The skirt was filled out with a full hoop underneath. She decided to just wear small shorts under the skirt because her friends explained how hot the hall gets, especially considering the temps were seasonably warm for this time of the year.

She slipped on small socks before putting on her chucks tennis shoes. She wanted comfort and was afraid someone would step on her feet. Besides the dress was so big she didn't think anyone would find or see her feet.

Her hair was her favorite part of the night. She went to Rissa's stylist, Kathy, at Cutting Edge. Kathy did a fabulous job putting her hair up like Cinderella going to a ball. It was coiffured with curls through her head and swept up to keep it off her neck. She had wispy pieces framing her face and her long bangs were swept over and blended in with the look. The entire look tied in with the velour choker wrapped around her neck.

Lilly did her own makeup because she didn't wear a lot and didn't want anyone overdoing it. Yet she did splurge and got a mani/pedi with the girls the night before. She loved how she had time for girl stuff with girlfriends. In Kansas she had friends but all they ever did was dinner and drinks once in a while. Or maybe coffee here or there. They also seemed to only talk about their careers or maybe bring up a guy they met over the weekend. But it just wasn't ever anything too personal.

Yet Rissa and her new friends loved to laugh and cut up. Sometimes there was a little gossip about who broke up with who and is now dating her or him. But for the most part it was just picking at each other and laughing over something corky someone in the group said or did. They were also there to show support for each other and were good listeners when someone needed to vent.

Lilly never shared her crazy ghostly past with the girls because she didn't want them thinking she was crazy and no longer wished to hang with her. Yet she did fill them in on Tripp. They couldn't wait until they got to meet the hottie. Lilly had no idea when that would be because it seemed like he was never coming back to town. The two of them talked over text a few times. There was serious flirting going on. Yet things never got too personal with them.

The plan for the evening was to have supper at Lisa's and then go to the Ball. She was waiting on her front porch with her grandmother's beautiful shawl wrapped around her when Zeke and Rissa emerged from their house. The short ride to Lisa's was filled with the girls complimenting each other about how beautiful the other looked. Zeke's eyes were smiling as he listened to the two chatty girls. He wondered what he was getting himself into with these two? Yet, he didn't mind. They were both gorgeous and they were his dates for the evening…or at least Rissa was but Lilly would only be for part of the evening if it all played out right.

The girls were feeling awkward walking into Lisa's in their gowns until they realized they were among the majority. Most of the occupants were dressed in similar time period clothing. There were several men dressed in colonial garb escorting women dressed in a variety of styles.

After dinner the trio went to the American Legion where the event was held every year. The Ball was in the hall and hosted by the La Guiannee, a French societe (society) that has been in the Prairie du Rocher area since the town was established and even before that because it was brought over with the French as the first fort was being constructed.

Lilly was in awe as she looked around the lavish decorations. Royal blue silk was draped throughout the room. The beams that held up the roof were wrapped and looked like pillars. There were two very royal looking chairs placed at one end of the hall for the new King and his Queen when announced around the midnight hour. The stage was on the opposite end and was being set up by a band of many pieces. Yet her favorite part was the beautiful chandelier hanging from the middle of the room.

Lilly felt the room was different from the Ball in 1754, yet there were many similarities like the chandelier and the royal silk. The atmosphere was also the same, only a bit more modern. The attendees were setting up their tables with tablecloths and candelabras before unpacking their food to the tables.

She looked over to where Diane was setting up their table. She had so much food laid out one could hardly see the top. Lilly laughed because she now understood what Diane meant when she said she had the food covered.

Lilly and Rissa hugged the Rocher Girls and met a few of their dates before each one went on and on about each other's gowns. Diane wore a beautiful yellow dress which Lilly loved. Gina's gown was a full skirt of soft pink and white. Tania's peach was the envy of most and Teresa's was a soft sage color that complimented her olive complexion. Lisa showed up with Rissa's Aunt Doris. Apparently, Doris just arrived back in town after being on holiday in Europe for the last three months.

A few minutes later the lights dimmed and the lead vocalist for the band started off by welcoming everyone. Lilly was so excited as she looked around at all the people. Yet her excitement was short lived when she spotted Edmond Brader staring at her from across the room. He gave her a nod. She quickly looked away. She realized she was holding her breath and quickly released it. She wanted to alert Rissa but didn't want him seeing her doing so.

She joined in with the girls' chatter and acted as if nothing was wrong. A few minutes later she asked Rissa to walk with her to the ladies room. Once inside she filled her friend in on Edmond being there. Rissa was angry. She was going to ask Zeke to have a word with him. Lilly asked her not to. Rissa promised to not let him get close to her, but she knew that was impossible because several songs had people switching partners throughout the dance.

Rissa reassured her all was going to be well as they exited the bathroom. Lilly looked over at their table and there stood Tripp…in all his glory. He was speaking with Zeke and looking hot as hell…figuratively. He was dressed very colonially and reminded Lilly of the man she met in her dreams a few months ago.

Chapter Fourteen

Lilly could have stood there staring at his profile all night. Yet she quickly changed her mind when she spotted Edmond making his way to her. She moved rather quickly towards her table.

She grabbed Tripp's attention when she stood in front of him. "Hi," she said and gave him a confused look. "I didn't know you were going to be here."

Tripp looked at her and was speechless. She took his breath away. She looked like something out of one of his crazy dreams. Regaining his composure, he took her hand in his and bowed over it before kissing the back of it. "My fair Lilly, I believe I have never seen a more beautiful creature."

Lilly had the grace to blush. She knew her friends were looking at her. Before she could reply, she suddenly flashed to another Ball and another handsome man kissing her hand. For some reason she felt the two of them were one and the same. She mentally shook herself and replied to Tripp with a grin. "Hi. Why didn't you tell me you were coming into town?" She gave him a confused look.

Just then Rissa stepped up to the couple. "I'm sorry Lilly, we wanted to surprise you!"

"We…who's we?" She asked with confusion while looking back and forth between the two.

Tripp smiled, showing off pretty white teeth. "Well, it was actually my idea. I asked Rissa if you both were going to be at the Ball and she hadn't thought about it. So I encouraged her to go and bring you so I might get to dance with you."

Before Lilly had time to process the meaning behind what he just said, the first song was announced. She looked up at Tripp as he held his hand out and asked her to dance. She didn't know what to think as she gave him her hand and joined in on the dancing.

The dance was similar to the dance she and Dane danced the first time they met. She thought it was odd but it was like she knew the dance well. So did Tripp which was even odder.

As the dance went on, she spotted Edmond out of the corner of her eye staring intently in her direction. The last thing she wanted to do was let Tripp know about Edmond lurking about in the shadows…here and at her home. They almost came to blows once and she was sure Tripp wouldn't hesitate to confront the creep.

One thing was sure, she wasn't going to save the day by dancing with Edmond again. He was a snake and she didn't trust snakes. So her plan was to stay close to Tripp throughout the night.

Hours later, Lilly was fanning herself trying to cool down and catch her breath. She was sure she danced every dance, only breaking when the band did. The band was great and the dancing was right out of 'Gone with the Wind.'

It was crazy, the band walked everyone through each dance the first time it was presented. Yet, she and Tripp didn't need any instructions. It was like they were born to know the steps. There were even a few times she and Tripp believed the instructor had the moves incorrect but they played along to the new steps if it involved a group dance.

She assumed she knew the dance steps from when she dreamed of meeting Dane the first time. Yet she didn't dance all the different dances that she did tonight. Plus how did Tripp know the dances so well? When she asked him if he had ever done this type of dancing he stated, "Only in my dreams." She took that to mean he hadn't.

Lilly was shocked at the number of grade school and high school kids that were in attendance. If she had to guess she'd say one in every ten were younger than sixteen. She found this was a good thing because they would be the next generation to keep the Ball alive. What was more amazing was the seriousness they applied to the dancing. They didn't jack around like you would expect from a bunch of kids at a dance.

Not able to cool down, Lilly excused herself and explained to her group that she was going outside for some air. She was glad Tripp stated he was going to join her. She didn't want Edmond following her out the door and there was less chance of that if Tripp was with her.

She couldn't explain how happy she was that Tripp had come tonight. She had a horrible feeling that Edmond would have been all over her if he hadn't.

But she wondered where Tripp stood with Selene. The second they stepped outside she had to ask. "So what's up with you and your girlfriend, Selene?" Before he could reply she continued. "I mean I'm surprised she isn't here, especially on the night of the annual Ball." She tried to act nonchalant but wasn't doing a good job with it.

He grinned and could see the jealousy eating at her and he was very pleased by it. As a rule, he hated dating a girl that was the jealous type, yet he found he liked seeing this side of Lilly. "Are you saying you wish I would have brought Selene along?"

"No…I mean, I don't care." She rolled her eyes upward. "I don't care, but you probably shouldn't be hanging out with me when you have her to go back to." She was babbling. "I mean if you were mine, I would be very angry if you were hanging out with another girl." Shut up Lilly, she told herself.

Tripp just grinned at her and stepped a little closer. "Lilly, Selene and I are just working together." Before she could interrupt, he continued. "I know it looked like more and honestly, she tried to make it more…but how could I be interested in another woman when my heart is set on someone else?"

He was moving closer and talking in such a soothing voice she didn't catch most of what he was saying after the part where he wasn't interested in the other woman. All she could focus on was his lips as they came closer and softly brushed across her. She felt a tingle from the top of her head to the tips of her toes. He barely pulled back and looked into her eyes before moving back in for a deeper kiss. Lilly closed her eyes and let herself be buried in that kiss. She opened her mouth so her tongue could mate with his.

The couple lost all consciousness of their surroundings as the kiss went on and on. It was crazy but she felt like she knew his mouth…knew his kiss. Tripp pulled back just as the door opened and Rissa and Zeke stepped outside. Lilly looked guilty and Rissa chuckled. "Whatcha doin?" she asked with laughter in her eyes.

Lilly had the grace to blush as Tripp announced. "Kissing this lovely lady."

Rissa laughed. "It's about time."

Tripp smiled. "I agree."

There was an awkward silence before Zeke announced, "So they are cutting the King's Cake if you guys are ready to go in." He put his arms around Rissa. "I plan to be first in line so I can make this lady a Queen."

"Woo-hoo…Let's do it then." She shouted as she followed Zeke through the side door.

Lilly made to follow, pausing to look back at Tripp who was looking off at the far side of the building. "Tripp, are you coming?" She asked.

He turned and followed her in through the door. He took her hand and walked with her to their table. She had no idea that under his calm demeanor he was seething.

He had spotted Brader tucked in between a cluster of trees watching as the two couples were chatting outside. The way he was buried in the trees pretty much said he didn't want to be seen. Hell, the bastard had probably been there the entire time he was kissing Lilly. Good, he hoped the son-of-a-bitch got an eye full. What disturbed him the most was he wasn't sure if Brader was spying on him or Lilly. One thing was for sure, he wasn't letting the bastard ruin his night.

"Come on Tripp, let's eat cake." Zeke stated a few minutes later as he led Tripp to the King's Cake line. The men were among many gentlemen in line hoping to find the first bean in the King's Cake. Normally this wasn't something Tripp would partake in but he liked the idea of being the King on the Court if Lilly was beside him.

Looking at the line of men in front of him, he noticed Brader was one of the first. Who in the hell was he planning to make his Queen if he got the bean first? He better not have his sights on Lilly.

Deciding not to let Brader get to him, Tripp moved forward to grab his piece of cake. Something deep inside of him told him he was going to be the first to find the bean. Walking back towards the table he bypassed Lilly and her friends as he felt the bean in the cake. Looking in her direction, he made eye contact with her and winked. He didn't wait for her reaction because the first bean found was King and the three to follow made up the court. So he needed to declare his bean before any other gentleman did.

Ruthie, the event coordinator was the lady to meet if you found a bean. She announced the first bean was found when Tripp handed her his bean. She explained to him that he needed to choose his Queen and put their names on the sheet of paper she gave him. The crowning would begin after the remaining beans were found. Tripp had no doubt Lilly would be his Queen and wrote her name down on the slip of paper.

Lilly was excited but not surprised Tripp found the first bean. She knew the night was going to play out very similar to her dream. She smiled as he walked over and once again bowed over her hand and asked if she would be his Queen. She nodded with a smile as he kissed her hand.

The remaining three beans were found and one of them belonged to Edmond. Lilly was surprised when he asked Diane if she would attend the court with him. Lilly didn't know Diane well enough to discourage Edmond's attention, but she would put the bug in Gina's ear. She prayed Gina would warn Diane that the man was a snake trying to destroy their town.

She decided not to worry about it for now because she was going to be Tripp's Queen. The coordinator announced the members of the court to join the retired King and Queen at the stage. Two small girls, Kaylee and Bella, were the court's Pages. They were around the age of six and would lead the retiring King and Queen, followed by the court, to the throne at the other end of the hall floor. Tripp and Lilly were to be the last to join the group and the crowns would be passed to them before they took their seats on the large chairs.

Lilly watched while each couple was introduced and the Pages would make their way back to the stage and escort the next couple. Lilly was excited when it was their turn. That excitement went into shock when she heard Ruthie announce. "Our new reigning King and Queen for the year 2023 of our Lord is…King Daniel Geofrey and Queen Lillian Bienvenue."

Lilly almost stumbled when she heard Tripp's real name. How odd that she didn't realize 'Tripp' was a nickname. Had he ever mentioned it when they were younger? She can't remember if she ever asked…how weird.

Her breathing was getting heavy and she told herself to smile and calm down as she made her way to the chair. Geofrey? Why didn't she know his last name? Why didn't she wonder what his last name was when she ran into him back in October? So many questions. Her head was spinning. Daniel Geofrey…really? She wondered what his middle name was? Then a memory suddenly popped in her head when she ran into him at the fort. She was coming out of her stupor and called Tripp…Dane. He said 'no one ever calls me by my middle name.'

She had to know. As all the newspapers in the area took their picture she smiled straight ahead and asked without moving her mouth much. "What's your middle name?"

"What?" He asked as he turned to look at her.

"Mr. Geofrey," This was coming from Ruthie. "Can you please look ahead at the camera please?" She asked sweetly.

Tripp did as he was told and felt like a child being scolded. A few minutes later the couple was to dance the King and Queen's Waltz for the first few minutes before the court was to join them. Lilly couldn't focus on the dance; she was still in shock from what she found out. How did she not ask him his last name…ever?

After the waltz began Tripp asked her to repeat her question. "What is your middle name?"

He chuckled. "What an odd question to ask at such an odd time. It's Dane. I thought you knew that. You called me that when we saw each other up on the tower."

She looked at him with so much confusion. "How come I never knew your real name?"

"I'm not sure I ever knew you didn't. But you have to remember we were only friends for one week in the summer before we were going on to high school." He stopped because they had to turn and pause for a picture of them dancing for one of the area newspapers.

He continued. "Anyhow, we didn't really ask about names because we were kids and we knew first names. Yet when I ran into you months ago, I found out your last name because you talked about inheriting your grandfather's house…the Bienvenue House. I asked Rissa if that was your last name and she said yes."

"Odd but I didn't even ask you what your last name was then." She was still baffled.

"I guess I wasn't worth the conversation." He stated, with a grin.

She slapped his shoulder just as a cameraman snapped a picture. Great, that was probably going to be on the front cover. "It wasn't like that."

Tripp smiled. "I get it. You just lost your grandfather and everything was changing. You had a lot going on." He twirled her around before continuing on. "We only saw each other twice and both times Selene was hanging on me like a monkey. Plus, our texts were more flirting than questions about our lives."

"See, admit it she has the hots for you."

"I only want you to have the hots for me." He whispered in her ear as the dance ended.

Walking towards their table she stopped him before they completely left the dance floor. "Tripp…or should I call you Daniel?"

"I'm partial to Tripp."

"Before you leave town, I have to show you something. Can you come by tomorrow?"

"I can come by tonight if you have a spare room?" He grinned at her raised eyebrows. "Well, you are Rissa's neighbor and that's where I am bunking tonight." He kissed her cheek. "So, if you aren't too tired you can show me what you need to show me tonight." He whispered in her ear.

She was hot and he was making her even hotter. Her voice was raspy when she replied. "If I'm not too tired tonight." She gave him a shy grin.

He took her hand and squeezed it before walking with her back to the table. Had he turned around he would have seen the evil look Brader was giving him. If looks could kill…the dark-eyed man would have accomplished his goal.

An hour later Tripp offered to take Lilly home and Rissa readily agreed. She hugged him and whispered something along the lines of if he didn't show up at the house she would understand why. She promised to text him the door code to her house just in case.

As they pulled up in the driveway Tripp asked if she was okay with him using a spare room to change out of his colonial garb and grab a quick shower. She agreed as she watched him grab his suitcase. She planned to do the same but first she wanted him to meet Moose, who came over rather quickly when he caught sight of Tripp.

Lilly smiled as she watched the two Alphas. Moose sniffed Tripp to get his scent and Tripp was hesitant and didn't want to upset the two-hundred-pound beast. It took a few minutes before Moose gave his okay and let Tripp give him some attention.

Lilly showed him the way to the spare bedroom and pointed out the bathroom before closing her bedroom door. She sat on her bed and was feeling anxious, wondering what in the hell was she doing letting Tripp come over and possibly staying the night? This made her nervous and very hot. Especially when she heard the shower running.

"Hell." She whispered. She needed help getting out of her dress. She grabbed her phone and texted Rissa and asked if she'd help her. Twenty minutes later and her hair free from all the pins holding up the mass, she decided her friend wasn't going to answer. She knew she was going to have to ask Tripp for his help. The shower stopped about five minutes before and she decided to give him a few more minutes before she knocked on his door.

Just as she was about to leave her room, he softly knocked on her door. He was standing on the other side in a T-shirt and sweatpants and boy did they look good on him. He was surprised to see her still in her dress when she answered the door. "I was just about to ask you for your help." She looked down at her gown before looking back up at him. "I need help with the zipper, buttons, and ribbon. Rissa won't answer my text so can you help me please?"

He followed her just inside the bedroom. "My pleasure."

The way he said it sent ripples down her spine. She turned her back to him and lifted her long thick flowing hair. She felt his warm hands on her neck and wondered what they would feel like if he touched her entire body with them?

Tripp unlaced the long ribbon that held the top of the dress together. He took his time so he could enjoy every minute of the task. Behind the ribbon was a zipper to keep the gown together. He guessed the ribbon was for show. After unzipping the material, he was surprised to find nothing underneath. He softly ran a finger down her spine. Her skin was soft and flawless. He reached her waist and unbuttoned the two small buttons that kept the skirt intact before zipping the material down several Inches. He didn't realize he was holding his breath until she turned around and gave him a smoldering look. That was all it took to make him move. He put his hands in her hair and pulled her into a deep kiss.

Lilly let the gown fall to the floor as she ran her hands up the front of his shirt. Her last controlled thought was how she loved the feel of his hard body under her palms before she lost herself in the kiss. She never wanted it to stop. He must have felt the same way because he picked her up and let the rest of the dress fall to the floor as he walked over to the king size bed and laid her down on it before lying next to her...never once breaking the kiss.

He wasn't sure how much time passed as he came up for air. He was overwhelmed by the passion in her eyes. "I want to make love to you." He whispered.

She smiled. "I want you to make love to me." She replied before pulling him down for another kiss. She couldn't get enough of him and almost stopped him from pulling back until she felt his mouth on her breast. Her sharp intake of breath told him she liked what he was doing. For the next several minutes his mouth teased and taunted her. He kissed her everywhere she longed to be kissed.

She almost cried out as he said he would be right back, because he was going to get protection and was gone for what seemed like forever but was actually no time at all. Just about the time she started to get cold feet he was there to warm her back up. Seconds later they were back to where they started only this time it was her doing the teasing and tasting.

Tripp had enough and couldn't go another second without being inside of her. He rolled over putting her underneath him. He filled her slowly at first. As she wrapped her legs around him, he gave her every part of himself.

There was something beyond them happening in that moment. It was as if they found something they both had been searching for a long time. She had tears in her eyes when he whispered, "I found you again and this time I am not going to lose you."

She moved to keep up with his strong, fulfilling pace. The intensity was so strong she cried out when the explosion shook her to the core. She held onto him and let the pleasure run its course over and over. Her pleasure took away all his control and he let that moment take over and joined her in his own release.

Once the impact subsided a little, Tripp rolled them, while they were still joined, to lay on their sides all twisted up and staring into each other's eyes. Lilly looked at him and ran her finger down the middle of his lips. He had such beautiful lips. She said in a very quiet voice. "Please don't ever leave me again." He wiped the one small tear that rolled out of her closed eyes.

"I won't." He whispered back and kissed where the tear was. He could tell she fell asleep. He smiled and thought that was pretty endearing as he pulled away from her sleeping body and made his way to the bathroom.

A few hours later Tripp woke to Lilly kissing the side of his neck. He lifted her chin and went in for a long hot kiss. When they finished, she asked if he enjoyed what they had shared hours ago. He laughed. "So now you want pillow talk? I was all wanting to get mushy with you earlier and you were like a satisfied cat…got your milk and off you went leaving me with mixed emotions."

She laughed and chucked a pillow at his head. He retaliated by pinning her down to the bed and making love to her all over again. Only this time she didn't sleep afterwards, instead she laid in bed and tried to reason her discovery that her and Tripp's ancestors were once married. If she had to guess, there was something here that needed to be fixed for them to move on from their past.

Chapter Fifteen

The following morning Lilly found Tripp in her kitchen flipping bacon in a skillet. She fell back asleep in the early part of dawn and now it was after nine. When Tripp wasn't beside her, she wondered if he left or slept in the spare room. She looked through the open bedroom door on her way to the shower and could tell the bed hadn't been slept in yet he was still here because his bag was on the chair in the corner. This made her smile. So he did sleep in her bed…good.

Now looking at him by the stove she didn't think there was anything sexier than a half-naked man cooking for her in a kitchen. She took a moment to admire his shirtless, muscular back before it met with his sweatpants. She started flashing back to what happened in her bedroom only hours before and her cheeks felt flushed. With the exception of her dream with the man she was somehow sure was Tripp, she had never been made to feel as complete as she did at this moment.

She grinned as she spotted him giving Moose a slice of bacon and patting him on the head before popping a piece in his mouth.

"All things male will bond with the love of bacon." When he turned to her voice she nodded to Moose. "This just confirms it."

She gave a timid smile and he grinned. "Yep, your dog is crazy about me." He walked over and gave her a long, hot kiss before saying, "Good morning beautiful."

She smiled because he tasted like bacon. "I see you've sampled our breakfast."

"I'd rather sample you again." He said before dropping his arms and walking back to the stove. "I hope you don't mind that I took over your kitchen."

"Are you kidding? Do you know how sexy it is to have a hot guy cook breakfast for you?" She asked before sitting on one of the stools at the island.

He lifted his eyebrows and looked at her before placing a plate of food in front of her. "No, I can't say I do. But I can say I know how sexy it is having breakfast with you."

She smiled at his flirting. He sure knew how to make a girl feel good. When he placed the cup of coffee in front of her, she knew she was a goner. Yet first, before she let herself fall anymore in love, she was going to have to fill him in on their past...because she was sure he was her past and hoped he didn't think she was crazy.

She decided to put the one question to him that would confirm he was related to the first Lilly's husband. "So, I have a question."

"Really...I have a ton. Like what do you think it would have been like if we would have done what we did upstairs last night when we were fourteen?" He grinned and popped a piece of bacon in his mouth.

She laughed. "I guarantee it would have been a lot of fumbling and awkwardness."

He shook his head. "Yeah, but man what fun it would have been." He gave her that sexy dimpled grin that melted her everywhere.

"Okay, so back to my question. I remember you have only one sibling, a brother...right?" At his nod. "I remember you would talk about him when we hung out. He didn't come with you the year we met...right?"

"Correct...so why all the questions about my brother?" He was a bit confused.

"I'll fill you in. But what is his name?"

"Jay Jay." Just as she was about to react, he continued. "His real name is Jasper, but when I was younger, I always called him Jay Jay...then Jay as we got older."

At her odd expression, he asked. "Why?"

She didn't know how to respond. Deep down she knew he was going to say his brother's name was Jasper. Yet hearing it out loud sent chills up her spine.

"Just curious." She started and started picking at her food.

The next twenty minutes consisted of small talk and flirting over breakfast. When she was done, she stood up and took her half-finished plate to the sink where he joined her and helped her clean up. Neither said a word for several minutes. He knew she had something on her mind and he was giving her time to sort it out.

She put the dishes away as soon as he finished drying each of them. After the kitchen work was finished, she walked over to him and hugged him for several moments. He finally pulled back and looked at her. "I hope that wasn't a goodbye hug." He gave that cocky grin again. "I'm not going to lie, I was hoping to spend the day with you before I have to go back tonight."

"I am hoping you spend the day with me before you go back also." She took a deep breath and pulled away from him. "But first, I would like to show you something in Grandpa's study." She stated before leading the way to the study.

She asked him to have a seat on the sofa before retrieving two different items from the desk. Turning to him, she handed him the Bienvenue Genealogy Book. "Ever since I arrived here, after my grandfather passed, I have had a lot of crazy things happen. I want to share these things with you but I am trying to decide how I should begin. So I think I'll start with our family tree in the back of the book." She nodded towards the book he was holding and asked him to flip to the back of the book as she sat down next to him.

"Look right here." She pointed to the first Lilly and Daniel were married. "It says my... many greats over... aunt, by the name of Liliane Bienvenue, married Daniel Dane Geofrey at Fort de Chartres on 28 June 1754." She looked up at him. "This is 'many greats over' uncle to you."

"How awesome." He smiled at her. "See it was destiny that brought us together."

"Umm, I think more than you realize." She stated before continuing on. "So like I said, odd things have been happening. It started with the day I arrived. I need to back up a second and tell you I didn't know about this book until the following day." She took a deep breath and released it. "Anyhow, I stopped off at the cemetery to put flowers on my grandma's grave before I met up with my family." She stood up and started pacing. Tripp was clueless to what was going on so he let her explain at her own pace.

"While I was at the cemetery..." She paused and looked at him "Please don't think I am crazy about what I am going to tell you." She threw her hands up in the air. "Hell, I may be crazy...but know that I believe everything I am saying to you." She took a deep breath and continued.

"So okay, I was walking back to my car and something drew my attention to the back side of the cemetery. It's the part where the older graves are...pre-Civil War. There was a family plot surrounded by a gated fence beckoning me towards it." She smiled at him. "I can't tell you why I walked in that direction because truth be told…I'm a chicken-shit."

She felt a little more at ease by his sweet smile. "So, like a tough-girl, I walked over to the fence and right on through the open doors. Looking back now I have no idea where this boldness came from. But it was like I knew this place." She paused. "There in front of me was a monument with your last name on it…only I didn't know it was your last name. Hell, I didn't know of anyone with that last name…until recently."

She knew she was sounding crazy so she decided to bite the bullet and continue. "That's not the part that makes me sound crazy…there is a monument there with Geofrey's name on it. If you don't believe me, I can show you…even though I really don't want to go back out there." She threw up her hands and started pacing quicker. "I mean I need to go back out there because I want to put flowers on my grandparent's graves."

"Lilly…sweetie." He was looking at her with patience. "Calm down honey. I know the monument. I've been out there with my father before."

She smiled and calmed down a bit. "Okay…good." Then she started pacing again. "So anyway, I was staring at the three graves and I was looking down at Liliane's husband's grave, mind you I had no idea these people ever existed." She plopped down in the recliner across from him. "Tripp, I had an out of body experience." At his raised eyebrows she continued. "I know it sounds crazy but that's all I can say."

Tripp looked at her oddly. "Okay Lilly. Take your time and start at the beginning."

Lilly did as he said. She started off by explaining to him how she must have fallen into the fence because she was leaning against it when she woke up. She went on to explain how people were flashing through her mind. When that all cleared, she was at the fort…only not present-day fort but the fort centuries ago. How at first no one could see her, then it was as if suddenly they could.

She went on about how the military man approached her and how she realized now he was Tripp's ancestor. He looked so similar to Tripp and he hugged her as if she belonged to him. She explained to him about how the evil man came along and took his place sneering at her. She looked up at Tripp. "He had a hunting bow in his hand." She started to tear up. "Then Daniel, or Dane as he was called, had an arrow in his chest and there was blood everywhere." She looked at Tripp with tears in her eyes and whispered to him. "He says to me, 'Lilly...my love. You will always be my forever. I will find you.' And then he dies." She was softly crying as Tripp pulled her off the chair and hugged her.

They were silent for several minutes before he pulled back to look at her and ask, "Are you okay?"

She pulled away, nodding because she was embarrassed. She assumed she became emotional because she met Daniel Dane Geofrey from the 1700s. She felt him as if he were real. She felt the love in her heart and the loss from him dying in her arms. It was surreal the intensity she had felt for the man...she never knew but had known.

Lilly leaned against the deck. "Sorry, this has all been a bit traumatic." She clears her throat. "Moving on. So I am here for just one night and dream of being at the Ball. Kind of like the same Ball we were at last night...only it was at the fort and in the 1700s." Taking a deep breath she looks at him. "The evening played out much like it did last night. You or I should say your ancestor Daniel Dane became queen and my ancestor became his queen." She smiled.

He grinned at her. "Did they end the evening as we did?"

Lilly tossed a pillow at him. "No...that wasn't to be done back then."

She smiled because she knew he joked around trying to make her relax. "The following day I noticed my family ancestry book for the first time. If you look at all the Lilly's in the family tree you will see some rather odd things. Like when one dies, another is born...the same day. Plus, they never married...with the exception of the first Lilly, who was married to your ancestor, but they never had children."

Tripp interrupted her. "Well, if you are afraid you will be an old spinster...I will make an honest woman out of you." He teased.

She smiled and thought he had to be the cutest guy she had ever known. "Umm...I may hold you to that." She picked up the letter her grandfather wrote her and handed it to him. "Please read the letter my grandfather left me. I'm going to grab another cup of coffee." She rolled her eyes with a smile. "Someone kept me up half the night and I need some serious caffeine. Would you like a cup?"

"I think it was you who kept me up. And yes, I would love a cup."

"Whatever." Was all she said before leaving the room.

He chuckled and looked down at the letter and began reading it. Several minutes passed before he finished. He sat back and tried to take it all in what Lilly's grandfather was implying. It seemed a bit far-fetched. Yet then again, how many crazy dreams had he had over the years that always involved this area? There were dreams where he was commanding a group of soldiers. He dreamed of the Ball on several different occasions…only not like the Ball last night. Many of his dreams were like he was in a dated time period. There was also the dream that he had for years of getting murdered by the town creek and even across the tracks. His dream always had him lying dead as a woman cried over him. He didn't know who the woman was. When he was younger, he thought it was his mother. Then as he got older and would have the recurring dream, he realized it was someone who loved him as a woman does a man. Only he never saw her face.

He looked up as she entered the room and handed him his coffee before sitting across from him on the recliner. "So…what did you think of Grandfather's letter?" She asked.

"Wow." He shook his head in confused wonder. "It's a bit surreal."

"Do you think it's a bit far-fetched?"

"I don't know what to think. If this is true it's definitely bigger than us."

"Well, there's more." She paused and sipped her coffee.

He remained silent waiting for her to go on. She didn't disappoint him.

"I played around with different information Grandfather left me. But things got real the day I saw you at the fort." Taking a deep breath, she began her story of going to the tower and dreaming of Lilly and Dane's last day together. She explained everything she experienced with the exception of her and Dane making love. She wasn't ready to share that with someone she just made love to only hours before.

She went into detail about the death of Daniel and how it is believed Edwin Berger was the man behind the killing. She didn't bring up the gold just yet because she needed to see how he was going to react to everything she told him. She gave him a brief description of the Phantom Funeral and her dream of being Lilly in France. When she was finished, she looked at him intently. "So do you think I am crazy now?"

The last thing he thought of her was crazy. He felt he could now understand this strong pull he has always had to her since the first time he saw her years ago. He often thought of her over the years and when he met up with her in

October, all those crazy emotions he felt as an adolescent resurfaced…only now they were stronger and more mature.

The last few months were the hardest staying away from her. Yet he planned all along to be with her. He just needed to settle things where he was before making Prairie du Rocher his permanent home. He could tell she felt something similar to what he felt when they danced that night at Lisa's.

That was why he spent so much time in Champaign…so he could tie up several loose ends to a variety of jobs he was working on. This gave him a little more free time to come back to Lilly and do some serious dating. Plus it gave him time to work on the issues with the levees.

"Lilly, I think you are adorable and I think there is something going on here. To be honest you aren't the only one having crazy dreams about the past. I have been having some odd ones also." He took a breath before explaining to her all the odd dreams he had had since he was a teenager.

When he was finished, they were both very quiet for a few moments. Lilly was the first to break the silence. "There's more."

"Your aunt's journal that your grandfather spoke of in his letter?" he asked.

"There's that. I read most of the entries of the first Liliane, Lilly Elizabeth, that's how I keep the different Lilly's apart. Anyhow, she does speak of a few things that confirms what I already put together. Then the next Liliane…Maria, I use their middle names to keep them apart, I started on her entries but haven't gotten too involved with her yet because time got in the way and I don't want to push through everything I find. I was waiting to have time to really document everything."

"So, you believe all your 'Lilly ancestors' are involved?"

She shrugged. "I don't really know. But Lilly Maria did have a friend who saw the Phantom Funeral. And speaking of that, I truly believe that it is your ancestor, Daniel Dane Geofrey, Commander at Fort de Chartres and married to my aunt Liliane who is the deceased in the procession."

"Why do you think that?"

"Just that it all ties in together. He died on July fourth…which is when the people see the Phantom, when the moon is bright…give or take a day or two. I came to this conclusion because I looked at dates throughout time and when people say they saw the Phantom on the Fourth but charts show the full moon may have actually been a few days before or after. But I will add that when I flashed back to the night Daniel died the moon was bright and full and it is documented that he died on the fourth…which was a full moon in 1754."

"Okay, but I am still not buying the Phantom Funeral bit or that it was my relative that is the deceased. But I will add that I am going to stop by my parent's house this week and see what info dad has on our family tree." When she tried to interrupt him, he stopped her. "Don't worry, I won't tell them why I am wondering. I'll just say I'm tying it to my work at the fort."

She smiled. "Thank You. This is so odd that I feel that the less people who know…the better. As of right now it's just you, me, Rissa and my Pops. He's actually the one who looked up the Geofrey tree and found there was still a line to present day. He's going to freak out when I tell him you are related to the Daniel Dane that he found who was married to Liliane Elizabeth."

"Really…So what does he think about all of this?"

"He agrees there's something there. But before I go on…where did you get the nickname Tripp?" She asked.

He grinned. "I was always tripping over everything as a small child. My dad started calling me that when I was young. I guess you could say I liked the attention I was getting from him because of the name. After that I refused to answer to any other name. My mother was frustrated but finally caved and started calling me Tripp so I would answer." He chuckled. "When I was in first grade T-ball, the coach wanted our first name printed on the back of our shirts. I wanted my nickname on the shirt so my mom decided to make it more like a name and added the extra 'p' on the end. And then it was all history from there."

She smiled and thought about how cute he was. She could only imagine him as a cocky little boy insisting on everyone calling him Tripp. "Sounds to me like you were a bit spoiled." She stated.

"You think?" He smirked.

She stood up. "Probably still are." She picked up her grandfather's letter from the table and put it back inside her grandfather's desk drawer. She leaned against the desk again. "There's more."

"Really. You have had a busy few months."

"You are not kidding. Yet most everything happened in the first few weeks. It's been silent since then." She walked over to the window and looked out at the bluffs for a minute. "So the day I saw you at the fort and I had whatever it is called…a premonition, out of body experience, I…whatever it was. I was sitting on the tower edge one minute and the next I was in the 1700s with your ancestor Daniel Dane Geofrey. He was the commander of the fort and I was his wife."

She looked back at him. "It's definitely in your family's blood to use nicknames over given names." She rolled her eyes. "This would have been a little easier if you all would just use your birth names."

She smiled when she heard his chuckle. "Anyhow Dane, I'm going to call him that to make it less confusing, took me into the basement of our quarters. It's actually the holes we use to climb in at the fort. Only there were houses on top and the basement was for storage. He took me down there and wanted to show me something." She breathed heavily thinking about how this part freaked her out the most. "He had chiseled out a small hole in the wall where he hid a bag of gold…gold from the bluffs."

Tripp gave her an odd look. "Lilly, this is getting a little far-fetched. I mean I believe you believe all of this but I am just not sure all of this is happening."

She smiled. "I agree with you but hear me out." She proceeded to tell him about Philippe Renaut and his search for treasure and how he came up with finding lead and that it was mostly on the Missouri side of the river. She went into detail about why Daniel left that evening with Running Wolf.

"Well that puts a wicked twist to the story. So did this Edwin kill for the gold or for the girl? I mean if it was me, I would kill for the girl." He said in a flirting tone.

She rolled her eyes at his jest before answering him. "I have no idea. And like you I was almost doubting myself. So I decided to go to the fort and see if I could find the hole Daniel chiseled out and had placed the gold in before covering it back up with the rock." She grinned. "I dragged Rissa along as a lookout. It's a good thing the place is pretty much deserted throughout the week."

"Is the hole sealed up from the restorations they've done out there?" He asked.

"No and that's the crazy part. It is one of the holes that hasn't been touched. It's the first one on the right as you enter through the gates." She grinned at him. "You should've seen me climbing down in the hole. I can promise you it was a lot easier when we were kids."

He lifted his eyebrows and agreed with a nod of his head. "I can only imagine."

"But I did it. I made it in the hole. Then I had to dig around because everything looked so different."

"And did you find the hole? If so, I want to see it. Don't leave me hanging." He stated as he watched her walk over and open her safe.

Once she got it opened, she left the door slightly ajar and continued. "Tripp, I bet I was in that hole for an hour and I was giving up hope. My arms were tired from reaching up and stabbing at the edges of cemented stones with a butter knife in that dark little room that is under the stairwell. And low and behold...I found a loose rock."

She shook her head. "I prayed there weren't cameras on me. Not that I was vandalizing anything but it sure wouldn't look good me stabbing at the wall like that." She took a deep breath. "Anyhow I found a loose area and once loose it didn't take much for the stone to give and inside was a dark hole."

"No shit? Sorry...I can't believe you found the hole. So this confirms that the events of that night actually happened."

"There's more. I wanted to take a picture of where the hole was exactly located so I would be able to find it again if I ever needed to. But because it was fairly dark under the stairwell, the flash went off." She looked at him intently. "When I looked to make sure the pictures were taken correctly, I noticed there was something on the whole picture." She reached into the safe and pulled out the bag of gold. She walked over to him and handed him the bag. "This is what I found inside."

Tripp was shocked when he opened up the bag and poured out the handful of gold nuggets onto the coffee table. "Dear Lord Lilly, shit just got real!"

She smiled because he was reacting similar to how she reacted when she first saw the nuggets. "Yes. It's crazy, I never would have thought the gold was still there. I just assumed Lilly Elizabeth grabbed it when she went back to France. But what's odd is I should have known she didn't take it with her because I dreamed about the day she left and remember all the way up to the part where she was crying on the boat. So I think my memory took me that far so my subconscious brain would tell me to find the gold...only I just thought I needed to find the hole to prove I was at the fort in 1754."

She blew her hair out of her eye and smiled as she plopped back down into the recliner. "Then I dreamed of her in France when she was old and I remember thinking about the bracelet that was melted down and made from the gold Dane asked me to take from his pocket right before he died. I...or

179

she," she shrugged, "it's so confusing because I was there but it was her." She rolled her eyes and tossed up her hands. "Anyhow one of us put the gold in the pocket, but because he was dying, we never really thought about it. I…or I guess Lilly found it when she got to France." She threw up her hands again. "Does that make any sense?" She laughed.

He chuckled. "Actually, it does." He picked up a piece and looked real close at it. "Do you think it's the real deal?"

"Yes, because my dad does and this is an area he specializes in."

He whistled. "I'm speechless." He put the gold back into the pile and walked over to the window and looked at the bluffs. "To think there could be gold up in those bluffs. Crazier yet no one has found any, or admitted to finding any, in all these years."

As she walked over towards him to look at the bluffs also. He slid her in front of him and put his arms around her waist. "I know and I really don't know what to do about it. If I alert whoever it is one alerts about it, they are going to ask me where I found it. I can't just tell them in the bluffs because I have no idea where in the bluffs. And I can't say I found them at the fort because I'd have to show them and that's trespassing and vandalism. And every gold-digger…literally, would be chiseling away at our history. Plus the property, the gold property, will technically be owned by the state."

She looked up at him. "And then who knows what will happen to the gold." Looking back out of the window. "I'm not greedy by any means and have no desire to climb the bluffs and try to find it. Yet I want to keep the gold because it belonged to our ancestors and they wanted me to find it." She turned in his arms and hugged him. "I think they needed us to find each other." She stated.

He hugged her and was a bit overwhelmed by all of this. He did agree there was something way beyond them that was leading them down a very surreal path. He felt in his heart they needed to see this through and figure out why these occurrences were repeatedly happening to them.

They were suddenly interrupted by Moose coming into the room with his leash. Lilly chuckled as she walked over and took the leash from his mouth. "He gets put out if he doesn't get his walk in." She explained.

Tripp smiled. "I have an idea. Why don't we take him out to the fort and have a look around? Maybe you'll have another out of body experience and we can get a few more answers to all of this crazy stuff."

"Sure, easy for you to say. You're not the one who takes a two-minute nap in a tower and ends up in another century for a day."

"Trust me...I would love it."

She smiled. "It was pretty cool to see what it was all like. I wish I could describe it but there's no way I could do it any justice." She clamped the leash to Moose's collar. "Come on, baby, let's take you for a walk."

Chapter Sixteen

Their drive to the fort was nice because the warm January day allowed for the Jeep's windows to be rolled down. Moose loved sticking his head out the backseat window. It was a comical picture because even though Lilly's jeep was a four door, Moose's head was so large it made the window look very small in comparison.

They walked around the fort holding hands while Tripp took over control of the Saint Bernard's leash. Lilly was grateful because sometimes when Moose spotted another animal, like a squirrel or a cat, he would pull her along like he forgot she was attached to the other end. She was sure one of these times he was going to pull her arm out of its socket.

Lilly filled him in on everything she remembered about the dream. Oddly, she was finding her memory suddenly becoming a bit hazy. She wondered if she was losing it because she never really lived it. She was glad she decided to start the entries into the journal of her life including the dreams. She was at first hesitant because she didn't want any future Lilly Bienvenues to think she was crazy. Yet she decided it needed to be done in case she didn't stop whatever was going on.

They approached the area where she found the bag of gold. They didn't climb down into the hole because there were others walking around the fort and didn't want to draw any attention to themselves. There was really no need to climb down. She stood on the edge and showed Tripp right where she chiseled out the rock. And by the look on his face, he was fascinated that someone thought to hide it there. He also stated he was duly impressed.

They climbed the tower and even went into the chapel. They walked around the little museum and looked at the pictures and artifacts. It was crazy because they knew what most of the artifacts were and what they were used for. Was it because they've both been in the museum before? Or maybe their love of history? Lilly thought it was their subconscious mind letting them know they lived in the time the tools were used.

The walk around the park took a good hour. They even walked to the back of the fort where the large levees towered. Tripp pointed to a few spots where the side of the levee walls looked like the dirt was being washed away. He explained that it was a breach from the other side pushing through the inside of the mound when the river rose and pushed its way through and washed away that part of the levee. This was one of the many things that needed to be repaired. This was also what the state no longer wanted to pay for.

He explained how the Mississippi was the longest river in the United States and it drains forty-one percent of the US watershed. It also transports millions of tons of materials up and down the river yearly. The levee systems started in Louisiana as early as the 1700s and didn't come this far up until the early to middle 1900s. People that lived along the river did what they could to keep the flooding out. Over the years and with technology always improving, the levees were rebuilt higher and better because more and more people altered their waterways to drain into the good Ole' Mississippi, causing more water pressure and flooding to occur. That and global warming near the top of the planet was melting and adding more drainage into the river...thus causing under seepage of water under the hills adding pressure to open channels which led to serious flooding across the levees.

Lilly could see how passionate he was when he explained, "People up north think only of themselves and build higher levees that squeeze together the water route to avoid flooding up there but making it impossible to avoid down here."

According to Tripp there were many things that caused the levees to become damaged and even break. Yet his theory was that every area along the river was unique and needed different things to improve the flooding to their area.

Like a farmer with land for miles and miles could get by with letting the water flood over and taking pressure off the river in a year when the river flooded. The federal funding would need to compensate the farmer for the loss of crops or not being able to plant at a higher scale than if there was a crop produced. Or the government could even offer a large amount of money to purchase the land and then they would have complete control of the land. Of course, that would be the last option because farmland was needed because the country was growing and expanding and the farmland which they took away was keeping the country fed.

His theory was that each spot along the river had different needs to keep it thriving. The small towns and cities had other options for keeping the flood waters out. And that was what PORT was about…getting people together to preserve the lands where they lived. One thing was for sure, it wasn't fair to tell small communities they needed to leave so they could save bigger cities. Everyone should be treated equally.

Tripp put his arm around her waist and pointed to the large mounds. "The river has a job to do but when you overload it, you are setting it up for failure. It will flow downstream and wipe out everything in its way. Many people running our state want to give up and make people leave their homes, their history, their lifestyles and move to higher ground. While this may work for some it didn't work for most. These people have businesses, they farm. Their history is here. Their deceased are buried here."

He shook his head. "It's a lot about money. It always comes down to money. To them it's better to let the angry river wipe everything out and move on downstream." He took a deep breath. "There's so many questions and someone needed to come in and stand up for the people along the river." He looked at her before continuing. "Every disaster that life deals people shouldn't just be pushed away. What happens when it widens so big it decides to take out the larger cities that sit along the river…like St. Louis or Memphis?"

Lilly let him collect his thoughts before asking. "What does your organization PORT do to try and stop them from forcing an evacuation?"

He took her hand and walked away from the face of the levee and headed in the direction of her jeep. "We have several ideas…but that's just it. We know there is a solution and we want to find the correct one. So PORT wants to sit down with every organization from each side and come up with a solution. May it be rerouting the water flows that were man-created, or asking the farmland owners, minus the houses and business areas, to allow pressure drainage in times of highwater. The plan was for there to be a fund for extra income for the farmer losing a crop or not being able to plant. These seem a little more practical than building higher and higher levees that are just breaching."

"So why isn't this happening? Like I mean why haven't you all sat down and talked about it?"

"Well PORT is new and we are working on it…it just takes time. Plus, then you have assholes, like Brader, who work for departments that want to wipe everyone out."

He opened the door and let Moose into the back seat before climbing into the front passenger seat. "For some reason he wants everyone out of these areas."

"You have no idea why?"

"No!" He answered, as she pulled out of the fort parking lot. "But I plan to find out. Do you know he personally buys up large amounts of land along the bluffs once the government restricts a town to rebuild after a flood?" She shook her head as he continued. "The people get bought out at market value after a flood occurs. The government then buys up a chunk of land on top of the bluffs and starts a community. The flooded homeowners get a decent rate to live in the community, mind you these people used to live on acres and now they are on top of each other. Some like it, some hate it. Then the government is sitting on this land with nothing to do with it. Eventually they decided to let farmers or any non-residential business buy the ground for a decent price. And for some reason Edmond bought a lot of it."

She glanced his way to give him a confused look before returning her eyes to the road. "I definitely think you're onto something. Edmond is a snake and he's up to no good." A few seconds later she continued. "You know he reminds me of Lilly and Daniel's nemesis Edwin. I mean they don't really look alike, yet the dark eyes and black curly hair are similar. Besides you don't really look like Daniel yet your stance reminds me of him. So that could be the same as Edmond. He could be an ancestor of Edwin's. Hell, even their names are similar."

Tripp smiled and grabbed her hand after she shifted gears on the manual. "Honey, I think that's a bit far-fetched."

She shrugged, "I think all of this is a bit far-fetched…so you never know."

Lilly fell asleep a few hours after Tripp left to go back to Champaign. At first, she had trouble falling asleep because she kept thinking about the night they shared…then she recaptured the day they shared together. Then she was excited with anticipation about the following weekend because he asked if she would come up to Champaign and go with him to his parent's house and collect genealogy information. So it was no wonder it took her awhile to fall asleep.

She dreamed she was sitting on a blanket having a Fourth of July Eve picnic with Tripp. Only it wasn't Tripp. It was Daniel. But wait...she wasn't sure if it was Daniel or Tripp? Geez, why did everything have to be so confusing, she wondered as she spread her lovely dress around her. Looking back up she realized it was her love, Daniel, sitting across from her.

She was grateful her summer riding habit was short sleeved and the shirt didn't have layers and layers of material, for the day was hot and humid and she was sure she would pass out from the heat if she had to endure so much clothing. Looking in the direction of the little house that sat tall on a limestone wall, Lilly hoped her mother didn't look out the picture window to see she was without her hat. The house sat far enough back and her mother's vision wasn't the best so she doubted her mother would notice.

The spot they picnicked along the town's creek was a bit secluded with a few trees blocking the view of any passersby. So unless a passerby wished to water their horses, which wasn't uncommon at this part of the town creek, she didn't worry much about being caught with her hat off. It was such a ridiculous rule for a lady to always have a hat on when taking an outing with a gentleman caller. The ribbons and feathers that adorned the wide brim did nothing but blow in her face and make her head hot. Sometimes it was hard to use proper etiquette when the heat was stifling.

Looking over at her dashing Daniel, her breath caught in her throat at how handsome he was with the loosened cravat around the neck of his crisp white shirt tucked into his black trousers. Every day for the last six months she thanked the Good Lord that Daniel Geofrey wished to court her. Every girl, including herself, in Prairie du Rocher had hoped the prodigal son would look their way when he moved back to the area after studying at the College of William and Mary in Williamsburg Virginia.

Lilly didn't really remember him before he left for college a decade past. He had only been thirteen to her eight years. The last thing she would have paid attention to was a boy...even a handsome one with sandy brown hair and startling green eyes. Yet she paid a lot of attention to him now, as a man of twenty and four.

She smiled as she thought of the first time she laid eyes on him. Sunday Mass at St. Joseph's Catholic Church. He walked in with his two brothers and his parents. She remembered her heart stopped at the sight of him as he walked past and sat in the pew in front of her family's pew.

The church was fairly small so everyone noticed the family's entrance. The small log-structured building was filled with friends, neighbors and family, yet all she could do was stare at his profile. There was no way she could explain what the sermon or gospel was on that cold February day. All she could do was wonder if this was what she read about once in a dime novel. They called it love at first sight.

When the time came to greet the neighbors of the congregation by acknowledging one another, Lilly held her breath when it was her turn to make eye contact with the handsome newcomer. He took her breath away when he turned to her and looked her in the eyes and smiled as he gave her the proper greeting.

She wasn't sure she even replied yet she was sure the skies opened up and bolts of lightning struck the two of them right then and there. Never had she been impacted by a male in all of her nineteen years. If truth be told she always believed she'd end up a spinster with what she had as choices around town…that was until Daniel came back to town.

Now, months later, here she was sitting across from him picking at the grapes he placed on the expensive china his mother packed for the outing. She was suddenly nervous, which was odd because from the moment he made her acquaintance, that Sunday Mass several months before, they have spent quite a bit of time on the weekends together. She smiled at the first few times he came calling, he seemed just as nervous as she. Soon they became comfortable with each other during their long walks and the time they spent fishing together. It was as if they knew each other forever.

Daniel laid back on his side and propped his head up with his hand as he stared at the beautiful creature in front of him. He wondered how he became so blessed to have caught her eye? From the moment he shook her hand in church he knew he was going to marry her someday. He wanted that day to be soon. He dreamed of them always together. He longed to touch her silky hair and kiss her lips. He wanted her to be his everything. To one day see her swollen with their child.

He knew the time was right because everything was coming into order. His entire reason for coming back to the area was his offer from Rudloff Law to practice at their firm in St. Louis. The original agreement was to work in the heart of the city, which is what he had been doing for the past several months. Yet now his boss, Mr. Carol Rudloff wanted to open an office on the Illinois side of the river. He wanted Daniel in Belleville, Illinois. The village was now the St. Clair County seat, taking over from Cahokia.

Daniel was excited because he would be in charge of the firm. The courthouse in Belleville was a small wood building, nothing like the beautiful massive courthouse that was recently built in St. Louis. Yet he believed in time, Belleville's court house would be just as big and beautiful as St. Louis.

There was just one last thing he needed to complete his almost perfect life. Making Lilly his bride. He could see the two of them settling in the house his boss was having erected on the tract of land next to the courthouse. His plan was to make his offices on one side and a house on the other. Daniel could live in the house for as long as he worked for Rudloff and the rent would be very cheap.

In the end it would be perfect because as of right now he only got to see Lilly on the weekends because he had to stay in St. Louis throughout the week. This way he could be with her every day...and every night. He liked the thought of that.

He had been planning for this moment for weeks now. Tomorrow was the Fourth of July and his boss was fine with letting him take off for a few days because of the holiday. So he made his way back home this afternoon and asked Lilly to go on a picnic with him.

"Daniel, why are you looking at me so oddly?" She asked with a smile in her voice.

Daniel sat up and smiled at her. "It is not an oddity that I look upon thee, but yet it is a look of love you see in my eyes my fair Lilly." He leaned across her and picked up her hand and kissed the back of it.

She was shocked whenever he touched her hands, it was still like it was the first time they touched hands, as if a jolt of lightning was racing through her body. "I feel the same as you." She whispered shyly.

She watched as he shifted himself to balance himself on one knee. "Lilly, if you mean what you say and your love is as my love for you…" He reached into his pocket and pulled out a simple, beautiful, one-stoned diamond ring. "Liliane Maria Bienvenue, will you do me the honor of becoming Mrs. Geofrey?"

Lilly put her hand to her mouth. She was shocked and excited. "Of course, I will marry you." She stated as he slid the ring on her finger. He stood and pulled her into his arms and swung her in a circle before setting her back down and kissed her.

"I asked your father last weekend and he granted his permission." He paused and held up her hand and rubbed the ring with his thumb and finger. "It's the craziest thing. I wanted his permission before I purchased a ring. Well, after he granted it, he left the room and reentered a few moments later with a ring in his hand. After handing it to me…" He looked up and gave her a confused look. "He said it seemed appropriate that I give you the ring because of the inscription on the inside."

Lilly looked at the ring closely. She remembered this ring…but how? Has her father shown her it before? No, that wasn't it. She suddenly flashed to a different time…an earlier time when another man proposed to her by a river. She wanted the image to go away because every time she was with this man something bad would happen and she was afraid she would suddenly leave this place. Yet, she felt it was okay now because she had Tripp. Wait…Tripp was later. Shaking her head, she focused on Daniel. She looked back at the ring and smiled up at him as she took it off. She knew it was going to be engraved before turning it over. "From My Beloved Daniel."

"I know, isn't that crazy? Your father said it was an inheritance from your great-grandfather's sister who married a distant relative of mine." He shook his head. "I believe that to be a true sign of our happily ever after."

Lilly was thoughtful for a moment. Had she known that Daniel's ancestor was married to hers? She couldn't remember. Yet that was because she wasn't really this Lilly. She was just dreaming she was this Lilly. But she didn't want to remember that because she wanted to stay here. She was grateful when Daniel spoke and brought her back to focus.

"I know we have several things to discuss and we can do that later. But I would like to tell you that my boss has asked me to start up a second firm, under him, but at a different location."

"Oh my goodness Daniel, that would be wonderful."

"Well, the thing is it's in St. Clair county. A village above Cahokia. Yet, before I agree, I would like to make sure you are fine with the move."

Lilly was a bit taken back. She hadn't expected to have to leave her little town. She knew she would rather be with him every day than to only have him on the weekends though, so she placed her hands on his cheeks and stated. "My love, I will go to the ends of the earth for you."

He touched his forehead to hers and stated, "How did I ever get so blessed to have you?"

Before she could reply, they heard a voice from behind them. "Well, well, well, what do we have here?"

Lilly cringed at the familiar voice. When Daniel spoke, his voice sent warm lightning bolts through her…but when she heard Edwardo Brigman's voice, she always had cold eerie chills, right down her spine. She turned to see the devil himself with his black evil eyes looking down at her from his massive black horse.

Before she could reply Daniel answered him. "We are having a private moment Brigman, so you can move along." His voice stated he wasn't backing down if the other man thought to intimidate them. Knowing both men, she was sure Edwardo would cower before taking on Daniel.

Edwardo looked back and forth between the couple and wanted to put a bullet between Geofrey's eyes. The son-of-a-bitch comes into town and ruins all his plans. Lilly was his and he planned to have her. He just had to get rid of the bastard who stuck a ring on her finger minutes ago. It sickened him to see her all over the bastard after sliding the diamond on her finger. He tipped his hat and looked at her, "Lilly." He nodded and turned his horse in the direction of town.

Lilly looked at Daniel and could see the anger in his eyes. She put her hands to his lips and whispered. "Don't do or say anything related to that man. This is our moment and I want to remember every minute of it." She reached up and kissed his soft lips. He took over and deepened the kiss.

The next hour was spent with the couple making plans for their future. As the sun slowly descended behind the bluffs, Lilly and Daniel walked hand in hand towards her home, making plans for the future. He walked her to her door and set the picnic basket down while he gave her a quick kiss and hug before they parted ways. "You've made me a very happy man on this day, Liliane Bienvenue."

After hugging him goodbye, Lilly breezed in the house all happy and giddy. Her parents were waiting at the kitchen table. They were smiling because they knew Daniel was proposing to their daughter during their picnic. They could tell by her expression, she said yes.

She looked up at her parents and thought about how different they looked since only seeing them a few weeks ago at Christmas. Only that wasn't who she is now and they weren't her parents then but they are her parents now. They looked a little different only she knew they were the same people by the way they held themselves.

They were still a handsome couple, with her father looking younger than his forty years and her mother not yet reaching his age for another couple years. Her skin was still young and beautiful with the touch of sun that kissed it daily when she was working in her gardens.

She smiled at her parents and asked, "Why are you looking at me like that?" She teased because she knew, they knew, he proposed. She slowly lifted her left hand up to brush away a lock of hair that fell near her eye. The hair wasn't bothering her but she knew her parents were wanting to see her ring finger and she was being nonchalant.

"Oh my Lilly-Bear." Her mother said as she rushed over and hugged her daughter. "I'm so happy for you and I believe it is destiny. Did you read the inscription?"

"I did." She replied as she hugged her back.

Her father refused to be left out and hugged his only daughter. "So when do I get to walk my little girl down the aisle?" He asked.

She smiled at him. "No date yet, but we hope soon. Daniel has a job offer to continue working for Mr. Rudloff, running a second firm in St. Clair county, in the village of Belleville. Apparently, they moved the county seat from Cahokia to there and Mr. Rudloff is wanting to open an office there with Daniel in charge."

"Oh…so does that mean you will be moving away?" Her mother looked at her daughter with sadness in her eyes.

"Yes." She answered as she took her mother's hands. "Mother, it is only a few hours ride from here to there and Daniel has promised me we will be home every other weekend."

Her mother turned to her father. "I'm guessing you knew about this Mr. Bienvenue?" She asked her husband with a touch of anger.

Her father looked back and forth between them with a sheepish grin. "Um…I think I hear some mooing…I need to run out and give some hay to Suzy." With that he was out the door.

Lilly joined her mother in the kitchen. She looked around and suddenly realized she wasn't in the Bienvenue house. She wondered if her mother would think she was crazy if she asked why they were in this house? Surely she would. She really needed to know what day it was?

All confusion was suddenly forgotten as her father came rushing back in and slamming a wooden bar over the large metal hooks that protruded from the wall on both sides of the door. He called out for her brother, Tylere, to come quickly. Lilly was startled to see a gawky boy emerge from the stairs leading to the upper attic. "Yes, father?"

He whispered loudly, "Help me seal up the house and Catherine please lock the windows. Lilly, distinguish the lights. I heard shouting coming from the town that there was an Indian raid happening. Then the bell rang."

Everyone quickly did as they were told. When everything was sealed up and lights out except for the lantern her mother used to light the way, the family quietly made their way to the two upstairs bedrooms. Her father and brother had every gun they owned plus ammunition in their arms. The plan was for her father and Lilly to watch out the open windows in her bedroom that covered the front and right side of the house while her brother and mother took watch at the opposite side of the house that covered the back and left side of the house. Her father intentionally built the house in this fashion for just this purpose…to protect them from any raids.

Her father and sixteen-year-old brother each had a musket close by while Lilly and her mother had a pistol ready to go in case the intruders came close. Everyone had a window to look out and that covered all four sides. They stood back to not be noticed. The full moon's light made it possible to see if anyone tried to sneak up on the house. They could hear shouts in the distance and what appeared to be many horses and riders running together. Gun fire was randomly heard.

Lilly was pacing in the darkened room. She hated when the Fox Tribe came near the town and went on a raid. As a rule, most of the local natives were friendly and worked beside the community. Yet the Fox were a different lot and when they see something they want they would just take it.

It was just after midnight when Lilly's father felt the fighting was done because they heard nothing in the last hour. It was decided that one person in each room would stay awake and look back and forth between the two windows in each room to make sure nothing was amiss. He suggested Lilly nap while he took the first watch but she insisted she wasn't tired and he should sleep until she became tired herself. He agreed because he was having a hard time keeping his eyes open. Her brother was taking the first shift watching out his bedroom window.

An hour later Lilly was yawning and trying to keep her eyes open. She didn't want to wake her father because she knew he was going to need more than just an hour of sleep. She tried occupying her mind as she twirled the beautiful ring around her finger. She couldn't wait until she and Daniel were married.

She wondered what her friend Agatha was going to say when she showed her the ring at this evening's festivities. This year marked the forty-sixth year the United States became an independent country. The evening will be filled with food, dancing, a parade, and her favorite…fireworks.

Lilly was smiling as she looked out the window. She was glad the evening was relatively cool. It didn't help that the mosquitos were bad this time of the year near the water's edge, but having the sweetgrass hanging in the open windows did keep the hungry monsters at bay. She watched as the very bright moon shone on the town creek that flowed behind her homestead. She looked out to the area where Daniel proposed to her only hours earlier. She prayed he and his family were safe from the raids. She walked over the other windows and made sure all was calm before going back to the other window and looking once again at her favorite spot.

Lilly suddenly tensed up as she noticed someone lurking about in the cluster of trees where she and Daniel picnicked earlier. She started to wake her father just as she spotted Daniel and his brother Denis, on horseback, riding up from the area opposite of the trees. She was wondering what they were doing as she watched him direct Denis to check the other side of the house. She realized he was making sure they were safe. She ran across the hall to let Tylere know it was just Daniel's brother riding up on his side.

Rushing back to her room she leaned out the open window. "Daniel." She whispered loudly and waved to him trying to get his attention. After a few moments he spotted her and rode up under her window.

"Lilly, what in blazes are you doing hanging out that window?" He asked as he tried to calm his prancing horse. "Don't you know the townspeople just stopped a bunch of natives from raiding the homes?"

She knew he wasn't angry at her…just worried. "I know. I told Father to take a nap and I would keep watch."

He shook his head and grinned. "So you decided it was okay to hang your head out the window and shout out to me like Juliette?"

"Romeo, Romeo…" She laughed quietly. Then she remembered that someone was in the trees. "Dane," she whispered down to him. "Right before you arrived, I was getting ready to wake Father. I think someone is in our trees." She nodded in the direction of the cluster of trees that sat off from the side of the house. She didn't want to point in case whoever was there would see her doing so.

"Okay love…stay here and keep your head inside." He stated before adjusting the pistol that sat in front of him as he backtracked in the direction he just came from so he could throw off whoever was in the trees. She worried a bit because she knew whoever was in the trees had the advantage because they were hiding and he was out in the open.

Lilly could hear her brother talking to Denis out his window in the other room. She decided to walk across the hall to let Denis know what Daniel was up to. Just as she started to turn away, she noticed a flash through the air and then…as if in a slow motion, Daniel fell backwards off his horse and to the ground. She stood still for a second just as the rider climbed on a big black horse.

Something jolted her as she screamed and ran down the stairs to the door. She was having trouble getting the thick board off the frame. Once she got it open, she ran out the door. Her family and Denis heard her screams and rushed to see what happened.

Denis was just coming around the house and saw her running and pointing towards the lone horseman who was emerging from the trees, "He hurt Daniel." She shouted, never slowing down.

Lilly heard Denis dislodge a bullet in the direction of the horseman before he took off away from the creek into the wooded area. Denis didn't follow, instead he turned his horse to get to his brother.

She reached Daniel before anyone else. She fell next to his fallen body. She was shocked to see an arrow protruding from his chest. "No, No, No…not again." She cried as she looked up into his beautiful face. He was looking at her with such pain and regret.

"Please don't die on me again…please." She whispered.

His voice was a harsh whisper. "Please Lilly, always remember my love for you." His voice was barely a whisper. Daniel slowly reached up and wiped at the tears falling down her cheek. "My sweet love, you've owned my heart from the moment we met." He coughed. "I will find you again in another time…this I vow. I love you my sweet Lilly."

Those words were said once before. She knew what her reply was before she said it. "I promise you Daniel Dane Geofrey, you are and will always be my forever." She cried over and over as her sweet beautiful Daniel died in her arms…again.

It was several moments later when her father lifted her from Daniel's side. He was surprised at all the blood on her dress. He looked over and noticed there wasn't much blood on Daniel's chest. He was confused until he spotted the hole in her dress on her right side below her ribs. He looked up at Denis. "Help me get her inside. She's been shot." That was the last thing Lilly remembered.

Chapter Seventeen

Lilly sat up straight in her bed. She was crying and panting. Her blankets were twisted and caught in her legs. It took her several minutes before she could calm her racing heart.

Dammit, the dreams were happening again. Ugh, she was hoping the death of the man she loved wouldn't happen again. It was too vivid, too real. She loved going back but the pain she felt every time she did wasn't worth it.

This time was worse because now she felt as if this Daniel was her Tripp. It made her realize her feelings for him were strong, making the pain from this loss so much more intense. Looking at her clock it was barely five in the morning. She untangled the covers from her feet and decided to stay up...she knew there wasn't going to be any going back to bed for a while after that dream.

Moose looked up at her from his bed on the bedroom floor before putting his head back down and closing his eyes. She patted his head as she passed him. As a rule, he didn't like to be woken up before the sun started coming out so she left him alone.

Lilly knew what she had to do. She had to finish reading Liliane Maria's story. She turned the lights on in the study and because she was a bit spooked, she pulled the blinds down in the room. She grabbed the diary and sat in the recliner and read where she left off months ago.

The last entry she read was Lilly Maria's friend's Phantom Funeral spotting. The next several posts were summarizing her life before she turned eighteen. It was crazy to think about how life was back then. No modernization yet they maintained relationships with each other that weren't hidden behind a screen as most people did today.

Lilly scanned through several entries until she came across the first one that mentioned Daniel.

3 February 1822

My Dearest Confidant, for this journal, is who I speak to about every true emotion I have.

Today has brought on the happiest day of my life. I met the most beautiful man I have ever set my eyes upon. His name is Daniel Geofrey. In all of my nineteen years I have never believed in love at first sight...until that moment.

Lilly read her aunt's story as if she knew it. Her aunt's words and entries continued on for many pages about her love for Daniel and their courtship. Lilly's heart was filled as she read the sweet things he did for her.

Her aunt wrote very well, yet it was hard to sometimes make out what she was saying because it was a different time and the way people spoke was so different from the way they spoke today. It took her over an hour until she got to the first entry after Daniel proposed and died.

17 July 1822

My Dearest Diary,

So much has happened and I feel as if I cannot go on any longer. I've lost him. For he is gone forever. The Lord has taken him to the heavens and has left me here to feel the hurt.

Daniel proposed to me two weeks ago at our secluded spot by the creek. I was so overjoyed. The ring he gave me once belonged to his uncle, many generations ago and was given to my aunt of many generations past. Ironically, our ancestors were in love as we were. The inside of the rings says, 'From My Beloved Daniel.'

I cannot describe how happy I was at that moment. The ring was proof we belonged together. We had plans to move to a neighboring village and start a new life.

I cannot believe that just a few hours later he was gone from me. I cried over his body as an arrow was protruding from his chest. My world stopped.

Lilly had to get up and grab the box of tissues. Geez, she shook her head in wonder and sat back down. "I can't believe I keep crying over people who've been dead for centuries." She said out loud to herself.

I saw the murder and I even know who did it. Yet he has denied it. It was Edwardo Brigman. I know it was him because I saw him ride off as I was running to my fallen Daniel. It may have been the back of him but I know his stance. I know his horse because he actually came upon Daniel and I at the river after Daniel proposed to me only hours before.

In the midst of all of the chaos, I got shot from a ricocheting bullet that Daniel's brother shot at the murderer. It hit me below the ribs on the right side of my body. I never felt the bullet lodge into me. I was too focused on getting to my Daniel.

Lilly lifted her shirt and looked down at the small, round, jagged, birthmark that was below her ribs on the right side of her body. She now knew in her heart the birthmark represented the wound she received in her past.

I was sick with fever and did not get to attend my beloved's funeral. When I awoke from the disillusioned state of fever I was reminded of my loss. I wished then and there that I would die myself so I could be with my Daniel. God had other plans for me for I recovered against my will.

I tried to explain to my father that it was Edwardo who put an arrow through Daniel's body. My father wanted details. I explained that I actually hadn't seen the man's face but could tell by his stance it was him. My father stated I should not accuse unless there was no doubt and seeing only the back of a man's head leaves doubt.

I could tell he believed me but considering we were under an Indian attack hours before he explained that many will believe my Daniel was murdered by a native. My father also added that Brigman was not the nicest man and they would be better off to leave the situation as it is. Apparently he and my father were not in favor of each other because he approached my father asking for permission to court me when I turned eighteen and my father denied his request. His reasoning was the man was too old for me in his years of twenty and seven. He confided to me on this day that he could see evil in the man's eyes and would never allow his daughter to be in attendance with the man.

I agreed with my father, yet I felt so angry and believed justice should be served. I felt like I couldn't move forward until Edwardo paid for his crime. I believe that God will give him his just due and I cannot wait until I see it unfold. I am also saddened with myself that I have such anger and hate in my heart.

Damn, Lilly thought, Lilly Maria had a bit of a temper. This made her smile because that was how she would feel towards the man also. Lilly went on to read several more readings. Her aunt's entries weren't nearly as many as when she first received the journal and met Daniel. Her writings lacked the passion she showed in her earlier entries.

Lilly started to skim over the words, just as she was about to lose interest one caught her eyes.

4 September 1822

Dearest Diary,

I am sure I am going to pass through the gates of hell and I cannot care. Edwardo Brigman has died on this day and I will surely go to hell alongside him because I am elated that the deed is done.

Lilly had to pause for a moment. She hoped that she wasn't reading a murder confession from her aunt's diary.

It was in the late morning and I was sitting near the spot along the creek where Daniel proposed to me, yet close enough to the house so my father could watch out the window and know I am fine. I cannot lie, I was sad and just needed the time alone. I was there for about an hour when I heard someone approaching the area I occupied. It was Denis, Daniel's brother. He was walking from the direction of our house so I am to assume he spoke with my parents before coming to me.

He asked if he could join me and I nodded my approval. I was shocked by what he had to say. He said there was a body found this morning along the banks of the Mississippi by the old abandoned fort down the road. It was Edwardo Brigman.

I cannot tell you the joy that surged through my body. Justice had been served. I could hardly focus on what Denis was saying, but I had to hear the rest of the tale. He went on to say that Delbert Tockstein, who happened to be one of my father's friends, was going to fish the cove near the bank. As he approached the river, he spotted a man lying along the bank. He first thought the man was sleeping. After shouting at him and receiving no answer, he concluded all was not well.

Moving closer he immediately noticed the man's scalp was removed and the entire head was open. He said Delbert heard screeching and looked up to see the buzzards circling the dead man. This made him jump into action and get help. Because Denis lived the closest to the fort, he was where Delbert first came to. Denis wasted no time and told Delbert to get help in town while he jumped on his horse and rushed to the river's bank.

While he didn't want to be descriptive about the murder, he did tell me Edwardo experienced a brutal death. I hoped he did and didn't have a problem saying that to Daniel's brother.

I know this makes me sound sacrilegious but I do not care. I believe Denis feels the same. What he said next made some of my anger dissipate. Denis explained that I was his only confidant and to repeat to no one…so I only share with you, Diary, because you are so hidden no one but myself will read your words.

Denis went on to say that while he was staring at the body, he looked over as the native by the name of Wolf Running approached him and said… "Evil deserves to die. Justice has been served this time but hasn't erased what is to come. Your brother needs to defeat him before he can move on." Denis said he stared at the man's retrieving back and tried to understand what was being said. Had Wolf Running killed Edwardo? And how can Daniel kill Edwardo next time?

Denis explained I was the only one who he confided in about Wolf Running. He also said that he could tell there was something in the dead man's hand. He knew he had to pry it open because maybe it would be a clue as to what happened. He was shocked to see a fairly large gold nugget in the hand. He didn't know where it came from or how Edwardo came to have it in his hand but he felt he couldn't tell anyone because he read about the Carolina Gold Rush and how it made people crazy and how they would cause destruction to nature and anything in its way.

I looked at the nugget as he showed it to me and I said to get rid of it…gold brought greed and greed killed. He agreed. Denis and I talked for a little while longer. I told him the hardest part was I never got to go to my beloved's funeral. I then did one of the hardest things I ever had to do…I removed the beautiful ring Daniel gave me when he asked me to be his bride and gave it to Denis. Denis didn't want it but I explained that it hurt too much to wear it and I needed to move forward.

That night I decided to move on with my life. I made a decision from that day forward to do something that made a difference. I wanted to change the world.

Lilly spent the next hour reading how a few years later her aunt moved to Belleville and started working at a small school house. She went on to circulate the importance of education and fought for more involvement in education. She also became one of the first female writers in her time. She would submit articles to newspapers throughout the states, via stagecoach and trains. The articles were about the importance of education and also the lifestyles of the Midwest.

Lilly was excited to read that her aunt was a journalist. There was definitely something in the Bienvenue line that gave them a love for writing. She stopped for a bit and searched her aunt on the web and while there wasn't a lot, because it was so long ago, there were a few articles posted that were written by her.

Lilly spent another hour reading the rest of Lilly Maria's diary entries and was sad when she finished the last one. Her aunt never married. She often referred to her beloved Daniel and pined away for him until her death on 1 November 1897. Amazing that a woman in that time period lived to be ninety-four years old.

Her aunt also wrote about how she learned to read and write the French language and was able to interpret the first Lilly's words. She wrote about how eerie it was that the two Lillys had an almost parallel romance with men by the name of Daniel Geofrey.

Lilly grabbed her notebook and wrote down key clues to her aunt's writings. One of the important ones was there had been a Running Wolf in Lilly Elizabeth's story and a Wolf Running in Lilly Maria's story. Lilly underlined those names several times. She felt like the native man was somehow important in all of this.

Lilly looked up and watched as Moose made his way into the room. She smiled and hugged the big dog before taking him out into the back yard. She leaned against the doorframe and looked out at the huge bluffs that hovered over the town. If those rocks could talk, they would have the answers to all the questions she had.

The first would be what was the deal with Daniel getting murdered? And most importantly what does it have to do with her? She let the dog back in and decided to start documenting everything she knew, what her grandfather documented in his notes, and what information she retrieved from the journal.

She unplugged her phone and scrolled through the messages she received that morning. The first was Sawyer stating he was excited she was coming to Champaign in a few days. He thought it was cool she met up with Tripp again and was looking forward to hanging out one evening. Lilly smiled because she was just as excited to see him.

She replied "yes" to Rissa who wanted to come over for lunch and "get the scoop." Lilly smiled.

She answered a few emails from her colleagues at the paper, before scrolling through a new assignment her boss was sending her way. In the middle of reading the emails her phone alerted her to a FaceTime call from her mother. She smiled when her parents came on the screen. "What a pleasant surprise."

"Hello Lilly-Bear." Her mother said. Lilly suddenly remembered her mother called her that often. Even her other mother liked to call her that. Yet, that was weird because she only had one mother and each mother was the same…weren't they?

"Hi momma…how's it going, Pops?"

"Good, good." There was a slight delay in the connection so her parents would repeat themselves thinking they were losing connection. "So your mother and I have a new dig."

Lilly made her way to the living room because the connection was better there. "So where's the dig?"

"Virginia. It's connected to the original College of William and Mary." He smiled. "Remember when we took you kids and your grandparents there?"

Lilly did. She was very young but that visit was when her love of history started. Williamsburg, Yorktown, and Jamestown was where it all started and she had been completely fascinated with it. Oddly enough, she felt like she remembered that Lilly Maria's Daniel went to that same college. She noted that in her notebook also.

The conversation went back and forth for several minutes. She filled them in on hanging out with Tripp over the weekend. Of course, his spending the night wasn't mentioned. She went on to explain to her father that Trip's real name was Daniel Geofrey. The ancestor to the Daniel Dane Geofrey from the 1700s.

"Really. How come we never knew that boy's real name?" he asked in wonder.

She shrugged. "I guess he was only here a week and not local. Plus, I always thought his real name was Tripp." She thought about it for a second. "And maybe we weren't supposed to know."

Before they could reply she had an incoming facetime call from Tripp. She smiled at her parents, "That will be Tripp now."

Her mother giggled. "Okay sweetie, we will talk to you soon. Love you."

"I love you too." She replied before clicking over.

Tripp's handsome face appeared and her stomach started fluttering.

"Good morning, beautiful." he smiled.

She smiled. "Hi yourself and I don't think there's anything beautiful on this end. I haven't even combed my hair."

"Trust me you look incredible." He gave her that dimpled grin.

"So guess what?" She wanted to change the subject because he was making her feel shy with his compliments.

"What?" He asked with a chuckle because he noticed her blush.

Lilly knew he probably couldn't talk long so she gave him a quick summary of her dream and about her aunt's entries in the diary. He was stunned. He wanted her to give him all the details where together over the weekend. He was fascinated by the mystery of what was unraveling in their past. They chatted for a little bit before he promised to call her later.

The drive to Champaign a few days later helped Lilly collect her thoughts. She thought about how fast the past week went by as she finished up several jobs for the paper and even made time for her friends. She and Rissa took the dogs for their daily walks. Lilly was blessed because Rissa was fine with watching Moose over the weekend.

Lilly spent quite a bit of time going over the information she had on the Phantom Funeral. That was the title she labeled the notes that had anything to do with the Bienvenue and Geofrey family. For some reason she felt like it all came back to the Phantom.

She felt like something was making the funeral repeat itself. It had to do with the death of Daniel...of that she was sure. Plus, both murders involved two natives. One named Running Wolf and the other Wolf Running. She didn't believe that to be a coincidence.

She even noted that both murderers had similar names and both knew about the gold. Both also wanted each Lilly of that era. Plus both men killed Daniel with an arrow to the chest and both times each Lilly of their time saw it happen.

She was hoping to read the entries of the next Lilly…Lillian Francis, born 1 November 1897, the same day Liliane Maria died. This Lilly was her grandfather's great-aunt. This aunt also had a different spelling to her first name. Lilly assumed it was their way to Americanize the name Liliane.

Lilly decided to wait until she caught up on all her notes before moving on to the next generation. Things were getting too complicated as it was. And truth be told it was all a bit overwhelming.

Lilly smiled as she pulled into the driveway of Tripp's house. Her stomach fluttered as the handsome man walked outside of his ranch style house to greet her. He had her door open before she could get her keys out of the ignition.

Tripp was so excited she was here. He gave her a long hug as soon as she stepped from her car. "Hi, I missed you." He whispered into her ear.

She smiled and took a deep breath, loving the smell of him. "Hi, I missed you too." She pulled back and looked up at him. "Are we going to hang out in the driveway? If so, can I get my coat?" She smiled with a shiver.

"I can keep you warm." He flirted.

She reached up and gave him a quick peck on his lips. "Then warm me up inside…I'm freezing," she said with a promise in her eyes. Tripp was happy to oblige.

The weekend was one of the best Lilly had ever spent in her life. She and Tripp spent three glorious days together. She was sad to see it end as she pulled into her driveway. With that thought, she was glad to get home because she missed Moose and her friends.

After dragging her large suitcase into the house, she sat down on the living room sofa for a few minutes. Looking around she couldn't be any happier than she was in this house. Tripp's house was nice, but small and slightly enclosed. Not like the openness she felt here.

She sighed as she laid her head back on the cushion. Driving could be so exhausting. Even though she didn't mind the drive because she got to spend the weekend with the man she was falling head over heels in love with. She and Tripp went all over the place on her visit. They met up with Sawyer one evening and had dinner at Tripp's parents' house the other. That had been an enlightening evening that started with both of his parents greeting her with open arms.

Tripp's father, Elgee, was a very handsome, tall gentleman with a full head of snowy white hair. His eyes were the same as Tripp's beautiful soft green ones. Elgee hugged her and stated how nice it was to see her after all these years.

His mother, Jeanette, was a very attractive lady with natural brown hair that had only a hint of silver flowing through it, giving it a highlighted effect. She had soft, tanned skin and very pretty blue smiling eyes. Lilly hoped she looked this good in her forties.

Jeanette mentioned how excited she was that one of her boys finally brought a girl to the house…making the number a little more even. She rolled her eyes at Lilly and said something about being a 'boy mom' was sure to earn her wings one day. Lilly could only imagine.

Lilly thought it was cute when his mother called Tripp…Daniel. She mentioned how she refused to call him by his silly nickname any longer. She went on to say how she played his game as a child but he was grown now and needed to "man-up" and get over it if someone wanted to call him by the name he was blessed with. He chuckled and mentioned that most everyone at his place of work called him Daniel.

Tripp's brother Jasper joined them as well. Lilly never met Jasper because he didn't come to the fort the year Tripp did. She was a bit taken back at how good-looking Jasper was as well. He was also a big flirt.

"Lilly, I'd like for you to meet my brother Jasper…or Jay Jay." Tripp stated.

His mother threw up her hands. "See another nickname." She rolled her eyes.

Lilly laughed as she shook his hand. "Nice to meet you." As she pulled her hand away, she turned to Tripp's mother. "I personally like the name Jasper so I agree. Now Tripp may be a problem because even though I love the name Daniel, I've only ever known him as Tripp so it may take me some time to try and correct this." She stated.

His mother smiled and looked at Tripp before stating. "I like her, Daniel." She smiled at Lilly. "It really is nice to have another woman in the house. For a while I was thinking these two were gay and that's why they refused to ever bring any ladies here." She quickly continued to clarify. "Not that we have anything against either one being gay." She lifted an eyebrow at the boys. "It would just be nice to know something about their personal life."

Everyone laughed and Jasper was the first to reply. "Mom, we aren't gay we just haven't found anyone as perfect as you."

Tripp rolled his eyes. "Suck ass...I mean butt. Sorry mom." He rushed on so she wouldn't scold him for cursing in front of her. "Speak for yourself Jasper. Lilly is as close to perfect as one can get when compared to mom."

"Now who's the suck...?" He couldn't finish because Tripp's dad interrupted.

"Enough with all this blarney." He grabbed Lilly's hand and walked her into the family room. "My son tells me you are doing some research on the Prairie du Rocher history. So I grabbed everything I could find from our family history and have it waiting in here for you."

The rest of the evening was going through old family trees and journals...before and after having dinner. Tripp's father was funny yet serious as he told several crazy stories of the Geofrey men.

There apparently have been several men murdered in the Geofrey line. There were two with the name Tomas', three Daniel's, and three Mathews. Many have died odd deaths over the centuries. A few in the wars, which were the two Tomas'...they were father and son. The three Daniel's died a century apart in the town of Prairie du Rocher. He mentioned that if he would have known this, he probably wouldn't have given Tripp the name Daniel.

Lilly asked if they had ever heard about the Phantom Funeral. When they all shook their heads she explained what she knew, minus anything too personal. She also brought up that their ancestor was married to hers. They thought that was pretty awesome.

The evening went on fairly late and Lilly did get a lot of insight into the Geofrey line but there didn't seem to be anything too unusual that took place that was outside of the fact that the two families kept meeting up and everyone named Daniel kept dying.

That thought made Lilly turn to Tripp's mother and ask, "What made you decide to name Tripp...I mean Daniel...Daniel?"

Jeanette shrugged. "I really cannot remember." She turned to look at Elgee. "Do you remember Dear?" she asked.

Elgee took his glasses off and had to think about it for a minute. "I really don't know. It definitely wasn't because of the past Geofrey men being named

Daniel because I didn't get into the whole family history thing until you boys were small. That's when I first found out about the fort and started doing the reenactments."

Elgee looked over at Jasper. "Now Jasper, your name came from your grandfather of course." He looked back at Lilly. "I really have no idea. That was so long ago."

Tripp chuckled. "Thanks, dad, for implying I'm old."

Lilly chucked as she thought about that evening. She loved being with Tripp's family. She loved being with Tripp. She was hating to admit it because she felt vulnerable…but she was definitely falling in love hard and fast.

She closed her eyes and remembered how incredible their lovemaking was. How he knew just what she liked even when she didn't know it herself. They worked, she thought. They just worked.

It wasn't all about the sex. They had so much in common and their beliefs were traditional in a lot of ways. They appreciated the old school values and after their many talks Lilly felt if they ever had children they would be on the same page when it came to raising them.

She chuckled and stood up and stretched. She probably needed to slow down a bit, she was thinking about kids and having a family and she has only been romantically involved with the man for a week. Yet, she knew in her heart they've known each other forever.

Chapter Eighteen

Winter in Southern Illinois could be harsh and this was one of the years for it. There wasn't much snow but by mid-January the cold was so bitter even Moose didn't wish to take his daily walks. Lilly knew he loved watching the squirrels and any other creatures that visited the fenced in yard so she made him up a makeshift bed in front of the patio window where he could look outside.

She and Tripp spent every weekend together in Prairie du Rocher. Mostly due to PORT trying to get a large meeting set up with everyone involved in the levee systems from Missouri and Illinois. His hope was for all involved to come up with a solution, a sound solution. The task was a trial because trying to get that many people in one spot at one time was nearly impossible.

He hoped members of all government agencies…federal, state and local, who had anything to do with the river and levee system, would show up along with both governors and all the bordering town mayors. There were also the levee commissioners and basically anyone who understood what was happening and had a plan. Lilly was impressed at how devoted he was to the people. When she mentioned this to him, he wrapped his arms around her and gave her a peck on the lips. "Now more than ever because someone I am crazy about lives here." Geez, she thought, he knows how to warm a girl's heart.

Spring eventually showed up in Prairie du Rocher. This was Lilly's favorite time of the year. She and Tripp worked hard on the weekends to get the house ready for summer. Lilly was busy planting flowers and trimming trees. The Magnolia needed to be cut back a bit because it was so large it almost hit the rooftop so Tripp hired a tree trimmer they met one evening at Lisa's to cut back the branches.

The tree trimmer's name was Ron Wolfe…but preferred to be called Wolfe. Wolfe apparently had roots that went further back then the French Fort days. Lilly thought it to be true because he looked very American Indian with his nice tan and flawless skin. She had to admit she did think it was a bit odd that he had the name Wolfe, considering each of her encounters into the past had a native named Wolf in their story. Yet she was sure the natives of her past were spelled like the animal and this gentleman's name wasn't.

Tripp and Wolfe became fast friends. So much that Lilly started asking him to join them for dinner at least one night every weekend. Wolfe was single and loved home cooked meals so he was happy to oblige.

Some nights she would ask Rissa and Zeke over as well. It was nice how everyone became fast friends. Yet Lilly was bummed because she thought Wolfe needed someone to pair up with. She wished her friend Diane would show an interest in Wolfe, but Gina informed her that Diane was spending a lot of time with Edmond...and that worried Lilly.

Tripp wanted to do something special to get the PORT gathering going so he scheduled a luncheon for April fifth, at the American Legion Hall. The luncheon was funded through PORT. Lisa was doing the catering. He joked he would make everyone content with Lisa's chicken and maybe there wouldn't be much fighting between the two sides. Lilly thought his plan just might work.

When the morning of the fifth arrived, Lilly stood in the middle of the Legion Hall and was excited for the meeting, but nervous for Tripp and PORT. The place looked great with the tablecloths adorning each table and the catering was set up at the end of the hall, opposite the stage. There were charts on easels and information about PORT on the tables. The check in line was at the entrance to the room. Everyone attending had to RSVP. There were over one hundred and fifty expected...including the Missouri Governor and a few lobbyists from each state.

Looking around she thought about how the place looked completely different from the night it was converted into a Vintage Ball. She, Rissa, and the Rocher Girls all came and helped set up the evening before. Wolfe arrived later, after he finished his work day. Jasper and his friend Cooper came straight to the hall as soon as they arrived in town. Cooper was a college buddy of Jasper's and was tall, dark and adorable according to the Rocher Girls.

The plan was for the men to stay at Lilly's for the few days they were in town. She had to admit she was excited for the extra company. Lilly smiled when Gina walked over to her and nodded towards the far corner of the room. Lilly was happy to see Diane hanging out with Cooper.

Lilly lifted her eyebrows and asked Gina. "So what's up with Edmond?"

"Well," She looked back to make sure Diane wasn't going to walk in on them. "He's been blowing her off for the past several weeks. And he's coming to this meeting tomorrow and basically told her he needed to get back right away so he wouldn't have time for her. She's upset and said it's time to move on."

"Thank the Good Lord!" Lilly said.

Gina replied, "Amen."

Lilly kept an eye on the pair throughout the evening and there was indeed chemistry. She didn't see the pair after they finished setting up because she and Tripp went home and Jasper, Cooper, and Diane went to Lisa's. It wasn't until two in the morning that she heard the two men use the code on her front door. She was still smiling this morning at the thought of Diane and Cooper flirting.

After taking one last glance around the hall, she turned to exit the room when she came up short because standing in front of her was her brother Sawyer. She was very surprised and shrieked before running to him to give him a big hug. "What are you doing here?" She asked with much excitement in her voice.

"I was told you were here?" He stated as he hugged her back.

After returning his hug she pulled back and looked at him confused. "I didn't know you were going to be here."

He grinned. "I know, I asked Tripp to not say anything…so I could surprise you."

She was shaking her head. "Did you come here for moral support?"

"Kind of. I actually joined PORT a few weeks ago. I've been wanting to do it since Tripp was trying to sell me on it during the weekend you were in Champaign." He rolled his eyes at her. "You know me, I have to research something over and over before I can make a decision." he paused before continuing. "I love everything about the group. Plus Tripp mentioned there wasn't an engineer in the group and my input would be over the top." He chuckled. "He used those words…over the top?"

Lilly hugged him again. "That's awesome. I am so excited for us."

"Us?" He raised an eyebrow.

She laughed out loud. "Yep, I also am now a part of PORT because Tripp stated having a freelance journalist in the group…with a minor in marketing, would be 'Over the Top' as well!"

"Great now my 'over the top' doesn't seem so important if everyone gets a 'over the top." He chuckled. "I'm just kidding. If Tripp is the company's membership recruiter, they picked the right man for the job."

"Who's the right man for the job?" Tripp asked as he came in and joined the siblings.

"Apparently you." Lilly said as he walked over and gave her a quick kiss.

Tripp shook hands with Sawyer and the two men made idle conversation for a few moments before they dived into what Tripp hoped the outcome of the meeting would be.

"I'm just hoping at the bare minimum everyone agrees there is a problem that needs to be solved that doesn't involve people leaving their homes. I have a few homeowners coming today that will speak about how important their homes and lands are. I also have a couple of business owners speaking on behalf of their communities and how important it is to find a solution."

The next hour was organizing everyone from PORT who came to work the luncheon. Lilly rolled her eyes as Selene came in and slithered her way to Tripp, like a snake. She hugged him and spoke clearly enough for Lilly to hear about how much she missed him. Tripp wasn't nobody's fool, he pulled away from her advancements and offered a polite greeting.

Not long after, another snake entered the room, Edmond Brader in all his glory. The man really did make her sick. She couldn't explain why, but he just did. It was probably because his evil eyes reminded her of the murderers that killed both Daniels in the past.

An hour and a half later the hall was packed and everyone raved about how wonderful their lunch was. Lisa blushed when Tripp asked everyone to give Lisa a round of applause for the great meal. It seemed Lisa was going to have a few more fans of her chicken.

Shortly after the meal was finished, Tripp started asking for different people to come and speak at the podium. At the end of each speaker's speech the floor was open to ask the speaker any questions. Jasper, Sawyer and two of Tripp's college buddies, who have been with PORT from the beginning, stood on the stage and helped with the answers.

As Lisa was cleaning up, Lilly helped her. Walking back and forth from the hall to the kitchen that was located in the bar area, Lilly was surprised to see Edmond Brader sitting at the bar talking with Selene. They looked like they were in a heated discussion and Selene seemed angry. Lilly backed away from the kitchen window just as Selene turned and stomped away from Edmond and went into the direction of the ladies room.

Many speakers had important information to pass on. There were town mayors who talked about their towns and communities. One Mayor asked why the northern areas were not punished for their interference in adding to the waterways that caused the southern states to be wiped out by flooding? He went on to say that the high-grounds were known to be in the middle of a drought year while the river towns would have thousands of acres of flooding. He explained that this was due to no control up north. Too many waterways dumping into the river, causing flooding to the towns and farm ground on the lower-ground.

One government official stood at the podium and stated that floods killed people. That was countered by a lady standing up and asking how can anyone justify the very minimal number of deaths that occur due to flooding compared to all the things killing people in our country today. She listed many facts to back her question. Her opponent didn't counter. Instead, he sat down and was silent.

One by one, people spoke. Most blamed flooding on the rerouting of waterways by many states throughout the United States. Lilly was shocked at several things she learned at the luncheon. Like how apparently there are thirty-one states and two Canadian provinces rerouted their waterways to dump into the river. It was one thing if it was a natural flow but to reroute the water to stop flooding in one's area yet cause flooding to the lower areas was just not right.

Lilly was standing next to Tripp as they listened to a store owner speak about the importance of keeping their town alive. The gentleman's name was Louis and looked to be in his early forties. Louis owned a hardware store about one hundred miles south of Prairie du Rocher. The town was almost three hundred years old and his family was one of the founding families. He explained that his town, Creed, was in 'Small Town, USA,' His business was in demand and needed in the town.

He went on to explain that if he was forced to move out, the closest hardware business was over sixty miles away. He stated that buying him out was only a temporary fix because a man his age wouldn't be able to find work that paid any decent wages. He went on about how there were hundreds of thousands of residents and businesses that would be affected by trying to kick everyone out. He felt the solution was to reroute the waterways. He went on and on about the different ways it was possible.

Louis ended his speech with one final thought that Lilly thought was very clever. "Are you going to sit there and tell me that there isn't a way?" He looked intently at Edmond Brader. Lilly wondered if that was a coincidence or if the gentleman knew Edmond was against them. Lilly looked back at Louis as he continued in a strong, almost angry voice. "In 1817 when this country was raw and there weren't any tools or technology like there are today…the Erie Canal was built. Think about how the waterways were shifted and re-routed then."

He looked around the room. "Now let's go up the river a little bit from where we sit today. I know a few of you are here from St. Louis and you also are worried about your livelihood because you are next to the river." His eyes met Edmond's again. "In 1868 a man by the name of Andrew Carnegie did what everyone believed impossible. He built the first massive steel bridge to cross over any impossible waterway." He looked around at the faces in the room. "This bridge is still being utilized today. It's the Eads Bridge and it was the first to bring our two states together." He paused. "Now think about life back then and how an impossible situation became a possible solution."

He shuffled through his papers for a second before continuing. "There are over six-hundred thousand people affected by the flooding in this area. And it seems to me you can't take from one what you can't take from all. If there's a problem that's not getting fixed correctly and you are only putting a band-aid on it then in the end the entire country is affected. So how in the hell is our government able to buy all these people out? I would guess the taxpayers are paying for it. Seems like a hell of a lot of money…this is all just my opinion. Maybe we should do what we did a few years ago and print more money and make the US dollar not worth a damn thing."

He started to turn to exit, then stopped and turned back to the microphone. "Seems to me we all live to preserve our livelihood for the next generation. And shoving people out of their homes without fixing the problem isn't preserving anything. With the population growing as fast as it is and shoving people together is a disaster waiting to happen. Look at the coronavirus a few years ago…the hardest hit were the overly populated urban areas. Remember the social distancing they put in order? That's because people should have room to breathe and not be shoved together like a bunch of cattle on stock market day. I believe people trying to kick people out of their homes is just a selfish fix for the ones who are doing the booting and later that night those crooked bastards have their own nice, warm, open space mansions to go home to."

Lilly smiled as he walked off the stage not waiting to see if anyone wanted to ask him any questions. For the next hour she listened to the many ideas people had. Every once in a while someone spoke against moving forward with controlling the flood waters. There were so many good ideas presented and Lilly hoped they would figure out a way to join forces and unite on a solution for the flooding and levees.

When the prearranged list of speakers came to a close and the floor was open for anyone wishing to address the crowd, Lilly cringed as Edmond walked up and took the stage. He introduced himself and many in the crowd started mumbling softly to their neighbors. Lilly looked around the hall and noticed many upset faces. Apparently she wasn't the only one who had a dislike for the man.

Edmond's voice was loud and strong. "I work for Advance Ground Engineering. We are a branch hired by the federal government to oversee and decide the maintenance of the Mississippi Levee District. I understand many of you do not wish to leave your homes. If I was in your position, I would feel the same way. Yet you need to start thinking about your children and grandchildren. How this continuous flooding will be nothing but a nuisance to them. The stress and worry every time the water rises and having to move out of their houses. There are spots along the river that could be a danger to residents if the levee breaks. How would each and every one of you feel if you were responsible?"

Lilly wanted to go on the stage and slap him. His cocky way of trying to put guilt on the residents was sickening. As she listened to him going on and on about how much better their lives would be if they relocated to a higher ground she was shocked by how heartless he was. He acted like it was nothing for these people to give up their home…their roots. She wondered if he liked the control of putting fear in these people.

When he was finished speaking a gentleman in the back stood up and stated, "Shoving people out of their homes isn't the answer. Just like Louis stated there's a problem that needs to be fixed. This is 2023, there should be a solution. Either way it will cost the people tax money so we need to do it right."

Lilly could see Edmond getting angry by the way he was clenching the podium. "I can assure you the small towns along the river that have resettled to higher grounds are most happy with their decision."

Lilly looked into the room and watched as a middle-aged woman stood. "Excuse me, my name is Dawn Walken and I have to disagree with you. I am a resident of New Valmeyertown. I was a resident of the original Valmeyertown and my house was submerged in water in the flood of 93." She took a deep breath and was wringing her fingers. Lilly wanted to hug the sweet lady and tell her it was going to be okay. "We didn't want to leave. The government took advantage of our vulnerable state and made it seem like our new location would have the same atmosphere as our old town."

Dawn's voice started to raise in anger. "We moved up into a glorified subdivision. We sit on top of each other and most of us do not know who our neighbors are because so many young families move to the area because the value is cheap. The scenery is pitiful and we no longer have our beautiful sunsets." She turned and looked at Edmond and pointed her finger at him. "And let me tell you mister, almost all of us wish we had never moved away from our homes." With that she sat down.

Edmond explained that he wasn't around during that time so he did not have many facts of the town relocating. Another man stood up and said, "Well you were around when Roots almost went under water and what did you do? You damn near threatened the people to get out or they were going to be forced to and receive a severely under market value for their homes and lands."

"Sir, I believe you have me mistaken for someone else." Edmond tried to move on but the man wasn't going to allow that to happen.

"Bullshit because I was one of the people. I know you know who I am so don't act all innocent." He looked around at the crowd. "Trust me, if we don't do something he will take away everything. He cannot be trusted."

Edmond lifted an eyebrow and looked at the man. "Sir, that is defamation of character. I would hate to have a serious problem."

Just then Jasper walked up to stand next to Edmond and spoke loud enough for the entire room to hear him without a microphone. "It cannot be defamation of character if what he says is true. Were you involved with this gentleman in the town of Roots four years ago?"

Edmond glared at Jasper before walking off the stage. As he passed Tripp he sent him a glare and then smiled an eerie smile at Lilly as he passed her and

215

made his exit through the stage door. Lilly looked up to see Tripp smiling. She turned to look into the crowd and see Louis stand up and start clapping. Almost everyone in the room followed suit.

It took several minutes for the crowd to calm down. Tripp took the microphone and spoke to the crowd. "Friends, I have met and talked to each one of you personally and have gotten to know you all. I invited Brader to the meeting because I didn't want anyone thinking we are sneaking around and trying to do things behind their backs. I find that being up front works the best in the end."

He looked over at a few men who thought it would be better to move everyone out of the flood plain. "Not everyone is in agreement about what we should do. And it takes all sides to see every angle to come to a solution for the problem. PORT is for all of you to join and try to come up with a plan that is as solid as the steel used in the Eads Bridge. Then when we have a solution we give it to these officials." He indicated to the government officials sitting at a table along the wall. "These men aren't necessarily against us but we have to prove to them that what we think will work…works."

Hours later there was a party going on at Lisa's. Tripp, Jasper, and Sawyer were celebrating their success at the meeting. They had over one hundred new members that signed up at the meeting and committed to helping PORT move forward. Everyone who signed with the group stayed behind after the meeting and Tripp outlined how they were going to move forward.

Every town was assigned to an area within fifty miles of where they lived or worked from. Each area was called an Area Group and had a number assigned to it. This helped organize each area. Every Area Group already had a Group Leader who Tripp predesignated before the meeting took place. It had apparently taken him over two years to meet with people in all the River Towns along the Mississippi and find the perfect person to put in charge.

Each Area Group would work together in their general area to submit where their flooding problems were and what they thought would be the best solution to the flooding problem in their area. The geography in every area was different, so Tripp felt there could be a different solution to each different area. Each Area Group would also recruit people in their communities to join PORT. These people would be placed in a specialized branch of their Area Group. Some could work on advertisement and social media. Others would do fundraising. Lilly's favorite was Area Group Media. When all areas were submitted on what they believed their fix to the problem was, Sawyer would come in and see if there was a geological solution that could put all the puzzle pieces together and see if they couldn't somehow fit together. She was impressed by all the work Tripp did for PORT.

Chapter Nineteen

Lilly looked around Lisa's bar at all her new friends and couldn't believe she has only known everyone for less than six months. Zeke and Rissa were slow dancing to the jukebox while Diane and Cooper were playing pool in the far corner. Jasper was flirting with the bartender Bethany. Her favorite part of the night was her 'Rocher Girls' were trying to teach a drunken Tripp and Sawyer how to play Euchre…and not very well she might add.

Lily looked up at the digital beer logo clock above Tripp's head and was shocked it was 12:04 am. She knew Moose probably needed to relieve himself, but she didn't want anyone to leave their good time. She quietly walked out the front door and sent a text to Tripp saying she was going to walk to the house real quick and let Moose out. She would be back ASAP.

The walk wasn't far and she took her time because the night was a little chili but yet beautiful for early April. Lilly looked around as she made her way down her street. It was crazy how pretty the Bienvenue house looked in the shining moon's light. Lilly was just bummed because the Magnolia needed a good tree trimming.

This suddenly confused her because Wolfe had just trimmed it. As she stepped on the porch, she realized her grandfather's study light was on. That worried her because she knew she never left that light on when she went out. She noticed a small movement inside and her first instinct was she was being robbed. She stood to the side of the open window and peeked inside. To her shock there were two women inside having a conversation over tea. She didn't know what to make of it. It was like they were making themselves at home.

Lilly didn't know what to do. She decided she needed to find the town cop and have him get to the bottom of this. Yet as she turned, she noticed her laptop was no longer sitting on the desk. In its place was a vintage typewriter. Next to the typewriter was a tiffany lamp. She looked all around the room and noticed a flowered sofa and a large trunk in the corner. Nothing like the room she was in earlier in the day.

Lilly was at first shocked and she wondered where Moose was? She prayed he wasn't hurt. Looking in the window once again she wondered if she knew these people?

It suddenly dawned on her…she was dreaming one of her crazy dreams of the past. She smiled and relished in the dream. She enjoyed going back, yet wasn't quite sure what time period she was in and who the two women were having tea in her grandfather's study. Lilly stood back to not be noticed but close enough to hear what the women were saying.

"Well Cheri, I agree, your mother-in-law needs to respect you and your decisions." This came from an attractive lady who looked to be in her late thirties. Her hair was blonde and cut to the shoulders and flipped up at the ends. Her dress landed right at the knees and was boxy. Lilly wasn't sure but she thought she may be in the early sixties timeframe.

The lady, who Lilly presumed to be Cheri, replied. "I just am tired of being pushed around and told what to do. That woman is not my mother."

Lilly had to smile as she looked at the women. They must go to the same stylist because their hair was the same style, only Cheri's seemed to be a little darker. Yet Lilly wasn't sure because she was looking at each of the women's profiles.

"Mine tried that. She even tries to tell me the correct way to raise Franklin. Well, I tend to do the opposite." She snorted before taking a sip of tea.

Oh my, Lilly thought, this was her great-grandmother and Franklin was her grandfather Frank.

"Same here Helen. I told Dean I was done with listening to her and if she didn't stop I wasn't going to allow Butch over to her house anymore." Cheri stated in a stern voice.

Lilly watched from the dark porch as Helen got up from her chair and walked over to grab a book from the shelf. "I have one better." She pulled out a book and walked back to sit down with it placed on her lap.

Cheri gave her a confused look. "The Taming of the Shrew." She chuckled. "Yes, that would describe your mother-in-law but I'm not sure how that book will help you?"

Helen smiled as she opened the book. "I chose this book for many reasons. First the title was appropriate and second no one in the family would ever have the desire to read it." Lilly almost gasped when Helen reached into the open book and pulled out the gold bangle bracelet. Apparently, she hollowed out the pages on the inside so she could use it as a hiding place.

"Oh my." Said Cheri. "Wherever did that come from?"

"I received it when Ellen was born. It comes from a long line of Bienvenue aunts. My mother-in-law mentioned it to me when I was pregnant. It would seem that if a female was born in the family and was named Lilly, the bracelet would automatically go to her. Well Laurence and I were the only remaining family to carry on the name and the only one able to have any more children. But I guess Aunt Lillian was hesitant to give me the bracelet because I don't think she liked me much."

Cheri leaned forward to get a better look. "So how did you get it?" she asked.

Helen smiled. "I gave Ellen the middle name Lillian."

Cheri chuckled. "Clever." She stated.

"I know. But since Ellen passed as an infant the bracelet should go to Franklin. Yet I don't see any need for Franklin to have it. The way he's been pining away for that Miller girl is ridiculous."

"Ashley?" Cheri asked and Helen nodded. "I had no idea. I mean I thought she was with that Badger fellow?"

"She is, but I think she's just trying to make Franklin jealous." She huffed. "Tramp."

The two women gossiped for a few more minutes before Cheri placed her tea back on the table and stood up stating it was after one in the morning and she was needing to go to bed because Sunday mass was going to come early. Lilly didn't want to be caught so she hid around the corner of the house and watched as the other woman walked down the road to her house.

Lilly knew what she had to do. She waited for what seemed like forever to give Helen time to go up the steps and into her bed. Plus, about another half an hour to go to sleep. She knew the front door wasn't locked because her grandfather used to talk about how there wasn't much crime in Prairie du Rocher and they never locked their doors. She wasted no time walking into the front door and heading left through the study door.

Lilly was glad she had her phone with her because she used the light to see her way around the study. She was tempted to take a pic but didn't want the flash to alert anyone. Plus, she didn't want to take any chances on altering the course of history.

It took her several minutes to find 'The Taming of the Shrew' book her grandmother replaced in the line of books on the bookshelf. Lilly grabbed the bracelet and stuck it in her pocket. She went on to find the book 'The Clock That Spun Backwards' just as her grandfather requested.

After finding the book she quickly walked over to the desk and started looking for something to write with. Lilly froze when she heard someone coming down the steps. She quietly wedged her way between the desk and the wall hoping to not be found. She could hear a man grumbling in the kitchen and what sounded like water running and pills shaking in a bottle.

It was several minutes before she heard the retreating steps going up the stairs. Lilly let out a quiet breath and waited several minutes before going to the desk and finding a pen and paper.

Grandfather, it is I Lilly. Today is…

Lilly looked around the desk and found an ancient digital clock that said it was one 1:43 in the morning. She shined her light quickly around the room and spotted a calendar with the days marked off hanging on the wall next to the desk. Even though Saturday, 4 April 1970, wasn't marked off, Lilly knew it was early the next day, Sunday morning the fifth, because Cheri had mentioned Sunday mass.

5 April 1970 (5 April 2023 my time!) You were correct! Your mother was wanting to melt down the bracelet and it was hidden in the book. I found the bracelet and I am going to plant it under the Magnolia. You are right on so many levels. I have been time traveling and I haven't come up with any answers as to why this is happening. By the way my old friend Tripp…he's Daniel. One last thing, the first Daniel found gold in the bluffs. I believe that's why Edwin Berger murdered him…that and he wanted Lilly.

I Love you so much and Miss You Every day! Love, Your Lilly-Bear.

Lilly put the paper between pages sixty-nine and seventy just like he asked and returned the book to the shelf. She knew she had to hurry because as she was writing down the date, she remembered she needed to go and help save her grandmother.

Lilly quickly left the house and kneeled down in front of the Magnolia Tree. There weren't any surfacing roots so she had to guess where to bury it. Which wasn't an easy task because it was very dark outside. Once she felt it was good enough, she jumped up and dusted her knees before taking off. She ran through the dark streets wishing the moon was a little brighter so it would shed more light on the roads.

Everything was so different than in her time. She was panting as she made it to the corner of the Creole House. Climbing the fence, she hid behind the old building. She had a great view of Lisa's which wasn't Lisa's yet. It was a rough looking two-story brick building. It lacked the charm Lisa's had.

She also had a great view of the Brickley Mansion. *Wow,* she thought, *it's beautiful but so run down.* She decided her best course of action was to sneak through the yard and hide by the mansion to make sure Badger takes her grandma there before getting her grandfather involved.

She snuck around the old out buildings and across the dark yard. She turned her run into a jog because she almost fell on her face twice. She finally made it to the mansion and took her time looking inside each window but couldn't see anything because it was just too dark. She decided to take that time and find the secret exit that was supposed to lead her grandparents to safety.

She came to the conclusion it had to be the balcony on the side of the mansion because that was the only one that didn't have a window, only a door, so she was sure it was a hallway and isn't that what her grandfather wrote…a hallway? Darn, she couldn't be sure.

Next she looked around for their means of escape. If they exit the balcony, there weren't any stairs that led to the ground. She looked all around the house and when she came up with nothing she flashed her camera light quickly into the door of the summer kitchen that was a couple yards away from the mansion. It took her a couple seconds but her eyes landed on a ladder laying amongst the debris.

To her dismay the door was locked. "Figures, every damn lock in this town is unlocked except for this one." She mumbled. Lilly looked around and found an old board and broke the glass on the door window. She looked around to make sure no one heard her.

She reached in and after several minutes and the thought of giving up, she unlocked the door. It wasn't like it was a modern lock so how in the hell was she to know how to unlock it. Eventually the flipping of the lever gave way and she tried the doorknob and it opened the door.

Lilly froze as she heard voices. She ducked down and scooted on bent legs over to the side of the small house to look in the direction of the mansion. She started to panic. There was her very young grandmother and who she assumed was Badger, walking towards the side entrance of the mansion.

Lilly held her breath as she heard her grandmother ask, "Are you sure the others are coming?" She looked back towards the front of the tavern.

"Yes Ashley, they are coming soon." His voice sounded so much like Edmond Brader's voice, Lilly had chills go up her spine.

Lilly watched as the couple went inside and a few seconds later a lantern was lit. Damn, she thought, that was the lantern the bastard starts the fire with. As much as she would like to stop the flames from destroying the house, she knew not to mess with history any more than she already was…or was she? Isn't all of this supposed to have already happened?

Deciding not to dwell on it, Lilly quietly made her way into the abandoned summer house and as silent as one could be, she dragged the tall ladder out and around to the side of the mansion below the exit door she was supposed to lead her grandparents through. She was just grateful the door was facing the bluffs so no one could look over and see her. After placing the ladder against the balcony, she looked in the window of the lower level. She could hear Badger walking her grandmother through the house and describing how each room was put to use while holding another lantern. She could see the other lantern sitting on a small table by the front door.

Lilly did get to see a glimpse of the house but wasn't really looking. She was in awe, staring at her beautiful grandmother. She looked young and flawless. No wonder her grandfather was jealous she was with Badger.

As Badger started backing her grandmother up the steps Lilly panicked. Her grandmother was trying to push past him to get down the steps but he wasn't letting her. The last thing she saw was Badger forcefully shoving her grandmother as they disappeared up the steps.

Lilly took no time to step into action. She ran across the yard and through the half-opened iron gate. She spotted her grandfather, a very young version of her grandfather, exactly where he said he would be in front of the tavern.

She approached him and grabbed his arm and said, "Grandpa, you have to save Grandma? He's got her in the house and he's going to hurt her." Her grandfather looked at her like, *who in the hell are you?* Lilly tried to remember what she said to get him to listen to her.

"Pardon me?" He asked and she rolled her eyes.

Lilly pointed in the direction of the mansion and shouted, "Badger…is hurting Grandma Ashley." When he still didn't move, she pushed him and said, "Go to Ashley!" She yelled as she pointed to Brickley Mansion.

That was all it took. Lilly watched him shoot off and cross the street and leaped over the wrought iron fence. "Damn," She whispered, "Grandpa has got it going on."

No time to waste, Lilly followed her grandfather, only she went via the fence gate. She hustled through the yard and climbed the ladder to the upper balcony. She tried the door, to be prepared to lead the way when the time came, only the damn door was locked, also. She rolled her eyes and thought, 'you've got to be freaking kidding me.'

Lilly's anxiety level was reaching its maximum level. It only worsened when she heard her grandmother scream and then two men fighting. She was in severe panic mode a few minutes later when she saw the reflection of dancing light coming from the lower level. She knew Badger threw the burning oil on the bottom part of the stairs. She raised her eyes heavenward and silently asked God to help her.

Lilly was shocked when the door suddenly gave way. She looked up and thanked God for his help as she opened the door and stepped inside. The pressure from the door caused the flames to jump up the stairwell in her direction.

Standing there in front of her was her grandfather holding her grandmother wrapped in an old quilt with her face buried in his chest. She motioned for him to follow her as she stepped back to the balcony. She quickly exited the ladder and watched as he set her grandmother down on the balcony and pointed towards the ladder. Ashley quickly climbed down and Frank followed. Frank paused to look around for Lilly but she was already rushing towards the tavern. He picked up Ashley and went in the opposite direction to hide under the bluffs.

Lilly sat down on the front bench in front of the tavern and closed her eyes and panted for several minutes. She could not believe how she spent the last several hours. She was shocked and amazed that her grandfather's prediction or premonition came true.

As she opened her eyes, she noticed the lights in the tavern were on. She could hear noise inside so she stood on the bench and turned towards the big window behind her to look inside. She was a little amazed and very relieved. There inside were the friends she left hours ago. She wondered how long she had been gone? She had her answer when she looked above Tripp's head and read the time on the digital clock…12:05 am. She looked over at Tripp as he looked at his phone and then up at the picture window she was looking through. He spotted her looking inside and held up his index finger asking her to wait for him.

He said his goodbyes to everyone and walked out the front door and took her hand. "I'll go with you to let Moose out."

The following morning Lilly found herself making breakfast for three hungover men. They had no idea they were getting such a treat because they were still dead to the world. She decided to make everyone breakfast and texted all her local friends.

She was humming away as she scrambled the eggs. She was overjoyed by what she experienced only hours ago. Saving her grandmother and seeing her grandfather was incredible. Then with her adrenaline up, she capped her night off with a fun, semi-drunk Tripp in her bed. He was actually a fun lover when he was intoxicated.

Yep, she actually helped her grandfather save her grandmother and that put her on such a high. She almost thought it was a dream this morning until she looked at her discarded jeans in the hamper that she had worn the evening before. The knees were covered in dirt. Who would have thought dirty jeans could make a person so happy? That and her clothes smelled like smoke…only confirming she was at the Brickley Mansion while it was on fire.

She still had about thirty minutes before her friends arrived and instead of waking the sleeping bears upstairs, she walked into the study. She was too anxious to wait any longer. She walked over to the bookshelf and found the 'The Clock That Spun Backwards' book. She opened it to page seventy and to her delight there was a slip of paper. She knew in an instant it wasn't her letter to her grandfather and she knew it hadn't been there months ago because she checked after reading her grandfather's letter.

She sat on the sofa before reading it. First she noticed the date and realized he received the letter the last April 5th he spent in the house.

5 April 2022, 7:45 am

Oh My Sweet Lilly-Bear,

You cannot know how excited I was to see your letter. It would seem we are onto something. I cannot believe it has been fifty-two years since your grandmother and I found each other. I was excited to read that the young gentleman that practically lived at our house for that one week, so many summers ago, is your Daniel.

I have to tell you my thoughts…something is causing the Daniels to die, at an early age, if the headstones are correct. I believe he has a repeated murderer and you need to stop him before he murders your Daniel, July 4th, 2023.

I feel like it is a love triangle of some sort. Or if your message is accurate, it's death over greed. You need to find out because I feel it will continue to repeat itself until the murderer is disposed of before your Daniel is. I believe this because Liliane Maria talks about a native saying this. And the natives always have a special insight.

I Love You my sweet girl and know I have always believed in you and know you have strength to see this through. Keep God close to your heart because I think there is evil lurking your way.

Love, Grandfather

Lilly let a few tears fall as she folded the letter and placed it inside the safe. She didn't want to put it back in the book because she was afraid it would somehow disappear. Plus if she went back and wanted to send a letter again then this one shouldn't be in the book.

She pulled her phone out of her back pocket and walked over to her grandfather's journal and opened it. She flipped through papers and looked at her phone to see if anything was different. There was a new page added since she took a picture of his journal months ago. It was the slip of paper she left for him hours ago. With shaking hands she ran her fingers over it as more tears gathered in her eyes.

She nearly jumped out of her skin as Tripp came up and hugged her from behind. He chuckled and nuzzled her neck. "Sorry baby, I didn't mean to scare you."

She smiled and turned around and hugged him. They stood that way for a while before he pulled back and noticed the tears in her eyes. He ran his finger over one that fell onto her cheek. "Are you okay?" He whispered.

She nodded and pulled him back in for another hug. When she finally pulled back, she broke the contact and sat on the edge of the desktop. "So guess what."

"What?" He replied before sitting at the desk chair and leaning forward to pull her to him and wrapping his arm around her waist to pull her forward. He rested the side of his face on her waist, as she stood between his legs. His hands ran seductively up and down the tight leggings that covered her thighs.

She ran her fingers through his soft hair and smiled. "I had another moment."

"Really…another dream?" He was distracting her and making it hard for her to think.

"No, this one happened outside of Lisa's last night." She knew that would grab his attention.

Tripp sat back and looked up at her. "Where was I?"

Lilly took the next ten minutes explaining to him about her adventures last evening. Tripp was fascinated. "So you're saying it was like time stood still?" At her nod he continued. "I'm not doubting you but how do you know you didn't just dream it?"

"I wondered that also but this morning I noticed the dirt on the knees of the jeans I wore last night. It was from when I was burying the bracelet. And they still smell like smoke from the fire." She stood up and walked over to the book shelf. She pulled out both books involved. He chuckled at the hollowed-out book because he heard people did that but had never seen one.

Lilly walked over to the unlocked safe and pulled out the letter her grandfather left her. He read it and was a bit taken back. He believed everything she had told him from the beginning and he knew there was something beyond them that brought them together. Yet, he had to admit it still shocked him every time he heard something. He did smile at her though and said, "So your grandpa approved of me…yes!" He stated, with a silly arm gesture.

Lilly smiled and continued, "I was just looking through Grandfather's journal when you walked in." She picked up the slip of paper lying inside the book and handed it to him. "This is what I wrote to him hours ago…look at the date."

Tripp did as she asked. "Damn." He looked up at her. "This is crazy-shit."

"I know." She said with frustration.

"Now what?" He asked as he pulled her onto his lap and started kissing the side of her neck.

She had a hard time concentrating when he did things like that.

He whispered in her eye softly. "Do you know what I want?"

She smiled as his mouth came back down her neck and kissed her behind the ear. "I think it's obvious." She replied in a raspy voice.

He whispered in her ear again, sending tingles up and down her spine. "I want…" he used the tip of his tongue to softly lick her earlobe. "Breakfast."

"What?" She laughed and pulled back, slapping his shoulder.

"Come on. I've been smelling bacon since I came down stairs." He ducked as she laughed and threw a sofa pillow at him. "What did you think I wanted?" He laughed as he pulled her through the door into the kitchen.

Chapter Twenty

April showers did bring May flowers to Prairie du Rocher. It also brought another number to tally to her age. Her friends surprised her with a birthday party at Lisa's. Her parents and siblings even made it into town. She decided twenty-seven was going to be a great year for her.

Lilly loved that the days were turning longer and the spring colors were everywhere. With the nice days, Moose wanted longer morning and evening walks. Lucky for him Lilly was happy to oblige.

As the evenings started getting warmer, she kept the walks to early morning or later in the evenings because Moose's heavy coat contributed to him getting hot fast. Sometimes Rissa joined her on her walks but lately she was busy because she and Zeke were flipping a large house that had much work to be done to it. So it's been pretty much just her and Moose unless it was a weekend and Tripp was home.

She chuckled, thinking about Tripp and home and how it just sounded great together. She was crazy in love with him and couldn't wait until they said the words to each other. Considering it has only been a little over five months since they started seeing each other she wondered if it was too soon to say those three little words?

Lilly had to admit she was in such a happy place, with her life…at this moment. She was sure if anyone looked out their window and watched her walk by, they'd think something was wrong with her the way she kept smiling to herself. Yet, she didn't care because the night was beautiful and she was in love. Lilly made her way towards Lisa's. As she crossed the side street, she was happy to run into Tania's nieces. The girls were thirteen and named Dusti and Kylie. These two may be twins yet they were as different as night and day, in looks and personality. They jumped up from the bench in front of Lisa's as she approached and rushed over to pet Moose. Lilly smiled because he was loving it as much as they were.

"Lilly, can I take Moose for a walk?" Asked Kylie.

Dusti nudged her. "I wanted to take him." She glared.

Before the girls could get into a big spat Lilly came up with a compromise. The deal was one would get to hold the leash while the other walked along. Then once ten minutes passed, they would switch and walk the same path back. The girls were fine with the plan. Lilly rolled her eyes as she watched Kylie set a timer on her phone as Dusti took the leash.

Lilly sat down on the bench and laid her head against the bottom of the window sill before closing her eyes. This was the exact place she sat when she helped her grandfather save her grandmother. She was pretty bummed out because nothing much had happened since. She guessed everything was going to come to a head on the Fourth of July.

Which is why she and Tripp were planning to spend it in Champaign. She didn't need to see any Phantom Funerals. If truth be told she was thinking if nothing happens to Tripp on that night then maybe the curse would go away. She came to this conclusion because she read everything she could find on the funeral procession.

Before she let herself nod off she opened her eyes to see Daniel walking towards her. Of course, Sleeping Wolf was right beside him. This made her smile because Sleeping Wolf stuck to Daniel like he was his protector. Lilly scooted over as Daniel sat next to her.

"Hello my fair Lilly." Daniel said in that deep baritone voice she loved so much. How he looked so much like Tripp. Wait…why was she confusing the two? Tripp comes into her life later. Yet, she smiles because now she knows they are one and the same person.

Lilly looked around a bit confused. Everything seemed different than a few minutes ago. She glanced behind her and looked at the large picture window that should have the words 'Lisa's Market Street Grille' splashed across it. It was the same window but the name 'Larry & Carol's Tavern and Theatre' was painted on the window instead. Looking in through the glass, she noticed some old looking fans with belts attached, making the fans spin. *Yep,* she thought, *definitely not Lisa's.*

Suddenly she knew where she was, she was with Daniel and they were getting ready to watch a film at the theatre upstairs. It was titled 'The Butcher Man' and she was excited because she rarely got to watch a picture film. Yet, now that she was engaged, her mother permitted it.

She smiled as she looked down at the beautiful ring Daniel gave her. It apparently has been passed down to him from the Geofrey side. The inside of the ring was inscribed *'From my Beloved Daniel.* Lilly chuckled, so did that mean only a Daniel in the family could pass the ring to a bride? She smiled and decided they would name their first-born son Daniel.

Her mother came from around the corner. "Hello gentleman." She smiled at Daniel and Sleeping Wolf. "Are you ready to go upstairs and view the film?" She asked in such a prim, yet sweet voice.

"Yes madam." Daniel stood and nodded his head to her.

"I'm still not sure why the theatre is open on a Tuesday night. I guess Larry figured most people were off tomorrow for the Freedom Holiday, so why not try to make a few extra bucks. You know how Larry is…always business." She looked around at several young people in line to go up the steps to the theatre that occupied the upper level of the tavern. The hour was almost 9:00 pm and the movie was to start as soon as the last bit of daylight left the little town. This was so the projector light would show up on the screen while in darkness.

She looked towards Lilly's hand. "Since you are officially engaged, I will permit you to attend the film without a chaperone." She gave Daniel a stern look. "Don't make me regret this decision, young man."

Lilly smiled. She must be dreaming again. She liked it when she dreamed of going to the past. She looked around and took everything in, from the gas street lamps to the horse and buggies going by Lisa's…or wait…Larry & Carol's Tavern.

"I won't madam." Daniel was nervous around Lilly's mother.

Lilly's mother turned to Sleeping Wolf. "Sleeping Wolf, I hope I can count on you to make sure Daniel stays a gentleman and doesn't take any liberties with my Lilly-Bear."

Sleeping Wolf smiled because he could see the slightest bit of humor in her eyes. "Yes, Madam. I will play chaperone." His speech was perfect English because he was raised as a local.

"Good enough." She turned to Lilly who stood and hugged her mother. Lilly took in her scent of roses. She loved her mother and was so glad she approved of Daniel.

"I will be home after the movie Mother. I don't wish to stay up too late because tomorrow is the Fourth of July celebrations and I want to be well rested."

"Very good dear." She smiled her goodbyes to the gentlemen and walked off towards the direction of Bienvenue House.

Lilly smiled as she watched her mother leave. Her mother, Morgan, acted a bit stern but she was the sweetest lady and very involved in the town. Lilly's father, Jules, was a town trustee and her mother was the voice behind him. Since society wouldn't acknowledge the intelligence of a woman, Jules took his wife's ideas and made them happen.

The perfect example was that the town had electricity that was allowed to be used only a few hours in the evening, to conserve it. It was because of her mother this became possible. It all started when Morgan and her friend took the Mountain Iron Railway to St. Louis for a bit of shopping one day.

Morgan was impressed with all the electric lights the city had. So over the course of the next six months she would inquire within the large city how the lighting worked. The men she spoke to didn't mind sharing their knowledge with the beautiful lady. Then one evening she presented Jules, on paper, how the town could benefit from this. It would be a one cylinder diesel engine with a cowhide belt.

Lilly's father had been impressed. He took it to the board and implied it was his idea and pushed for the new electric plant. The town bought the idea and when it was finished, to her mother's dismay, her father bragged to everyone how it had been his beautiful wife from the beginning. Many believed her Papa was telling a tale. Yet most people who knew Morgan Bienvenue believed it.

Looking around, Lilly just wished the lightning could be used for more than a few hours in the evening. It wasn't so bad this time of the year because the days were long and it didn't get dark until nine in the evening, so the lights would stay on until ten...even sometimes eleven. Yet in the wintertime the lights were shut down around sixish. But she knew she shouldn't complain because at least they had electricity.

Just as Lilly turned to ask the gentlemen if they were ready because the show was to start soon, she spotted Edgar Brimley and his cronies walking by in front of the trio. Lilly took a deep breath as she waited for the confrontation.

Edgar was the son of the town Marshall. He and his pals were the town bullies. The Marshall turned a blind eye on his son's deed. According to her mother, Edgar was privileged and undisciplined. Unfortunately for Lilly, he set his eyes on her. When she didn't reciprocate and directed her attention to Daniel Geofrey, Edgar went crazy.

The trio were almost always together. The red head, Woody…nicknamed after a red-headed woodpecker, was a disgusting fuzzy headed, rotten-teeth, severely under educated and overbearing guy who along with his uncleaned, unkept, greasy headed wife, Julia, liked to start disputes with everyone in the little town. They had a large brood of children, six in all, that they couldn't afford to keep fed and clothed without becoming a financial burden to their families. It was known to all the local businesses that the couple and their children would steal them blind if they weren't watched carefully.

Beans, the tall and lanky third person in the group was the quiet one. He's the one who looked shady and dangerous. He was the one Lilly didn't trust the most.

Yet it was Edgar who put the most fear in her. As he walked by the trio, he tipped his hat and smiled at her before looking at Daniel and Sleeping Wolf and nodded a greeting. Neither man replied. Lilly took a second to look at Daniel's face…she cringed at the anger she saw there.

Daniel had reason to despise Brimley. He has repeatedly tried to do everything he could to hurt their reputation around town. He started horrid rumors about Lilly that made her seem unclean. Thank goodness that everyone who knew Lilly, which was most of the town, didn't believe the horrid man.

Once he couldn't get anywhere with that, he and his buddies stole some tires from Mr. Conrad. They somehow got ahold of one of Daniel's Jaxson hats that had his name on the inside and left it at the crime scene. Unfortunately for the gang and fortunately for Daniel, Mr. Conrad and Daniel were together all evening playing cards the night the theft happened so the older gentleman knew it couldn't have been Daniel.

There was a witness that saw the gang at the scene. Yet a day after the witness was questioned by the Marshall the witness changed his story. Many folks in the town didn't need to know why the man changed his story, they knew he was threatened. Lilly just wanted to know how they had Daniel's hat in their possession?

After the couple had been dating over a year, she believed Edgar had finally let it go. What she didn't know was that Daniel confronted the man a few months ago as he had him by the throat and threatened him within a second of his life if he didn't stay the hell away from them. Edgar squirming and promising over and over that he would back off. Later Daniel explained to her that he had a nice chat with the man and he agreed to back off.

Lilly was glad she had Daniel as her champion. There had been a time she didn't think that was possible. Their actual courtship started when she was eighteen, yet she always knew she and Daniel would be together one day. Since the first time she laid eyes on him, at the age of twelve, she knew he would one day be hers. When she explained this to her mother, her mother was a bit taken back. Lilly never showed any interest in boys and this particular boy was four years her senior.

So she explained to Lilly, who in turn explained to Daniel, that they couldn't start dating until she was eighteen. This made Daniel laugh because the sixteen-year-old had no interest in the twelve-year-old. When he stated to her that she was just too young for him she politely told him one day he was going to chase her like a wild puppy.

Over the next six years she got his attention and kept it. Every time Daniel would start dating someone, Lilly was there to make it difficult for him. She pulled a few pranks to discourage any of the older girls from pursuing any type of relationships with her Daniel.

The worst, yet probably the best prank she pulled, was the time she heard he was taking Betsy Prune on a picnic the following day. Lilly prepared for the picnic as well by visiting Farmer Dean's pasture the day before.

That next day she hid behind Betsy's neighbor's house waiting for Daniel to pull up. After he arrived and was inside the house, she very quickly replaced the contents in his basket with some of Farmer Dean's cow dung.

Her plan worked perfectly. The couple was back within thirty minutes and Betsy was upset. As he tried to walk her up the driveway, she stopped him and stated she wasn't sure what kind of sick joke he was playing but she wanted no part of his antics. Daniel was at a loss for what to say because he had no idea how the dung came to be in the basket.

Her plan was solid…until a few days later he came to her house and confronted her in front of her parents. Apparently one of Betsy's neighbors spotted her switching the food and told the Prune family what they saw. So after Betsy forgave Daniel, he hightailed it over to Lilly's house in a rage. He was tired of her trying to sabotage his love life.

Ironically all the trouble that came from that day turned into her favor. Lilly was halfway into her sixteenth year and after seeing him so mad at her she decided he wasn't the one for her anymore. She stared at him blankly and gave him an apology and stating she was finished with him and he no longer had to worry about her intruding on his life before turning and walking from the room.

Truly for the next year she wouldn't acknowledge him anywhere. If he passed her on the street and tipped his hat at her, she would look straight ahead and ignore the gesture. At first it amused him. Eventually it started to annoy him because this was completely different from the girl that followed him everywhere and tried getting his attention.

Once he caught her mother's slight smile as Lilly gave him the cold shoulder as he was greeting the two of them outside of Conrad's grocer. He was put out and decided to play her game and treat her as she was treating him. That only worked until he saw her talking to another local boy…Cade Schmitz.

Lilly and Cade were sitting in front of the iron fence wall that bordered the Brickley Mansion and the Creole House. At first, he was surprised at how pretty she looked in her yellow dress and white bonnet with her hair pulled back. Then a new feeling surfaced as she smiled at the boy. Some unknown feeling of hurt and betrayal creeped over him. How dare she tap her fan on Cade's arm? She was being such an outrageous flirt. Did she not care that the entire town could see her making a fool of herself over the boy?

He knew he was being foolish. She wasn't doing anything inappropriate yet he didn't like it. She was supposed to only have eyes for him.

Over the next few months, Daniel started thinking about her all the time. He started making excuses to be at the same places she was. Like helping at the 'bobbing for apples' booth at the church social. Even as far as making an excuse to go into Conrad's Grocery after she got a job there serving the soda pops. She barely acknowledged him but he kept trying without seeming to try.

It took him several months to break her down and get her to talk to him again. It happened in the fall about a month before she was to turn eighteen. He spotted her raking leaves outside her house. He made a point to walk over and talk to her. She tried to ignore him but he wasn't having any of that.

Finally, she turned to him and propped up the rake and leaned on it. "Daniel Geofrey, what is it you want from me?" He was taken aback by the hurt and anger he heard in her voice.

He stared at her for several long moments before replying. "I want you to look at me…again, like you look at Cade Schmitz."

He wasn't sure how, but her face became angrier. She turned and started raking again. He rushed over and stood in front of her so she would stop and talk to him. "Lilly please?" He gave her pleading eyes.

Lilly didn't know what to think. One minute she had the plague and the next he was wanting her attention. She didn't trust him to not hurt her again. "Daniel, please leave. I'm not trying to be mean but I don't understand this game you are playing and I feel like it's way above me. So go and find Betsy and get married and raise some babies. I don't have time for this."

Just as she started to turn away, he grabbed her hand. "Lilly, I broke it off with Betsy months ago." He saw the surprise in her eyes. "It wasn't fair to her to let her think my feelings were with her when they were with someone else."

She looked at him long and hard. "What are you saying Daniel?"

He looked away and started stuttering a bit, but when he looked into her eyes, he knew the truth. "Lilly, I have been thinking about you for months. I've even been having crazy dreams of us together. I would like to ask your parents if I can have their permission to court you."

Lilly said nothing for several minutes. She was trying to keep her excitement in line. "Daniel, I turn eighteen in a month. If you are serious, then I think you need to prove to me in that time why I should allow myself to be in your presence."

He was confused. "What do you mean?"

She smiled at him. "You figure it out." With that she and her rake walked back to the house.

The next month brought more happiness to Lilly than she would have ever believed possible. Daniel treated her like a princess. He brought her flowers daily and they went on many walks. He planned romantic picnics and took her to all the town events that occurred.

Lilly smiled over the memory as she looked at Daniel and smiled. "Are you both ready?" She looked over at Sleeping Wolf, who yawned. She laughed because no other Native American has ever been named more accordingly. Sleeping Wolf was always tired.

Lilly loved Sleeping Wolf as much as the Geofrey family did…only they loved him longer. He was considered a son to Mr. Geofrey because Sleeping Wolf's father and Mr. Geofrey grew up together like brothers.

Sleeping Wolf's mother died bringing him into this world. Then at the age of seven his father died. The Geofrey family took the young Native-American in as one of their own. If anyone felt any prejudice towards the child they would be shredded over by most people of the community. Truly most people treated him as they did everyone else.

Daniel pulled her out of her thoughts as he took her by the elbow and led her up the steps into the theatre. Lilly pointed out where she wished to sit and Daniel led the way. They sat down on each side of her only Sleeping Wolf left a seat open in between them. She guessed to give them a bit of privacy in the dark theatre. Not that Daniel would try and take liberties with her but he did hold her hand throughout the show.

The movie began and Lilly became excited to hear the reel spinning in the room behind her. She quickly became absorbed in the black and white comedy. She had only been permitted to attend the theatre a few times and she took every bit of it in.

The movie was about a butcher wanting to court a store owner's daughter. Yet another worker wanted to court her as well. The movie was silent but everyone knew what was happening by how well they dramatized everything with their body language.

Lilly laughed as food was being scattered over the floor of the grocer and flour was flying everywhere. It amazed her that people could do these silly things and make it so people could watch it. Whoever invented and created anything to do with the picture show had to be a genius.

After the show was over, Sleeping Wolf made an excuse not to walk with the couple to Lilly's house. He knew they wanted a few minutes alone and they appreciated the gesture. Lilly felt like her life couldn't get any better as she walked down the street, hand in hand, with her true love.

The couple talked about their wedding day and how she was going to take the train into St. Louis in a few days and pick out her wedding gown. Daniel talked about the house he was wanting to show her on the other end of town. It was recently vacant and the bank had ownership.

Just as they started to turn onto Lilly's street, three guys with faces covered by burlap bags and holes cut out for eyes and mouth came up and pointed a gun into Daniel's back. One of the men grabbed her hair and had a knife blade to her neck. Lilly wanted to scream but she was too scared.

A masked face whispered to Daniel, "Walk fast or he'll slit her throat."

Daniel did as he asked because he believed the man would do as he said and he wasn't taking any chances that would hurt Lilly. He was trying to think of a way out of the situation. He knew Sleeping Wolf would be coming soon because they preplanned for Daniel to have a little alone time before the two would take the horse and buggy back home.

Lilly was scared as they walked down a back street with a knife pointed at her back. They crossed the tracks and made their way to a secluded spot on the other side. Lilly watched as one of the men held the gun next to Daniel's head while the other whipped out a large knife. She flinched as he took the knife and ran it down Daniel's neck, cutting the skin. She started to scream but felt pressure on her neck from the knife blade.

Daniel wasn't stupid. He knew once he was cut that they weren't going to let either one out alive. His only choice was to fight. "I know who you are, Brimley." He looked up at the man in front of him. "I could smell you before I saw you, Beans." He said right before he headbutted the back of his head to the front of Beans' forehead. Bean's threw his hand up, gun and all, towards his forehead causing it to shoot up in the air.

Just as Daniel swung his hand wide and slammed into Edgar's hand to dislodge the knife, Lilly stomped on her attacker's foot before shoving away from him. He dropped the knife but held her tight so as not to let her get away. She looked up to see Woody's face before he pulled the mask back down. Edgar's knifed hand jerked back and swung wide, lodging into Daniel's chest right next to his heart.

It seemed as if everything happened in slow motion for Lilly. She screamed as no other woman had ever screamed. She pulled away just as Sleeping Wolf jumped over the tracks and threw a knife that landed in Edgar's throat. Woody and Beans took off just as several local townsmen came running because they heard her scream and rushed to the sound.

Lilly slid next to Daniel and put her hands over his chest trying to stop the blood from pumping so fast. Yet it just kept running over her hands. She looked up at his sweet face and whispered, "I can't keep doing this."

Daniel looked at her and replied softly. "I know my love. I just do not understand why it cannot be." He closed his eyes and was gone.

Lilly kissed his lips and said a silent goodbye. She turned to see Sleeping Wolf beside her. He lifted her up just as the marshal came and shouted "What happened to my son?"

Sleeping Wolf turned and looked at him. "You gave your son freedom to hurt others. Now your son hurts others for the last time." He looked over at the enemy and watched him take his last breath. How he wished the devil would have died before his friend and broke the spell.

He turned Lilly into the direction of her house when the marshal tried to stop them. There were at least twenty men to intervene. Sleeping Wolf heard one say, "Marshall we've had enough of you and your family bullying our town…"

Sleeping Wolf didn't hear the rest because he was slowly walking Lilly to her home while she stared straight ahead. Neither said much until they rounded the corner that led to her house. Sleeping Wolf broke the silence. "Lilly, you have to stop this. It is because of this love that it keeps happening. You have to break the curse. Evil must die first."

Lilly suddenly remembered another native friend saying similar words to Denis, Daniel's brother of the past. Lilly wondered if it was because she loved Daniel that he kept dying? Maybe she was the reason. Maybe she is supposed to only know love but not have it.

She turned and looked at Sleeping Wolf. "Please take me to the theatre, I can't go home yet. I need to think."

"Lilly, I think you need to go to your parents." He stated.

Lilly looked at him. "We both know I am not her…so I must go back so she can grieve. Please take me back…" She gave him a lopsided teary grin. "Besides, I have to get my dog."

He looked at her oddly and nodded.

As they walked, they could hear all the commotion at the other end of town. They knew more people were finding out about the murder. "Sleeping Wolf, do me a favor?" As he nodded, she continued. "Encourage me in the coming weeks to marbleize the Geofrey headstones at the cemetery. They need to be remembered."

He nodded as they approached the bench in front of the tavern. Lilly sat down with exhaustion. She closed her eyes as if she was sleeping.

Chapter Twenty-One

Several minutes later she woke to Moose barking in the distance. She smiled and opened her eyes because she knew she was back home. She looked up and was surprised to see Wolfe standing in front of her leaning on a post. "Hi." She stated. She wondered if she was in the past. She looked around and didn't think so. Yet why was Wolfe in front of her and how come he reminded her of Sleeping Wolf? Their coloring and stance was similar…yet they really didn't look that much alike.

He smiled. "Hi, how was your nap?"

She gave him an odd look. "Nap?" She shook her head to clear her stupor.

"Looked to me you were pretty far away and by the tears that were rolling down your face, it wasn't a good dream?"

She patted under her eyes to collect any moisture before shaking her head because she was suddenly uncomfortable. "I don't remember." She needed to change the subject because she was suddenly awkward. "So what are you doing out here?"

He smiled and Lilly felt like she wasn't fooling him. "I noticed two little girls walking Moose and they explained how they each got a ten-minute turn." He chuckled.

She smiled back and more at ease. She liked Wolfe and believed he was a good guy. It was just that sometimes she would see him staring at her and she felt like he could see into her soul. "Yes, they even set a timer."

Just then the two girls and the big dog approached from around the corner. Lilly and Wolfe listened as they chatted on and on about all the adventures that had had with Moose in twenty minutes. Lilly thanked them for taking him for a walk and said her goodbyes.

She was surprised to see Wolfe following along. She looked over and said, "I'm good Wolfe, you don't have to see me home."

He shrugged. "Imagine how bad I would feel if something was to happen to you and I didn't walk you home when I could have?"

They chatted for several minutes before they arrived at her house. She looked over and Zeke and Rissa were sitting on their porch swing. "Hey guys." She waved as she and Wolfe walked over to chat. Moose trotted ahead of her and made his way over to greet Maverick.

Zeke was the first to speak. "So you found her…great. The bastard left about five minutes ago."

Lilly was confused and even more so when Wolfe replied. "She was sitting in front of Lisa's, waiting for two little girls who took Moose out for a walk. Good thing we left when we did or he would have seen her sitting there and who knows what."

"STOP!" Lilly practically shouted. "Stop talking like I'm not here."

Rissa smiled. "Sorry sweetie. We've been stressed. Wolfe stopped by for a chat and spotted your stalker down the road. When you didn't answer your calls, which by the way you need to take your phone with you more often, anyhow…I knocked on your door and when you didn't answer I used the code and went inside." She took a deep breath. "There was no Moose and no leash so I assumed you were on your walk. So Wolfe went to find you while we stalked the stalker."

"Wow." Lilly had to shake her head to process what her friend just said. She took a deep breath. "It was Edmond…correct?"

Rissa nodded. "Yes."

Lilly looked over at Wolfe. "Why didn't you tell me this instead of letting me be a jerk about you walking me home?"

He shrugged. "I didn't see the need."

Lilly shook her head and decided she just wanted to go home and go to bed. She was having a hard time dealing with people right now. She had a lot to think about with the entire Daniel dying thing. She had to sort through everything and see if she was the cause.

She picked up Moose's leash and thanked her friends for looking out for her. She made her way home and locked the house up before going to her bedroom. Once she hit the bed, she looked at her hands and remembered them trying to stop the blood…but couldn't. She didn't think she could watch Daniel die again. And yet in a few months the Fourth of July landed on a full moon. Lilly took a deep breath to try and stop the tears…but no such luck.

Two in the morning Lilly found herself unable to sleep. She knew what she had to do. She had to read about the third Lillian's life. Lillian Francis...her actual namesake. Turning on the lamp next to her bed, she left the room to head downstairs to collect the diary from the study before climbing back into bed.

Lillian's first entry wasn't until after the events of Daniel's passing. She stated she never really thought about the book because when she received it at the age of eighteen, she was too involved with her daydreams of being courted by Daniel to pay the book any attention. She began with a summary of her days growing up in the little town. She also wrote about her obsessive love for Daniel. Lilly chuckled because Lillian was a typical awkward twelve-year-old stalker. Next came stories of her flirtatious flirting with Cade Schmitz...who was a close second to Daniel in Lillian's opinion. Lilly wondered if her aunt wouldn't have been better off just sticking with Cade and not having the loss she was going to receive down the road?

Yet Lilly knew that didn't happen and Lillian confirmed it in the next chapter where she went on about their courtship and engagement. Lilly started crying when she read her aunt's idea of the perfect wedding gown.

The next entry was the night Lilly just lived hours ago. Lillian was descriptive in detail and Lilly felt like she was going to be sick. It took her some time to compose herself and read on. The only reason Lilly was putting herself through this was because she wanted to find out the ending.

Her aunt didn't disappoint her as she went on to say Marshall Brimley and the rest of his family were removed from the town. Woody and Beans went to a federal prison and Woody's wife still blabbed around town how her husband was innocent. It was so bad that people rudely ignored her on the streets. Eventually she moved out of town with her brood.

Sleeping Wolf had a hard time with his friend's death and became somewhat of a recluse. That's what everyone thought because no one ever saw him again. Lillian just hoped he moved away and met a nice woman and got married and had a dozen kids.

Lillian couldn't attend the funeral because she didn't want to remember her Daniel laying in a coffin. It was bad enough that she had to remember him dying in her arms. She took to her rooms and didn't come out of her mourning for months. It was actually Sleeping Wolf who pushed her into the first step of healing by coming to see her before he left town. He made her understand that

Daniel would be devastated to see her that way and that she had a job to do...take care of the plots and get the best memorial money could buy.

It was actually the journal that made her move on. By reading it she realized there was a curse and that was why she encouraged a niece to be named after her...to break the curse. The problem was she could tell no one because she didn't wish to be placed in an asylum.

So she wrote her story and sent the ring back to the Geofrey family. She eventually left the area and went into the medical field and became a nurse during World War Two. She never married and was quite content.

Lilly finished the diary and was suddenly sad. The last entry from her aunt was a summary of her life and all the great things she did and loved. She wrote about how her heart still belonged to Daniel. Lilly was overcome with emotions. She felt like maybe it's some kind of forbidden love and they aren't meant to be.

One thing was sure, she couldn't have Daniel die in her arms again. She...herself would need to be committed to an asylum if she went through that again. She buried her head into her pillow and cried herself back to sleep.

The first weekend in June was a Prairie du Rocher village holiday. It was the summer Rendezvous at Fort de Chartres. This was the fort and town's biggest celebration of the year. Lilly was excited to visit the fort during the event. She hadn't been to a reenactment since that summer she met Tripp.

Rendezvous was also Lisa's biggest celebration of the year. She had dinner and drink specials all weekend long and great local bands to perform every night. The town hosted a parade on Saturday evening. It was like Rendezvous kicked off summer for many people.

Lilly and Tripp went to the fort celebrations with Rissa and Zeke on Sunday. They loved all the reenactments and the French Troops marching around. The cannons shooting their loud noises startled Lilly, at first, but she got used to it. She loved all the teepees and white canvas tents that were set up by people trying to sell their wares. This festival was so much bigger than the fall one she and Rissa attended right after she came back to town.

She explained to the men she and Rissa were going to do some shopping. The guys were in line to grab a jug of 'Old Fashion Root Beer' so they waved them off. Lilly needed space from Tripp and this gave her an excuse to breathe.

The poor guy didn't know what to think. She was hurting him and couldn't help it. For the last few weeks, ever since the third Lilly's story, Lilly knew she needed to pull completely away from Tripp. She was sure there was a curse on them if they stayed together and he would die. She thought it over for hours and knew she couldn't just break it off until after the Fourth of July because it would just happen on the next Fourth of July that landed on or close to a full moon. The problem was she was having a hard time letting him go and was also giving him mixed signals.

The dream happened a month ago and she discouraged him from coming down two of the four weekends. He knew something was up…he just wasn't sure what it was. She wanted to confide in Rissa but she also didn't want to put her in the middle of it. She just didn't know how to let him go.

Lilly and Rissa were shopping at one of the teepees that had some great fashion vintage trinkets for sale. Lilly looked up to show Rissa some cute earrings just as something made her look over two teepee's down from where she stood and watched as a lady slapped at her hands like she was disgusted by the outside dirt. The lady turned and walked over to the flap that covered an entrance into the teepee and disappeared inside.

"I like them." Rissa said. When Lilly continued to look past Rissa's shoulder, Rissa followed suit. Seeing nothing too important, she turned back around and whispered to her friend. "What? Please tell me you aren't seeing a ghost or having a vision?"

Lilly chuckled and looked at her friend. "Geez Rissa, I'm not a witch!" She stated, before lifting her eyes as if to say 'Really?'

Rissa chuckled. "Like the crap you've been experiencing isn't witchy?"

Lilly pretended to think about it then shrugged. "Maybe."

"So what were you looking at?" Rissa asked, pointing her thumb behind her.

Lilly turned her around and nodded at the teepee. "Two teepee's down." When Rissa nodded, she continued. "I'm pretty sure I saw Selene walk into it."

Rissa turned her head sideways to give Lilly an odd look. "Nu-uh?"

"And guess what she was doing?" When Rissa shrugged, she replied. "Dusting her hands."

Rissa busted out laughing and most everyone surrounding the retail tent looked their way. Rissa and Lilly decided to find the men and ask them if it was possible. They were disappointed when they didn't find them by the root beer tent. They spent the next hour trying to find them in the crowd of people.

It was just as the celebration was coming to an end, they spotted the men by the entrance. Tripp was busy doing PR for PORT with a couple reenactors who lived just up the river.

When he finished, Lilly pulled him to the side and explained to Tripp what she saw as they started making their way to the parking lot. Tripp stated that it wouldn't surprise him and acted like he didn't care. This on one hand made her feel good that he could care less but on the other hand shouldn't he be wondering why Selene was in town and didn't tell him?

Lilly decided if he didn't think it was a big deal then she shouldn't worry about it. Yet as they were exiting through all the gates, she looked up to see Edmond Brader passing by her dressed as a colonial man. He had the nerve to ignore Tripp and Zeke but smiled and gave the girls a greeting before walking on.

Lilly didn't say a word until they got into Tripp's pickup truck. "Okay, you don't think it's odd that Brader is here?"

Tripp grinned at her. "I knew he was going to be here. He has been a reenactor for a few years."

"So where is his tent or teepee?" She asked.

He lifted his eyebrows at her. "And why would you want to know that?" Rissa and Zeke chuckled from the back seat.

She laughed. "Stop, I'm being serious."

He looked at her and grinned. "If I had to guess, I would say his teepee would be in the same place you saw Selene."

Lilly's expression was priceless. Rissa looked just as confused and Zeke was still chuckling as Tripp pulled out of the field road that was being used as a parking lot. He waved at the local FFA worker who was collecting the money to park the vehicles.

Lilly wanted answers. "So what's this all about? Is Selene and Edmond an item?"

Tripp was nonchalant when he answered. "For about two years now."

"WHAT?" She nearly shouted. "Then why would you let her work at PORT?" This made absolutely no sense.

Zeke answered. "Haven't you ever heard the expression…Friends close, enemies closer?"

Lilly turned around to look at him. "You knew this also?" Before he could reply she looked at Rissa. "Did you?" Her friend shrugged and shook her head before glaring at Zeke.

Rissa spoke. "I have a question…if the two of you knew this…why didn't we?"

Zeke answered for himself. "Tripp asked me to keep it to myself."

Before Rissa could tear into him, Lilly looked over at Tripp. "How long have you known about this?" He instantly became nervous by her calm voice.

"I suspected from early on, when she first joined. That's why I let her hang around me." He reached for her hand and while she didn't move it, she also didn't respond to his grip.

"How long have you known this for sure?" She was looking straight ahead and her voice was void of feeling.

Tripp realized his mistake immediately. He should have told her as soon as it was clarified. She confided in him about all the crazy shit happening to her so he should have done the same. Yet he knew she had enough going on and he didn't want to add to it. Plus he could feel her pulling away from him lately and he was wanting to give her space. Yet, it sure as hell wasn't going to look that way. "I've known since the PORT Luncheon. She was spotted staying with Edmond at the Conrad B&B. I also asked your brother to do a little snooping to see what he could find out. He texted me a few days later to say that Selene had been Edmond's secretary for two years and the relationship didn't stay a working relationship long. We believe she was planted to either sabotage paperwork or just to spy."

When she didn't say anything, he took his hand away and continued. "Lilly, I'm sorry I didn't tell you. I guess I figured you had enough going on."

"It's fine." was her reply. Yet everyone in the truck knew she was upset.

After parking in her driveway Lilly waved goodbye to her friend and went into the kitchen to let Moose out. She had wanted to take him to the fort today but all the walking on such a hot day was just too much for him.

Tripp walked into the kitchen and leaned against the counter as she stood by the French doors waiting for Moose to finish. "So are we going to talk about this?" He asked.

She continued looking out the door as she replied. "What's there to talk about? I can share everything with you…everything. Everything I told you was huge and surreal…but I did it anyhow. Yet you didn't trust me enough to let me in on something that was important." She looked over her shoulder at him. "It was important...but not huge."

Guilt made Tripp toss up his hands. "Give me a break. You are going to be all pissed off because I kept this from you...are you serious?"

She let Moose in and turned to him. "Isn't it getting close to the time you need to leave to go back home?" She hoped he didn't hear the tears in her voice.

"Wow...just like that. Get the hell out because I pissed you off...Fine." He turned and walked towards the stairs to retrieve his stuff. He paused and took a deep breath before slowly letting it out. He didn't turn around when he stated, "This isn't about Selene and Edmond. I can feel you pulling away and I don't know why. We've been through so much...I just can't believe you are going to throw it all away."

Lilly opened the door and walked out the patio doors and sat on the back porch swing. A few minutes later she heard Tripp's truck start and back out of the driveway. She held her breath until she could no longer hear the engine purr. It was in that instant she let the tears fall.

Chapter Twenty-Two

The Fourth of July in Prairie du Rocher was huge this year because it was 2023 and the moon was full so the Phantom was supposed to show its ghostly head. Lilly couldn't wait for the crappy day to just go away. She no longer thought of it as this wonderful day that celebrated the birth of a nation…she just thought of it as death. She was frustrated seeing all the cars driving by and people camping out in neighborhood lawns. All because they hoped to see the ghost…her ghost…her nightmare.

She was so done with anything and everything to do with the Phantom. The ghost has done nothing but destroy her and her aunts' lives. This thing was so beyond them and had completely taken over any happiness she felt and was slowly turning her into a bitter person. It didn't help that she emotionally felt three men die in her arms…three murdered men. And now she can't be with the one she loved because of this Phantom Funeral.

Lilly sighed as she tried to hold back her tears. The last month had been miserable for her. She missed Tripp so much. She wanted to call him so many times but knew she couldn't. She loved him too much to see him die.

The hardest part was ignoring his calls and text. Every message was so sweet and loving. He told her he knew what she was doing by keeping them apart. He was right in his assumption, but she wasn't going to tell him that. She just needed him to let go so it would be a little easier for her to let go.

She knew her friends were clueless as to why she pushed him away. Well, except for Rissa. She also figured it out and was trying to get her to admit it. But Lilly couldn't admit it because if she did Tripp would push his way back in because he'd know she still loved him.

Lilly was frustrated when Moose came around the corner with his leash in his mouth. Ugh, she didn't want to go outside. She just wanted to crawl under her covers and sleep away the night. Even though her entire family was in town, she refused to go and wait for the Phantom. Her siblings didn't understand, but Greg and Lauren knew enough to respect their daughter's wishes. All Lilly wanted to do was cry into her pillow as she did every night.

Yet, here it was after nine pm and Moose approached her with his leash and wasn't taking no for an answer. It was probably more aggravating because even though it was dark out, she still felt she had to put on a bra and shoes. She guessed he wouldn't be out long because once the fireworks started…she was sure he'd drag her back home.

Tripp parked behind Lisa's and found Wolfe waiting for him inside the restaurant. The guys shook hands and Tripp patted his back before taking a seat across from him. He was here at Wolfe's request but he already planned to be in Prairie du Rocher on the Fourth. He was going to prove to Lilly the Phantom wasn't going to get him. He knew that was why she was pulling away. He believed with his entire heart she loved him and wanted to be with him. She somehow got it stuck in her head he was going to die if they stayed together. Well, he planned to prove her wrong.

Tripp looked at his friend. "So, how is she?"

Wolfe smiled, he guessed wrong. He figured they'd have at least five minutes of small talk before his friend would bring up Lilly, but instead he cut right to the chase. "I wish you'd all tell us why the two of you aren't together. Honestly, she's a complete mess. She rarely leaves her house, but to take Moose on walks. She's quiet when she is with us…it's not good." He lifted an eyebrow. "So what's up?"

Tripp didn't know how much he could tell his friend without sounding crazy. "Honestly Lilly is spooked. Since the early 1700s she and I have had some crazy shit in our families." He explained to his friend everything Lilly was going through with their past connecting and separating. He went on to explain how they all died on the Fourth of July and oddly enough it could be connected to the same Phantom Funeral everyone was in town for on that very night. He stated that Lilly feels that if they stayed together, it's a bad omen and he would die.

Tripp didn't know what Wolfe would think about all of this but he knew he could trust him. So he was surprised when Wolfe said, "I wouldn't take what she says lightly. My ancestors go way back…especially in this area and they believed omens last until they were completed." He gave his friend a stern look. "I even feel a connection to the two of you. I have also dreamed about the two of you in the past." He smiled at his friend. "So what are you going to do?"

Tripp took a deep breath. "I am going to be at her door at 12:05 AM. Then I am planning to tell her we will break up for a month before the next full moon that lands on the fourth. Do you think she will buy it?" He asked nervously?

Wolfe chuckled. "Let's hope." He turned serious. "Brader has been driving by her house and sitting in different areas several times in the last four weeks. He's up to something and we need to find out."

Tripp looked around and was glad they were the only ones in the restaurant. Not surprising because the entire tri county was at the fort and the cemetery trying to catch sight of his funeral. "You're FBI, what can we do with the bastard?" Tripp knew that was another thing he was going to have to explain to Lilly. His friend Wolfe was an agent for the feds and has been working with Tripp to try and bring down Brader. They knew he was up to something and was going to find out what it was. But Lilly was going to be angry when she learns that Wolfe and his family have been friends for years. Wolfe and Tripp's father met years ago at the fort during their reenactment days. She was going to be even more upset when she realized Wolfe wasn't a tree trimmer, they just made that up to have a reason for him to be around…plus Tripp was happy for the free labor.

Lilly was walking along the sidewalk across the street from Lisa's. Never having a clue Tripp was in town much less inside of the restaurant. She was too busy looking over at where the Brickley Mansion once stood and tried to conjure up the image of it in her mind as she stopped by the fence to stare in its direction.

She almost jumped out of her skin when she was approached from behind and felt a hard object pushed into her back. *Not again,* was all she could think before she heard Edmond's voice next to her ear. "If you want to keep your puppy safe, tie him to the fence or I'll blow his brains out."

Lilly believed him and hurriedly twisted and clamped the leash to the fence as Moose was growling and trying to get to Edmond. He grabbed her by the back of the hair and pushed her through the gated fence. He was still whispering in her ear as he kept pushing her in front of him. "I know you know where the gold is and you're going to show me." He shoved her in the direction of the bluffs.

Lilly had no idea why he thought she knew and said as much. This made him all the more angrier. "Bullshit. I went back too, you know. I dream about how you and I were supposed to be together but you whored yourself out to him. I saw you that night at the dance when you floated into the air and vanished. I was also there for each of the murders, yet...I never got to see it through. I never knew what happened after I killed your precious Daniel. But I did see you take the gold from his pocket that first time and I knew you knew where the mine was." He shoved her as she came closer to the bottom of the bluff where the mansion once sat.

Lilly lost her footing and fell. He grabbed her hair and stood her up. "Edmond, I don't know where it is...I swear."

He put the gun to her head and looked her dead on. "Then I'll put a bullet between your beautiful eyes."

She knew he meant it and she needed to borrow some time. Hopefully Moose would get loose and get help. She knew she had no choice but to play his game. She pointed to the rough trail that led up the side of the bluff. She didn't know what she was going to do once they reached the old water tower that was nothing more than a big flat-top barrel that sat up on the hill. The tower was the furthest she had ever climbed...and that was when she was a kid.

The two men were discussing different ways to trap Edmond when Selene rushed through the back entrance door. "Tripp thank God I spotted your car before leaving town. We need to talk." She panted as she tried to catch her breath.

Tripp lifted his eyes. "Selene, I thought I explained to you months ago that we have nothing more to say and whatever comes out of your mouth I refuse to believe."

She held up her hand. "I get it. And I am sorry I was suckered into Edmond's crap...but you have to listen. It has to do with Lilly."

She had his attention now as he set up and glared at her. "What about Lilly?" He asked in a quiet voice.

She started talking fast. "I just went by the B&B to see if he was there because he said he wasn't coming here this weekend and I didn't believe him." Pausing for a big breath, she continued. "He wasn't in his room, but the owner let me in because he just assumed we were there together because I stayed there with him in the past. So I went into the room and he had all these papers

251

scattered. There were photos all over the place of Lilly. There were a few of you as well, but not many."

While she caught her breath Tripp took a second to look over at Wolfe who was doing some quick texting, probably alerting the boys to the area. Tripp was already moving his chair back as Selene continued.

"Anyway I started to freak out when I saw a box of bullets turned over on the bed. There were also maps drawn up about possible gold mines in the bluffs and there was also a gun case…" Just then she was interrupted as the bartender Ryan opened the door between the restaurant and bar. "Tripp, you better take care of Moose across the street…he's about to rip the entire fence down"

Both men almost knocked Ryan down as they rushed through the bar area and out the front door. Tripp was the first to approach the dog and got him untied quickly. "Where's your Momma Moo…?" He didn't have time to finish because Moose took off towards the bluffs like a bat outta hell. Tripp was glad he had a hold of the leash because it took everything for Tripp and Wolfe to keep up.

Tripp was wishing Moose would quiet down but there was no calming the big dog. He was charging in the direction of Lilly and growling like he was ready to do some damage. Tripp had a hard time holding his leash. As they got closer to the water tower, Lilly must have heard Moose because they heard her yell for Moose to stay back.

They heard her pleading with Edmond to not hurt her dog. Wolfe tossed Tripp a small pistol and pointed in the direction he thought Lilly was. He motioned that he was going to go around the back. Tripp was going to see how close he could get without being spotted. But first he whispered his commands into Moose's ear to try and calm the angry dog down.

As Tripp made his way to Lilly's voice, he heard her pleas once again for Edmond to not shoot Moose. Moose started snarling again. Tripp couldn't calm the dog down and Moose jerked his leash out of Tripp's hand causing him to lose his footing. Edmond pulled Lilly in front of him and was using her as a shield so Moose wouldn't attack. He figured the only reason Edmond was sparing the dog was because he didn't want the gunshot to be heard or because he needed Lilly to cooperate and Moose was his leverage.

Edging closer, he could see Wolfe coming up the other side. Tripp was relieved there was a full moon, yet that could work against him if Edmond spotted him. It sucked that Lilly was a shield because he couldn't get a shot off. Especially because Edmond had the barrel touching Lilly's temple.

Suddenly, Tripp lost his footing again along the steep side of the bluff and slipped a few feet down. Edmond heard the twigs breaking and turned to the sound and found Tripp holding on to a low branch of a tree. He shoved Lilly away from him as he stood looking down at Tripp and pointed the gun at him with his right hand as he pulled out a knife from his pants waist. "The pleasure is all mine...to kill you again. You have done nothing but make my life hell for centuries."

At that moment Lilly knew she couldn't handle losing him again. Without thinking she jumped in front of Edmond to get the gun away. He turned just as she leaped and brought the knife around and thrust it into Lilly's chest as she knocked him over and rolled over to the edge of the metal water tower. Moose didn't waste a second. He leaped over Lilly's lifeless body and sunk his teeth into Edmond's throat. Edmond didn't have a chance against the large dog.

Tripp yelled and rushed to Lilly. She was completely unconscious. Wolfe was already calling for a medic and helicopter. Tripp got to Lilly's side and spotted the blood covering the front of her. He ripped at her shirt and used it to apply pressure to the wound. The blood didn't seem to be stopping. Tripp had tears in his eyes as he begged her over and over to not leave him.

Wolfe explained they needed to get her help as he took his shirt off and replaced her soaked shirt by pressing it tightly to her chest just as Tripp picked her up and stated that the ambulance was never going to find them up in the bluffs so he was going to get her to them. He held her wounded chest close to his to keep the pressure on the wound as he quickly ran down the side of the bluff with Lilly in his arms.

Wolfe rushed over to Edmond and called Moose off. Moose looked up at Wolfe's command then turned to see Tripp's head disappear down the hill. Wolfe used his native tongue and commanded Moose to stay...the dog listened. Wolfe looked down at the limp body of Edmond and was sure he was dead. He checked the pulse on his wrist and found there was none. "The deed is done." He stated, as he stood up and grabbed Moose's leash before walking climbing back up the water tower and turned to face the little village.

There in front of him he watched what everyone was there to see...more than forty wagons and thirteen groups of soldiers with a casket sitting on the back of the wagon, heading towards the town's cemetery. This was the opposite direction of what had always been recorded. The procession made its way to a gated gravesite and one by one each dissolved into the ground at the tomb.

He looked down at the dog sitting next to his legs and patted his head. "Good job, Moose. I believe Lilly and Daniel's past is put to rest…but now I just pray it also begins."

The hospital waiting room was filled with friends and family of Lillian Bienvenue. There was pacing, a lot of coffee drinking, and too much silence as Lilly's loved ones came to pray together. Every time a doctor walked by you could hear a pin drop.

Lilly had been in surgery for over an hour and it wasn't looking good because she lost a large amount of blood. Everyone teared up when Lauren started losing it in the corner. No one knew what to do or say.

The doctor finally came into the room and asked who was there for Lillian Bienvenue. Everyone stood and he smiled and lifted his eyebrows, but didn't say anything about the protocol of only so many in a surgery waiting room. He cleared his voice and said, "The bullet lodged in her right lung and came in at an odd angle which did a lot of damage. That and the blood loss is what is making it hard to gauge the outcome." Lauren let out a deep sob at the news and tears came into everyone's eyes. "I will add that she's young and healthy so that's in her favor. But the next twenty-four hours will tell us more." He patted Greg on the back. "I wish I had better news." He explained that it was just too early to let anyone in but that they would keep everyone updated on any progress.

Tripp looked at Sawyer and said he needed some air and left the room. He walked down the hall and out the exit door and found a quiet bench on the side of the building. He prayed. He prayed as he had never prayed. He begged as he had never begged and he cried as he'd never cried before. He was completely torn up inside. He wanted this final chance with Lilly. He wanted her more than he had ever wanted anything.

Hours later, as a shadow from the parking light glow casted over him, he looked up to see Wolfe standing in front of him. "It is done my friend. I have seen the spirits of your ancestors put to rest. Your evil is gone forever."

Tripp didn't care that his friend saw his tears. "But what good is that if she is gone?" He ran his hands through his hair and down his face before shouting into the dark night. "What in the fuck is my purpose without her?"

Wolfe smiled and put his hand on his friend's shoulder. "Why do you believe she's gone? She is still here."

Tripp looked at Wolfe with a lost expression. "The doctor said she's in need of prayers and I think he was trying to let us down easy…" Tears were coming back. "It's not looking good, Wolfe." He choked before burying his face in his hands.

"My friend, listen to what your God tells you." With that he turned and walked away.

Tripp was confused by his friend's words, yet took a deep breath and followed his advice. It was in the next several minutes he found a voice in his heart letting him know that Lilly was going to be okay. He truly could feel it.

Several hours later, Tripp poured himself another cup of coffee and looked towards the waiting room blinds and was surprised to see the sun was up and looked to have been for several hours. His phone died hours ago and he honestly could have cared less if it was charged or not. He looked around the waiting room and smiled at all the sleeping bodies. It was only him and Greg awake. As he made eye contact with the older man, he was surprised Lilly's father motioned for him to follow him out into the hall.

Just outside the door, Greg spotted a couple chairs and sat down. Tripp decided to stay standing. He was anxious and tired of sitting. Greg was the first to break the silence as he looked at Tripp and stated, "Who in the hell would ever believe such a crazy tale as yours and my baby's story?"

Tripp ran his hands through his hair. "I know. I just can't believe it's really real. This stuff is made for the movies…not real life."

Greg smiled at him. "You know she's going to be okay!"

Tripp gave him a small smile. "I do. I have faith in God and in the fact that we came this far and now this curse or whatever it was is finally over. Whatever evil was lurking above us is gone…" He tapped his heart, "I feel it here."

"I was relieved when your friend Wolfe pulled me aside and told me what Moose did." His smile grew. "I think that sweet dog deserves a big rawhide."

Tripp grinned and agreed. "He truly saved the day. If he wouldn't have raised such a fit we never would have known Brader had her." He shook his head and shuddered. "I can't imagine what the bastard would have done to her."

"We can't think about that." Greg stated before changing the subject. "So what about the gold?"

"I think we need to let Lilly decide on that." Tripp leaned against the corridor wall and smiled at Greg. "I have a question."

Greg grinned because he knew what the young man was going to ask. "Yes?"

Tripp stuttered for a second but then asked Greg if he could have his daughter's hand in marriage. Greg decided the boy had been through too much to make it rough on him, so he readily agreed.

Both men looked over as they spotted Lilly's doctor going into the waiting room. They hurried to follow him in. The doctor turned to Greg as they entered behind him. He smiled and let the men know that Lilly was awake and it looked as if she was going to pull through. Both men said a quick thank you to the Good Lord before waking the others to let them in on what the doctor just said.

Lilly's doctor smiled as everyone cheered but then they hushed because he wasn't finished. "She will be in ICU for a few days so you will all get to see her soon. Yet it's been a long night and I think most of you need to go home."

He looked at Lauren and Greg, then over to Tripp. "You three are more than welcome to stay, but let's encourage this crowd to go home. Hospitals still use the six-foot social distancing rule and your group is really breaking it." He smiled and said he was checking on his patient one last time and they could see her soon.

A few hours later Tripp was the first to see Lilly. Lauren and Greg thought it was only right. He was choked up at how small and vulnerable she looked. He couldn't believe a few hours ago she took a bullet for him. He sat on the chair next to her bed and just stared at her. He held her hand as his thumb brushed across it back and forth. Her parents peeked in and Lauren couldn't handle seeing her baby just lying there helpless so Greg thought it best if they just sat in the waiting room until she woke up.

Tripp was surprised and grateful as all the nurses came in and out of Lilly's room, never saying anything to him about being in there too long. They just let him sit there for hours, every once in a while asking if he needed anything. Greg peaked in once to give him his phone that someone took the time to charge. He glanced down to see a text from Wolfe saying that Selene was in custody.

It was finally in the early afternoon when Lilly woke to Tripp holding her hand and rubbing his thumb over her skin. He smiled at her and said, "Hi."

She mouthed, "Hi." and licked her lips because they were so dry.

Tripp's eyes filled with tears. "I love you." He smiled.

She smiled back as she whispered. "I love you," before falling back to sleep with a smile on her face.

It was over an hour later before she woke back up and smiled because he was still there.

"Will you marry me?" He whispered.

She smiled again with tears in her eyes as she whispered back, "I was afraid I was going to be the only Lilly that didn't get asked by Daniel." She looked down and smiled as he slid the diamond ring that graced so many Lilly Bienvenues' hands. "Yes, I'll marry you!" She entwined her fingers through his and fell back asleep.

Chapter Twenty-Three

4 July 2024

Lilly and Tripp were swinging on the front porch of Bienvenue House. He was busy rubbing Lilly's belly as she was trying to get comfortable. Rissa and Zeke made their way over from across the street and sat on the lounge chairs. Not long after, Wolfe stopped by, followed by the Rocher Girls. Lilly smiled as Lisa pulled up when she spotted the crowd gathering on the porch.

Lilly looked around at all her chatty friends and couldn't believe how happy she was. It had been a year to the day since she was shot. And while she missed some of the visions of the past, she was glad she no longer had them. She was sad that she no longer communicated with her grandfather, but she knew she was blessed to have had the opportunity when she did. She was just relieved that nothing more ever happened after that horrific day.

Once Lilly got over her anger with Tripp for not explaining who Wolfe really was, which didn't take long because she realized life was too short, the trio wondered if the first Daniel Dane Geofrey put the curse on them while dying by declaring *I will find you again in another time...this I vow.* Lilly prayed if that was the case then hopefully, the curse was broken.

The tourists were excited because a few people hanging out by the cemetery apparently saw the Phantom Funeral go to the cemetery and disappear around the area of the older graves. Many were disappointed because they were at the fort or on the road leading to the fort instead of the town cemetery so they didn't see anything worth talking about. Yet now everyone was excited and couldn't wait to see it again on the next full moon that fell on the Fourth of July...at the cemetery. Lilly truly believed they were going to be disappointed when it didn't happen...but let them believe. Every town needs their ghost.

The months following that horrid day, she and Tripp sorted out what they thought happened. Lilly wrote about it in her diary but omitted anything about the gold. She kept the diary locked up in the safe along with the gold she found at the fort. She wasn't sure what to do with the gold but she knew it was going to go to a great cause one day…maybe even to help preserve the historical fort. She also wasn't sure if she would ever tell her kids about the experience, but she was sure she wouldn't tell them about the gold. Gold made people evil.

Lilly believed it was greed that motivated Edmond. He apparently knew about the gold and truly thought Lilly knew where it was. She remembered he said he went back in time also, so maybe that was how he knew…she just wasn't sure and no longer wanted to think about it.

According to Selene, Edmond was trying to force people out of their homes because he wanted to buy up the bluff land so he would have all the gold rights to the land he owned. Wolfe convinced Selene that Edmond was disillusioned about the gold and she seemed to buy that story. It helped that it was implied that as long as she kept quiet about anything gold, there would be no charges pressed.

As far as Edmond, after researching through his family history, Wolfe found out he was related to all the evil men in Lilly's Aunts' past. So Lilly believed for some reason he dreamed of the past just as she did. Yet nothing was confirmed.

Tripp and Lilly married two months after Lilly was released from the hospital. To make sure no more history was repeating itself, Tripp had her pregnant within the first month they were married. The couple decided the Bienvenue house was perfect for them and Tripp opened his own business right in the middle of town. It was out of this office he also ran PORT. He was happy with the progress PORT was receiving and prayed that soon people would feel safe in not having to leave their homes.

Rissa decorated the baby's room in many shades of blue. It matched the same shades Rissa had in her own nursery. Lilly stated the ultrasound could be wrong and she would have to redo everything. Her friend just laughed and stated she would really go crazy then…because she loved pink. Lilly just laughed and rolled her eyes. She was excited that her best friend was expecting a baby boy two months after Lilly and Tripp's baby was due.

Tripp was laughing at something Zeke said, just as Lilly felt something similar to a 'pop' on her lower stomach. Suddenly, she was releasing pressure and her legs were getting damp. She looked up at everyone and stated, "Oh no...I don't want a Fourth of July baby."

Eight hours later, Tripp was holding his beautiful baby boy and smiling from ear to ear. They refused to name the baby after any past family members on either side. Yes, he was a Fourth of July baby and Tripp took that as a sign to not hate the day, but to embrace everything in the past that brought them to where they are today.

THE END